A J HEALY

TOMMY STORM

AND THE GALACTIC KNIGHTS

Quercus

First published in Great Britain in 2009 by

Quercus
21 Bloomsbury Square
London
WC1A 2NS

A CIP catalogue reference for this book is available from the British Library

ISBN 978 1 84724 755 1

This book is a work of fiction. Names, characters, businesses, organizations, places and events are either the product of the author's imagination or are used fictitiously. Any resemblance to actual persons, living or dead, events or locales is entirely coincidental.

10 9 8 7 6 5 4 3 2 1

Designed and typeset by Rook Books, London
Printed and bound in England by Clays Ltd, St Ives plc.

By the same author

TOMMY STORM

for MF

THE SCOOP

If you just want to know the story and want to know it fast, then feel free to skip the footnotes and boxes of information sprinkled throughout.

Curiouser and Curiouser

But if you'd like to know as much as possible about the world of Tommy Storm, then the footnotes, the boxes and the Extra Bits at the end of this book are for you.

The Story So Far . . .

Tommy Storm and the Galactic Knights (*TS2*) is the sequel to *Tommy Storm* (*TS1*). A reminder of what happened in *TS1* is set out below.

So if you plan on reading TS1, *look away now . . .*

TS1 is set in 2096 – a time when it's *always* raining on Earth due to climate change and a time when Earthlings have known for some years that intelligent life exists elsewhere in the Milky Way. The book opens with an invitation – Earth is requested to send five children to a training school called IGGY located in the middle of the Milky Way. Here they will join other children from across the galaxy and receive training for a dangerous and secret mission. For various ignoble reasons, Tommy Storm, a 'loser' aged eleven and a quarter, is chosen as one of the five Earthlings to attend IGGY.

Tommy blossoms at IGGY and is put in a dorm with four 'alien' kids who go on to become his closest friends. Following a series of challenges and adventures, Tommy and his four friends are crowned IGGY Knights and save Earth from destruction. *TS1* ends with the IGGY Knights leaving the galaxy on a mission to save the universe from the Terrible Future Calamity (the TFC).

1

Deadly Buzz

The IGGY Knights were in a spot of bother.

Tommy Storm, Marielle, Woozie, Rumbles and Summy were hanging upside down in a dimly-lit cell, their feet and hands bound, their mouths gagged.

Tommy, a slight boy of fourteen who looked about twelve, was a mix of many races, with spiky, black hair and dark eyes. But right now he wasn't a pretty sight. Covered in cuts and bruises, his black trousers were torn, his black shirt ragged.

None of the other Knights looked quite so bad. Marielle – petite, blonde and human-like – retained a certain grace despite her shredded clothes and swellings. Woozie and Rumbles showed no sign of bruising (being furry), while Summy, a small, dragon-like creature, sported a ripped T-shirt and a smattering of welts beneath each wing.

Tommy opened his eyes. His right one was swollen from a blow he'd received hours – *or was it days?* – earlier. He looked around – all the others were asleep – and winced at the all-pervasive odour. A drop of perspiration trickled down his arm.

For the umpteenth time he tried to wrench his wrists and ankles, but they wouldn't budge. Alas, there could be no doubt. They were bound with tinderwire – an extremely flammable substance that's much too strong for any creature to snap with their hands. Tommy eyed the taut wire. From his hands and feet, it stretched vertically to a high metal rafter, looping round it before angling down to a hook low down on the cell wall. There were four other hooks beside this one – each holding a length of tinderwire attached to an IGGY Knight. Marielle's hook was right next to an orange plug socket.

He tried to call out – nothing more than 'Mmuuuuuuuhhhhhhhhhhhhhhhhh' escaped from the gag across his mouth.

SSCCHHHIIIISSSSSSSSSSSSSS!!!

A burst of steam rose up from a stack of white-hot rocks across the room and the temperature rose a notch. Tommy blinked a bead of sweat from his eye and waited for the steam to clear . . . There, on a table below, were the IGGY Knights' curved swords (known as flashscimitars, or scimmies for short).

He closed his eyes – picturing, concentrating – trying to tap into that inner power known as the Surge. *If I can lift the top scimmy and make it cut the tinderwire . . .* He fought and strained, sweat rolling off his brow. But five minutes in, the greatest reaction had been a vague levering upwards of the blade.

Just then, the cell door began heaving open. Tommy opened his eyes and the blade collapsed, the faint metallic sound drowned by his effort-quitting gasp.

Three creatures entered the cell.

The first was fearsome and bull-like with a chainsaw tail that buzzed when she eyed the captives. A muscular arm stemmed from her chest, gripping a baseball bat.

The second creature was smiley and furry and licking a lollipop the size of a dinner plate. He leant against a wall and surveyed the scene contentedly.

And the last creature was small and twitchy. 'All right, you layabouts,' he cried. 'Rise and shine!' He had what looked like a speaker under his arm and, with a jabbing smack, he plugged this into the orange socket next to Marielle's hook.

Marielle had woken and muffled sounds filled the air as Woozie, Rumbles and Summy followed suit. Tommy looked over at his friends. *At least we're alive!*

'Sorry to have left you *hanging around* for so long,' said the small, twitchy creature with a chuckle. 'Now, can any of you numbskulls remember my name? Well?'

The IGGY Knights (now also known as *the FiiVe*) tried to answer, but their mouths were still gagged.

'It's Nack,' said the creature with the chainsaw tail. 'Nack Jickilson.'

Nack smacked his head down hard on to the table top. 'Duh!! Shotputtska, I wasn't asking *you*!'

Shotputtska swung the baseball bat violently towards her buzzing tail, splicing half an inch of wood off the end of it. 'How was *I* supposed to know?'

'So, yeah,' intoned Nack, shaking the grogginess out of his head and addressing the FiiVe. 'Now you're sure of my name, be sure that I *will* get the truth out of you *this* time.'

There were two heavy metal tables in the cell. The FiiVe's scimmies rested upon one. Taking a seat, Nack placed the speaker on the other. 'This is a lie detector,' he said, tapping the speaker. 'It's called *PoF!* – which stands for, Pants on Fire!® – and it's fitted with the latest Auntie-Porki-Pi™ technology, so no fib, however small, will go unnoticed. When I turn it on, it'll make a loud buzz any time anyone in this room tells a lie.' He pointed at Rumbles. 'Shotputtska, cut down that three-armed, hairy oaf. I reckon she's ready to sing.'

Nack Jickilson was human-like, except that the dark,

receding, just-got-out-of-bed hair tufting from his jittery head also sprouted out along the length of his back. His eyes looked as though they wanted to pop out of their sockets and his black eyebrows twitched dementedly.

With her chainsaw tail, Shotputtska cut the tinderwire holding Rumbles aloft. The charcoal-furred bear fell to the floor in a heap. Meanwhile, Nack slid a poker into the white-hot stones on the far side of room.

Once Rumbles had been tied to a chair and her gag removed, Nack returned to his seat opposite Rumbles, holding the fiery red poker aloft. 'I have yet to decide where I'll stick this if you tell me so much as *two* lies.' One of his eyes was twitching, as though wanting to leap out of its socket and ram the poker into Rumbles itself. Nack motioned to Shotputtska. 'Remove the gags from the others . . . Now,' he said, addressing the four hanging Knights, 'if any of you says a word out of turn, I'll stab your furry friend with this poker.'

Shotputtska flicked on *PoF!*.

'I'm not afraid of you,' said Rumbles, eyes gaping up at Nack.

PoF! made an angry buzz.

Nack smiled, together his eyebrows forming into a *V*. 'That's your first lie gone. No more chances . . . Tell me why you came here, to Planet Skanger, and searched me out. You work for a rival criminal, don't you? Else you're with the Universal Police and want to bring me in.'

Rumbles eyed the orange-hot poker nervously. 'I told you before,' she said. 'We all told you . . . We're trying to save the universe from the TFC – meaning the Terrible Future Calamity – which is due to destroy the universe and everything in it in less than eighteen years. And we don't know where to start. We don't even know what the Terrible Future Calamity is.'

Nack looked over at the lie detector. It was silent. He thumped it to ensure it was still working. Rumbles continued in a splurge of nervous energy: 'In the three years since we've left IGGY, we've visited many galaxies and talked to lots of scientists, geography teachers and paw readers[1] – with no success. So when we heard about you – a notorious criminal genius – we thought we'd seek you out. We hoped you might be able to come up with some scrap of information that might point us in the right direction.'

Nack stared at *PoF!*. It hadn't made a sound.

'We've had a few faults with this lie detector,' he said. *PoF!* buzzed loudly. Much to Nack's fury. 'Stop wasting my time!' he yelled at Rumbles. 'I'm a very busy man!' Again *PoF!* buzzed – which made Woozie laugh out loud. 'How dare you laugh at me!' cried Nack. 'I'm an extremely important person.' *BUZZ!!* 'Worthy of immense respect.' *BUZZ!!*

Nack plunged the poker into Rumbles's midriff. But the bear-like creature was big and the poker had grown cold. 'Stop!' she cried. 'Ha-ha-ha! You're tickling me! Stop!'

Nack flung the poker across the room in exasperation. Then he slammed his head against the table top. Twice. 'Aaaaghhhhh!' he screamed – which seemed to exorcise his temper. When Rumbles stopped laughing and Nack eventually spoke, it was with a chilling calmness. 'Enough . . . Shotputtska, let's kill the lot of 'em right now! You can lay each one out on the table and cut them in two with your tail.'

'There's no need for that,' said Rumbles with a giggle (she found it hard not to laugh at serious things so soon after a tickling).

'What? You think I'm joking! You think I won't have you killed?'

1 Similar to palm readers.

'No, I—'

'So you think we'll set up some stupid, over-elaborate way to kill you, giving you time to escape?'

'No, of course not,' said Rumbles. *PoF!* buzzed. 'Hey, don't mind that machine! You're right, it must be defective.'

Nack turned to the furry, smiley creature who'd just taken a big bite of the lollipop. 'Doogle, jump up on the table there and show these people we mean business.'

Doogle climbed on to the table and sprawled across it. Shotputtska, meanwhile, climbed up to the rafters and looped a length of tinderwire round it. She grabbed hold of its free end, then waited, chainsaw tail buzzing with anticipation.

Nack gave a nod and Shotputtska pushed herself off, swinging in an arc towards the furry figure of Doogle sprawled across the table. Doogle wasn't watching. He was turned towards Nack, whispering: 'She's not going to hurt me, right? We'll just pretend – to scare these kids – like we agreed.'

'Of course,' said Nack. 'She won't touch you.'

PoF! gave a loud buzz. Doogle heard it, realized his mistake and in the same instant knew it was too late . . . A split second later, he was chopped down the middle, from groin to neck. Tommy saw a shard of lollipop nestling in the freshly opened guts.

'You think I'm serious now!?' cried Nack to Rumbles and the other IGGY Knights.

'Please!' cried Rumbles. 'I told you *everything*.'

'Yeah, I know,' replied Nack. '*That's* why it's time to kill you.' He turned to Shotputtska who was clearing Doogle's gooey body parts off the table. 'Kill them all. Careful to kill one before you cut down the next.' Then he addressed the IGGY Knights. 'You'll all be dead in under five minutes.'

No buzz issued from *PoF!*.

2

Murphy's Law

There's a planet in a remote galaxy of the universe that revolves on its axis every twenty-four hours and travels round its sun every 365¼ days. This planet has a single moon and harbours (supposedly) intelligent life.

Down on this planet, in the year '2009', a great meeting was coming to a close, watched on TV by almost all the planet's six billion inhabitants. The only ones who missed it were either in bed, on the loo, or had failed to pay their TV licence.

A self-important man called Chancellor Rommel stood up before the assembly and everyone hushed. 'Vee haff only fifteen minutes left to make our choice,' he said.

This caused a stir of nervous comments from the crowd – 'Why didn't we start thinking about this sooner?' 'Yeah, we had *years* to come up with an answer!' And an argument began raging about who was to blame for the delay. It only subsided when Rommel shouted: '*Eleven* minutes to make our choice!' And he indicated to a large screen behind him. 'Zis projection vill remind you of da message vee received ten yearz ago.'

The projection looked like this.

REQUEST FOR HELP

It is vital that we come up with the Wisdom of Life, Death and The Universe in under 25 words. We would be grateful if your planet could help us by making a suggestion in precisely 10 years and 10 hours from the time of this message.

Note:

- If you come up with a good answer we will shower you with riches.
- Please put your 'wisdom' into the sock provided.

Rommell waved his arm. The projection disappeared. 'Then, some veeks later, ve received ze following message.' A new projection appeared.

CORRECTION TO PREVIOUS MESSAGE

When we said 10 years and 10 hours, we meant 10 years and 9 hours . . . to come up with your 'wisdom' in under 25 words.

Note:

- If you make no response or if your answer is 'not good enough', then your planet and solar system will be crushed by THE HAND.
- Please write your answer on to a postcard and put it into the toaster attached to this note – NOT into the sock.

'Why the change in time?' cried a voice from the crowd. 'We should have another hour to come up with our answer!'

'Who cares about the time!' yelled someone else. 'First they were going to give us *riches* for our answer, then it's: *oh, we're gonna crush your planet!*'

'It must be a bluff!' announced someone else, which

resulted in a deluge of voices.

Rommel reached under the podium and took out what looked like a two-slicer toaster. 'Vee discussed all dis,' he said. 'Vee agreed to choose an anszer and put it in da toaster. If it's a bluff, then vee haff lost nossing . . . By da vay, *ten minutes* to go.'

Once he had silence, Rommel called on the six chosen delegates to approach the platform. 'Da votes haff been cast,' he said. 'Each ov you haz da anszer proposed by da one billion people on dis planet dat you represent.'

One after another, the delegates opened the envelope in their hand and read out the 'answer' written on the piece of paper inside. These answers were:

1 Life is silly. Then you die.
2 Oh, to be rich and famous! With two big houses, four sports cars and seven marriages.
3 Eh, sorry . . . We don't know.
4 Death is not the end. It's the beginning (fingers crossed) – but still, please don't kill us.
5 Your aunt Agnes would like you to call her after the assembly.
6 Life is a mystery. A *whodunnit* we'll never know the answer to.

'Sank you,' said Rommel when the delegates were finished. 'Now I vud like you all to uze da electronic voting machines under your chairs to vote for your favourite out of dese six possible anszers . . . By da vay, we haff *five minutes* left to make our choice.'

As the assembly voted on its choice, over four billion TV viewers phoned in their votes at a cost of $4.50 each – votes which would have no effect on the proceedings, but which promised the chance of winning a two-week holiday in a prize draw (assuming the planet wasn't destroyed beforehand).

'Da assembly votes are almost in,' said Rommel as a projection of the number 60 appeared behind him. 'By da vay, *one minute* to go.'

60, changed to 59, then to 58 and continued counting downwards.

Someone popped an envelope into Rommel's hand and he opened it, eager to see what his planet had voted as Wisdom of the Universe. The bespectacled man's face registered surprise when he saw the answer. *Your aunt Agnes would like you to call her after the assembly*. Yes, a huge majority of the delegates had voted for Answer No. 5. Rommel shrugged – *democracy is a beautiful and mysterious thing.*

I should say two things here. One, the delegates had actually chosen Answer No. 4 ('Death is not the end . . .'), but a fault with the voting machine software meant that all votes for No. 4 read as votes for No. 5. Two, the 'answer' known as Answer No. 5 was there due to a clerical error. A nervous administrator, who'd received a call from a very irate woman professing to be Delegate Five's auntie ('He said he'd call me last week!'), mistakenly put the auntie's message into the Answer No. 5 envelope and inserted a slip of paper into Delegate Five's message box that read: 'Anything that can go wrong will go wrong.'

Rommel lifted the postcard and held it, poised, over the toaster. By now, the projection behind him was at 12.

'Eleven . . . ten . . . nine . . . eight . . .' The entire assembly chanted down the numbers with increasing excitement – caught up in a fervour of New-Year's-Eve proportions. They all saw Rommel drop the postcard into the toaster. They all cheered when the digits reached zero.

Then silence.

Everyone digesting the situation. Nothing happening . . .

Nothing happened! We're still alive!!

Then the cheering resumed, louder than ever.

'Bluff! Bluff! Bluff' cried a section of the assembly with boisterous enthusiasm.

One group took to chanting, 'Right answer! Right answer! We gave *the* right answer – to the wisdom that we know!' Over and over they sang these lines, and as more people joined in, they all clasped hands, knocking chairs aside, dancing in a circle to the rhythm of the words.

All over the planet, TV viewers joined hands in the same chanting dance. The song reached such a crescendo that no one noticed something strange happen – with the exception of an overly thin girl called Twigletta who stayed watching the telly because she was waiting to watch her favourite show, *Almerica's Next Super-Vain Model.*

The TV image was fixed on a close-up of the toaster. Except the toaster was no more. It'd melted into a puddle of silvery-black goo and was bubbling away like acid, eating into the podium.

Unfortunately, all of the world's astronomers, bird watchers and peeping toms were singing, dancing or falling out of trees at that very moment, so not one telescope on the planet was being looked through. Had Twigletta raised the alarm and the authorities been called super-quickly, one of these determined telescope-wielding observers might've gazed up at the night sky and seen what looked like a giant hand – ten times the size of the planet's solar system – appear from the blackness of space.

But the revelry continued and Twigletta panicked – dashing to the fridge to gorge on a stick of celery.

Seconds later, the planet, its sun and planetary neighbours had been extinguished. With one crush of the hand, all voices, bar one, were silenced.

This solitary voice boomed out across the emptiness where once a cheering planet had revolved. 'I AM DEATH. DESTROYER OF WORLDS.'

3
KILLJOYS

Shotputtska dropped the baseball bat and heaved Rumbles's shackled body on to the table.

'What? What did I do?' cried Rumbles. 'I told you the truthskeys.'

'Not another word,' said Nack, stuffing a gag into Rumbles's mouth as Shotputtska began tying tinderwire to the four table legs, so she could bind Rumbles in the shape of an X (making it easy to cut her down the middle).

'And we'll chop this one next,' said Nack, pointing at Woozie. 'He sniggered at me.'

'Wasn't laughing at *you*,' protested Woozie. 'I was laughing at the lie-detector.'

'Well tough! You die next.'

During Rumbles's interrogation, Tommy'd noticed a few sparks flying from the plug that connected *PoF!* to the wall whenever the lie detector buzzed. *Perhaps* . . . 'Excuse m-me, N-Nack,' he ventured.

'Hey, stutterface! Didn't I tell you not to speak? Another word and we kill you next.' No buzz.

Yes, the stutter that Tommy'd once had on Earth and then lost during his time in the Milky Way was back. It'd made its first appearance about nine months into the IGGY Knights' mission and, apart from a few brief periods of respite, had become progressively worse over the following two-and-a-bit years. Though he assured his fellow Knights it was 'no b-b-big deal', the stutter's inexplicable return had devastated Tommy.

Ignoring Nack's 'stutterface' jibe, Tommy continued addressing the jittery, wild-eyed man. 'If w-we're going to d-die, then p-please, answer me w-w-one question . . .' He was careful to phrase his words so they wouldn't form a lie. 'N-Nack, how c-come you're so n-n-notorious and s-successful at what you d-do?'

Nack looked up. 'Listen, mangle-mouth. If you think you're gonna distract me from having you and your friends killed, it won't work.' And he banged his head off the table as if to prove his point.

No buzz.

'I'm n-not trying to d-distract you. You d-don't have to stop your w-work. Please, I'd r-really like to hear y-you answer th-the question.'

Nack looked over at the strange spiky-haired boy hanging upside down. 'How come I'm so notorious and successful?' Tommy nodded. Nack pondered. ''Spose it's cos I have such courage.' *BUZZ!!* 'Plus I think ahead . . .' Another buzz and more sparks coming from the plug – some of them almost hitting the tinderwire tethered to Marielle's hook.

By now, Rumbles was tied to the table in a star-shape (since she had three arms) and Shotputtska was climbing up the rafters again. 'I love chopping furry lumps down the middle,' she said.

'Mmmmuhhhhhhh.' Through her gag, Rumbles was trying to say, 'Hey! I'm not a furry lumpskeys!'

' . . . And I'm cunning,' continued Nack. 'I use my intelligence in a very focused way.' *PoF!* made no sound in response.

Fizzlestix! Tommy had to come up with something else.

Quick! Shotputtska was on a rafter, pulling on the length of tinderwire fastened round it. 'And are you h-h-happy?' asked Tommy.

'Happy?' Nack was confused for a moment. 'Yeah, I'm totally happy.' A loud buzz, some sparks. 'Couldn't be more happy if I were a pig in Mairrdd.'[2]

At this, *PoF!* buzzed frantically, the plug spat a dozen sparks – one of them landing by Marielle's hook. A flame appeared and it raced up the length of tinderwire as though it were a dynamite fuse. Up to the rafter it ran, around the loops and down towards the binds that held Marielle.

Shotputtska pushed herself back off the far rafter to get a swing at Rumbles, her tail revving loudly.

Marielle felt a shooting burn, first around her ankles, then around her wrists – the flame zipping through her binds – and next thing she was falling to the floor. Released.

VVVRRRRRRRRMMMM!!!! Shotputtska's tail snarled as her backward flight was checked and she started swinging down towards Rumbles.

Flying headfirst towards the ground, there was no time for Marielle to feel shocked or disoriented. Instinctively, she somersaulted in the air, landing like a panther on the table that held the scimmies.

'No!!' cried Nack and he smacked his head off the table and leapt for the baseball bat on the floor.

VVVRRRRRRRRRRRRRRRRMMMMMMMMMM!!!! Shotputtska swooped down, her tail thundering, poised to strike. Five metres from Rumbles . . . four metres . . . three . . . two . . . Rumbles's eyes looked like Nack's – ready to jump out of their sockets. *I'm going to be chopped down the middleskeys!!*

2 Mairrdd is a very stinky planet, beloved of pigs.

SSSCHWWWIPPPPP!!

'Waaaahhhhh!!'

BAMMMMMMMM!!!

VVVRRRRRMMMMSSSSCCCRRRRAAAARRRR!!!

'Shyyyysen!'

Let me explain those noises in REVERSE ORDER.

Shyyyysen – which sort of means *darn-it* – was uttered by Nack as he went to hit Marielle with the baseball bat and found himself falling through the floor of the cell. This would've been particularly alarming since the cell was suspended over a pool of crackodiles.[3] Luckily for Nack, Marielle caught hold of his arm and hauled him up. The baseball bat, however, plummetted and was swallowed whole by an eager crackodile before it hit the pool.

VVVVVRRRRRRRMMMMMSSSCCRRRAARRRR!!! was the sound made by Shotputtska's tail as it cut through the floor of the cell. She dropped to the pool below and, to her credit, managed to cut two crackodiles in half before providing a light snack for the rest of the pack.

BAMMMMMMMM!!! was the sound of Shotputtska's torso as it whumped against the side of the heavy metal table on which Rumbles lay, causing Shotputtska to fall, tail-first, towards the floor, next to where Nack was standing (he'd moved here to fetch the baseball bat).

'Waaaahhhhh!!' was the cry made by Shotputtska as her perfect trajectory towards Rumbles was halted, she realized that the length of tinderwire in her hand had gone limp and the edge of the table zoomed straight for her.

3 Best described as crockodiles strung out on 'mouth-snapping' drugs.

SSSCHWWWIPPPPP!! is the sound made when a scimmy cuts through taut tinderwire. One lash of Marielle's scimmy was all it took.

Five minutes later, Nack was tied to a chair, the FiiVe standing before him, all rubbing their wrists and ankles.

'Poooweee!' exclaimed Woozie. 'Something stinks round here.'

'Yeah, you!' said Nack. 'All of you stink!' *PoF!* made no sound.

Summy knelt down in front of Nack. 'Any help or ideas can you give us?'

'About th-the TFC,' added Tommy.

'No,' said Nack. *PoF!* buzzed. 'I don't care what that says!' cried the hairy-backed fellow. 'I'll tell you nothing!' No buzz.

'Then we'll torture you lotskeys, till you tell us.' *BUZZ!!!*

Rumbles's threat was a lie because a rule applied to all in the universe who wished to be officially recognized as a Good Guy, a Good Planet or a Good Galaxy. This rule was called The Sorry-To-Be-A-KillJoy Convention and it prohibited torture no matter what was at stake (even if someone might have information that'd stop a planet exploding or would admit what they really thought of your hair). Only one exception to the Convention existed . . . Boys or girls could torture their younger brothers and sisters 'so long as the torture is administered for no good reason'.

'You can't twist my nose,' said Nack. 'Or stub my toe. Or give me a wedgie up over my head.' No buzz.

'What if we tied him down and poured r-e-t-a-w over his face till he felt like he was drowning? Then he'd tell us soon enough.' (R-e-t-a-w tastes the opposite of water. It's made of

OH_2 instead of H_2O.)

Unfortunately, every idea the FiiVe came up with constituted a form of torture. So Tommy offered Nack some of the 'bribery' jewels they had on board *Swiggy*. Maybe the 'carrot' would work better than the 'stick'. But Nack had become defiant and wasn't thinking straight.

'I don't want your damn jewels!' *BUZZ!!* 'I won't tell you a thing.' No buzz.

It was Woozie who came up with an idea that wasn't banned by the KillJoy Convention. The thought came to him when he noticed Nack's clothes. The weaselly fellow was wearing a yellow backless vest (to accommodate his hairy back) and dark shorts.

Half an hour later, Nack's attitude had changed. 'Please! Anything. Just scratch my belly button! I'll tell you anything. And my bum. Just give it a scrape!'

So what was Woozie's suggestion? To give you a clue, it was administered by Summy – down the front of Nack's vest and down the back of his shorts . . . Yes, you guessed it . . . Good ole'-fashioned itching powder.

'OK! OK!' cried Nack, eyes boggling out of their sockets. 'I heard *something*. Once. Presumed it was a solar-urban legend . . .'

'Go on.'

'It was just some drunk in a bar rattling on about the TSC . . . Said it stood for Terrifying Slaughter Countdown. That's why—'

'W-wait! T-*F*-C – that's wh-what we're after. Stands f-for *Terrible F-Future Calamity*.'

'OK, maybe he said T*F*C. He was definitely talking 'bout something *Terrible* destroying planets blah blah blah . . . Aaaighh! Someone scratch my belly button! Please!'

Tommy nodded and Rumbles gave Nack a quick scratch.

'And who was this guy? Where can we find him?'

Nack started laughing, speaking between cackles and surges of itchiness. 'How can I . . . put this . . .? I . . . had him . . . *whacked* . . . For . . . talking back.' No buzz.

'Dead, you mean, he is?'

'What do you think, thicko?'

'Hey! A thicko I am not!' retorted Summy.

'Course not – sorry!' exclaimed Nack, continuing in a rapid please-scratch-me voice: 'One o' the last things he said was *wisdom*.'

'W-w-wisdom?'

Nack nodded. 'I swear . . . Said it could stop EARTH being des–'

'Earth?'

'Yeah, EARTH – he said it could stop it being destroyed.'

'Are y-you *sure* about th-this?'

'No, stutterface, I'm making it all up cos I've nothing better to be doing!' *BUZZ!* (*PoF!* took no account of sarcasm.) Realizing he might not be scratched again if he annoyed these kids too much, Nack adopted a more reasonable tone. 'I didn't believe him,' he continued. 'Wacko, I thought. He's a wacko . . . Then I had him whacked.'

Tommy glanced over at his friends – a look of worry and bewilderment. Nack, taking this as a sign he might get no more scratches, continued: 'An' I didn't mean to call you *stutterface* . . . You're just *verbally challenged* is all.'

A little later, the FiiVe were about to unplug *PoF!* and take it with them. ('Useful in the future, it could prove.') Nack had answered all their questions, including giving Rumbles a recipe for making a type of Swiss Roll. 'So there's nothing important you've forgotten?' asked Tommy, dangling a sachet of itching powder before the hairy-backed man.

Nack shook his head, then seemed to remember something. 'The Beast!' he exclaimed, and started laughing uncontrollably. It took some time for the laughter to quell and for Nack to explain himself. 'If the universe is to be destroyed, then the Beast will know about it. May even be behind it.' His voice became jittery and nervous. 'The Beast – it's also called . . . the Demon . . . or the . . . the Fallen One.'

The FiiVe exchanged glances. On a previous stop in another galaxy, some creatures had claimed that *the Demon* would know all about the TFC. But apart from gibbering in fear about cloven hooves, horns and a forked tail, these people could shed no light on the Demon or its whereabouts.

Nack Jickilson, it turned out, not only knew where the Beast resided, but had a map of how to get there tattooed on his thigh. Printed in large letters above it was the word *Hellsbells*. Below it, in tiny letters were lots of instructions.

'The map's been passed from criminal mastermind to prison inmate and back again through the ages,' Nack explained. 'In case the authorities ever track us down and try to bring us in . . . If I zoomed off to Hellsbells, no namby-pamby policeman's gonna follow me . . . Not that I'd land on Hellsbells. Oh, no! I may be bad, but I'm not *mad*.' *PoF!* gave a soft buzz.

They placed some tracing paper on Nack's knee and copied the map. And Rumbles stared at the instructions below the map (she'd perfected a photographic memory). Then the FiiVe bade farewell to Nack, gave him one last scratch and made for their spacecraft. As they closed the cell door, Nack's voice regained its swagger.

'I'll get you! No one humiliates Nack Jickilson. Just you wait. Revenge is a dish best eaten hot. With a sauce of *pain*! Yes, I'll get you. Specially you, stutterface. Just you wait!'

4

Up a Creek

The silver, Lancaster-bomber-like spacecraft charged with ferrying the five IGGY Knights on their mission through space was known as *Swiggy*. Once they left Planet Skanger (Nack Jickilson's abode), the Knights set a course for Hellsbells, feeding the traced map into Swiggy's Hmmm-I-Wouldn't-Start-From-Here® Navigator and the information Rumbles had memorized into the automatic pilot. This included detailed instructions on how to avoid various obstacles on the way to Hellsbells, such as the Khyper Zip (an asteroid 'zip' rather than a 'belt'), the Mirage Galaxy (looks like a 'rest-stop galaxy', but is in fact a vacuum-whirlpool) and the Bermuddy Triangle (use your own imagination).

Given that their journey would be speeded up considerably due to a number of speedy-uppy-zones along the way, the FiiVe reckoned it'd take ten days to reach Hellsbells. This gave them all time to relax, shower and, as Rumbles put it, 'catch up on some chow' (she cooked up so much Castor-Pollox Curry it lasted nearly three days).

A week into the journey, a small warning light started flashing in Swiggy's cockpit. Unfortunately, no one noticed it.

'The Beast does not place dice'
(Quote of Einbert Alstein, discoverer of theoretical SUZs)

When travelling through space, objects experience a drag known as the Drag Kween Co-efficient, which slows them somewhat – much like trying to run in ludicrously high heels. There are, however, zones in the cosmos (known as speedy-uppy-zones or SUZs) where objects experience the opposite of a drag – like roller-skating with a 10-force gale blowing behind you. These zones are not of uniform shape and are practically invisible, so if you're not armed with a special map, your odds of finding one are 'less than the chances of throwing 333 dice and having them all land with the number 6 face-up' (according to Einbert Alstein).

The Boys' Dorm was bright and cosy and fitted with two bunks and a pull-out couch. One entire wall was made of glass, looking out to space, while the ceiling and other walls were covered in beige corduroy (with button-down pockets for storage). 'Boys' stuff' lay across the purple-carpeted floor and a ladder led through an opening in the ceiling to a glass-balled floating globe bathroom, attached like a barnacle to Swiggy's outer skin.

When the warning light began flashing in the cockpit, Tommy was waking from a nap on the top bunk. He jumped to the floor, landing with a jolt. *Ow!* He swivelled his ankle. It was OK. I really have lost my nimbleness, he thought. It was weird. Before they left the Milky Way, he'd thought himself co-ordinated and acrobatic. But in the last few years he'd become a klutz. His fellow Knights usually got the better of him now in scimmy fights and other contests.

He glanced into the bottom bunk – no sign of Woozie –

and walked across the Dorm, looking better than he had a week earlier. The cuts and bruises were almost gone, and his hair was 'mad-spiky' rather than 'crazy-spiky'. Yet as he spotted his reflection, Tommy winced. *I'm so short and scrawny!* And he wished he could look his actual age (fourteen). *Aaaigghh! I look about twelve!*

Then he caught himself. *There's a universe to be saved and here are you fretting about your looks!* He gazed past his reflection, through the glass wall. A dazzling galaxy drifted by and the question that'd soured his dreams swirled towards him . . . *Wisdom.* He kicked a ball towards a poster of Raccoon Squelch on the far wall. It took three goes before he hit the MilkyFed's favourite poster-girl smack in the face and a section of wall swivelled open ninety degrees. He walked through into Swiggy's Lounge.

Hmmm. No one about . . . He meandered between giant cushions to the other side of the room and tugged on a rope hanging by some shelves. A distant jingle sounded, followed by a muffled sigh. Then the shelves revolved inwards, revealing the Girls' Dorm – with Summy at its centre, perched on a small stepladder, leaning over a near fully constructed globe.

'Say a word do not,' said the small, dragon-like creature. She was kind of pink yet sort of blue, though some could argue she was greenish. With purple eyes. From the side, whenever she smiled or opened her mouth, at least fifty gleaming teeth were visible.

Tommy watched in silence as the flying kangasaurus eased a piece of jigsaw into place. 'My planet a model of, this is,' she said, rustling the small wings on her back and climbing down the ladder. 'One million in excess of jigsaw pieces. And finished this morning later I will be.' Tommy knew exactly what the jigsaw was as Summy'd been boring them all about it for months.

The Girls' Dorm mirrored the Boy's Dorm, except that the corduroy on the walls was a rusty colour and the poster on the door was a picture of Take This (a MilkyFed boy-band).

'All right is everything?' asked Summy, stuffing her short arms into her pouch and stepping on to the cream carpet which was half-covered in girls' clothes and other female debris.

'Can you g-give me a piece of w-w-wisdom?' asked Tommy.

Summy looked surprised, then her face set in an expression of deep thought. '*Repeating themselves often are history teachers*,' she said finally. 'Now please. To finish this jigsaw I want.'

Hmmm. The kangasaurus was a history and geography nerd, so her idea of wisdom came as no surprise.

Swiggy's cockpit was up the steps from the Lounge, beyond the beaded curtain. 'R-Rumbles?' Tommy called from the foot of the steps. 'Any-w-one?' Receiving no answer, he turned away, missing his chance to enter the cockpit and notice the flashing warning light.

He looked in the GalleyKitchen – nothing but a three-foot pile of dirty plates by the sink – and checked a dozen other rooms, having no luck till he reached the SwotStudy. There, amidst the laden shelves, a big, furry creature was sitting on a swing suspended from the ceiling, staring at a ginormous screen. 'And what about Pavalavalovian Pieskeys?' she asked.

'One wheelbarrow's worth of meringue,' replied the screen in a high voice. 'Plus ten pawfuls of cream, a vat of custard and a trailer-load of fruit.'

What's new? thought Tommy. Rumbles was consulting *Swiggapedia* for recipes.

'H-hey!'

'Wha – Aaargghhh!' Rumbles fell backwards off the swing, knocking over a desk and a pile of books and landing in a heap.

'S-sorry! Didn't m-mean to f-f-frighten you,' said Tommy, offering his furry friend a hand.

Rumbles, who was taller than a lanky basketball player, was pear-shaped and had three arms (one of which stemmed from his back) and feet like loaves of bread (unsliced). His fur was charcoal, his wide eyes orangey.

Since Rumbles was both male and female, I'll refer to him as 'he' or 'she' depending upon her mood at that exact moment (which may even change mid-sentence).

'You didn't frighten me,' said Rumbles. 'That's the way I always dismount the swingskeys.'

As they righted the table and were gathering books, Tommy asked the thunderbumble for a piece of wisdom. After some contemplation, she answered: 'Eat much, drink lots and be cheerfulskeys. But don't go overboardskeys today or you might die tomorrow.'

When they looked up Wisdom in Swiggapedia, they found two definitions:

1 A good judgement or understanding of what is right or true.
2 Learning or knowledge acquired by study and experience.

Tommy was more impressed with the thunderbumble's answer than with Swiggapedia's.

. . . The One-Eyed Man Is King

Swiggapedia took up an entire wall of the SwotStudy. When off, it looked like a fish tank housing starstarfish, planetmackerel and other species. When on, it resembled a giant computer screen and you 'navigated' by touching the screen with your hands, feet or tail.[4] (Tommy usually turned gravity off in the Study when using Swiggapedia so he could 'navigate' more easily.) As Swiggy flew past galaxies, Swiggapedia automatically downloaded any information in the airwaves which had been generated by 'ordinary locals' – although it gave no guarantee that such info was 'accurate . . . or sane'.

'Hey, someone's calling you,' announced Rumbles.

Sure enough, a silvery light was flashing atop the intercom by the door. Tommy hurried over, in little doubt who it was. 'Hey, W-Woozie,' he said, pressing the intercom button.

'You up yet, ya lazy sod?' Woozie Wibblewoodrow's voice crackled out at him. 'Forgotten 'bout our rocket-blade race? Or are ya too human to go through with it?'

I should explain . . . Many people from the Milky Way (known as MilkyFederans) use the word 'human', where we humans would use the word 'chicken'. Its use originates from the fact that down through the ages humans always became really scared whenever a MilkyFed flying saucer overflew Earth.

'I'll t-take you any t-time, W-Wibblewoodrow!' retorted Tommy.

Woozie guffawed, echoing, 'I'll take you any time,' in a perfect Tommy impression (but leaving out the stutter). Then he added: 'Yeah, right! If you're not here in eight minutes then you've officially *humaned* out and you forfeit the

4 Some 'pages' allow voice-interaction once you've navigated to them.

race to me.'

'F-fine. I'll b-b-be there.'

Once Woozie was off the line, Tommy paged Marielle. A blue light flashed atop every intercom in Swiggy. But there was no answer.

At this point, the warning light in Swiggy's cockpit started making a throat-clearing sound – like somebody politely looking for attention.

Following a hunch, having descended to the bowels of Swiggy, Tommy found himself in a narrow corridor with two fast-moving travelators running side by side in opposite directions. He jumped on to one, lost his balance and landed on his bum. He was whisked past half a dozen doors till he reached one labelled 'Octuballia Training'.

He dived through the swing door, landing face-down in a small room with a glass bottom. He shook his head and glanced about. The room was empty save for a couch made out of freeze-dried potato and a trapdoor in the transparent floor, out of which protruded a long, rubbery sock like an elephant's trunk. Beneath him (just as he'd guessed), Marielle was floating in a squash-court-sized space, scimmy in hand, wearing a padded helmet and facing a creature that looked like a furry black ball with eight arms – each wielding a sword or a flail or a saucepan.

The young Earthling couldn't help pausing and admiring Marielle. The petite elquinine moved with speed and intensity, somehow remaining graceful all the while. Her eyes – one bright blue, the other hazelnut brown – were shadowed under the ridge of her helmet, yet Tommy could sense their fire.

By now, the warning light in the cockpit was making a loud tinging noise – like someone hitting a glass with a spoon, calling for attention before a speech . . .

Tommy found the OcTr control panel on the wall and did some twiddling. *This should freeze the Octuballia and halt the session.* But, next thing, eggs the size of watermelons were whizzing across the court, Marielle was being tossed about like confetti[5] and the Octuballia had begun fighting with a maniacal fury. (Tommy'd actually increased the Fury level from *LostMyKeys*, past *ThatDriverDidn'tWaveWhenILetThemIn*, all the way up to *FemaleScorned.*) Two of the meleggs hit the blonde girl before the Octuballia cracked her helmet and the contest halted.

'You trying to kill me?' cried Marielle when she'd climbed out of the zero-gravity court through the insanely tight rubber trunk to the normal gravity conditions of the CouchPotatoGallery.

'N-n-none of the b-buttons were l-labelled on the OcTr control p-panel!'

An argument ensued, in the midst of which, Tommy blurted, 'Who are y-you to–? The G-GalleyKitchen is a p-pig-sty. You're supposed to b-be on w-washing up this w-week.'

'I always wash up on the *last* day of the week.'

The row ended when Tommy helped the blonde elquinine out of her helmet (which had wedged on super-tight) and whacked his head off a wall.

'W-wisdom,' he said, once he'd recovered. 'Can you give me a p-piece of w-w-wisdom?'

'Is *that* what you halted my duel to ask me?'

'OK, f-f-forget it!' cried Tommy, pushing through the

5 Caused by blasts of air in the zero-gravity enclosure. (A magnetic field kept the Octuballia fixed in the centre of the court.)

swing-door and falling on to a travelator.

Marielle's face appeared around the doorway, watching Tommy recede into the distance. 'Once said, a mean comment cannot be taken back. It's out there forever . . . THAT'S MY WISDOM!'

Tommy rounded a corner and the elquinine disappeared from sight.

Rocket-blades in hand, Tommy stood outside the door of the WallSphereOf-Death(ish). He could hear Woozie calling out (in a perfect Tommy Storm impression): 'Seven minutes forty-four seconds . . . forty-five seconds . . . forty-six . . .'

The Earthling had been in such a rush to get his rocket-blades that he hadn't ventured inside Swiggy's cockpit and seen or heard the warning light. Nor had anyone else. Travelling at many times the speed of light had become the norm for all the IGGY Knights and they frequently activated the automatic pilot for over twenty-two hours a day.

Tommy planned to join Woozie just as the furry wibble-wallian got to seven minutes fifty-eight seconds. But Woozie never got that far. He halted the count when a shrieking alarm began sounding in every cabin, corridor and crevice of Swiggy, screaming: *NOOOO! IIIIIIII! NOOOO!*

'Emergency! Emergency!' cried Woozie, bursting through the door. 'The WAP alarm!' The reddy-brown creature's big green eyes were agape, his button nose sniffing the air. He looked like a small, hairy human, yet for once he wasn't smiling, wasn't revealing those gleaming white teeth. He scanned left and right, spotted Tommy whisking away on a travelator and – scurrying after him – saw his good friend jump at a doorway, miss, hit a wall and crash face-down on to another travelator zooming in the opposite direction. Ordinarily, Woozie would've stopped to help, but this time he jumped through the doorway Tommy'd tried to enter and disappeared . . . For the IGGY Knights had never known the WAP alarm to sound for real.

WAP stands for Without A Paddle – as in, 'up a creek without a paddle'. WAP alarms never go off by accident (unless set off inadvertently) and only sound on MilkyFed craft for disasters such as the captain being sucked out of the cockpit, an imminent crash or a craft bereft of handkerchiefs and dock-leaves running out of toilet paper.

Rumbles and Marielle were already in the cockpit when Woozie arrived, chewing on the pair of dog tags at the end of his leather necklace. The WAP alarm was so loud it made the wibblewallian grind his teeth into the silver tags.

'Can we turn it down!?' he shouted.

Rumbles and Marielle said something inaudible and all three began scrambling with various dials before someone found the right one and reduced the volume.

'THAT'S MUCH BETTERSKEYS!' cried Rumbles, ears not yet adjusted.

Summy appeared. 'A false alarm this better not be!' she cried to everyone's surprise. 'My planet jigsaw – from the WAP alarm, such a shock I got, that into it I fell. Completely it's ruined.'

Then Tommy appeared – frenzied and red-faced. 'Wh-what is it?' he asked.

'My jigsaw!' replied Summy.

'N-not your silly j-jigsaw. I mean the W-W-WAP alarm!'

Summy was about to reply that her jigsaw wasn't silly when she knocked a lever and a screen lit up. It explained the problem with three flashing words.

For a time no one said a word. Things were worse than any of them had feared.

In the years since they left the Milky Way, the IGGY Knights had stopped off in just seven galaxies. In each case, they went into Stealth Mode and eavesdropped on the galaxy's inhabitants before making the decision to land. And the reason for such precautions . . .? Well, the FiiVe were charged with saving the universe from the Terrible Future Calamity (the TFC) – a reasonably important task – and they had no wish to fail merely because they'd stopped off for shampoo on an unknown planet and ended up getting eaten by the locals.

Hence the fear that passed through the IGGY Knights as they stood in Swiggy's cockpit and saw three words flashing on a screen.

OUT OF FUEL

'How did–?'

'You'd think we'd get some warning firstskeys.'

'We d-did. Looks like that w-warning light's been g-g-going off for hours.'

Swiggy was still moving fast through space and could keep going for an indefinite length of time. But without fuel she was like a glider. With no acceleration. Any time they pressed the brakes and her speed reduced, that would become her new speed till the brakes were pressed again and her speed reduced yet further. The Auxiliary Power would ensure that lights, central heating and vital systems (including automatic pilot) could continue for at least three weeks.

Turbo Boost

Swiggy's fuel system required only very small amounts of 'fizz' in order to convert organic matter into fuel via a POP!fzzzzsshhhhh!! chain reaction. In practice, this meant that if you dropped a jelly-cola bottle or poured a mouthful of fizzy drink into the fuel chute once a week, Swiggy'd continue flying normally so long as the garbage bins were emptied into the fuel drum or an IGGY Knight went to the loo at least once a day (the toilets' exit pipes led directly into the fuel drum). Sometimes Tommy could actually feel Swiggy travelling faster after Rumbles had 'used the facilities'. Turbo boost, she called it.

'C-can we reach Hells-b-b-bells on Auxiliary Power?' asked Tommy looking at Summy.

The dinosaurus nodded. 'But further not much.'

Rumbles had another suggestion. 'Why not veer towards the next galaxy we see insteadskeys?'

Woozie shook his head. 'Cos if it's uninhabited and we can't find any fizzy stuff when we come to a halt, then *that's it*. We're finished.'

It was Marielle who vocalized what they all knew, but feared to admit. 'We've no choice. We have to keep going . . . To Hellsbells . . . *Without* the usual precautions.'

'W-without *any* p-precautions,' Tommy muttered.

'We won't be able to go into Stealth Mode,' said Woozie. 'We need fuel for that.'

'And if fizzy fuel there we cannot find,' said Summy. 'Never again will Swiggy take off.'

The cockpit filled with unspoken dread. For Marielle was right . . . They had no choice.

5

Not One (A Bit About the Mission Thus Far)

In the first three years of their mission, the FiiVe had attended countless interactive lessons given by the Milki Masters who'd trained them before they left the Milky Way. (This was made possible by a combination of tutorial holograms and grow-sss-goo movies.)

The most senior Master of the Way was a scaly, orange kangasaurus called Lord Beardedmoustachedwiseface-oh – who went by the nickname of Wisebeardyface. He focused on the TFC and on putting the lessons of the other Masters in context.

'Your mission is to save the universe from the TFC,' declared the orange dinosaurus with monotonous regularity. 'Do not let *anything* deviate you from this course.'

Wisebeardyface's classes usually took place in Swiggy's Lounge, with the old Master standing on the coffee table, bowing his head (since it would scrape off the ceiling) and the five IGGY Knights seated on giant cushions in a semi-circle before him. No less than three times as tall as Tommy, Wisebeardyface had scaly skin and his beard trailed down almost to his (two) feet. His tail was festooned with grey triangular slatey things that grew larger as they continued up the middle of his back, then shrank to nothing as they approached his neck. His face looked like that of a kindly dragon.

In one of the first classes, Wisebeardyface explained the course their mission should take. 'Yes, we set you off in a particular direction, but you must chart a course of your own. Since the TFC is scheduled to destroy the whole universe, we believe that you will find evidence of it on your travels. And once you have a sniff of the trail, you must stick to it, follow it, hound it down with every ounce of resolve you possess.'

It wasn't till they were eleven months into the mission that the FiiVe decided to deviate significantly from Swiggy's pre-set course (following a reference they'd found on Swiggapedia). Over the next couple of years they ended up flittering from galaxy to galaxy based on various tips (none of which revealed anything about the TFC), until they heard about the notorious criminal Nack Jickilson and decided to seek him out. Throughout these travels, Tommy was aware of a point made by Wisebeardyface in an early class.

'And yet, when you discover the nature of the TFC – *that* is only *half* the task completed. Maybe less. For you will have to use all your skills and cunning to put a stop to it. What sacrifice that will entail, I cannot say.'

In one of the more recent classes, the old dinosaurus admitted: 'There are lots of theories, but we do not know what the TFC is, specifically.'

'Then how do you know there really is a TFC?' asked Woozie.

'Or that it's due to happen in eighteen years' time?' added Tommy.

'We feel 102 per cent certain that a TFC of some description is scheduled to happen,' replied Wisebeardyface, stuffing his short arms into the pouch in his belly. 'This is because a DSM Messenger made it to the Milky Way and told us Milki Masters that it was so. Other DSM Messengers have come to us in the past and the gist of what they have said has always been true . . . Yes, it could be argued that the TFC may not happen in precisely eighteen years' time. It may not be for twenty-three years, or alternatively, it might be in just fourteen years' time.'

'In that case,' ventured Marielle. 'Might it just as possibly happen in eight years' time or, say, in only three years' time?'

'Hmmm . . .' Wisebeardyface scratched his beard and took out a cigarette. 'Could someone get me a drink of cherry-mango-crush-surpreez – in a *very* tall glass.'

'Five out of Six Harbingers use it'
(Slogan for Costmost Cosmos Anti-Dandruff Shampoo)

DSM Messengers (Don'tShootMe Messengers) were creatures who carried important (bad news) messages tattooed on their heads, having travelled for millions of years from distant galaxies. By the time they arrived at the Milki Masters' door they'd be too old to speak and their head would have to be shaved so the message could be viewed. Invariably the Messenger died soon after and it was incumbent on the Milki Masters to tattoo the same message on the head of a MilkyFed citizen and then blast them out of the Milky Way in the direction that the Messenger had been heading, so that the message could be relayed to more distant galaxies. It was estimated that thousands of other galaxies would've relayed the message in this way *before* it reached the Milky Way – hence the Chinese Whispers Effect (meaning that small variations or inaccuracies could've crept into the message).

Since the birth of the Milky Way, six DSMs had arrived at

the Milki Masters' door, each with a different message. The first had to do with the dangers of meteorites, the second with the dangers of nuclear weapons, the third with the dangers of bicycles without lights, the fourth with the dangers of unremitting irony and the fifth with the irony of unremitting danger (this one was difficult to read because of a septic boil on the scalp of the Messenger). The sixth one had to do with the end of the universe (the TFC).

The old dinosaurus lit the cigarette and took a few anxious puffs while Rumbles disappeared to the GalleyKitchen. The other IGGY Knights knew by the look on the dinosaurus's face that he didn't want to be spoken to, and so they were relieved when Rumbles returned with a metre-tall glass, half-filled with a purple, crushed-ice juice drink.

Wisebeardyface took it with barely a nod of thanks, turned away and pulled something from his pouch. The FiiVe heard a glug-glug pouring sound and when Wisebeardyface turned around, the glass was almost full.

'Oh, and you might need *this*keys,' said Rumbles, handing over a ridiculously long straw (twice the length of the couch).

Wisebeardyface put the (bendy) straw in the glass and then, reclining on the sofa, with one end in his mouth, he proceeded to suck. Amazingly, he was able to smoke his cigarette at the same time and only experienced two choking fits before he'd drained the glass.

He stared into space (literally) for about ten minutes and then quite suddenly he jumped back on to the coffee table and started singing, 'She'll Be Coming Round The Comet When She Comes' while performing the Can't-Can't (a dance – with opposite movements to the Can-Can). At last, having bumped his head off the ceiling on numerous occasions, fallen off the coffee table twice and sung nineteen verses of the song, the old dinosaurus burst into tears. 'It is really, really tough being head of the Milky Way,' he wailed. 'I have not had a holiday – a real holiday – since . . .' He never finished the sentence. Instead, he blurted: 'Corona Borealis is the only woman I ever loved. But then . . . she died in a spacecraft accident, before seatbelts in cockpits were made compulsory, before the medical advances that could have . . .'

Rumbles went to give the old Master a hug, but unfortunately, Wisebeardyface chose that very moment to throw up a bellyful of purple liquid.

While Rumbles showered and the others cleaned up the mess, Wisebeardyface crawled face-down on the coffee table and fell asleep. The FiiVe couldn't wake him for two days (they were afraid to whisk him back into the silver lesson-container-case and end the class, in case something happened to him in his current state). When he finally roused, the FiiVe gathered round the bleary-eyed dinosaurus as he downed a bucket of steaming BlackholeJavaCoffee®. 'I am most sorry about that,' he said, with a rasping voice. 'I do not know quite what came over me.' Then, wiping his lips with a hanky from his pouch, he looked at Marielle. 'What was the question again?'

'Er,' said the elquinine. 'I was just wondering if it *might* be possible that the TFC could happen in, say, eight years' time or three years' time?'

Wisebeardyface belched and then, in a voice that strained to sound upbeat, he said: 'Do everything in your power to stop the TFC *asap*. Do not waste a minute. Why yes, take a breather, recuperate for a few hours now and again if you must. But remember that *even one day* lounging about is one day nearer the TFC and *one day* that can *never* be reclaimed. The future of every planet, every star, every creature, yes, the future of every single living thing depends on you stopping the TFC . . . So, with all this resting on your shoulders, let me give you some advice – *the most important* advice I can give you . . .'

Looking deadly serious, the old dinosaur stood tall, bumped his head on the ceiling and crouched a little. If anything the look of seriousness becoming even more serious. 'Do not waste so much as one day!' he cried. 'Not one!' As the words, *Not one* flew from his lips, a flame of fire roared from his mouth, hitting Swiggy's ceiling and fanning outwards, so that for a moment the whole room was encircled in flame.

Tommy dived for a silver case on the floor and prised it open. The flame vanished like a snuffed-out candle and Wisebeardyface disappeared into the case with a whoosh – Tommy immediately slamming it shut.

The young Earthling would've felt quite pleased with himself except that he ended up sprawled on the shag-pile rug, between the coffee table and the couch. And, alas, there could be no doubt. The smell of stale vomit hadn't quite gone.

6

A Dish of Revenge

In the days following the OUT OF FUEL debate, Swiggy whizzed along a handful of speedy-uppy-zones and passed through an asteroid belt known as Devil's Buckle where the 'asteroids' consisted of Pluto-sized body parts. The FiiVe flew through hairy nostrils and snapping mouths and past squished eyes, thrashing tails and clenching hands. At one point, Tommy thought they were going to be stamped by a particularly large clubbed foot with mouldy moon-sized toenails, but Swiggy managed to steer them safely out of danger.

That evening, the FiiVe sat down to a meal of cold soup and raw veggies. It was a bit sad, but the hob and cooker were out of operation.

'G-glad I'm not on w-w-wash-up,' laughed Tommy at one point, seeing the mountain of pots, pans and dishes in the sink and remembering there was no hot water.

He meant it as a joke to lighten the mood. But Marielle heard only sarcasm. 'Very funny,' she retorted. 'I said I'd do it before the end of the week.'

Woozie tried to cheer everyone up by producing some flippety-flapjacks he'd 'baked' – claiming them to be a wibblewallian speciality.

'Uuugghhh!'

'Pppffaawwww!'

Sitting at the table-booth in the GalleyKitchen, everyone spat out mouthfuls and almost doubled over.

'Disgusting are these.'

'Told you they wouldn't cookskeys without an oven!'

'They're fine!' said Woozie, trying to down a mouthful. 'OK, maybe they need more sinsinammon.'

That same evening, Tommy went looking for Marielle. He felt bad about their dinner-time misunderstanding and wanted to apologize. But when he peered into the Ammunition Hold, he saw that the elquinine was inside chatting to her parents (they were actually dead, but they'd left the elquinine a case of interactive holograms so she could sit and chat with them about schoolwork, romance or appropriate modes of dress). Not wanting to intrude, he went looking for Woozie. But the wibblewallian was in the WallSphereOf-Death(ish) with one of *his* family interactive holograms, playing an argumentative game of charades (his brothers were notorious cheats). Coincidentally, Rumbles and Summy were also off doing family hologram activities, so Tommy ended up alone in the semi-domed, glass-walled room on the underside of Swiggy, known as the Bellepoch Studio (pronounced *Bellypock*).

Tommy's parents had died when he was a baby and they'd never got to make any interactive holograms for him. Normally, Tommy didn't think about this very much, but this particular evening, he had the palpable sense of being an orphan. He took up his electric violin and played a 'happy' piece at half speed, purposely out-of-tune. He tried – and failed – to picture what his parents would look like if they'd lived to this day.

Later, as Swiggy continued avoiding seen and unseen obstacles, Tommy lay in his bunk and tried to put his parents out of his head by thinking about Marielle. When this failed to cheer him, he considered the one subject that no one seemed prepared to talk about.

The Beast.

As images of dragons and monsters drifted into his head, he fought them off. In the midst of this battle, he somehow fell asleep.

Next afternoon, a misty shadow appeared on the SickoWarpoSpeed Viewfinder. Seated in Swiggy's cockpit, Tommy and Woozie eyed the strange form.

'Think this is itskeys?' asked Woozie, imitating Rumbles.

Tommy nodded, adding: 'Which would you p-prefer . . . to meet the B-B-Beast on your own or to eat a p-pair of Rumbles under-p-pants?' He found humour a good way to combat fear.

'Would they be clean or used?'

Tommy never got to answer because at that moment the other three arrived through the beaded curtains.

'Is this Hellsbells?'

'S-seems to b-be.'

As they drew closer, they could make out a sickly-lit form. It looked like a planet with a third of its 'skin' peeled back, revealing the crown, eye-sockets and nose of an animal-like skull filling the inside. And the skull had two horns (one cutting through the planet's crust where it hadn't peeled back). The grisly form was shrouded in mist and overlooked by a pale moon.

Woozie gulped. 'OK to apply the brakes . . .? Remember, we'll be stuck at whatever speed we slow to. And if we actually bring the craft to a halt . . .'

The wibblewallian bit on one of the silver dog tags hanging round his neck – not wanting to finish the sentence. The IGGY Knights looked from one to the other and nodded uncertainly. Woozie pressed the brakes.

Swiggy cruised forward, Hellsbells swelling before the IGGY Knights. Tommy looked for some trace of emotion in its looming moon-crater eye-sockets. And found none.

Soon Swiggy was moving at a crawl and Hellsbells was so close that nothing else was visible through the cockpit windscreen. A patchwork of sickly stubble – weeds and barren trees – was now visible across the planet's crust.

'Stopping . . . stopping . . .' Woozie pulled the handbrake with a dramatic flourish. 'Stopped!' Then silence, till Woozie added: 'No going back now.'

They appeared to be stationary over one of the skull's nasal cavities.

'Should we take the jeggs down from here?'

'A good idea that sounds like.'

'Except—!'

Marielle was pointing to a sign in the distance.

Hellsbells

NO ENTRY

Don't Even Try

Protected by Fantastic Forcefield Technology

Go Away If You Know What's Good For You

And If You Don't, Then Still Go Away

As in the Milky Way, most writing in the cosmos was covered in Twaddle or a similar substance – so everyone could 'see' it in their language if MayksScents4UsNow or a similar substance had been sprayed into their eyes. (The FiiVe's eyes had been sprayed in the Milky Way – see TS1 *for more.)*

Summy was peering into a monitor. 'Yes, a force field there is. Incredibly strong the readings indicate.'

'So how do we get in?'

For the next two hours, Summy sent countless messages from the cockpit in an effort to get some response from Hellsbells. She tried using walkie-talkies, flag signals and even smoke signals. Meanwhile, Tommy, up in a gun turret, used a large spotlight to spell out messages in Morse code. When that failed to elicit a reply, Woozie fired several rounds with the tomato machine gun and Marielle and Rumbles shot off a number of cream pies from the missile launcher. But the tomatoes and cream pies just hit the invisible force field and stuck to it as if it were a pane of glass.

'N-no response.'

'All we've done is create a big mess.'

'What if we don't get throughskeys?'

'The Auxiliary P-Power will r-run out in a few w-w-weeks.'

'Meaning what exactly?'

'Meaning *S*-Swiggy will stop p-p-producing oxygen . . . And we'll su-suffocate.'

After another hour of fretting, the FiiVe decided to 'relax' for a while. Rumbles locked herself in the GalleyKitchen with a large book – *Good Foreign Food Cooked Cold.*[6] Summy went to see what she could retrieve of her jigsaw ('All woes I forget when a jigsaw doing'), while Woozie stuffed a few

6 'Foreign' being any food not from the Milky Way.

flippety-flapjacks into his pockets ('In case I get peckish') and set off with his rocket-blades to the WallSphereOf-Death(ish).

Marielle was going to disappear to the Ammunition Hold with her clarinet, but changed her mind when she saw Tommy marching out of the Boys' Dorm, violin in hand. Instead, she opted to soak in a (cool) bath.

The FiiVe were so preoccupied that they didn't notice a spacecraft whizzing towards them – syringe-shaped with a shark-like fin on its 'back' and a sharp, steel hook for a tail. Inside the craft's bridge, a small creature was reclining on a sofa, his foot firmly wedged in a clamp.

'Yahhh!' he cried. 'I'm still too cold for revenge. How long to impact?'

'Thirty seconds, Mr Jickilson . . . Accelerating to ram speed.'

Nack Jickilson could see Swiggy in the distance, drifting around Hellsbells. He leaned forwards and turned the screw on the clamp. 'Aaaaaghhhhhhhh!!!' Oh, that felt good. The pain. It made him hot. 'Sherbet! Quick, get me some sherbet!'

A creature rushed forward with a bowl of sherbet just as Nack whumped his forehead on the clamp with a cry of: 'Revenge! Revenge!'

'Adjust trajectory,' said the captain from behind Nack Jickilson. 'Take account of their orbit.'

'Roger,' said another voice. 'Trajectory adjusted.'

The captain's voice raised an octave. 'Don't call me Roger!' (Although his name was Roger, he insisted on being called Captain.) 'We're going to slice them in two.'

'All riiiiight!!!!' cried Nack, shuddering with exhilaration. Then, remembering something, his face turned cool. 'Just don't run into the force field!'

'No danger. Set to miss it by twenty degrees on the starboard side . . . Our fin will slice through them in . . . six seconds . . . four seconds . . .'

As Swiggy swelled across the windscreen, Nack Jickilson inhaled the bowl of sherbet, all coolness gone. 'Aaaaaiiiiiiiiiiiggggghhhhhh!!'

'Two seconds . . . one second.'

Oh, revenge could be hot, yet sweet.

7

Storm's Storm (a bit about growing up on Swiggy)

OK, so you know the IGGY Knights had visited seven galaxies during the first three years of their mission. But since many of those adventures are for another book, you're probably wondering how on Earth (or, more accurately, *how in the universe*) the FiiVe had been filling their time. The simple answer is: training and learning; searching for clues; mapping the universe; surviving and growing up.

By now, the FiiVe were all equivalent in maturity to fourteen-year-old humans. Swiggy's designers had taken this into account, which was why Swiggy had two separate mini-dorms (male and female) and a pair of tweezers attached to a chain in the SwishBathroom. As Summy often put it: 'Less smelly and more messy is our dorm.'

In recent months, Marielle had abandoned pigtails and pulled all her hair into a single ponytail. Her sweatshirts had become more clingy and she generally wore denim dungarees full of bulging pockets. Summy rarely wore more than a T-shirt with a nerdy slogan (such as, 'Adult-free Zone'), although she frequently sported a robotic speaking parrot (called Edwina) on her shoulder. Despite Summy's warnings on the dangers of piercings, Marielle now had one in her belly-button ('There are no parents to stop me'). She called Summy a copykatt[7] when, six months later, the winged kangasaurus had a tiny silver dumb-bell inserted through the end of her tail. 'Very different is a tail piercing to your jewel belly-button,' retorted Summy.

Woozie enjoyed using *the gals*' newly acquired bras as slingshots whenever he got hold of them, which usually resulted in a ferocious pillow fight. On one occasion, he caught Marielle in a bad mood and ended up with a black eye for his troubles 'These are my personal artefacts,' cried Marielle, feeling bad as Woozie's eye grew darker and hoping that *artefacts* was the correct word to use in this situation.

Woozie, who'd become an accomplished impersonator, had his own 'artefacts'. The dog tags that always hung around his neck had been fashioned by the wibblewallian from Milky Way silver after he'd taken some metalwork classes. They consisted of two razor-blade-sized pieces of silver – *IGGY Knights* engraved on one, *Always* on the other – strung on to a leather necklace. Dog tags aside, the main changes to Woozie since leaving IGGY were the short ponytail he'd grown through his reddy-brown fur and the fact that he sported leather wristbands. Plus he stopped being afraid of spaghetti.

Although Rumbles continued to wear nothing but a mustard-coloured pair of undies, the greatest transformation in her, according to her fellow Knights, was that she no longer mentioned them when they went missing. It was a strain for her not to, but she'd had a serious think about it soon after Swiggy left IGGY and reckoned that a mature Knight shouldn't be worrying others with thoughts of

7 'Copykatt' is a word copied directly from the word 'copycat' – they both mean the same thing.

undies. She also tried to cut down on using cute wordskeys, but this generally failed unless she was being interrogated or was telling jokes. (She maintained that both situations felt remarkably similar to her.)

Since Rumbles was both male and female, he slept in the male or female dorm, depending on her mood, ignoring Summy's insistence that 'much too hairy are you to sleep in this dorm'. Summy's attitude was almost certainly influenced by the fact that the three-armed bear had begun to do number sevens when she went to the toilet – in addition to her established repertoire of ones, twos, threes, fives and sixes.

A.K.A

At some point, historians realized that the IGGY Knights' (favoured) middle names were:

- ★ Frederick (Tommy)
- ★ ickle (Marielle)
- ★ ice-ICE-baby (Woozie)
- ★ Vera (Rumbles)
- ★ eisenhower (Summy)

From then on, they were often referred to as *the FiiVe.*

One person whose appearance had altered little was Tommy. Yes, he was a tad taller, a smidgen broader, but his face still looked part Asian, part West Indian, part South American, part Middle Eastern, part Celt, part Maori, part Inuit and part Liverpudlian. And he continued to wear black trainers, black trousers and a black shirt beneath a fray of black spiky hair. By now, his voice had half-broken (it sounded croaky sometimes) and he frequently searched in the mirror for evidence of facial hair (there was none). Occasionally, when stressed, he'd get a smattering of zits across his shoulder blades and would have to avoid doing shoulder stands till they disappeared.

As a result of the FiiVe's recent scrapes and adventures, the young Earthling now had a ξ-shaped burn mark across his left palm and a finger's-width scar across his right cheek-bone (it added to the look of menace when he was angry).

Back in the Milky Way, Tommy'd taken up the electric violin. Despite his failing co-ordination, his playing had improved over the ensuing three years. Once, as Swiggy'd hovered, stationary, outside a galaxy, Tommy's co-ordination had returned (briefly), and his playing had been 'almost masterful'. Yet ordinarily, even with stumbling fingers, he could channel feelings into his trusted violin. Whenever he felt angry, unsure or frustrated, he'd disappear into the Bellepoch Studio and conjure up a wild, fuming piece of music. The crazed sounds from these solo performances made the other IGGY Knights think of someone frantically searching for shelter in a thunder storm. They referred to such mini-concertos as *Storm's storm*.

Not all Tommy's violin-playing was 'stormy'. He sometimes played mischievous, playful tunes – which was how, soon after they left IGGY, he persuaded each of his fellow Knights to take up an instrument. Rumbles took up the double-bass and the castanets (her three arms allowing him to play both at the same time). Summy started 'tinkling' on the piano and Woozie elected for the drums. ('In the bathroom please practise,' Summy would yell. 'With the door shut well!' To which Woozie would reply: 'That's rich coming from you, outta-tune-piano-gal.') Marielle took to the clarinet, but wouldn't let anyone hear her play. At some stage, she realized that IGGY's Ammunition Hold was soundproof, and even though it only had a narrow, slitty window looking out to space, this is where she played – eyeing the slice of blackness as stars, comet trails and distant flashes were tossed across it.

Tommy was probably closest to Woozie. They teased each other good-naturedly (Woozie often saying dumb things in Tommy's voice) and enjoyed trying to outdo each other with PreferYuck questions whenever circumstances got hairy – such as, *Would you prefer to kiss a dead thunderbumblian chef on the lips for three minutes or to be locked in the loo for an hour after Rumbles has done a number six?* They had a minor row once about who got to sleep in the top bunk in their dorm, but compromised – swapping every three months.

Tommy's friendship with Rumbles was quite physical – in the sense that they often had play-fights and would occasionally indulge each other with a big hug. His bond with Summy was how he imagined it might be if he had an older sister who was incredibly nerdy.

The relationship between Tommy and Marielle had shifted from what it was in IGGY and they irked each other with increasing frequency (Tommy's most frantic violin concertos usually took place after he and Marielle had had a row).

The first nine months of the mission had been great. The Earthling and the elquinine often stayed up late chatting and almost kissed on a few occasions. One opportunity was aborted when Tommy clunked over a glass of juice as he moved in closer. Another time, Woozie wandered out into the Lounge, bleary-eyed, wondering what time it was and the moment was lost. A tongue-tied lack of nerve accounted for the third lost chance. Afterwards, having departed meekly to their separate dorms, they both lay in bed and fumed at their cowardice.

The last occasion was preceded by a stop-off in the Cadeaux Constellation for fuel and supplies. During the visit, Tommy disappeared and returned to Swiggy with a small gift-box. Later, in the Lounge, he presented it to Marielle. 'Just something I came across,' he said.

She opened the box and lifted out a white silk handkerchief with red polka-dots. TLM was printed in small letters in one corner (it stood for *Thunder Lightning Merchandise*, but Marielle presumed it stood for Tommy Loves Marielle). She was about to kiss the spiky-haired boy when the other IGGY Knights bustled in with bags of long-life groceries.

It's unclear why they didn't kiss that night – perhaps because there was so much work to be done (maintenance to Swiggy, purchasing more provisions). But whatever the reason, it made Tommy think that Marielle didn't want to kiss him. And his slightly changed demeanour as a result made her act a bit different, which then made him act a bit *more* different.

This altered behaviour was compounded a few weeks later when Tommy's stutter re-emerged. Whatever confidence he'd had in romantic scenarios sank without trace, so he no longer 'put himself in the way' of potentially scary one-on-one situations with the elquinine. Yet somehow he came to see this as Marielle avoiding *him* and formed the belief that she had no interest in him now that he was 'afflicted with a speech imp-p-pediment.'

Minor irritations flared between the human and the elquinine over the next year or so, but nothing too serious – nothing, that is, until the Elquinine Concerto Incident.

The IGGY Knights' adventures in the first three years of their mission may not be for this book, but it's important to note that the FiiVe understood all the languages they'd come across. It was as if the Talkie Max and Talkie Wax technology embedded in their tongues and ears (enabling them to understand *each other*) used a technology that was common across the universe. This made Summy wonder out loud whether language-comprehension technology had originated somewhere deep in the heart of the universe and been spread to all galaxies, including the Milky Way.[8]

Origin of the Specious Theory

The fact that the FiiVe could read signs and text wherever they went (all were covered in Twaddle) supported Summy's comment and chimed with a theory called the *HmmmMaybeIt-Didn'tHappen-In96Tempus-fugits Theory*[9] which suggested that the very first Milky Way creatures had great-grandparents with criminal records in far-flung galaxies.

A tempusfugit, by the way, is the time measurement used in the Milky Way, equal to 90 Earth minutes. I will endeavour to convert all times in this book to Earth time (minutes, hours, days, months, years etc.).

8 Talkie Maxes and Waxes are described in detail in *TS1* – as are lots more details about the FiiVe (so if you haven't done so already, do yourself a favour and read *TS1*!).

9 Postulated by the renowned Milky Way scholar, Dr Femmy Blass, it's sometimes referred to as the BotanyBay Theory by serious botanists (and by a number of giggly botanists).

8

Trap? Or Party?

As Swiggy swelled across the windscreen, Nack Jickilson inhaled the bowl of sherbet. 'Aaaaaiiiiiiiiiiggghhhhhh!!'

'Two seconds . . . One second.'

Somewhere between seven-tenths and eight-tenths of a second later, the (by now) enormous view of Swiggy disappeared from sight. Completely. One moment it was there. The next it wasn't.

Nack Jickilson had just enough time to say, 'Wha—? . . . Aaaaggghhhhhhhhhhh!!!' as his spacecraft flashed passed Hellsbells, through a cloud of mist the size of Iceland and straight into the path of the pale moon.

Tommy was in the Bellepoch Studio playing his violin, thoughts of death and failure on his mind. There were many ways to die, he thought, but just to sit here, waiting for the oxygen to drain out of Swiggy, was a particularly feeble and embarrassing way to go.

For the first twenty minutes, he'd thrashed angry, violent music from the violin, his co-ordination seemingly returned (however briefly). If you could see music as colour, the Bellepoch would've splashed full of red, orange and yellow, with streaks of black. But, his anger spent, the music slid into a slow, sad lament. He thought of his planet – Earth – and wondered if it really matters where you come from. Don't most living creatures want the same things . . ? He thought of his parents – would he see them after he died or was death just a nothingness, like the nothingness before you were born? And then, however much he fought it, however much he tried to push it away with the music, a vision kept appearing, that stung him to his heart.

It was a close-up image of Marielle, side-on, in the Store Room. From Year One of the mission. She and Tommy had just had one of *those* conversations – speaking fondly of their home planets, of happy memories, of loved ones passed away. And despite the honesty, neither of them cried, managing to surf over the memories in a state of happy recall. For the most part. At one stage, Marielle stopped speaking mid-sentence and looked away, out at the stars. Her lips pursed, her cheeks flushed and her eyes . . . her eyes fighting to quell a force brimming within her. This, this was the moment . . . The moment Tommy was going to reach out and take the achingly beautiful elquinine into his arms. The moment he was going to tell her that, no matter what, everything would be OK. The moment he returned to a thousand times and whirred forwards from – to a myriad of possible endings. None of which resembled the *actual* ending.

For in the real, once-only moment, he hesitated.

And then the internal intercom had crackled on with the hooting sound of a Minor Emergency followed by a voice over the system 'Could you bring up some loo-rollskeys asap?' And the moment passed.

Yet it wasn't lost entirely.

He remembered it now – *always* – as a picture. Black and white, with smudged corners. Marielle, side-on, looking out at the stars.

When Swiggy shot forward without warning, the Bellepoch had no red or yellow colours splashing about its interior. Instead, it was brimming with ghostly shades – soft wisps of cream, speckled with white and black, like the mist outside – rising and falling in concert with the boy-in-black's gentle, see-saw hand.

As Swiggy came to a halt, the ghostly wisps dissolved to nothing. Tommy dropped the violin and bolted for the door.

The cockpit was alive with chatter. Marielle was holding forth (in wet shampooey hair), wearing nothing but a high-tied bath towel. She was the only one who'd seen the sight of Swiggy heading straight for Hellsbells' force field.

'Instead of splattering against it, we shot straight through!'

'D-d-deadly! So we're inside the p-perimeter!'

'Once again at a standstillskeys.'

'Still yet *there* is the force field – *inside* trapped we are!'

The IGGY Knights were just as startled as Nack Jickilson at the turn of events (OK, maybe not quite so startled).

Once they finished speculating on exactly what'd happened ('Magnetism, say would I, to move us caused.' 'What if it's a trap?'), and the Uh-O2-Monitor confirmed that the atmosphere inside the force field contained Oxygene[10] and no detectable poisons, it was agreed that they should try to enter Hellsbells in their jeggs.

10 Identical to oxygen except for a tang of onions.

Jeggs are not much longer than a family car with a fin arcing down two metres from the underbelly and the wings arcing back in a similar curved style. The FiiVe's jeggs were metallic grey, each tailored specifically for its owner, with their name printed in black letters along the side.

Tommy, Marielle, Woozie and Rumbles huddled in the JeggHold. They'd all taken showers (cold) and freshened up, which only added to the sense of nervous excitement – they could've been setting out to a party rather than venturing into unknown and possibly lethal territory.

Wear Clean Undies in Case of an Accident

(Four times voted Best Motherly Advice of All Time *by the MilkyFed)*

Like Earth mothers, MilkyFed mothers were always bossing their children with suggestions such as: 'Don't go out without a dufforce coat' (in case of meteorite showers); 'Speak with your mouth full' (some species consider *not* speaking with a full mouth to be an insult to the chef); '*Untidy* your room' (tidy rooms were thought to be a sign of an untidy mind – and vice versa); 'You're not going out in *that* skirt!' (long skirts were thought to be very risqué – the shorter the skirt, the more formal it was thought to be).

The clean undies advice came about because most serious Milky Way accidents made it into MilkyFed newspapers, and the Freedom of Embarrassing Information Act required that the state of the victim's undies be fully described in the article.

Having synchronized watches, the four friends exchanged hugs in silence.

'Meet b-back here in time for d-dinner if we get split up,' said Tommy, trying to sound light-hearted. Trying to put thoughts of *the Beast*, *the Demon*, *the Fallen One* out of his head. He squeezed Marielle's shoulder. 'No w-way you're getting out of that w-w-washing up.' It came out less funny and affectionate than he intended.

Woozie broke the moment. 'Anyone want a flippety-flapjack? My pockets are stuffed.' This caused the other three to hurry towards the jeggs and begin clambering inside. After a puzzled shake of the head, the wibblewallian followed suit.

The word STORM was printed in large letters on the side of Tommy's jegg and this was surrounded by a few stickers – one of which was a picture of Earth with 'Probably the best planet in the universe' above it. The jegg's cockpit was like that of a fighter plane except for the rubbery claxon to the side and the funky-shaped steering wheel in the middle. It was cramped and Tommy stretched out his feet to the pedals and surveyed the dials and screens. He pulled the glass roof shut and pressed on a pedal. The cabin filled with loud music – folk, injected with a mad dash of rock. (The radio was set to *Local* – 'Hellsbells FM' had appeared in the radio display.) The lyrics rang out loud.

The devil went down to–

Summy's voice cut through. 'For you all here will I wait. Swiggy minding. Good luck!'

It took some seconds before the music returned.

I bet you didn't know it, but I'm a fiddle player too.
And if you'd care to take a dare, I'll make a bet with you.

The side of the JeggHold levered upwards. Tommy kicked the pedal again and the music died. The blackness of space – broken only by a swirl of mist and a sickly, stubbled corner of Hellsbells – stared back at them.

Woozie's jegg surged forward, halting in the distance. He was followed by Marielle and Rumbles in turn.

'Hey, dopey!' cried Woozie over the communications system. 'Whadya waiting for?'

Tommy wasn't sure what he was waiting for as he eyed his three friends – grey specks in the mist. He always liked to pause before leaping off a precipice. But this was different. A sense of foreboding hung about this place and he wanted to preserve these precious moments when everything was still OK (sort of) and his friends were still around him.

'Don't worry,' said Marielle, with an edge of sarcasm. 'I'll protect you.'

'Me tooskeys.' (No sarcasm.)

Tommy closed his eyes, uttered a few silent words, and pulled hard on the throttle. He shot out of Swiggy, into the mist, arcing past his friends. 'Just g-giving you slow-coaches a head st-st-start,' he crowed, accelerating away.

The three jeggs chased after him, Woozie letting rip a 'YeeeHIIIIII!!!' as they rounded the stubbled horizon and disappeared from Summy's sight.

9

The Darkest Well (a bit about training on Swiggy)

Training and learning had been a big part of the last three years. Quite apart from their lessons with Wisebeardyface, the FiiVe had daily interactive lessons with the other Masters of the Way – Miss Zophria LeWren, Crabble, MonSenior and Lady Muckbeff.

The FiiVe learnt more Milky Foo skills (the martial arts of the Milky Way), including how to chop their hands through dry balsa wood and how to let a Gemini Jelly dissolve in their mouths without chewing. They became practised in the forgotten art of Brilliant Memory Skills, improved their scimmy-fighting technique and came close to mastering the subjunctive tense.

Crabble (a potato-shaped man with electric-blue hair) taught them how to make explosives and how to hack into various computer and software systems. When he thought they were mature enough, he trained them in the vital art of how to pretend to have a limp.

MonSenior, the most ancient Master of them all, introduced the FiiVe to poetry, break-dancing, darts and how to resist the effects of drugs such as truth serums and cough mixture. A poem oft recited by the old tutor contained a line that 'spoke to' Tommy. '*We are all in the gutter, but some of us are looking at the stars.*' And so he learnt it off by heart.[11]

Lady Muckbeff was a white, bear-like creature who always wore a smelly green coat with the hood pulled up over her head. She'd shown contempt for the FiiVe in the Milky Way, before they were chosen as IGGY Knights, and her attitude appeared to have changed little since then. Tommy always felt that she reserved a particular dislike for him. Lady M's initial classes focused on literature – taking in revered Milky Way works such as, *Scorpio & Juliette*, *The Importance of Being Eridanus*, *Men Are From Musca*, *Women Are From Serpens* and *What A Load of Castor Pollux*. She also taught the FiiVe how to combat dysentery and, try as they might (since the classes were often painful), the FiiVe couldn't escape the fearsome lady's lessons on escapology. Her favourite saying was: 'The treasure thou seekest dost be in the cave thou fearest most' – which prompted lots of (quiet) jokes about pirates and torches.

To Tommy's surprise, the six-legged Master turned out to be an accomplished violinist and she gave the young Earthling several lessons. Usually she chided him for clumsy finger-work, but, one time, when Swiggy was hovering just outside a galaxy, she declared: 'Fie! Thy fingers dost be fast and nimble – faster and nimbler than mine . . . Thou couldst indeed be *masterful* . . . But thou lackest that which wouldst raise thee to the highest realms.'

'And what is that?' asked Tommy.

11 Some historians claim this line resonated with Tommy because he learnt a similar line by Tim-id Oscar while at school on Earth where stars were not visible due to constant rain ('We are all in the gutter, but some of us are looking at the clouds').

'Pain, suffering and inner turmoil,' replied Lady M.

Hmmm. This wasn't the answer Tommy expected or wanted. Yet he couldn't help asking: 'And why is *that*?'

Lady M smiled, enjoying his discomfort. 'Alack, the brightest light must hast the darkest shadow . . . Fortruth, the greatest music doth be sourced inst the darkest well.'

After this episode, Tommy chose to take no more violin lessons from the disagreeable master.

The main skill Miss LeWren concentrated on was the Surge. On IGGY, the beautiful, bird-like master had explained that, 'Ze Surge . . . eez ze life force, ze positive energy within yourself. By successfully channelling eet you can do anysing you want.' By the end of the third year, Tommy'd mastered a few elements of the Surge. He'd lifted a cup using only his mind (though its contents had ended up spilling down his shirt), and he'd tied his laces without touching them (though they'd come undone as he was bounding down the stairs from the cockpit, felling him flat on his face) and he'd once bent a dessert spoon into an L-shape (only to find it was Marielle's 'special spoon' – given to her by her parents before they died).

The other areas covered by Miss LeWren were calligraphy, culinary skills and Universal Signs.

Woozie, it should be said, did extraordinary impressions of all the Masters, frequently entertaining his fellow Knights with extended sketches. Lady Muckbeff's *Thine Break Dancing Class* was a favourite, as was Miss LeWren's *Beauty Teeps Forrr Rrrreally Ugly People*, not to mention Crabble's *Hmmm, yes, The-Birds-And-The-Bs* speech (so termed because bigtails, bums, bottoms and bras got frequent mention).

'I just gave you the finger'
(A warm compliment in many galaxies)

Waving goodbye is an example of a sign or a hand/paw signal used by almost all creatures throughout the universe. However, raising your hand to a waiter and pretending to write on it (which means, 'Can I have the bill, please' on Earth) means, 'I'm going to write to the health inspectors about closing down your restaurant' in 78% of galaxies. In the Sarko galaxy, clapping your hands means, 'That's the worst thing I've ever seen or heard' and in the ParaNoyd Sector, rotating your finger when referring to a spiral staircase means, 'Even though it seems like I'm talking about a spiral staircase, I'm really plotting to kill you.'

10
HOLD ON!

Tommy, Marielle, Woozie and Rumbles circled Hellsbells twice.

'That's the only way in I see,' said Marielle into her microphone, referring to a cave-like entrance in the skull's left ear.

'I don't like the lookskeys of that monster standing guard.'

'It's not a m-monster,' retorted Tommy. 'It's just a d-dog.'

'A dogskeys with three heads!'

Taller than a bus, the first of the creature's heads resembled a pit bull's, the second an Alsatian's and the third a Jack Russell's.

'*There's* a flat bit out of sight where we can land,' said Marielle.

Minutes later, the four (or FiiV as they were called in Summy's absence) were crouched behind a bony protrusion, raising their heads occasionally to snatch a glance at ThreeHeads. Prowling back and forth, she kept sniffing the air and squinting into the distance. Eventually, she padded off, leaving the way clear to the cave.

'Should we make a run for it?' asked Woozie, biting on his dog tags.

'No, we'd never make it,' replied Marielle.

'Did you see her teethskeys?' asked Rumbles. 'All pointy and glinty.'

'Maybe she's t-tamer than she l-l-looks,' suggested Tommy.

'There's one way of checking,' said Woozie, giving Rumbles a look.

It took the big thunderbumble a moment to understand. 'Oh, no, not againskeys!'

'Don't be silly about this.'

After much grumbling, Rumbles retrieved a nawhitmob from the glove compartment of her jegg. It looked like a cross between a miniature boar, a fluffy bunny and a chocolate brownie. (Nawhitmob stands for No Animals Were Harmed In The Making Of (this) Book. There was a plentiful supply of the cuddly creatures onboard Swiggy and they'd been bred specifically for purposes such as this.)

'I don't agreeskeys with this,' whispered Rumbles. 'It's wrong. This is nawhitmob number thirteenskeys since we left the Milky Way . . . Not counting the one I stood on . . . Or the two I fell on.'

Eventually, Rumbles pointed the little creature towards the cave and released it. It scuttled along the ground, its big chocolatey eyes fixed on its target, its little whiskers and fluffy tail vibrating to the padding of its paws.

It was halfway there when ThreeHeads spotted it, dashed over and ripped it limb from limb (blood dripping from the Alsatian and pit bull teeth). Then she licked two pairs of lips and surveyed all about her.

'Probably good we didn't make a run for it,' said Woozie.

'What if w-we all attack it at the same t-time?' suggested Tommy. 'We've g-got our s-scimmies.' (They were strapped to their backs.)

'Not sure I fancy that ideaskeys . . . She's as tall as a bus!'

'We could ask Summy to fire a missile at her.'

'*S*-Swiggy won't m-move, remember? And she's ow-outta range.'

They were stumped.

'Anyone for a flippety-flapjack?' asked Woozie, producing an armful from a pance pocket (built into his fur). 'They'll keep your strength up.'

'No wayskeys.'

'Ughh! I'd r-rather face ThreeH-Heads.'

'Yes!' exclaimed Marielle with sudden enthusiasm. 'Give them over here.'

'Hey, they're not all for you!'

Marielle had grabbed the entire armful and before anyone could stop her, she flung them over the bony protrusion, in the direction of ThreeHeads.

'You gone barking mad?' exclaimed Woozie.

Rather than apologizing, Marielle asked, 'Have you any more?'

'Yeah, q-quick,' said Tommy, realizing Marielle's game. 'H-hand them over.'

Soon they'd thrown every last one of the flippety-flapjacks towards ThreeHeads.

'Just stay still for a few minutes,' said Marielle to everyone, assuming a bossy captain-like voice.

When they looked out, ThreeHeads had collapsed on the ground, crumbs around her three heads.

'Nice w-w-work, Woozie,' said Tommy as they hurried past. 'You t-too Marielle.'

As they entered the cave-like opening, a cloud of squawking

oppobats streamed out. (Oppobats are like bats, only scared of the dark.)

'Aaaghh!' cried Rumbles. 'We're going to dieskeys!'

He was a little bit embarrassed when she realized they were just oppobats. 'I was talking filamosophically,'[12] she said. 'Some day we'll all die . . . Right?'

The cave was bright and smelt of wild jasmine with a little tame jasmine thrown in for good measure. It funnelled into a narrow passageway which curved back and forth, lit by flaming torches.

As they padded silently into the depths of Hellsbells, they had the feeling that thousands of eyes were watching them, hidden behind cracks in the flame-flickered walls. Every now and again, Tommy thought he heard a low growl from somewhere close.

And then a scream rang out – 'AAAAAAAIIIIIIIIIIII-IEEEEEEEEEEEEE!!!!' – like a dozen creatures being tortured to death. All the torches died. The FiiVe could see nothing. Only blackness.

'Er, anyone bring a torch?' asked Woozie.

'I was going to bring oneskeys.'

'I didn't ask who was *going* to bring—'

Woozie stopped speaking, for the sound of growling started to resonate from all sides of the passageway and each of the FiiV felt something swish past their faces. Like the fur of a yeti. Or the bristles of a giant spider's leg.

'Form a huddle,' said Marielle urgently. 'Back-to-back, so we're facing in all directions.'

No sooner had they done so than a thundering voice roared: 'GO! GO AWAY! . . . UNLESS YOU'RE

12 She hadn't used the word 'philosophically' very often.

PREPARED TO RISK EVERYTHING . . . EVERY-THING . . . EVERYTHING!'

They all felt the breeze carrying the words. As though they'd been spoken by a giant, wheezing creature. They stood in silence for some moments, scimmies drawn, ready to slash out at whatever came their way. There was no need to speak.

They all knew they couldn't go back.

Tommy had three possible reactions to immense fear – laughter (he'd crack a joke, sometimes inappropriately), unthinking bull-headedness (he'd rush headlong towards the danger) or quivering paralysis. Of the three, quivering paralysis was the one he fought most to avoid – since it just multiplies the fear and makes you more vulnerable.

And so, standing in the dark passageway, fear rising through his bones, Tommy sought in vain for something funny to say. But his mind went blank. And the beginnings of quivering paralysis were upon him. *No, no, got to do something!* Without thinking, Tommy Storm seized at the only option open to him and – much to the surprise of his fellow Knights – he surged forward, crying: 'Aaaaaaahhhhhh! Everything!! Everything!!'

It took some seconds before the others realized what was happening – confusion exacerbated by the fact that they were all facing different directions and had lost sense of which way was forward.

Tommy ran and ran through the darkness, hearing noises of deadly pursuit – rolling boulders, whizzing darts (which he shimmied from side to side to avoid). Every now and then, he'd feel the breath and thud of something just behind – as if he'd whisked under a falling tombstone. How he managed to find his way along the passageway, ducking unseen stalactites, turning corners, leaping over straw-covered chasms, was something he couldn't explain afterwards. 'Maybe the Surge,' was his only suggestion. As he ran, he entered pockets where gravity was twisted, so at times he was charging along the walls, at others he was actually careering over the dipping and peaking ceiling. Twice, a 'tombstone' grazed his shirt and once it actually caught him on the shoulder, causing him to stumble, but then he found the rhythm of madness once more.

And then, no more than sixty seconds – an unforgiving minute – since he'd left the others, his chest burning, an orangey haze licked against the passage walls. *Keep going! Don't stop now!* Brighter, brighter. He hurtled round a corner and out, out into . . .

'AAAAGGHHHHHHHHHHHIIIIIIIIII!!!'

He'd run out of the passageway into the yawning mouth of a great, steaming canyon. For a moment he saw himself as though in a cartoon – suspended in mid-air over a mighty drop, legs still moving. And yet . . . He *was* still moving. Ten metres, now fifteen, coming to a halt five jegg-lengths from the passageway.

And then he saw why he was 'suspended' in mid-air. His feet were perched on a beam of clear ice, no thicker than his arm – stretching from the passageway to the far side of the canyon.

FFFUUULLUUHHPPPP!!!

A waft of sulphur hit his nostrils and he looked down. Fiery magma bubbled far below. And from the canyon walls, bursts of steam rose up. He might've paused to admire the spectacle had the latest steamburst not passed through the ice beam by the passageway, melting it to within three paces of his feet.

'F-fornax!' he cried, as the beam continued to melt – so that he had to walk towards the other side of the canyon, and then run, to stay ahead of the disappearing beam-end. It was accelerating, catching him. *I can't! I can't! Unless –!! . . .* Dangling from somewhere overhead, twenty strides away, was a rope. Twelve strides away. Eight. Six.

Nooo!!

The beam gave way beneath his feet, the rope so agonizingly out of reach.

'YAAAARRRRGGGHHHHHHHHH – Uuuuuhhhhh!'

He'd fallen twenty, twenty-five metres when he caught the rope – and slid another ten, burning the skin off his palms, till he came to a stop.

It was even hotter here. A crater's-worth of magma gave an enormous belch, splashing up to lick the soles of his shoes and taking a mouthful of rope below his feet as if it were a length of overcooked spaghetti.

Tommy looked up to the source of the rope – a disc of rock protruding from the canyon wall high above. He snorted a nostrilful of sulphur, pulled his sleeves down over his palms and banished all thoughts of exhaustion (his lungs were still pounding from the run). Then he began to climb. And climb. And climb. Never looking down. The roasting heat turning cool, like a summer's evening. And the odorous sulphur softening.

He felt tired by now – really, really, really tired. Imagine not going to bed for three days and nights and then running an *uphill* marathon. If that doesn't make you want to take a nap, then imagine running the marathon backwards. While giving someone a piggyback. *And* wearing a ridiculously hot furry animal costume . . . This was close to the exhaustion Tommy felt. His hands bled (the sleeves wouldn't stay in place), his shoulder throbbed from the thud in the passageway. Every nerve and sinew trembled from the effort. Yet still the disc of rock was a penny high above.

'D-don't look down. G-gotta keep going.' This was his mantra and he used it to try to keep up some sort of rhythm. To try to block out the pain.

He managed to hold on for another six minutes – till the disc of rock was a distant bottle-top. Then his heart gave up and the rope slid through his hands.

11

Frayed Ends (Recounting the Elquinine Concerto Incident)

In that brief moment between consciousness and unconsciousness, as the rope slid from his grasp, a vision of Marielle's face filled Tommy's mind. And across her features, playing in slow – or was it fast? – motion was his view of the Concerto Incident.

Alas, his view, like that of Marielle, was only half the story.

In their second year on Swiggy, Tommy, Woozie, Rumbles and Summy each played a mini-concert on their preferred musical instrument for their fellow Knights in Swiggy's Lounge. They'd all practised hard and the four concerts had generated much excitement beforehand and standing ovations afterwards. But Marielle had refused to perform. 'The clarinet is still new to me,' was her only explanation. And whether it was due to shyness or down to doubting her abilities, they couldn't move the resolute elquinine, who took to hiding away in the Ammunition Hold more than ever (no one realizing she was practising the clarinet). Then, one day, after another barrage of attempted persuasion, she agreed to play everyone a *recording* of her playing.

At the appointed hour, after dinner, Tommy, Woozie, Rumbles and Summy plonked themselves on to cushions in the Lounge and waited. And waited . . .

'I'm a lady,' said Woozie at one point in a perfect Marielle impression, holding a Marielle action-figure.[13] 'It's my right to be late.'

Tommy shushed the wibblewallian with a look.

Summy and Rumbles finally made their way down to the Ammunition Hold where they found the dungareed figure of Marielle looking out of the slitted window, her face buried in a silk, polka-dot hanky. 'I can't do it.' After a lot of prodding and encouragement, they persuaded her to come up with them and to go through with the 'performance'.

'Now, I'm going to be over here,' she announced as she pushed a disc into Swiggy's music system. 'Please don't look at me when the music's playing.' She pressed a button and hurried to a large cushion in the corner of the room. There, she could huddle down with her back to everyone.

The music started . . . Soft, gentle notes, whiskering into the air like a rabbit daring to peek outside its warren. They frolicked onwards, a touch louder, before Tommy recognized the piece. It sounded different when played with a clarinet rather than a violin, but yes, how could he not have recognized it? *Adagio Fromagio* by Amadeus MozzarellArt – the piece he played when he was at his saddest, the piece that reminded him of his parents, the piece that made him think of all those he loved. The piece he'd once told Marielle was his very favourite.

13 Rumbles had made plastic action figures of each IGGY Knight during a period of 'extended bordedomskeys' months earlier. After an initial flurry of sketches from Woozie – involving tone-perfect impersonations of his friends – they now lived on the Lounge's shelves.

As the music swelled, he felt his heart rise with it. What a probing, sensitive touch the elquinine had. He was hearing the piece anew. Like seeing his favourite mountain from a new vantage point for the first time. Certainly, it was the same steep peak he loved. But here was a different face to it. Crags, shadows, rocky outcrops and dazzling reflections he never knew it had.

And maybe it was because they'd all been cooped up together for nearly two years, having to keep certain thoughts and feelings in check. Or perhaps he had a moment of weakness and felt the loss of his parents. Or he saw his life stretching before him and doubted if he'd ever be surrounded by such friends and such taken-for-granted happiness again. Or did the frayed ends of a recent tiff with Marielle stir a lake within him . . . ? Whatever it was, the music found a fissure in his heart and swam right in.

Tommy hurried into the Boys' Dorm before anyone noticed the welling in his eyes. He stayed there, looking out of the window at the stars and supernova cartwheeling by. The tears ran down his face to the haunting sounds, till, by the last note, he felt quite spent.

Ashamed of his tears and unable to articulate quite what'd happened, he stayed put during the standing ovation and didn't come out for supper. Instead, he fell into a deep sleep on the couch by the window – the deepest sleep he'd ever had on Swiggy.

Marielle had heard Tommy leave the room and felt his absence through the rest of the piece and through the rest of the evening. Momentary concern turned to annoyance, then to anger, then – by late evening – to resentment and, finally, to bitterness. *Even if he hated it, he could have the decency to say a kind word.*

Next morning, Tommy planned to congratulate Marielle on her playing and 'explain' how he'd had a tummy ache and didn't want to disturb everyone during the music. But as he approached the Girls' Dorm, rehearsed lines fleeing from his head, he overheard the elquinine talking to Summy.

'No! Why would I care whether he stayed and listened? . . . And don't you say this to anyone, but yes, I *did* have a crush on him. When I was young and immature. But I've long grown out of it. Thank goodness!'

Tommy went back to bed and stared at the ceiling. Now *he* felt hurt and angry.

When Woozie awoke, the wibblewallian asked his friend why he'd stayed out of the Lounge during and after Marielle's performance. Unfortunately, the elquinine chose this very moment to pass within earshot of the Boys' Dorm.

'I c-couldn't stand it a moment l-longer,' Tommy declared – as if this explained everything. And to Marielle, who heard the hurt in Tommy's voice as malice, it did indeed explain everything.

12
Fiddling, Not Kissing

The sound of wood being chopped. A rock wall reflecting light from overhead. Dry throat. Inane chatter and canned laughter, followed by annoying musical jingles. A buzzing fly. Warm blanket. *Beware*. Soft pillow. Strong thirst . . . These were the things Tommy became aware of as he swam towards wakefulness.

And then he awoke – fully – zapped by a sudden realization. *I'm in Hellsbells!* Still the chatter and laughter filling his ears. He jumped to his feet, ready to pick up the scimmy lying on the ground, ready to fight, to run, to . . . to . . .

'All righ'?'

Tommy looked over. The person who'd addressed him was a young girl in an apron, leaning against a tree, a pail of dirty water at her feet. She set down a mop, wiped her brow and removed something from her apron, pointing it over Tommy's head – the chatter and laughter died. Tommy looked up to see a large screen set into the rocky wall go blank.

'Like t'av the telly on when I'm workin',' explained the girl. ''Ope it didn't wake yuh.'

Tommy shook his head and the girl sighed. 'Only finish cleanin' an' it needs startin' again.' She picked a piece of paper off the ground, scrunched it up and threw it in Tommy's direction. It hit the rocky wall behind him, just missing a garbage-chute-like hole. 'I hear yuh fell off the rope,' she added from behind big black eyes.

Instinctively, Tommy picked up the ball of paper and, still eyeing the girl, smoothed it flat and posted it through the chute. (He was an obsessive recycler.) He noticed two little horns poking through her black hair.

'Lucky they caught yuh,' continued the girl. ''Ope yuh don't mind – I poured water on yer hands. An' yer shoulder was bruised somethin' awful . . . They should be better now.'

Tommy looked down at his hands – the cuts were gone – and swivelled his shoulder, feeling no stiffness.

'The water from this tree 'as 'oles in it,' explained the girl. 'If yuh look at a jugful you'll see thick, wormlike cavities runnin' through it. Cures all wounds. If you're thirsty, there's some o'er there.'

But Tommy had other things on his mind. 'My f-friends – are they all r-r-right?'

The girl nodded. 'Oh, yeah.' She pointed up at the big TV. 'I saw 'em on the screen. Waitin' close tuh where you left 'em.' Before Tommy could comment, the girl rattled on. 'You're the first person up here in an age. Nice t'av someone to talk tuh while I'm workin' . . . Very few make it as far as the rope. An' of them that do – none 'av ever been man enough to hold on tuh the very top.' Tommy's face must've looked downcast, for she added, brightly. 'But you did all righ'. Few even make it inside 'Ellsbells. How'd yuh get past the force field? Someone try to kill yuh? 'Tis the only way in without an invite.'

'Wh-who are y-you?' asked Tommy, moving closer. Despite her chattiness, the girl struck him as shy. She hadn't stopped leaning against the apple tree – as if it were her safety blanket.

'Me? Oh, I'm Elza.' This washergirl had an airy innocence to her voice and a wide-eyed expression, which made her look and sound quite dumb.

'Are y-you from Hells-b-b-bells?'

'No, not originally, but I been workin' here a while . . . What about you – where d'you hail from?'

'Earth.' Tommy spied the spring of water gushing from the side of the tree.

'EARTH??'

'N-no, *Earth*,' replied Tommy. (Elza's pronunciation had made 'Earth' sound like *ear-th*.)

'Yuh mean . . . the planet in the Milky Way!?'

But Tommy didn't hear the question, for he'd shoved his head into the path of the spring. Cold, soothing water hit his face and hair and he caught a dozen mouthfuls before he stood up, wet and sated. All tiredness gone.

'We heard yuh playin' the violin on yer craft,' said Elza. 'No one plays that well 'less they're in love . . . Are you in love?'

'What're you on about?' Tommy spluttered. 'No, I'm not.'

And he strode beyond the tree. They were on a rocky plateau in some sort of canyon, cliff-walls extending upwards into a silvery mist. The tree which (thankfully) blocked Elza from sight, grew straight out of the rock, full and green. And, not far from it, a wide tree stump thrust up from the rock, an axe on top of it. In the cliff wall, close to the mattress he'd slept on, was a man-sized hole. Above it, a large word was carved into the rock: *Beware*. And small writing below this (he stepped closer to read it): *What You Wish For*. The cave-like hole was the only obvious exit. *Although maybe* . . . Tied around the bough of the apple tree, extending away, was a rope. He followed it, twenty paces to the plateau's edge.

'Whhooooaaahhhh!' The world fell away over the brink – to a pinprick of orange far, far below – and he leapt back.

'Yuh'd wanna be careful,' said a voice. ''Tis a long way down.'

Tommy turned and saw an old woman shuffling towards his mattress. She could've been Elza's great-great-grand-mother. Wide in girth, she wore the same washerwoman's clothes. Tommy was on the point of asking her the where-abouts of the Beast when she began puffing his pillow and tucking in the sheets. *Better to ask Elza*. He looked about. But . . . she was gone

The mop and pail of water were still there. *Maybe she climbed into the branches of the tree.* He looked up, seeing nothing but foliage and . . . *the strangest hole*. Some way up the trunk, it was wide and bright. Straining his eyes, he made out something silvery-white and arching, but had no idea what it was.

''Tis a waterfall.' Elza was suddenly by his shoulder, leaning against the tree bough. 'Wouldn't advise climbin' in. Yuh'd never see yer friends again.'

Tommy looked at her, startled. 'Where did you go?' He glanced towards the mattress. 'And the old lady – where's she gone?' Now *she'd* disappeared.

'We work in shifts,' replied Elza. Then, with a laugh: 'Yer travel sickness's cured.' Tommy looked at her in bafflement. 'Yer stutter's gone,' she added by way of explanation.

'What're you on about – that's a mean thing to–' Tommy stopped. *It IS gone.* He looked at the young girl. '*Travel sickness*?'

She nodded. 'I used tuh get it somethin' awful. 'Twas the bad co-ordination I hated most. But lucky it always comes back *soon as* you stop movin' . . . 'Tis the stutter what takes a week or so tuh go ’way – ’nless you drink some ’oley water tuh make it go quicker.’

Wow! Tommy’s mind was racing. ‘But if . . . if it’s just travel sickness, why don’t my friends get it?’

Elza shrugged. ‘They say ’tis only species not used to high-speed space travel what get it.’

Hmmm, thought Tommy. Over the past few thousand years, his fellow humans had certainly travelled just a tiny bit through space compared to creatures such as elquinines and thunderbumbles.

It was amazing how much this news and the loss of his stutter buoyed his confidence. He was about to recall the times Swiggy’d come to a halt and see if these coincided with the times his co-ordination had returned when he realized he was getting side-tracked.

‘So, anyway,’ he said, enjoying the sound of his own clear, confident voice. ‘I’m looking for the Beast.’ Elza’s only reply was a wide-eyed, bamboozled look. ‘Can you tell me where I might find him?’ prompted Tommy.

‘Him?’

‘Yes, I’m hoping he can help me – they say he’s big and powerful, scares everyone.’

‘Oh!’ exclaimed the young washergirl. ‘Maybe yuh mean Beashto? He’s huge, wi’ teeth the size o’–’

‘Yes, yes!’

‘He’s through there,’ said Elza, pointing at the cave beneath the word *Beware*.

Tommy was about to hurry off when he paused. ‘Can you tell me anything about him?’ Elza looked at him blankly. ‘I’d be grateful for any help you can give me,’ he pressed. ‘*Any* advice at all.’

Again that wide-eyed look and Elza shrugged. ‘Be

yourself,' she said – almost as a question.

Tommy gave a grimace of thanks, snatched up his scimmy and was on his way when he heard the old woman's voice. 'Wouldn't bring *that* if I were you.'

He paused. The old woman, now by the tree stump, was pointing at his scimmy. 'Better to bring a gift . . . He kills people what bring weapons.'

'A gift?'

'Yer most valuable possession.'

Tommy's violin and bow lay by the axe on the ugly tree stump. Using the big screen on the cliff wall and following directions from Tommy, the old woman (who'd introduced herself as 'Bea') had located it on Swiggy and 'beamed it down' with the remote control in her apron.

When she stepped on to the stump and lifted the violin, Tommy saw that she had a tail, slightly forked at the end. Like Elza, her eyes were dark and little horns peeked through her thinning hair. 'Nice,' she purred, setting the violin under her chin and testing its strings with the bow. Strangled sounds filled the air.

'Careful!' cried Tommy, trying to snatch the violin.

But she twisted away and after a few more agonized sounds, she struck up a simple, cantering ditty. It sounded vaguely familiar.

'Very good,' said Tommy. 'Now give it over. I'm going to see Beashto.'

The old woman ignored the request. 'Gizza kiss,' she whispered, still playing. And she stepped off the stump, reducing the volume to a soft background trot, lips puckered.

'What?'

‘Kiss me.’

‘No!’ Tommy couldn’t hide the repugnance in his voice. The woman was wrinkled and shrivelled and, this close, gave off the smell of old breath.

‘Please,’ whispered Bea, eyes crinkling. ‘Just one li’l kiss.’

‘No!’ cried Tommy. ‘Give that back!’ And he tried to grab the violin. But Bea ducked behind the green tree and the soft, trotting music exploded into a wild, racing storm. Tommy rounded the wide trunk, finding Elza, violin and bow in hand. It looked like a single tear was running down her face. The old woman had disappeared.

Tommy stood and listened to the crazed music. The Beast – or Beashto – could wait a few minutes.

Elza was good, but he knew he could play better, and this cheered him somehow. He noticed that Elza, like Bea, had a long, forked serpenty tail. And though it twitched to the galloping music, it never stopped caressing the tree, as if it were a long-lost pet.

After a while, he ventured: ‘Er, please, I’m in a bit of a hurry.’ But Elza kept playing, making no response. The boy moved closer, raising his voice. ‘Give me back my violin. Please! I want to see Beashto!’

The violin stopped dead.

13

The Tooth, the Whole Tooth (and nothing but)

RRRRAAAGGGHHHRRRRR!!!

The roar – far in the distance – was loud enough to make the whole 'planet' tremble.

It was pitch-dark around Tommy, but for one in every forty-three breaths (he'd counted), a dim light would appear, giving everything a weak illumination. In those brief snatches, he saw that he was in another canyon on an island of rock some twenty metres across. The old woman had led him here through the cave-like hole in the cliff wall and then on further through the darkness before retreating. She hadn't said a word the whole way. *Still annoyed about not getting a kiss?*

The watery light, he realized, was from the pale moon passing overhead (the open-topped canyon rose high above the rocky island, emerging into space itself). All sides of the island seemed to fall away to darkness and there were no trees to hide behind (or in). Perhaps we walked across another beam of ice to get here, he thought. And now it's melted.

KUUUKKLAMM! A spotlight clanked on, pointing out of the darkness into his face. He couldn't see a thing.

A female voice, deepened through a microphone, intoned: 'How worthy are you to see the Beast?'

'Er, quite worthy,' replied Tommy, shielding his eyes

'*Quite worthy*,' repeated the voice with disdain.

'Eh, yes.'

'Hmmm . . . How much do you know?'

'About what?'

'*In general* . . . How knowledgeable are you? How much do you know?'

'I know lots,' said Tommy, trying to sound confident.

'That sounds likely!'

'It's true!' He thought of all the lessons from the Masters of the Way and of all his travels and felt a surge of confidence in his abilities (bolstered by the loss of his stutter). 'I know way more than a lot of people . . . I know an awful lot.'

'*Way more*?' Tommy nodded at the light. 'And are you *better* than a lot of people?' continued the voice.

'Better at what?'

'Better in general?'

Tommy thought about this. 'Well, I . . . I guess I – I did get chosen from billions on my planet . . . And then got chosen to be an IGGY Knight.' And now that his stutter had gone and his co-ordination was back . . . He looked up at the light more certainly. 'Yeah, I'm way better than most people.'

KUUUKKLAMM! The spotlight clanked off and, once again, Tommy couldn't see a thing.

RRRRRRAAAAGGGGHHHHRRRRRRR!!!

The roar – closer now – made the air quake. And when it passed, the ground began shuddering to a new sound – BOOOOOOMMMM! . . . BOOOOOOMMMM! – as if

Hellsbells were being slowly pounded by a moon-sized fist. As it drew nearer, even the pale moon seemed to lose its nerve, the lapse between visits stretching to fifty-one breaths (actually, Tommy was just breathing more quickly).

Be calm, Tommy told himself. Beashto won't eat you. Will he . . ? Ooohh, I don't want to die. Not now. Not yet. (He found it much easier to be brave when doing something, but this sitting, doing *nothing* in the darkness . . . *Aaaagghhhh!*)

Louder and louder came the BOOOOOOMMMM! . . . BOOOOOOMMMM! and with it, a strengthening breeze, moving one way then another – like the push and pull of the tide. The breeze became a wind, became a gale (clearly now, the breaths of a great giant). The rocky island began shaking so much from every BOOOOOOMMMM! that Tommy had to sit to stop from falling. (And at the last count, the frightened moon had hidden for *fifty-nine* breaths.) Tommy caught a moonlit glimpse of the creature as it approached. ENORMOUS and furry, it was moving on its fists and looked to be severed in half – no body from the waist down!

And then it – whatever *it* was – was towering over him (which was why the gale had dropped).

The deepest voice spoke, every syllable shaking the ground. 'FEE, FI, FO, FUM. MUSTARD, PICKLE, TOASTED BUN.' After this strange outburst, the moon passed overhead and Tommy caught a fleeting sight of the creature's face looking down on him. It had red eyes the size of office blocks, jagged teeth the height of skyscrapers and three ivory horns the length of jumbo-jet runways.

Then darkness once more.

'WHAT DO YOU WANT?' thundered the voice.

'Er, we – I – heard you might know something about the TFC . . .'

'WHAT DO YOU WANT?'

'Well, er, Beashto, I hoped you might be able to help me – us – to stop it.'

'WHAT DO YOU WANT?'

'Er, I just told you. To save everything from destruction.'

'WHAT DO *YOU* WANT?'

Tommy was unsure how to respond.

Again the question. 'WHAT DO *YOU* WANT?'

Tommy repeated himself a few times, but the question kept coming – with more urgency. And then he felt himself being picked up by a pair of claws and placed in something warm and squidgy. It felt like a bread roll the size of a bed. Then something heavy and slimy was placed along his torso. The pale moon chose that moment to flash past. *A pickle! I'm lying under a pickle!*

Darkness again. Then . . . *Uuuuggghhhhhhhh!* Something gooey splurted over him. Mustard. *Mustard!*

'WHAT DO YOU WANT?'

As the voice spoke, Tommy could feel himself being lifted up, up.

'WHAT DO YOU WANT?'

'To be alive!' he cried through a surge of panic.

'WHAT ELSE DO YOU WANT?'

'Er, apart from being alive? . . . To be happy! Yes, to find love one day and marry.'

'AND WHAT ELSE?'

'Er . . . To do whatever you ask of me . . . *Anything*!'

Beashto growled and Tommy couldn't hear a thing for some seconds. The smell of warm foulness hit his nostrils. *His mouth! I must be in front of his mouth!* A skyline of teeth and a river-wide tongue materialized from the blackness as the pale moon rode by. Then darkness once more.

'Eh, I want to be good – yes – to be a decent person, to be loyal and honest.' Again Beashto growled. 'I want to help my friends and make my parents proud.' Another growl and Tommy felt the air go clammy. *I'm inside its mouth!* 'I want to do great things. To scale wild heights. To–' He felt a heavy prod, something hard through the bottom bun. *It's a tooth!* 'I don't want to die! Please! Listen to me! I don't want–' He felt a prod through the upper bun. *It's biting down!* 'Noooo . . ! Nooooo!!'

The teeth pressed tighter, breaking through the bun to his skin. Pressing further, further.

'I want to be liked!!' he screamed. 'I want to be liked! I want everyone to like me, to love me, to think I'm great. Everyone to—'

He stopped mid-sentence. The teeth had released and he was being lifted away from the clammy mouth, down, down, down. And then he was back on rocky ground.

The rant had come from his very core and now, standing in the silence (the bun and pickle removed), he felt a sense of embarrassment. Perhaps even shock. Not to mention a little seepage from the mustard.

'YOU DARE TO COME HERE FOR HELP?'

'Er, em, yes,' said Tommy, his breath and composure somewhat recovered.

This was followed by a growl and then silence for half a minute, until . . .

'So, you have an off—?' This sounded like the old woman's voice – coming from high above.

'ER, AHEM,' said Beashto. 'YOU HAVE AN OFFERING?'

'Eh, yes.' Tommy searched along the rocky ground for his violin. 'This violin,' he said when his fingers found it.

KUUUKKLAMM! A spotlight clanked on, illuminating the violin as Tommy placed it on the ground.

Again, the silence.

'I WILL HELP YOU . . .' (Tommy breathed a sigh of relief) 'IF – *IF* YOU PLAY THAT FIDDLE BETTER THAN THE OLD WOMAN – BEA.'

'Deal!' cried Tommy with some excitement, in the knowledge that he'd already heard the woman play, in the knowledge that his co-ordination had returned. 'Deal.'

'BUT . . .' continued Beashto, 'IF – *IF* SHE PLAYS BETTER THAN YOU . . . THEN I GET TO . . . TO *PLAY* WITH *YOU*.'

'Play – what does that mean?'

'IT MEANS I WILL DRAG YOU DOWN TO THE SEWER AND I WILL BREAK YOU. I WILL STRIP YOU DOWN TO NOTHING, AND I WILL RIP YOUR HEART RIGHT OUT OF YOUR CHEST.'

Tommy gulped and steeled himself.

'Deal.'

The music soared through the dark canyon, cascading from the softness of lament to a crashing, wild fury and climaxing in a dizzying explosion of notes.

Illuminated by a single spotlight, Tommy whipped the bow from his violin with a flourish. It was the best he'd ever played and he half expected some applause, but there was nothing. Not even a 'well done'.

Then Bea was beside him and he handed her the bow and violin. To his surprise, she refused the bow. And so he stood back to savour the next few minutes. Apart from securing Beashto's favours, his imminent victory would be a well-deserved poke in the eye for the old woman. *A kiss from ME!? Who does she think she is?*

Bea stood rigid in the spotlight, holding the violin like a (decrepit) skater before a dance performance, her forked tail poised high.

And then it began. The most haunting, beautiful music Tommy'd ever heard. Bea's tail frittering across the violin like a bow with a life and a heart of its own. Rising to heights of wonder before plummeting to the depths of darkness.

When she'd finished (and she truly looked 'finished'), Tommy had tears in his eyes. Not for his own fate. But for the music that'd lifted him far, far away from the here and now.

Tommy was left sitting alone on the island of rock for some hours. Beashto had disappeared, but Tommy hadn't heard him go. For a long time he shouted into the darkness, receiving no answer.

'You were using metaphors, right? Ripping my heart out and all that . . . Right!? . . . And where are my friends? What've you done with them?'

His voice was almost hoarse when one whole side of the canyon lit up with an image of a bluey-white planet. 'Earth!' cried Tommy.

The image zoomed through clouds, over continents and seas to a great meeting in an auditorium. How can this be Earth? thought Tommy. There are no continents and no breaks in the clouds on Earth.[14]

Beashto (who was somehow towering above him again)

14 The Great Climate Enhancement had occurred on Earth during the twenty-first century, causing sea levels to rise above countries and the planet to be permanently shrouded in cloud (see *TS1*).

must've read his thoughts for he said, 'THERE ARE MANY EARTHS IN THE UNIVERSE.'

The movie – if it was a movie – continued. 'Vee haff only fifteen minutes left to make our choice,' said a bespectacled man.

The assembly had to come up with the Wisdom of Life, Death and the Universe – in less than twenty-five words – to save their planet from destruction. After a bad-tempered debate, six delegates read out six 'answers' to choose from.

Go for number six, thought Tommy. To his surprise, the delegates went for number five – *Your aunt Agnes would like you to call her after the assembly*.

It looked as though nothing was going to happen after the crowd counted to zero – except for rejoicing and bad dancing. But then . . . CCCRRRRRRUUUUSSSSSCCHHHH!!

The camera zoomed back to reveal a hand crushing the planet, its sun and its neighbours. A solitary voice boomed over the movie-speakers: 'I AM DEATH. DESTROYER OF WORLDS.'

And then the screen went blank.

'That was just a movie, right?' cried Tommy. 'Was it real? Tell me . . ! TELL ME!!' In his heart he already knew the answer. 'You killed, you killed . . . You're a monster! A sick, gutless . . . You're . . . AAAAAIIIIGGGHHHH!!'

'WHAT IS *YOUR* WISDOM?' asked Beashto.

'Huh?'

Once again the whole side of the canyon illuminated – this time the camera had panned out to reveal a sun surrounded by eight planets. The third planet from the sun was circled.

'Eh, I don't have any wisdom,' said Tommy.

'THEN SIT IN SILENCE AND WATCH ANOTHER EARTH – BILLIONS MORE PEOPLE – DESTROYED BEFORE YOUR EYES.'

'No! Please, no! Don't do it! These people – ordinary people. Have some mercy!'

'WHAT IS YOUR WISDOM?'

'I'm not going to be a part of this! . . . I don't care what you say.'

'VERY WELL.'

Despite Tommy's cries, the image zoomed through clouds, over continents and seas to a great meeting in a tent the size of Luxembourg. An elderly woman was sitting at a throne-like chair before the assembly. 'The Wisdom of Life, Death and the Universe in *less than* twenty-five words,' she said, holding the envelope aloft. 'This is our choice.' She opened it and read aloud: 'Eat, drink and be merry, for tomorrow you die.'

In the darkness, Tommy heard a faint voice (*Bea's?*) say: 'Wrong . . . *Today* you die.'

The crowd counted to zero – which, as with the last Earth, resulted in lots of rejoicing and bad dancing, and then . . . CCCRRRRRRUUUUSSSSSCCHHHH!!

The camera zoomed back to reveal a hand crushing the planet, its sun and its neighbours. A solitary voice boomed through the movie-speakers: 'I AM DEATH. DESTROYER OF WORLDS.' And then the screen went blank.

Tommy cried out. He felt dizzy, nauseous. And crumpled to the ground.

'WHAT IS YOUR WISDOM?'

'Huh?'

It was some hours later. Tommy'd wept himself to sleep, then woken to find a jug of holey water and food beside him. Having thrown the food aside, he'd downed the water and felt renewed.

'WHAT IS YOUR WISDOM?'

'Look, I'm just a boy. I know nothing of wisdom.'

'WHAT IS YOUR WISDOM?'

'Please! Please! Have some mercy.'

The canyonside illuminated, revealing a sun surrounded by eight planets. Again, the third planet from the sun was circled.

'WHAT IS YOUR WISDOM?'

'Listen to me! I have no wisdom! I have no—'

'THEN WATCH ANOTHER EARTH DESTROYED!'

'Nooooooo!! Wait! Let's talk about this. There must be a way. Some—'

'WHAT IS YOUR WISDOM?'

'I can't . . .'

The camera started to zoom in.

'Wait! . . . OK, OK, of course, yes, I have some wisdom, I have some . . .'

The camera panned back – till the third planet was but a speck. Tommy was trying to think. *Anything.* He had to save this planet and these people. Then it came to him. 'OK, yes! I have some wisdom, I have some.' He cleared his throat. *Please! Please let this save them.* And, stepping forward, he said: '*We are all in the gutter, but some of us are looking at the stars.*'

The image shuddered then zoomed in on the third planet, through clouds, over continents and seas to a great meeting in a tiered theatre. Two men were holding hands by a lectern in the middle of the stage. 'The Wisdom of Life, Death and the Universe in *less than* twenty-five words,' said one. 'Take it away, O'Flahertie.'

O'Flahertie plopped a bowler hat on his head, twirled a cane and said: '*We are all in the gutter, but some of us are looking at the stars.*'

A voice above Tommy (*Bea's?*) laughed, whispering: 'Right! And it's when you're looking up at the stars that you fall through the holes in the gutter, to the sewer below.'

The crowd counted down, greeting *zero* with a standing ovation and cries of 'Bravo!' O'Flahertie and the other man were just exchanging a kiss when . . . CCCRRRRRRUUU-USSSSCCHHHH!!

A solitary voice boomed over the devastation: 'I AM DEATH. DESTROYER OF WORLDS.' And then the screen went blank.

This time, Tommy couldn't even cry out. He just crumpled to his knees.

14
SACRIFICE?

'Like a drink afore yuh go?' Elza was standing by the big apple tree – her tail petting its bark.

Having passed out from retching or shock (or both), Tommy was back in the bright canyon lying on the mattress. He sat up. 'Go . . ? You mean . . . He's finished *playing* with me?'

'All I knows is yer free tuh go.'

'But . . .' Tommy stood up, stunned. 'All that stuff he said about breaking me, ripping my heart out . . .'

Elza shrugged.

Tommy wandered over to the tree stump, trying to digest Elza's words. He picked up the axe that was resting on the tree stump. Yes, it was good to be free. And surprising. But . . . He'd learned nothing of the TFC – unless the destruction of those Earths was linked to it. *All those billions killed!*

He smashed the axe into the stump – 'I'm not going anywhere!' – and sprinted to the cave entrance, not stopping till he came to the edge of that other great canyon. The pale moon passed and he saw that there was no way across to the island of rock. And so he cried out, calling for Beashto, insulting him, pledging his life, pledging his soul, anything – *Anything!* – to draw the creature.

After hours of calling, he returned to Elza, who was

spraying water on the apple tree and wiping its leaves with a cloth. The big screen on the cliff wall was on, showing some inane TV station.

'I have to see him!' cried Tommy.

'I'd just leave if I were you,' said Elza, looking up at the TV.

Tommy grabbed at her apron, pulling out the remote control and turning off the screen. 'I'm not taking *no* for an answer!'

'Yuh're alive, yer friends are alive, yuh're free to go,' said Elza, her tail petting the tree trunk.

Tommy grabbed her by the apron strings. 'I'm serious!' he screamed. 'Take me to Beashto!'

'Lemme alone!'

He began shaking the young girl and, as he did so, he pulled her from the tree. It felt strange – resistance, then sudden release – like delivering a new-born baby. And she was in his arms, a little shorter, a little wider, a different scent.

'Ugghh!' he screamed. It was Bea, the old woman, in his arms and he pushed her away. She fell on the ground, panting. 'Take me to Beashto!' he yelled, hardly missing a beat.

'No,' said the woman, looking shamed.

Tommy's anger soared – fuelled by shock. Or guilt. 'Billions of people's lives are depending – BILLIONS! TAKE ME TO BEASHTO!'

'No.'

He snatched up the axe. 'Take me!'

'No.'

'TAKE ME!'

And as he raised the axe, he must've stood on the remote

control, for the TV blared to life. 'Take me to Beashto!' cried the figure onscreen. Tommy turned to see an image of himself shaking Elza. That same figure pushed Bea to the ground. Then drew back an axe ready to strike her.

And at that moment, above the TV, he saw a vision of a man and a woman looking down at him in horror. The man had dark hair and brown eyes, the woman was blonde and green-eyed. Yet through their horror came a warmth and something else. Something stronger. Tommy turned away and dropped the axe, a wave of shame overcoming him. When he looked up again, the couple were gone.

He shook his head. The vision – he must've imagined it. Yes, the stress and anger of the last few hours was obviously making him hallucinate. For the couple he'd 'seen' had been Lola and Errol. His long-dead parents.

It took Tommy some moments to recover himself, but after he'd helped Bea to the tree stump, sat her down and said a dozen sorries, the old woman caught him by the wrist. 'There is a way,' she said, staring into his eyes. 'I call it Bea's Way.'

'That the Beast will help me?'

Bea nodded. 'In a manner of speakin'.'

'What does that mean?'

Bea released his wrist, reached behind the stump and produced a flat violin-shaped piece of wood which she placed on her knees. Then she took a strange knife from her apron and began smoothing the wood with it.

'I said, what does that mean?' pressed Tommy, growing impatient. 'I want to know Bea's Way.'

Bea stopped smoothing. 'Yuh *sure* yuh want tuh know?'

Tommy nodded. Later, he'd wish that he hadn't. For the old woman locked him in her gaze and proclaimed: 'If you sacrifice yerself fer someone else, then the Beast will help yer fellow Knights wi' the TFC.'

'Er, what do you mean by *sacrifice*?'

'*Die*,' replied Bea, standing and placing the piece of wood on the tree stump. She raised the knife with both hands and stabbed it full-force into the wood's violin-like heart. Then, looking up at Tommy: 'Meanin' you allow yerself tuh be killed tuh save someone else. Not pretend-killed where yuh're revived later or turn up in a new guise. But dead-forever-killed.' And she lifted the knife, the violin corpse rising with it. The knife had come right through.

Tommy tried to look unfazed. 'And the Beast definitely has some knowledge of the TFC?'

Bea nodded, twisting the knife to make a larger hole. 'Def'nitely.'

'And would the Beast definitely help my friends if I . . .' (his voice lowered) 'sacrificed myself?'

Bea pulled the knife free from the wood and nodded. 'Def'nitely.'

Now that Bea's Way had been explained, the old woman set down the violin corpse, walked over to the apple tree and leant against it. The years fell from her face. Her figure narrowed and lengthened. And she was Elza.

Tommy was about to slump on to the mattress in despair when Elza spoke – sounding less innocent than before. 'There is another way – if yuh don't fancy Bea's Way.'

Tommy spun around. 'That the Beast would help us?'

Elza nodded. 'It'd entail provin' yourself.'

'Proving myself – how?' Tommy was excited. Anything was preferable to Bea's Way.

Elza stroked the knife against her cheek. 'Yuh'd have to be man enough for a different type of challenge.'

'Yes, tell me, please. Please! How could I prove myself?'

'See the garbage chute?' said the young girl, pointing the knife over Tommy's shoulder to a hole in the cliff wall. 'Remember the piece of paper yuh posted through it?'

15
Behind You!

Tommy was back in the passageway where he'd last seen Marielle, Woozie and Rumbles, carrying a crate of clinking bottles. It was lit once more by flaming torches. He set down the crate, stood on top of it and pressed something on the passage-wall. A doorway opened in the rock and Tommy, looking down, saw a torch-lit pit full of scurrying, dustbin-lid-sized spiders.

'Tommy!'

He looked up at the cry. And there they were. His friends. Standing on two criss-crossing rocky beams, high above the spiders. Tommy leapt on to the nearest beam and hurried to them. He wanted to hug Marielle so badly. He wanted to kiss her and whoop and cry and laugh and yell, all at once. But he checked his feelings and forced himself to hug the elquinine no more than the others. They were so eager to hear what'd happened to him (and all so good at balancing), that they sat down on the beams and Tommy filled them in – still bottling emotions as best he could. He left out certain bits, like Bea's Way and the WHAT-DO-YOU-WANT? Episode (and made a lame excuse for the mustard stains on his clothes). The others speculated on how a hand could crush an entire solar system and then they filled him in on what they'd been up to.

'Just sitting here, watching TVskeys the whole time,' said

Rumbles. He pointed at a blank screen on the far wall.

'And skewering the odd spider silly enough to climb up to us.' Woozie grinned, brandishing his scimmy.

'We moved forward after you ran off,' said Marielle. 'And then that door shut and we were locked in here.'

They all eyed the door that Tommy had come through and seemed on the verge of moving towards it when someone brought up the question of fuel for Swiggy.

'No need to worry,' said Tommy, indicating the crate he'd been standing on. 'It's full of Fizzaholic Crater Dew.'

As though in response to this news, Woozie leapt up with a cry of 'Yahh!' and jabbed his scimmy over Tommy's shoulder. There was a squeaking squelchy sound and, next thing, Tommy saw a dustbin-lid-sized spider falling to the pit floor. 'He was just about to bite you,' explained Woozie, taking a tissue from his pocket and cleaning his scimmy blade.

'So what's this piece of paper Elza told you to find?' asked Marielle, returning to Tommy's story.

Tommy looked at Marielle, still having to restrain himself from hugging her. 'She said it's got a challenge on it,' he said. 'And if I can find it and complete the challenge – live up to the challenge, as she put it – then the Beast will help us stop the TFC.'

'And are you sureskeys the Beast – Beashto, or whatever his name is – can stop the TFC?'

'Weren't you listening?' exclaimed Woozie. 'The Beast is behind the TFC.'

'How so?' asked Marielle.

'Well, it's obviously his hand destroying them EARTHs.'

Tommy wasn't so sure. Booming as it was, the voice claiming to be DEATH, DESTROYER OF WORLDS seemed to have a different quality from Beashto's.

'Responsible or not,' said Tommy, 'I feel certain the Beast can help us find the source of the TFC. And maybe help us put a stop to it.'

'And this piece of paper,' said Marielle. 'What does it look like?'

Tommy shrugged. 'The only clue she gave me was that the word *triumph* is printed on the page.'

'Triumph?'

'You didn't look when you put it through the slot?' asked Woozie.

Tommy shook his head. 'It felt about this wide and this long,' he said, indicating a pretty average sheet of paper. 'Elza said half the challenge was to recognize it when I see it.'

'OK,' said Marielle, uncertainly. 'And where do we have to go to fetch it?'

Tommy looked at his watch. 'I'll explain when we're on Swiggy.' Then he ducked smartly – Woozie was skewering another giant spider.

Before they left, Woozie wanted to show Tommy something. 'This TV,' he said. 'Think they got every channel in the universe.'

'Billionskeys of them,' added Rumbles, reaching for a remote control hanging from a length of twine.

'And there's a show we found called *LostLosers*. Plays footage of people who've crash-landed on remote planets.'

Tommy indicated to his watch. 'Interesting as that sounds . . .'

But already an image had appeared of Nack Jickilson and others standing round a syringe-shaped spacecraft. There seemed to be a jack lifting up the craft slightly and someone was changing the tyre.

'It's live footageskeys. Unfortunately, there's no sound.'

'Deadly!' chortled Tommy, his demeanour completely changed. 'He looks pretty annoyed. *Ooooh* – that's gotta hurt!'

'He hit his head on purpose!'

'Aaaaiiigghhh!' cried Woozie in his best Nack Jickilson impersonation.

'They've been fixing that spacecraftskeys for at least two days. It looks almost mendedskeys.'

'Where do you think they are?' asked Tommy. It looked familiar.

'Looks like a moon surrounded by oxygen.'

ThreeHeads had made a full recovery by the time they made it along the passageway, back to the entrance cave.

'I've no more flippety-flapjacks!' whispered Woozie.

'No worries,' said Tommy. 'Let me handle this.'

'Which way did she go?'

ThreeHeads had moved out of sight.

Tommy walked calmly in the direction of the jeggs. The others stood watching inside the cave, holding their breath – Rumbles jumping when the cloud of oppobats flapped overhead.

Woozie saw it first. ThreeHeads running towards Tommy.

'Behind you! To your left!'

But Tommy just kept on walking. ThreeHeads leapt over him, slid in a semi-circle and pounced forward, all six eyes on Tommy's two. 'Sit!' cried Tommy, putting up a hand, palm out, in a firm fashion. 'Sit!'

ThreeHeads skidded to a halt and – to the astonishment of Marielle, Woozie and Rumbles – sat down hard on the bony earth.

'Good girl,' said Tommy continuing (backwards) to the jeggs.

As the other three ventured out, Tommy kept his eyes fixed on ThreeHeads, calling 'Sit!' in a firm voice whenever she looked like moving. 'Quick!' he hissed once they'd made it to the jeggs. 'Go! Go!'

Hearing his friends clamber in, Tommy cried one last 'Sit!' and scrambled up into his jegg. ThreeHeads came racing over, leaping at them like pigeons as they took off.

Back in Swiggy, Tommy explained the guidance Elza'd given him. 'ThreeHeads never attacks anyone from behind. Only from the front . . . But she's been very well trained. She'll sit for anyone if they say it firmly enough. Her real name's Barbarous-Wud-Howse.'

Summy was pouring half a bottle of Fizzaholic Crater Dew into the fuel tank and Rumbles was off doing a number seven, when an announcement sounded outside Swiggy: 'Force field opening briefly in seven minutes.'

'OK, on our way shortly shall we be,' said Summy who was mighty relieved to see everyone back on board.

'So where are we off to?' asked Marielle.

Tommy eyed the pretty elquinine with a look he hoped conveyed good humour. 'I'll tell you . . . *after* you've done the washing up.'

16
Why Me?

As Swiggy sped away from Hellsbells (following a map and instructions given to Tommy by Elza), Summy calculated that they had at least four days before getting close to the piece of paper they were after – 'assuming too late already we are not'.

Two days into the journey, Rumbles was fighting to remain upright on a hammock in the Lounge – the task made more difficult due to a certain wibblewallian standing on his shoulders.

'Got it!' cried Woozie, pushing one of the ceiling panels aside, a square of blackness appearing above him. 'Now, push me up.'

'You sureskeys you heard him?'

'Yeah. He's rousing. He'll be up soon and'll need some cheering up.'

Rumbles shifted her bodyweight so the hammock knifed down to the floor. When it sprang back up, she flung Woozie into the square of blackness. Two yells of 'Oww!' followed as the wibblewallian flew headfirst into a snake-like muddle of pipes, while the thunderbumble toppled out of the hammock and fell backwards into a cupboard.

Once Woozie'd got his bearings he whispered down: 'Come on up.'

It took Rumbles a few painful attempts to bounce through

the square of blackness and grab hold of a pipe. Woozie helped haul her up.

'Why didn't you let me go firstskeys?' moaned Rumbles, rubbing a sore bit.

'Cos I can't lift you,' hissed Woozie. 'Now, ssshhh! He'll hear us.' He pulled at the ceiling panel. 'You hid all the cream pies by the sofa?'

'Of coursekeys! Plus all the other stuff.'

'And you got the remote control?' whispered Woozie, setting the panel back in its original position. 'For the music.'

'No, it should be in your pocketskeys, remember?'

Now it was absolutely pitch black where Rumbles and Woozie lay crouched. But the ceiling looked perfectly normal from down in the Lounge.

Tommy spent the first two days of the journey in bed, sleeping fitfully, only getting up to go to the loo or to change his pyjamas because they were drenched in sweat. Later, he recalled four recurring nightmares:

1 Walking along a canal bank with his parents, feeling joyful when, without warning, a solar system appears and a hand crushes it.
2 Cantering music plays in the background. He and Marielle are in a candlelit cave. He leans in to kiss her and, just before their lips touch, she turns into the hideous form of Bea.
3 A voice repeats, 'WHAT DO YOU WANT?' over and over, as a giant tooth comes up through the mattress.
4 The other IGGY Knights are thanking him and hugging him. When they stand back, they disappear and he,

Tommy, is left tied to a post. A firing squad appears. They cock their weapons and fire.

Afterwards, he'd say that he relived the Hellsbells pain again and again so he could *cauterize* it. 'Otherwise, I'd've been paralysed by emotion for weeks and no good to anyone.'

When he'd dealt with the worst of it, he managed to convince himself that he wasn't to blame for the Earths he'd seen destroyed. He also persuaded himself that his final answer to the question, WHAT DO YOU WANT? (' . . . everyone to like me, to love me, to think I'm great') did not reflect his true self. . . . *That was extracted under duress. I only said it cos it's what the Beast wanted to hear.*

What are the chances we can get the Beast to help us? He agonized over this question, eliminating Bea's Way from his mind ('allow yerself tuh be killed . . . dead-forever-killed') and telling himself they'd complete Elza's challenge instead. And the vision he'd seen of his parents when he'd held the axe over Bea . . . That was just induced by stress. And yet, something about seeing them in Hellsbells – even if it was just a vision – made him feel sure he was right to put his trust in Bea, Elza and the Beast.

As for the possibility of more Earths being destroyed in the future, he couldn't banish the thought. So he had to fight it. And the only ammunition that worked was anger. He sat up, fished for his hologram diary and began writing (telepathically), rehashing grievances (*having* to attend interactive lessons, *having* to obey stupid, silly rules, being virtually imprisoned on Swiggy . . .) that'd been building in his fourteen-year-old head for months.

And Marielle . . . She managed to get under his skin more than anyone. That maddening power she had to annoy him . . !

The way she'd flick her hair (why would you flick a ponytail?) or bat her eyelids, so he'd get in trouble with a fool like Crabble for losing his concentration during Stink Bomb Disposal class – *that bomb going off wasn't my fault!* He flung the hologram diary across the room . . . *And she's always bossing everyone into playing silly games. Silly, silly, silly games!*

He leapt off the bunk, almost twisting his ankle and had to kick the ball fourteen times before it hit the Racoon Squelch poster and the door to the Lounge opened. He hurried through, returned clumsiness only souring his mood. It was time to give the elquinine a piece of his mind.

While Rumbles and Woozie were bouncing about on the hammock, Summy was in the BubbleNerdCapsule – a small glass room just below Swiggy's tail fin. From here, the kangasaurus could savour the view as the silver streak of Swiggy flashed through space.

There were spiral galaxies polka-dotted with black holes, elliptical galaxies that looked like glowing haddock and galaxies shaped like the letter S with a giant glow in their middle. Summy loved the spectacle and dictated reams of notes to Edwina, the robotic parrot perched on her shoulder.

'Extraordinary! A star just like that one – Arcturus – is in our own Milky Way.'

'Extraordinary! Extraordinary!' repeated Edwina.

Then she heard it. A loud whistle, summoning everybody. Issuing from the Lounge. Normally, Summy'd ignore such a bossy whistle, but she'd just made an exciting discovery in her efforts to disprove all aspects of astrology and was anxious to share it. She leapt up and exited the BubbleNerdCapsule.

Marielle sighed. She was in the Girls' Bathroom, tightening the plait in her pony-tail. She was bored. Summy was hiding away – no doubt, doing something super-nerdy – Tommy was probably still lounging about in bed, and if the sounds coming from the Lounge were anything to go by, Woozie and Rumbles were nude trampolining again. (This was the moment that Rumbles fell off the hammock.)

Was there any chance, she wondered, that one of them would organize a group activity – to cheer everyone up and get them all playing together . . ? *Hah!* About as much chance as a chocolate snowball had of surviving two seconds next to Rumbles! She sighed again. *Why is it always left to me?*

She leaned in towards the mirror and looked at her face. *Hmmm.* She wondered how a little make-up might look and fumbled in a glass cabinet, finding a thick pencil. Just for the heck of it, she circled her eyes. Then she undid her plait and combed some oil into her hair so that it hung back off her head. Finally, she descended the ladder into the Girls' Dorm, took off her sweatshirt and put on a cream-coloured nightie (patterned with a gold design) over her dungarees. Slipping two winding gold bangles around her bare arms finished the look.

She opened a pocket in the rusty corduroy wall, revealing a mirror on the underside flap. An Egyptian princess stared back at her. [15] She liked the look. And it gave her a great idea for a game involving all the IGGY Knights and one of the canoes in the UnderBellyPool. If she went out into the

15 Technically, she was trying to look like an ancient princess from the planet Nose (subsequently known as planet Missingnose). See *TS1* for more explanation.

Lounge and whistled loudly, she could round everyone up in no time . . . She might even rouse one particular lazybones.

Tommy arrived in the Lounge just as Marielle put her fingers into her mouth and started whistling loudly. He put his fingers in his ears and called out: 'Can you s-stop that infernal r-r-racket?'

Unfortunately, she couldn't hear him (with the whistling), but when she spotted him, she stopped whistling and smiled. 'I've an idea for a game. If we all go down to the UnderBelly and—'

But if Tommy'd been irked when he left his dorm, he was on the point of losing it now. That stupid-stupid stutter was back. 'F-F-Fornax!' he cried.

Marielle halted, a little shocked.

Fornax is a star in the Milky Way, but it has a very rude double-meaning in a number of MilkyFed languages. Many kids exploit this to the full by crying 'Fornax!' at inappropriate moments and then claiming to annoyed parents that, 'I meant the star.'

'What do you mean by that?'

Tommy approached the Egyptian princess. 'D-did you really have to m-make that infernal wh-whistling noise?'

So used was Marielle to Tommy's stuttering that she didn't particularly notice its return. 'It wasn't *infernal* . . . *!* I said, what did you mean by that? By that rude word you just—'

'F-F-Fornax? . . . I meant the s-star.'

Marielle's face grew crimson. 'You did not mean the star!'

'What? Y-you think I was s-saying something 'bout your s-s-silly game.'

'*Silly*?'

It was at this moment that Summy burst into the room.

'Complete nonsense is astrology. And prove it I just—'

'Be quiet, mutt-face!' snapped Marielle, determined not to be distracted.

'Well . . . to say of all the things! Mutt-face!'

'F-F-Fornax! F-F-Fornax!' squawked Edwina on Summy's shoulder – for she'd heard Tommy say it with her extrasensory ears and enjoyed repeating rude words.

'So, you think my games are *silly*?' Marielle had her hands on her hips, in that defiant way of hers, eyes flashing at Tommy. She was ignoring Edwina who was now saying *Mutt-face* repeatedly.

'S-sorry,' said Tommy softly. '*S-s-silly* was the wrong w-word . . . I meant *ri-ridiculous*.'

'How dare—'

'A mutt-face? Have you know I will—'

'Mutt-face! Mutt-face! F-F-Fornax! F-F-Forna—'

Marielle, Summy and Edwina were all mid-sentence when Rumbles and Woozie plunged from the ceiling – 'Geronimooooohhhh!' 'Oooops-a-dunglyyyyyy!' – pointing a remote control towards the shelves and landing on top of Tommy. Music started playing.

'Aghh!!' cried Tommy. 'G-g-gerroff!'

Marielle, Summy and Edwina stood open-mouthed before the tumbling, tussling pile of bodies. Rumbles had both Tommy's legs pinned, while Woozie had hold of one of his arms and was trying to hold it down, so he could grab the other. In the struggle, Tommy became aware of music, became aware that it was, in fact, *Pongs Like Teen Spirit*, one of the 'deadliest' songs of all time.

I feel thicko
And contagious . . .

Woozie started performing the most feared manoeuvre taught to Knights of the Way – the UpTheJumperUnder-TheArmpitTickleTickleDon'tStopEeeOhh. A regular human would've lost consciousness within seconds. But Tommy was well trained in the Arts of the Way and, although his co-ordination was a little off, inspired by the music, he sprang a DeadArmTwistEeyOhh move to wriggle free of Rumbles and spin from Woozie's clutches – landing on his feet.

And I forget
Just what it takes
But yes, I s'pose it makes me grin . . .

He thought he was free until – just then– a powerful jet of water hit him, knocking him onto his backside. Looking up, he saw that Marielle was holding a water-bazooka, aiming it straight at him.

'That'll teach you to call my games silly,' she shouted above the music.

No sooner had she said the word *silly*, than a cream pie flew over Tommy's shoulder and *SMACK!* straight into the elquinine's face.

'Sorry!' cried Woozie. 'I was going for Tommy.'

Then a mousse-bomb hit Tommy across the back of the neck – exploding everywhere. 'Gotcha!' yelled Rumbles, flinging two more baseball-sized 'bombs'. Fortunately for Tommy, he dived to the floor. Unfortunately for Summy, one bomb caught her square in the face (the other splatted Edwina to the ground[16]).

16 Where she short-circuited 'irretrievably' (from the effects of 'goo on the floor').

Within seconds, cream pies, mousse-bombs and kangasaurian quiches were flashing through the air – each of the IGGY Knights having got their hands on a stash of 'ammunition'. And no one was making any attempt to hide behind furniture. They were standing tall, throwing with wild abandon – emptying all their frustrations, all their fears and all their *everything* into every missile they flung. And having more of the same smacked out of them, every time they got hit (Tommy and Marielle reserving the most forceful barrages for each another).

Who started giggling first? No one is sure. But what the FiiVe were sure of, was that they all began laughing. And even as he struggled against it, Tommy couldn't help himself. For if anger obscures woes, laughter positively drowns them. And a part of him felt like drowning forever.

The FiiVe laughed so hard, they found it hard to stand. So hard they almost shut out the music. So hard they found it hard to throw . . . All ending up in a loose huddle, picking sticky lumps and blobs of goo off the floor – smearing them on any face within reach.

Our wee group has always been
And always will until the end.

17

Doing the Deed

In a cluttered office in the outer-reaches of space, a figure called Bobby J. Heimenopper stood before a glass case full of dust particles. At least they looked like dust particles. He wore a single rubber glove (*El Nerdo* stencilled across its knuckles) and a line of sweat gleamed above his top lip. 'Why can't I do it now and put them out of their misery?' he blurted, glancing at a toaster on his desk.

'No!' intoned a voice. 'I must see their wisdom attempt. They've had ten years and nine hours to come up with it.'

The voice came from a flickering image on the wall and whoever was speaking was using one of those scary voice-distorters favoured by kidnappers making ransom demands. His face was covered by a black bin-liner, with two small holes for his eyes and a slit for his shadowed mouth.

Heimenopper, who looked human apart from his tail and face (which was half-man, half-donkey), shook his head and brayed. 'But you tell me to destroy the planets whether their wisdom attempts are good or bad!'

The creature known as Bin-Liner seemed to smile at this outburst and a bonfire flared behind him, spitting and crackling as if in laughter. The image on the wall was of such quality that Heimenopper might've stayed staring at the dancing sparks had a loud beep not sounded in his office. The beep was followed by a protracted buzz and then a postcard emerged from the toaster on his desk.

Eyes closed, Heimenopper took the postcard and placed it before the spyhole camera so Bin-Liner could see it. Then he removed a pair of half-moon spectacles from his lab coat and approached the glass case. Etched into the glass, above an orange, rubbery, fist-sized circle were the words:

CAUTION
Probe-lab Wormhole entrance
Entry endangers destination life. Exercise extreme care.

Behind him, Bin-Liner gave a distorted laughed. 'Millions of years of existence, and this is the best they can come up with!'

The cause of Bin-Liner's mirth (as Heimenopper would later see) was the message on the card.

Having pooled the collective intelligence of our planet, this is our suggestion for the Wisdom of Life, Death and The Universe (in under 25 words) . . .

'Your aunt Agnes would like you to call her after the assembly.'

'I can't!' brayed Heimenopper, standing before the glass case.

'Do the deed!' barked Bin-Liner.

'No, I can't. I tell you, I won't do it any more.'

Bin-Liner's eyes hardened. 'You want me to cut off your money . . ? OK, have it your way.' He lifted up a bread-roll-sized crystal – dark at one end, light at the other. 'I'll just have to separate the mastervill and destroy *all* the EARTHs in one go.'

'No wait . . !'

'I thought you'd see sense.' Bin-Liner's image grew larger, blotting out the bonfire. 'Now, if you don't follow my instructions *to the letter* you won't get a penny more – understand?'

'Er, yes . . . Yes, I do.'

'Good . . . Now put the postcard through the shredder. *Without* reading it . . . After that . . . *Do the deed* . . . OR ELSE NO MORE MONEY.'

The image on the wall disappeared.

Heimenopper's office was dark apart from a glistening pinprick of light in the centre of the room. Gradually, the donkeyish scientist could make out the tiny specks of dust illuminated by the pinprick. Almost five million pressed against the inside of the glass. And now, separated from the others in the middle of the case, eight or nine lone specks. Hard to believe they were planets. Actual planets, billions of light-years away in space.

Even though he was the inventor, he still found it hard to believe that wormhole-miniaturization-glass-case-technology™ really worked.

He took a small bottle from the inside of his lab coat and took a swig. His insides hurt, his bank account hurt and Bin-Liner's voice still rang through his head. *Do the deed.* One last swig and then, with his gloved hand, he reached through the orange rubbery hole in the side of the glass case. The third speck of dust from the pinprick. That was the planet that held the six billion creatures. Creatures cloned and bred as part of some strange project. But live creatures nonetheless.

He was about to crush an entire solar system and – as ever at this moment – felt the urge to lighten the mood. He could say, '*I got your whole world in my hand*' . . . Or maybe, '*I make a good fist of my job*' or even, '*Oops, I did it again*'.

But, as ever, he stifled the urge. Better to say something dramatic – almost meaningful – in a ponderous, weighty tone.

'I am Death. Destroyer of worlds.'

He smiled momentarily. *Your aunt Agnes would like you to call her after the assembly.* He wished these people could have a reprieve. For, if nothing else, they had a sense of humour. Maybe not as funny as the planet that'd come back with the suggestion of '44 minus 2' *(seriously, that was their answer to the Wisdom of the Universe)* – but funny nonetheless.

Then he remembered the seriousness of the situation. The hare-brained hurdle was about to start. If he hurried he could place a bet.

Heimenopper squeezed his hand closed. *Ow!* Even at this size and wearing a purple rubber glove, extinguishing stars can give a nasty sting.

In a great amphitheatre somewhere in space, hundreds of bearded creatures sat at hundreds of tiered desks, all arranged in a crescent shape, facing a giant blackboard. The blackboard was filled with words and symbols and formulae – all scrawled beneath the heading WISDOM SUGGESTIONS.

Every now and again a bearded creature would look up from his book-covered desk and raise a hand. An elderly, bearded, bushy-tailed creature standing by the blackboard would point towards them and nod and write whatever they had to say on a sliver of blackboard.

Precisely fifty-nine minutes after a postcard popped

through the toaster in Heimenopper's office, a small creature appeared out of a trapdoor by the blackboard and the amphitheatre hushed.

'Er, Master OleSayjj,' said the creature, addressing the bearded elder by the blackboard. 'Less than a minute to the next EARTH-wisdom deadline.'

A chorus of voices rang out from the tiered desks. 'Waste of time!' 'They never bother to answer!' 'Told you we should've threatened them with *destruction* instead of offering *riches*!'

The bearded elder known as OleSayjj was covered in reddy-grey fur and looked half-man, half-twinkly-spaniel – with a smidge of fox thrown in for good measure. He raised his arms. 'Patience, friends . . . Who knows . . ? *This* EARTH may choose to answer. Let us pray they do, for they have had ten years and ten hours to come up with an answer.' He looked down at the small creature by the trapdoor. 'Balwick, you have the tele-sock.'

Balwick nodded and produced a large woolly sock. A sundial to the side of the blackboard lit up. Every creature in the amphitheatre froze and watched the shadow count down the seconds.

When the moment was reached, Balwick looked in the sock. Nothing. He turned the sock inside-out. Still nothing.

A chorus rose up. 'You see – waste of time!' 'That's over forty thousand waste of times so far.'

OleSayjj raised his arms to hush the gallery. 'Please! Even if we heard nothing from this EARTH, it was worth trying . . . Now, fear not. We will still come up with the wisdom necessary. And we *will* stop the TFC and save the universe. Or my name's not Jeremiah OleSayjj.'

18

Beware False Guiding Lights

Tommy felt a lot better. He'd convinced himself that the stutter's return and the loss of co-ordination *proved* they were linked to travel sickness – meaning they'd go away again whenever Swiggy stopped. And he'd managed to deal with the final nightmare knocking about his head – planet Earths being destroyed.

What I saw must've been a once-off for my benefit, he assured himself. No one would keep destroying planets for no reason. *Right?* Whatever the answer, the best thing (in fact, the *only* thing) he could do was to complete Elza's challenge and get the Beast to put a stop to the TFC. *And moping around, feeling sorry for myself or getting angry with other people isn't going to help!*

And so, after the food-fight clean-up, he exchanged high-fours with his friends. 'S-sorry about the extended l-lie-in. I'm b-back.'

He still wondered about the very existence of other Earths, but found nothing helpful on Swiggapedia and gave up asking his fellow Knights for their thoughts after Summy suggested: 'Like a bad rash Earths perhaps are.'

That evening, the Knights sat down for a hot meal ('The cookerskeys working again!') and had a serious chat about

Elza's challenge. The first order of business was to come up with a name for the sheet of paper they were after – the one with the word *triumph* printed somewhere on it. Having ruled out *Elza's Parchment* and the *Elzic Scroll*, they settled on the *Deadly Scroll* ('since Deadly means *super-dangerous* or *brilliant*') .

They also decided to cram in as many interactive lessons as possible that might help with the Deadly Scroll.

Marielle found a class given by MonSenior where he outlined the difference between wisdom and knowing lots of facts ('Wisdom means looking beyond *facts*. It is seeing, truly seeing, from the best vantage point that facts can give you').

When Tommy scanned the small, silver cases in the Masters of the Way Vault, the one he eventually removed had the following etching on its front:

— QUITE IMPORTANT LESSONS —
LESSON No. 2,317
'Guiding Lights'
Tutor = LBMWF-O[17]
(To Avoid Nightmares Do Not Attend Before Bed)

'A Guiding Light is what we call an individual who shows you the path to averting the TFC.'

The day after the food-fight, the IGGY Knights were sitting in large hammocks suspended from the ceiling of the DroneDroneClassRoom, paying differing amounts of attention to the tall, bearded kangasaurus before them.

'When you find a Guiding Light,' intoned Wisebeardyface, 'throw yourself, heart and soul, into the challenges, the ways,

17 Stands for Lord Beardedmoustachedwiseface-Oh – Wisebeardyface's real name.

the paths they show you.'

One Knight paying scant attention to the old Master was Woozie. 'Hey,' he whispered angrily, twisting in his seat. 'You eating chocolate snowballs?'

'Er, no,' said Rumbles, a ring of brown and white sticky stuff around her mouth.

'We're s'posed to be saving 'em for special occasions!'

'Quiet!' roared Wisebeardyface and a snarl of flame escaped from one of his nostrils. 'As I was saying . . . Follow the Guiding Light completely . . . But beware *false* Guiding Lights. Individuals who may want to trick you for reasons of their own . . . In other words, be cautious. *Very* cautious.' Marielle gave Tommy a look. 'Time wasted pursuing activities removed from the TFC,' continued the orange, scaly creature, 'makes the TFC all the more likely to happen . . . Remember . . . The future of the universe, the future of squintillions of lives may hang on your actions.'

After a few fiery sneezes, the lesson ended and the projection of Wisebeardyface vanished into a matchbox-sized silver case. Woozie's eyes turned fiery and he charged at Rumbles with a cry of: 'Hey! Chocolate snowball crumbs – by your hammock!'

'What? Where?' croaked the thunderbumble, feigning ignorance.

Tommy, Marielle and Summy laughed as they watched the ensuing tussle – thankful that the sombre mood, occasioned by Wisebeardyface's words, had been lifted.

19

More Than You Wish to Know

The biggest dump in the universe is known as LitterLoutt*Wot?* The name is said to derive from litter louts saying 'What!?' or 'Wot?' when their disgusting habit is pointed out to them. The area started off life as an inter-stellar park where creatures called sKumbaGs frequently dropped litter and then blamed local government for the mess. Later, the sKumbaGs were moved on to the PostKoncert constellation and six black holes were pushed into the area in an effort to clean the place up. Rubbish from thousands of galaxies is transported to LitterLoutt*Wot?* by enormous space vessels called dumptrux. They stop at a spot some fifty squillion kilometres above the circle of black holes and empty their contents. All the glass is automatically routed to one black hole. Paper, plastics and dead squirrels to another. Chewing gum and fluffy rugs to another. Gungy, smelly stuff and live squirrels to another. Fake things (legs, moustaches, paintings, diaries, etc.) to another. Everything else goes to the last and biggest black hole, known affectionately as BunterBilly.

'There's one!' cried Woozie, pointing to a speck in the distance.

Four and a half days out of Hellsbells, all but one of the IGGY Knights were in Swiggy's cockpit, looking out for a very specific dumptrux (this is both the singular and plural of the word).

Tommy peered at the sicko-warpo speed viewfinder. '*Y-You're An Idiot!*' he said. 'N-no, that's not the right wu-one.' *As you'll see from the box below, Tommy wasn't being rude.*

I Ate Your (Tasty) Gerbil!

Some time ago, people across much of the universe realized that ordinary spacecraft registration plates, such as kFrWxπ34e78, are difficult to remember – which was why most bank-robbery getaway vehicles went untraced. And so spacecraft registrations were changed so they'd be easily recalled. As people rarely forget insults or completely bizarre things, these formed the basis of most new registration plates.

The most requested registration plate ever was 'F#@£ Off!' (censored by publisher) and this was granted to an elderly lady called Miss Daisy when her name was chosen in a lottery.

'What's the reg. we're after?' asked Woozie.

'*There's-A-Funny-Smell*,' said Marielle.

'Catch the dumptrux we must, before its load it empties into LitterLoutt*Wot?!*' exclaimed Summy. 'Otherwise, history is that piece of paper – the *Deadly Scroll* mean I.'

And we lose our best chance of saving the universe from the TFC, thought Tommy.

'But don't go too close to the black holes,' said Marielle. 'Remember what Lady Muckbeff said.'

'Black holes doth spell death for eternity.' The IGGY Knights had heard Lady Muckbeff utter these words in Woozie's chosen class the previous afternoon.

'Isn't d-death usually f-for eternity?' whispered Tommy to Woozie.

'Fie!' cried Lady Muckbeff. 'Silence, I sayeth! Or extra homework wilst be thy punishment.'

Tommy was about to crack his usual gag about how all the lessons and work they did on Swiggy was already homework since this was their permanent home, but he resisted. Mainly because it wasn't funny.

'Hark, now, whilst I tell ye of black holes.'

As usual for these classes, the six-legged polar-bear-like creature was wearing a green coat with the hood pulled up. In order to make it seem like Lady M was really there, an awful smell whisked out of the case when the vision of Lady M appeared (*Eau de Coat*, as Woozie termed it).

'If ye fallest into a black hole,' said Lady M, rearing up on two legs, so her head almost hit the wooden beams near the ceiling, 'never, nay never, wilst ye return . . . The pain experienced wouldst be worse than being hit upon the head with a phonebook.'

'Ow!' said Woozie, biting on his dog tags at the thought of it. (Most phonebooks in the MilkyFed contain billions of names and can be up to twenty metres thick.)

After Lady M whisked back into the silver case – taking the Eau de Coat with her – Rumbles tumbled out of her hammock. 'Black holes sound a bit scary,' she said.

'Yes, avoidance the best policy is,' said Summy. 'Not that scared I am.'

'Of course n-not,' said Tommy.

'Just the rest of you about worried I am.'

Harriett Steptoe checked her co-ordinates and eased back the throttle. LitterLoutt*Wot?* was just a few minutes away. If she could dump this load quickly she might get home in time to catch an episode of her favourite soap – *The Sad and the Lonely*. Space looked dark and empty here. She gazed through the cockpit window – up, down, left and right – finally spotting a solitary star that blinked in the distance and inadvertently catching a glimpse of herself in the rear-view mirror. Sorrowful eyes, a squidgy nose, a soft mouth and thick, thick sideburns. *Why can't I be pretty like my sisters?*

As a kid, she never dreamt she'd end up driving a dumptrux for a living. She'd always imagined herself running a planet or inventing a new way to make toast that'd improve the lives of billions of people. Or perhaps opening a pie shop of her own. She'd always been good at making pies – it was the one thing her father used to compliment her on. Although he used to shout at her whenever she scoffed them without giving anyone else a taste.

Harriett reached under her seat and pulled out a bar of Dreamchoco. It felt good to eat whenever she felt like this. A bit down.

One bite, two bites . . . three. *Mmmmmmm.*

By the time the cockpit's Uh-Oh-Light started flashing, she had Dreamchoco all round her mouth. 'Danger!' said a computerized voice. 'You are approaching LitterLoutt*Wot?* Black holes can seriously damage your health . . . It's probably best to stay well back.'[18]

18 A lot of legal wrangling had taken place across the universe concerning the warnings that should accompany black holes. Much of the wrangling centred on the word 'probably'. The company that operated many of the black-hole-garbage-depots

Harriett stepped hard on the brakes, but because There's-A-Funny-Smell was such a big dumptrux, it took half a minute to come to a complete standstill.

'In position,' said the computerized voice. 'Ready to dump your load.'

Harriett's hand went to the lever marked *JustBeSure*. Pulling this lever would open the back of the dumptrux, releasing enough garbage to fill half a moon.

As ever, Harriett paused at this moment . . . All that rubbish. Where had it all come from? Imagine all the people who'd generated it. Think of all the activities the rubbish represented – eating, drinking, cleaning, constructing; throwing out the old, the unwanted, the things that had once been loved. She thought of joyous moments, of arrivals and birthdays, of presents being opened and packaging discarded. She pictured sad moments – parties ending, detritus like vomit on the floor. Then she remembered her father dying and, afterwards, when she had to clear out all his cupboards. *Two chest-loads of junk.*

If you want to know a people, she contended, don't listen to what they say, don't look at what they wear. Just go through their rubbish. That'll tell you more than you wish to know.

And with that, she polished off the last piece of Dreamchoco, scrunched up the wrapper and dropped it through a chute. It was part of the ritual. Something from her life would always be the very last piece of rubbish to go

claimed to have no responsibility for the billions of people who'd lost their lives over the years while depositing their rubbish. For aeons, the company stuck to the line that 'there is absolutely no proof that black holes are dangerous'. This position was aided by the fact that anyone who'd actually found a black hole to be dangerous (i.e. anyone who'd been sucked into one for all eternity) was unable to present themselves as a witness for the prosecution.

into the garbage bay before she released its contents to eternity (and it really was the size of a bay – think San Francisco Bay).

Just as Harriett pulled the JustBeSure lever, a metallic streak whizzed past the cockpit. The lever moved to the *open* position and Harriett peered into the *BowelsAway!* Viewfinder to watch the garbage flow from the dumptrux and down towards the black holes. This was the best part of being a dumptrux driver – watching the waste-wash waterfall.

But . . ? Of the garbage, there was no sign! She pulled the lever to the *closed* position then back again to *open*. Nothing. She did it again. And again. Still nothing.

Then she saw the metallic streak. This time it was heading straight for her . . . What Harriett didn't know was that this was a jegg and it was being piloted by Rumbles. If she'd checked her wing mirrors, she'd have seen an even bigger streak (of silver), circling behind. This was Swiggy, acting as an enormous sticky-tape dispenser, wrapping tape around the dumptrux, preventing its great bowel doors from opening. It came to a stop just as Rumbles shot past Harriet's cockpit and severed the sticky-tape from Swiggy with a swish of his wing.

'Deh-nahhh!' cried Rumbles, looping back towards Swiggy. 'What skill! No one can ever say I'm clumskeys again.' And with that she went to sound her klaxon, but somehow fired two missiles instead.

The first missile narrowly missed Swiggy, going on to zip within inches of Harriett's cockpit. The second went even closer to Swiggy (causing Summy to spill a cup of tea), then ploughed straight into Harriett's cockpit.

'Cripes! Double-cripes!!' yelled Rumbles, whooshing towards the stricken cockpit.

Plus ça Change

Ironically, a dumptrux would appear in that evening's episode of *The Sad and the Lonely* – the one that Harriett would miss. In the episode, a husband who's grown tired of coffee-mornings, detoxes, botoxes and giving his (ungrateful) kids lifts to far-flung planets, finds out that his wife has been 'oiling' her robot-secretary. In a fit of pique, he steals a dumptrux, empties its contents over his wife's workplace and is hailed a hero by the Men's Liberation movement. (In much of the universe, it's men who are expected to be the primary child-carers.)

20

In a Stew

Etched across the door were the words:

Bobby J. Heimenopper PhD MaD
PRIVATE – NO ENTRY

And when it opened, a tired, donkeyish scientist emerged on to a balcony that was one of hundreds hugging the inside of an elliptical-shaped building. He locked the door and proceeded along the narrow walkway, past other offices and storage rooms, to a liftwell. The lift, when it came, was made of glass and afforded him a clear vista of El Nerdo Lostalmost Physics Facility.

Floating in the outer reaches of space, El Nerdo was capped with a glass roof that funnelled light from a faraway sun and a recurrent meteorite onto its expansive Ground Floor. This floor, half hidden by luscious trees and rich vegetation, was made of marble and teemed with restaurants and people. El Nerdo's main feature, however, was some two kilometres tall and stood between the teeming floor and the glass roof. Known as the EARTH Wall, it consisted of thousands of screens filling the 365¼-metre-wide section of wall between all the balconies. Each screen was the size of a double bed. And each played live images from a different planet.

The lift had descended a single floor when it came to a halt, the doors opened and in hopped a worried looking kangalarsen (much like a kangaroo, but with buck teeth, grey hair, spectacle-eyes and a number of pens sticking out the top of its pouch). Heimenopper recognized the creature as Max Bohr, a scientist he'd usually just nod to (since the creature was referred to by many as Maximum Bore), but given how he'd just obliterated six billion lives, Heimenopper was determined to spread good cheer.

'Max. How are you?'

'Ah!' said Max, staring into his pouch as if the world was about to end.

'Can't be all that bad,' said Heimenopper as the lift began descending.

'You don't want to know. Trust me.'

'No, I do. Please. A problem shared is a problem halved.'

Something in Heimenopper's tone struck Max Bohr, for the kangalarsen smacked the lift's STOP button and pushed himself into Heimenopper's face. 'You can keep a secret, can't you, Heimenopper? I mean, you work on your own a lot, so you can keep a secret, can't you? Can't you!?'

Stuck between floors 188 and 189, with a kangalarsen in his face, Heimenopper had little option but to say, 'Eh, yes.'

'Cross-your-heart-and-hope-to-die, stick-a-laser-beam-in-your-eye?'

'Er, OK.'

Max Bohr stood back and burst into tears.

'What is it, Max?'

Between sobs, Max unloaded his big secret. 'I've lost an excessive number of planet EARTHs . . . Yes, we expect 8.3 per cent of them to destroy themselves with nuclear weapons, 13.4 per cent to wipe out all life with climate change and 22.8 per cent to lose all human inhabitants to elvisyndrome[19]. But I'm missing over forty thousand planet EARTHs. They've just disappeared, along with their suns and neighbouring planets.'

Heimenopper tried to sound calm. 'Oh, er, I'm sure you've made a mistake with your calculations, Max.'

'No!' cried Max. 'I'm SURE!!' He burst into tears again and it took some time before he could speak. 'I've checked back through all the video tapes, and all the EARTHs end the same way – *POOOFFF!!* The video goes blank and a voice, all pompous, says, *I am Death, destroyer of worlds.*'

'I'm sure the voice didn't mean to be pompous.' When Max looked at him oddly, Heimenopper changed the subject. 'Er, who else knows about this?'

'Just me. I've told no one – apart from you.'

'Max, listen to me,' brayed Heimenopper. 'Keep it that way. Top secret.'

Max Bohr started to shake. 'But . . . The EARTH Wall! Heimenopper, you know each screen picks a random EARTH every few minutes and displays images from it. Now screens are popping up blank for minutes at a time!'

'Max . . .' Heimenopper had such an urge to tell Max the truth. But then he thought of Bin-Liner and the money he owed, not to mention the fact that he'd probably be fired. 'Max, think about it . . . forty thousand missing EARTHs out of five million in the universe. That's less than 1 per cent . . . So people see a few blank screens – big deal! They'll just assume there's a problem with the signal. And that's if they even notice!'

'Hmmm . . . I don't know.'

19 This involves eating themselves to death with cheese burgers and milkshakes.

'They haven't noticed up till now, have they?' Max shook his head. Heimenopper continued: 'And you're the expert in this field – and it took *you* years to confirm it.'

'But . . .' Bohr's voice lowered to a whisper. 'Bobby . . . I'm due to retire in a few years. Been banking on a *full* pension . . . If the inspectors find out about the missing EARTHs . . .'

'There's no chance they'll find out. They're complete dopes.'

The kangalarsen's face lightened a touch. 'Hmmm.'

'See? You know I'm right!' declared Heimenopper.

'Well,' said Bohr, caught in two minds. 'I *have* been getting myself into such a stew. Not thinking straight.'

'Exactly! Now, speaking of stew, let's go get some lunch.'

And the scientist with the half-human half-donkey-face depressed the STOP button. The lift resumed its descent.

21

Worse Than Your Socks

The first thing Rumbles did on approaching Harriett's smashed cockpit was to shoot a TOR-bubblegum-PEDOE from his jegg. It hit the side of the vessel and exploded, forming a bubble around the stricken cockpit. Rumbles performed a parallel parking manoeuvre, easing the window of his jegg into the bubble. Once it was pressed hard enough against the bubble, he opened the window and jumped through the skin of the bubble into Harriett's cockpit. Inside, he found Harriett sitting motionless, strapped into the pilot-seat.

'No!' he cried. 'Please wake up! Don't be dead!'

He unclasped her seat-belt and lifted her, laying her gently on the cockpit floor. Pressing on her chest, he breathed into her mouth and licked the chocy-wocky off her face as Miss LeWren had taught them in LastAid Class. But it was no use. Harriett wouldn't respond.

By the time Tommy and the others appeared through the bubblegum, Rumbles was distraught.

'The temperature and pressure exceedingly low of deep space,' said Summy. 'Harmed her it has.'

'B-but there was another b-bubble besides the b-b-bubblegum one,' said Tommy. 'L-look. You'd hardly n-notice as you j-jump through them both.'

Sure enough, they now all saw that there was a transparent soapy bubble, just inside the bubblegum one. (Both bubbles were designed to be jumped through without bursting – in the way that bubbles can pass through bubbles.)

Summy examined data from the cockpit's pink triangle (much like the black boxes found in planes on Earth) and noted that the transparent bubble had deployed one millionth of a second after Rumble's missile had pierced the cockpit.[20]

This meant that Harriett would've been exposed to the elements of deep space for only a very short period. Still, considering the temperature at this point in space was about *minus* 269°C, even a tiny blast could spell trouble if you weren't wearing a scarf and mitts.

'We can't all h-help her at wu-once,' said Tommy, as Marielle took over Rumbles's attempts to revive Harriett. 'W-we should start l-looking for the Deadly Scroll.'

They drew lots to determine the order.

'Me and Tommy first!' cried Woozie when the curly straws had been drawn. Then he realized this wasn't a good thing and muttered *fizzlestix* under his breath.

Summy accompanied Tommy and Woozie through the thick, steel door at the back of the cockpit. It slammed shut behind them and they found themselves in a clanking utility room with a circular hatch in the middle of its floor. The hatch had a lever and, inscribed into its steel, were the words:

Property of The Universal Refuse Department (TURD)
DO NOT under any circumstances
open this GarbageHold hatch

20 The missile actually passed through this bubble on the other side of the cockpit as it flew off into deep space.

'Hmm,' said Summy. 'Reconsider perhaps we should.'

'The Deadly Scroll may not even be down there,' said Woozie.

'No, we've g-got to go down,' said Tommy, looking round at a bank of shelves labelled *Specialized GarbageHold Stuff*. 'It's the only l-l-lead we have.'

The shelves, it turned out, held various clothes and equipment, including togs, towels, extra-strong nose pegs and face masks (with built-in microphones and earplug receivers). Tommy and Woozie got changed before the Earthling pulled the lever on the hatch. It jolted from the three o'clock to the six o'clock position.

'Look!' said Woozie. '*Another* notice.'

Sure enough, in the three o'clock position, previously hidden by the thick lever were the words:

Seriously,
DO NOT under any circumstances open this hatch.

'Trying to tell us something, I think it is,' said Summy.

Ignoring the dinosaurus, Tommy pulled on the lever with all of his might. It swung round and the hatch opened – revealing another hatch underneath and another notice.

OK, you are either really stupid or really desperate.
Last chance . . .
DO NOT under any circumstances open this hatch.

Tommy looked up at his two friends then pulled the lever on this second hatch. It swung open.

If the three friends had been expecting to see something spectacular, they were bitterly disappointed. Nothing but a circle of lumpy greeny-purple gunge with a Dreamchoco wrapper floating on top. And the smell – worse than anything you could ever imagine.[21]

As they tightened their nose pegs, Tommy felt a surge of conflicting emotions. He realized his co-ordination had returned (*Elza was right!*) and he realized the craziness of what he was about to do (*How can we find a sheet of paper in THIS?*).

'Wow!' cried Woozie. 'What a pong! Even worse than your socks after a flashscimitar duel.'

Somehow this made up Tommy's mind – he gave the wibblewallian a friendly punch, held his face mask firmly to his face and jumped feet-first into the porridgey pool.

Summy'd flicked on the GarbageHold lights and these, together with his torch-helmet, meant the young Earthling could see dark blotches and dim shapes as he sank down, down. Something wriggly touched his neck – he lurched to the side, but saw nothing.

'Hey, furry-f-face,' he said into his microphone. 'You b-better not've changed your m-mind!'

Through his earphones, he heard Woozie's reply. 'Don't you be worrying. I'm in already. We should go in opposite direc—'

Aaaaaggggghhhhhhhhh!!!

The yell was echoing in his ears before Tommy realized that it belonged to him. No longer swimming in liquid, he was falling. Until – *WHUUUUMMMMPPPP!!* – he landed on something hard and lumpy.

Tommy'd assumed the GarbageHold was full to the brim with liquid, but he was wrong. The liquid at the top of the hold was

21 The society of INsANE Mathematicians actually calculated the formula for how smelly it was: {VeRY $x^{2.16}$ x 10 x π x 'smelly'}.

composed of WarmHelium which, like helium balloons, rises (it and TekeelahShotz are the only liquids in the universe which rise in gravity conditions). So, once Tommy swam through the bottom of the WarmHelium, he was bound to fall till he hit something.

'You OK?' asked Woozie. And then, before Tommy could reply, the furry fellow screamed. 'Aaaaaggggghhhhhhhhh!!!' Followed by the sound of a dull thud.

'I'm O-OK,' said Tommy. 'Howsabout y-you?'

Woozie seemed to be recovering his breath, when he gave a different kind of yell. 'Waaggghhh!! . . . A snaky thing!'

'Wh –? Wh-what is it!?'

'No, nothing. It's gone. Yeah, definitely gone.'

Having left Rumbles and Harriett, Marielle made it back to Swiggy. She could find nothing on *resuscitation techniques* on Swiggapedia and had little more success in the Medical section of the Masters of the Way Vault. The most useful thing she came across was a lesson in a different section.

— INTERACTIVE LESSONS —
LESSON No. 498
'Fixing Things – Innovative Techniques'
Tutor = LBMWF-O

She took the silver case into the Lounge and opened it on the coffee table. Immediately, Wisebeardyface whisked into view and Marielle started explaining their predicament.

The Silver Case technology was so extraordinary that a casual observer would've thought that the orange kangasaurus was actually in Swiggy's Lounge, sinking back on the sofa, with his feet stretched out on a pouffe, listening to the young elquinine. This is exactly what a very formal observer would've thought, except they might also have noticed the old Master holding a funny-looking cigarette and rooting about in his pouch for nothing in particular.

'Nothing on resuscitation!' exclaimed Wisebeardyface when Marielle had finished. 'Deary me. Most remiss. Hmmm . . . Well then, we will have to come up with a solution ourselves.' He asked Marielle to talk him through Harriett's symptoms, asking a series of detailed questions. 'What happens if she is held upside down? . . . Did anyone think of putting a slice of quiche down her trousers?'

Eventually, Wisebeardyface had an idea. 'I am not a doctor, so I can give no guarantees, but I saw it done once in a Grow-sss-Goo movie.'

Marielle took down some notes. 'And did it revive the person?' she asked.

Wisebeardyface took an anxious puff on his cigarette. 'I am afraid not.'

'What happened?'

'The patient exploded and everyone within a three-kilometre radius was killed.' The dinosaurus saw a look of fear cloud Marielle's face. 'But it *was* just a movie.'

Some hours into the search, swimming through islands of debris, Tommy eyed another piece of paper. They were hard to spot, being so covered in goo. The corner of this sheet was brown – doubly difficult to see – and it was caught in a castor of a shopping trolley floating in the sea of gunge. He reached for the paper, but its corner tore away in his hand and the trolley disappeared from sight. Something grazed his foot, then sank away. Like a hunting bird, he curled and dived.

'Supposedly, it's like hot-wiring a jegg.'

Rumbles looked blankly at Marielle. 'I've no idea how to hot-wire a jeggskeys.'

Marielle took the keys out of the dumptrux's ignition and searched under the dashboard for wiring. 'Got it . . . I think.' She pulled hard and both of her hands emerged, each holding the frayed end of a wire.

The pretty elquinine stretched the wires till they were hovering either side of the comatose pilot's chest. 'If these are the right wires, they should send a small blast of volts through her body – waking her up.'

'And if they're the wrong wires?'

Marielle decided not to answer that question. Instead, she closed her eyes, took a deep breath and pressed the frayed ends into Harriett's chest.

Six, seven metres down, Tommy caught hold of the trolley, bringing it to a halt. And yes, still jammed in one of its castors – half stuck to a can of spam – was something you couldn't tell was a sheet of paper. But Tommy recognized the edge of flat brownness and the torn corner.

He smeared what goo he could off the sheet, folded it in two and stuffed it down the back of his pants. This was getting ridiculous. He had so many sheaves of paper down there, his bum looked half the size of a wheelbarrow.

FFFFFZZZZZZZZZZZZZZZZZZZZZZZZZZZZ!!

A strange sound buzzed through the hold and all the lights died – including the torch on his head.

'H-hello!? . . . W-Woozie? . . . S-S-Summy?'

No answer.

Something slimy and wriggly swam between his legs.

'Aaaaaggghhhh!!'

The slimy creature curled past his chest. *It's OK. Probably just a fish.* Then he felt a slight pressure on his legs, his arms, his chest, his neck. *It's wrapped itself around me! It's curling tighter!* He wriggled, twisting, turning. One arm almost free. But then he felt a jab in his biceps – 'IIIIIIIIIIIIIII-IEEEEEEEEE!!!!' – and his arm went limp.

FFFFFZZZZZZZZZZZZZZZZZZZZZZZZZZZZ!!

The cockpit went pitch-dark.

'You still there, Rumbles?'

'Yes. Are you?'

Marielle resisted making a smart comment. 'I think we short-circuited the entire dumptrux. We've lost all power.'

'Say, am I dead?' This was a different voice. One that neither Marielle nor Rumbles had ever heard before. The voice reminded Rumbles of warm honey being raked across his back (which had been one of his favourite childhood treats).

'No. You're safeskeys.'

To Harriett, this voice sounded like a bear-like creature with three arms holding a damsel in distress (which had been her favourite childhood fantasy).

VVVVVVVVVVVVVVVHHHHHOOOOOOOOMMMM!!

The lights came back on.

'Hurrah!' cried Marielle. 'The power's back'

But neither Harriett nor Rumbles heard her. They were both too captivated by the vision in front of them.

VVVVVVVVVVVVVVHHHHHHOOOOOOOMMM!!

The lights flickered and came back on in the GarbageHold. So did a certain torch-helmet. It took a second to register the scene. But when Tommy did, he screamed.

'NOOOOOOOOOOOOOOOOOOOOOOOOO!!!'

There, six inches from his face, was a python-like creature, mouth open, ready to strike.

22

Goldilocks – No Kidding

'You wait six months for a falling star then outta nowhere one falls into your lap.'

On the planet Potboyler in the PI-DI Constellation, a middle-aged man sat at a desk in a poorly lit office and stared at the phone receiver he'd just replaced. He had big floppy ears and the look of a bloodhound. When he spoke, it was to no one in particular, for the room was empty save for his slightly overweight frame. If you'd been standing outside, looking in through the door with its frosted window frame and stencilled lettering – *Barlowe Sherlock Canusmajor Magnum Marple Farlowe PI* – you'd have thought Barlowe Farlowe (as his name was generally shortened to) was quite mad. For you'd've had no idea that a tiny microphone, embedded into the back of his askew tie, was picking up every word for posterity.

'On the slim chance I ever pen my life story,' was how he'd once put it.

DICTATED BY PI BARLOWE FARLOWE . . .

I was clean, shaved and sober, and I didn't care who knew it. The phone receiver certainly didn't, but that wasn't going to stop me staring at it like it'd committed a Class A misdemeanour. Two days ago, I'd been wondering if I'd have to eat baked-beings for the rest of my life when a call comes through from some patsy goes by the name of Max Bohr. No kidding. A kangalarsen if ever I heard one. He was more worried than a hen at a fox convention.

'Discretion,' he whispers. 'You know all 'bout discretion? Everything you do is confidential, right?'

'If the moolah's right,' I says.

'Oh, of course, I'd pay you handsomely.'

Turned out the quack had lost some planets. And we're not talking one or two moon-sized loo-lahs. We're talking forty thousand *real* planets. All called EARTH and all packed with living creatures . . . *And* he was willing to give twenty per cent of his future pension if I could 'find out where they went'.

'Thirty per cent or I hang up now,' I says.

He rolled like a puppy. 'Er, OK. Deal.'

'Deal,' I says, the devil in my heart crying, why the heck didn't you say *forty*?

'I'd decided I was going to forget about them,' he says. 'The planets, I mean. Say nothing. But then I thought, no, the inspectors – they're not dopes. If they find out, I could lose my pension!'

He gave me a pain in the head, but when a patsy's got moolah and you ain't had a case in six months, you'd listen to him talk about his nail-clipping regimen if you had to.

'About your fee . . . I'll wire you an advance right now,' he said. 'But please promise no one will hear about this assignment. It's top-top secret.'

'That goes without saying,' I said – which made about as much sense as a dame with a monkey wrench since it needed to be said.

So the money comes through and I start to do some digging. A few phone calls, a couple of bent tails later and I learn that EARTH stands for:

1 Earthlings Are Really Thick Humans, or
2 Exist And Ruin The Health (of the planet), or
3 Eccentric Auxiliary Required To Help

'It's the third one,' says Max Bohr when he calls back.

'Well, thanks for telling me *now*,' I say and I wring him like a soggy towel for all the skinny he can spill.

Turns out, a few billion years ago, his 'employer' – a physics facility called El Nerdo – gets a secret commission from some group called *CoW* to produce five million planet EARTHs based on some secret blue-print known only as *Jennysiss*. These EARTHs are to be scattered throughout the universe and given 'ideal conditions' for life to flourish. 'Course, this means El Nerdo also has to make five million suns of just the right temperature and place them just the right distance from the EARTHs. It also means they have to produce another set of planets to surround each EARTH, plus a moon for the planet – to shield it from asteroids and other cosmic splutterings.

Who or what is CoW? The *Council of Wisdom*, apparently, but more than that he won't – or can't – say.

What he will say is that CoW has so much money it's unreal, so El Nerdo keeps doing the job – even when CoW starts banging on about how they should be able to make all five million EARTHs in six days and 'put their feet up' for the seventh. Three months later, all the EARTHs are up and running (six days, my eye!) and CoW sends over six million cans of primordial soup (an extra million to cover spillage).

It's El Nerdo's job to pour a can over every planet. And each one's a different flavour – or scenario – and supposedly you pour it and leave it to simmer for a billion years or so and then – hey presto! – life starts evolving. And before you know it, you got beings walking round the planet who think they know the difference between a good cup of coffee and a mouthful of chicory.

Out of the traps, I decide to focus on two angles – the Jennysiss blueprint and the 'scenarios' of the planets that disappeared.

The Jennysiss blueprint is based on some planet called *Earth* which everyone's lost the co-ordinates for. Why's this planet so special? The answer is, it's not. Everything about this punk planet's average, which is why scientists call it *the Goldilocks planet*. It's not too hot, it's not too cold, it's just right. Meaning it's *just average*. And its 'intelligent' inhabitants – humans – are the averagest of all creatures in the universe.

But why? Why would being average matter and why would some anonymous grifter demand that five million *more* morasses of mediocrity be built?

If I could get the answer to that little conundrum, I could be halfway to solving the mystery of the disappearing planets . . . *And if my uncle were my auntie* . . .

So I pore over the 'scenario' info Max Bohr gave me like an adolescent studying a lingerie catalogue . . . The five million EARTHs and the cans of primordial soup were all made with *exactly* the same ingredients as Earth, except that every one differed from Earth in just one tiny detail.

Here are two sample EARTHs that disappeared.

Scenario (difference from Earth)	Outcome
Humans are complete idiots.	Global warming wipes out all human life by 2183.
Aliens do not visit the planet in 5,012 BC, accidentally leaving a crane behind.	The pyramids are never built and Agatha Christie's *Death on the Nile* is never made into a movie.

And two sample EARTHs that *haven't* disappeared.

Scenario (difference from Earth)	Outcome
Incompetent parents prohibited from having children.	Human race dies out early – indeterminate date.
Women physically stronger than men.	Exactly the same number of wars and incidents of football hooliganism – the perpetrators being mostly female. Main difference is that men don't do a poor job of cleaning the bathroom or the cooker, necessitating a 'redo'.

There are literally millions of these. (See *Extra Bits No. 1* for more EARTH scenarios.) They make about as much sense as a bicycle with no pedals.

So I sit in my swivel chair, catching up on my foot-dangling and stare at the damn phone receiver. I'm stumped. The afternoon passes and all I got to show for it's a face full of shadow and a bellyful of nothing.

At last I admit it. If I'm gonna crack this nut, I'm gonna have to dust down *I-Don't-Believe-Your-Alibi* – the biggest banger of a spacecraft known to dog or beast. Yeah, I'm gonna have to venture back into the big bad universe and bend some tails for real.

23
What's She Done?

After the darkness, the GarbageHold seemed bathed in light.

The python-like creature froze. Tommy could see its face perfectly, spotlighted by his hat-torch. Three finger-length fangs glinted in its open mouth. *It's going to strike!* For a split-second he thought of Bea's Way and his heart sank even further than you'd expect for someone about to die. *This won't even count as dying to save someone else! What a waste!* And then his heart rose a notch . . . *Why is it waiting? Just sitting there.*

The creature had one large owl-like eye and this had a glazed, dazzled look.

'Wwwaaaaaaaaaaaahhhhhhhhh!' cried Tommy.

Almost immediately, the pressure released around his body and the hairy pythony creature whipped away.

Tommy would later find out that the creature was an owlaconda. Such creatures paralyse their prey by biting them. Then they squeeze them to the width of macaroni before munching them. Only thing is, owlacondas (who share 23 per cent of their DNA with oppobats) are scared stiff of two things – orthodontists and brightness.

'Can'cha keep the noise down?' said a voice. It was Woozie.

Tommy heaved an enormous sigh of relief. He'd been so frightened he'd almost done a wee. Which would've been

OK. Wee would've been the cleanest liquid in this gunge. His right arm was still numb, but he decided to keep going downwards.

Half an hour later, his trousers full to the brim with paper, a voice sounded over the headphones.

'Out of the hold please get, Tommy, Woozie.'

'Smartest thing you said all day,' said Woozie.

'But there's more p-p-paper down here!' exclaimed Tommy.

'Just cos you've grown to like the smell, doesn't mean you can stay down here f'rever,' said Woozie.

'Ha-ha.'

Tommy relented when Summy explained that they wouldn't have to climb and swim all the way back to the top of the hold. The resourceful dinosaurus had found a monitor that pinpointed Tommy and Woozie (via their nose-pegs) and she directed each of them to airlock exits on the side of the hold. Once Tommy swam through his, the port-hole sealed, the rubbish was sucked out and the chamber started whisking upwards.

Tommy landed in the Utility Room just after Woozie.

'Here both you are,' said Summy. 'Excellent.'

'Wh-why are you c-closing the hatches?' asked Tommy. 'We'll n-need to go back d-down.'

'From Marielle, orders.'

'Since when is she the b-b-boss?'

Summy pressed a button on an intercom by the wall. 'Out of the hold are Tommy and Woozie. Sealed are the hatches.'

'Great. Thank you,' replied Marielle's voice.

'Hey!' exclaimed Tommy. 'We can't afford this kind of m-messing. We've g-got to g-get our hands on the Deadly S-Scroll.'

And he emptied all the paper he'd collected on top of the heap that Woozie had deposited.

'Uuuuggghhhh! Stink do the pair of you,' exclaimed Summy.

'They look like showers,' said Woozie, noticing some nozzles as he fought to get the last sheaves of paper out of his pance pockets.

Tommy considered buzzing Marielle on the intercom, but thought better of it. Best to shower first and confront her in person. Particularly as his arm was still numb. Maybe the shower would revive it.

He and Woozie had just pulled across a set of suede curtains and started their showers when they started floating into the air. 'Gravity off someone has turned,' cried Summy, her wings bristling against the ceiling.

'You don't say!' said Woozie.

'How're w-we supposed to w-w-wash like this?' asked Tommy. (Showering in zero-gravity conditions is a nightmare because the water doesn't fall downwards – it can go anywhere, depending on the intricacies of the nozzle.)

The floor began to shudder and a gathering, creaking roar meant they could no longer hear each other speak. Just as the roar reached a crescendo, it stopped. Replaced by a deathly silence. Then the heavy echo of a half-moon clanking shut. At the same moment, gravity returned and three IGGY Knights went *splat!* on the metal floor.

Marielle's voice sounded through the intercom. 'OK, done.'

'She could've w-warned us about the g-g-gravity,' said Tommy, rubbing his knee.

Summy opened the hatches. 'Heavens2murgatroyd!'

Tommy and Woozie hurried over, careful not to drop their

towels. When Woozie leaned over to get a better look, his nose-peg fell off. The three friends watched as it fell down, down, through a vast and empty hold, until it was so tiny it disappeared from sight.

'Wh-what has she d-done!?' cried Tommy, white-faced, charging towards the porthole that led into the cockpit. He heaved and heaved, but it wouldn't budge.

24
A Trick Question

'Hey! Are you two OK?'

Marielle had to shout a few times before Rumbles and Harriet came out of the trance that had them staring at each other.

'Oh, my!' exclaimed Harriett, hearing Marielle and realizing where she was.

'You OK?' asked Marielle more gently.

'Why yes, thank you kindly. I'm just fine 'n' dandy . . . What happened?'

Once they'd described all the events of the previous few hours and Harriett had explained what *dandy* meant, Rumbles went to get Harriett some food from Swiggy. He wouldn't hear of her fetching anything herself from the dumptrux larder.

Harriett was most alarmed to hear that two of Marielle's friends were wading about in the dumptrux hold. 'Mighty dangerous down there. I presume they're wearing nose-pegs?'

Marielle thought it best to come clean and tell Harriett they were looking for a single sheet of paper.

'But, my! You should be using the Dumptrux Search Sieve.'

Harriett took Marielle to a monitor and they started entering the Search Criteria.

Q. What kind of substance are you looking for?
A. Paper

Q. How many sheets or sheaves?
A. One sheet
Q. Can you stipulate how smelly this sheet of paper is?
A. No
Q. Are there any particular words printed on this sheet of paper?
A. Yes. 'Triumph' or 'triumph' or 'TRIUMPH'
Q. Would you like to start the search?

'No-can-do,' said Harriett just as Marielle was about to type *Yes*. 'We can't start the search till you get your buddies out of that there hold.'

Marielle buzzed Summy and asked her to tell Tommy and Woozie to exit the hold. Then, ensuring the *JustBeSure* lever was set to 'closed', she contacted Rumbles and asked her to circle Swiggy round the dumptrux, removing the sellotape that prevented the doors from opening.

'Doneskeys.'

'Out of the hold are Tommy and Woozie. Sealed are the hatches.'

When these confirmations were buzzed through, Marielle typed *Yes* into the monitor. A giant sieve levered into position beneath the dumptrux's underbelly and then a flashing sign changed from 'Gravity On' to 'Gravity Off'.

'That's so the hold's doors can open plumb into zero-gravity space,' explained Harriett as she and Marielle started floating.

Moments later, they were back on the floor, the GarbageHold was empty and garbage was spewing through the giant sieve towards the black holes of LitterLout*Wot!*. (You need to be very careful that you've got the Search Criteria correct before you put the search into operation because you can only do *one* search per load.) Marielle watched the monitors with curious fascination.

'My, how I love this sight,' said Harriett. 'The search will take time a-fixin'. An' then, whatever's found will be plumb cleaned an' disinfected 'fore it comes to us.'

A buzzer sounded minutes later. Marielle thought it was the search item arriving, but it was Tommy in the Utility Room.

'Hey! The p-porthole's locked. L-l-let us in!'

'No-can-do,' replied Harriett.

'Stop m-messing about! L-let us in!'

'When the garbage hatch opened, it triggered a health-n-safety time-lock on the porthole. Ain't a doggarn thang we can do for five hours. At least.'

'Wh-what!?' Tommy shouted. 'No way! Marielle! P-put Marielle on! Marielle, you m-may have thrown away our only chance to f-f-find—'

Marielle turned off the intercom and asked Harriett to disconnect the buzzer.

'A feisty critter,' said Harriett.

'He thinks he's right all the time,' said Marielle. 'Drives me crazy.'

Just then, Rumbles arrived in the cockpit with a tray of steaming-hot food, six plates and some cutlery (his three arms enabled him to act as a marvellous waiter).

'My, you're strong,' said Harriett.

'Oh, this is nothingskeys. I could carry twenty times this amount.'

As Harriett turned the cockpit dashboard into a dining counter-top, a cardboard box slid down a chute, landing on the floor. 'That there's the search item,' she explained. 'It always gets boxed oh-so neatly.'

Marielle set about opening the box while Rumbles tied a giant napkin round Harriett's neck and dished her out some

Lyra linguini with Pegasus porcini.

The cardboard ripped easily in Marielle's hands. Then she spied it. Half concealed by ripped cardboard, the only word she could make out was *Disaster*.

'She cut m-me off!' Tommy was so furious he ripped the suede shower curtain off the rails.

'I'm hungry,' said Woozie stripping open the Velcro-like seal on his dorsal pocket and taking out his dog tags (he hadn't wanted them to get dirty in the hold).

'Some biscuits I have in my pouch.'

Woozie pulled the dog tags on over his head and devoured six of Summy's biscuits. 'Mmmm! Will you have one, Tommy?'

'Our w-one chance to f-find the D-Deadly Scroll!' Tommy was having difficulty replacing the shower curtain – his arm was still numb, which didn't help.

Summy kicked at the heap of paper deposited on the floor. 'Perhaps in this smelly pile is the Scroll.'

'Yeah, r-right!' exclaimed Tommy. And yet he ended up sitting on the floor, in nothing but a towel, going through the papers with his two friends.

Three hours later, the pile was scattered round the Utility Room and three showers were going full blast (Summy'd repaired the curtain).

'N-nothing!' said Tommy. 'That's t-twice we've gone through the entire l-lot.'

'Not *nothing*,' exclaimed Woozie. 'We found a *105 per cent OFF Voucher* for all pizzas in the CasinoCasino Constellation . . . And what about that sheet you found with the torn corner? The page we can't read cos it's too dirty.'

'N-no,' said Tommy. 'I can make out the w-word *P-Prize*

in the headline. It's n-not the Deadly Scroll.'

'For sure you do not know that,' interjected Summy. 'To do with a prize might the challenge be something.'

'Your arm OK, Tommy? You're still holding it funny.'

'It's f-fine.'

Summy was first out of the showers and she lifted up the page with the torn corner. 'Soak this I will in informaldehyde.[22] A bottle of it I saw on the shelf by a basin.'

Tommy was still muttering about Marielle and holding his arm two hours later when Summy announced a breakthrough. 'Read it now we can!'

All the brown gunge had dissolved, leaving a visible page with a box in its middle . . .

The ChAOS Challenge: Lorry 22

WANT TO WIN THE ULTIMATE CHAOS PRIZE?

ANSWER THIS PUZZLE AND YOU COULD BE THE ONE TO TRIUMPH!

THE SCENARIO: A LORRY IS 5CM TALLER THAN THE UNDERSIDE OF A CERTAIN BRIDGE.

THE QUESTION: HOW CAN THE DRIVER PASS THE LORRY UNDER THE BRIDGE AND BE ON HER WAY IN REASONABLE TIME.

NOTE: THERE IS NO ALTERNATIVE ROUTE FOR THE DRIVER. SHE MUST PASS UNDER THE BRIDGE IF SHE IS TO MAKE HER DESTINATION ON TIME. SHE CANNOT TRY TO RAM THE LORRY THROUGH, BECAUSE HER CARGO IS FRAGILE AND SHE'D BE FINED A FORTUNE FOR DAMAGING THE BRIDGE.

– PLEASE CALL TO CLAIM YOUR PRIZE –

$\oint\{\Sigma(\pi \times e^3 \times \Delta(A + B) - \sqrt{63})\}$ = 'The number to call'.

22 A very strong cleaning agent, described by chemists as a 'casual cousin' of formaldehyde.

What's a l-l-lorry?' asked Tommy. (They no longer had lorries on Earth when Tommy was a boy.)

Summy explained what a lorry was (they're common in the Milky Way) and then Woozie had a few suggestions for the puzzle.

'What if you get a crane to lift the bridge?'

'That's not al-l-lowed.'

'Or blow up the bridge.'

'Definitely allowed that is not.'

'Or grease the lorry with butter so it can slide through.'

'It's still five centim-m-metres too tall.'

'Impossible to pass the lorry,' said Summy eventually. 'A trick question, you see.'

'Do you think this is the Deadly Scroll?' asked Woozie.

Tommy shook his head. 'N-not a chance.'

Woozie stared down at the page. He wasn't so sure. 'Whadya think ChAOS stands for?'

But the porthole to the dumptrux cockpit was swinging open and Tommy jumped up. Why were they wasting time on silly puzzles when the Deadly Scroll had been lost forever? At last he could give Marielle a taste of his mind.

25

CHAOS

'Yes, you're tuned to *ChAOS* – the most popular TV show in the universe! My name is FionaDeFridge and I'm here to welcome contestants as they arrive from all over the cosmos.'

FionaDeFridge was a robot, fashioned from a variety of household appliances. Her torso was a fridge (of course), her head an array of nuts and bolts and coloured mini-tiles. Her nose was made from a tap, a blue shag-pile rug formed her hair and her two eyes were fridge lights (they flared brighter when she spoke). One of her hands looked like a salad tongs, the other like a nutcracker. She had a vacuum cleaner for a tail and her legs were hidden beneath a long gold dress – though she seemed to float a centimetre above the ground and move around like a hovercraft.

As the TV cameras panned back, viewers saw that FionaDeFridge was hovering on an open platform, clinging to a can of hairspray, seemingly in the middle of space. (In much of the universe, cans of hairspray or deodorant are also fully functioning microphones.) Behind her, on all sides, a wild crowd cheered noisily.

'Yes,' she cried, eyes flaring. 'This is a one-off kids' edition of *ChAOS* – with thanks to our sponsor, *Wuhoo! Wormholes*™.' (A jingle of music blared.) '*Because the universe need not be big*.'

A procession of spaceships and bubbles zoomed into view, docked by the Arrivals Platform and disgorged themselves of kids. (*I say 'kids', but all the contestants looked about fourteen years of age.)* One group after another introduced themselves and revealed which puzzle they'd answered correctly 'to be here'.

Finally, DeFridge announced: 'OK, just *five minutes* to go till the cut-off time for entries to the show. So please check the labels on all your cans of tinned spam – and ring in with your answers . . . We'll be back after this commercial break with any final contestants who make the deadline . . . Don't go 'way!'

I should point out that time moves at different speeds in different galaxies (due to the Time Continuum Literary Convenience Torque), so when DeFridge said, 'just five minutes to go', this was true where she was. But in some parts of the universe, viewers would only have ten seconds till the deadline, while in others they'd have almost two months.

26

Ain't No Time

'Y-you opened the GarbageHold d-doors!'

'Would you like some linguine?' replied the elquinine. 'It's absolutely delicious. Well done, Rumbles!'

'Yes, Rumbleys, it's mighty tasty. Even second time round.'

Rumbles blushed to hear such praise from Harriett. 'Oh, it's nothing. Just something I rustled together.'

'I'd love to try it,' said Woozie.

'Also me,' said Summy.

'Hey!' cried Tommy. 'Am I t-talking to myself? The Deadly S-Scroll was the most important l-lead we've ever ha-had!'

'The *Deathly Scowl*?' intoned Marielle.

'The Deadly S-Scroll!' Tommy smacked his hand on the dashboard. 'The p-page with Elza's ch-challenge!'

Oh! You mean one of these?' asked Marielle, taking out three sheets of paper and putting her finger under the word *triumph*.

'Y-yes, that's exactly wh-what I—' Tommy stopped mid-sentence. 'Is th-th-that . . ?'

Marielle gave a victorious smile. 'One of these three pages should be it . . . I happen to think it's the third one.'

'And how d-did you . . ?'

Marielle grinned. 'If you must know, we used the Dumptrux Search Sieve. It took about two minutes.'

There was a stunned silence before Tommy realized the implications. 'You m-mean we crawled round that st-stinking GarbageHold for n-nothing!?'

'It wasn't too bad down there, was it?'

Tommy was too infuriated to speak. That cheeky elquinine smile didn't help. Plus his arm was feeling worse. He snatched the three sheets from Marielle and marched to the other side of the dumptrux cockpit.

'It's OK,' said Marielle. 'You don't need to ask politely . . . This is Harriett, by the way.'

Despite his fury, Tommy gave Harriett a fleeting smile and slumped to the floor, his back to everyone, the bits of paper clutched in his hand. Summy and Woozie thought they'd better leave him to it for a while and tucked into the linguine. They were most appreciative and introduced themselves to Harriett between mouthfuls. They didn't hear Tommy whisper, 'This is it' – a single sheaf clasped in his left hand.

It was Harriett who brought Tommy to the attention of everyone after they'd finished eating. 'My, for such a loud, fast-talkin' whirlwind of a guy, he sure reads slow.'

Tommy hadn't moved an inch from his position on the floor. Summy, who was nearest, hurried over to the crumpled Earthling. 'To nearly nothing his pulse has dropped,' said the kangasaurus, holding the dark boy's wrist and pushing open one of his eyelids.

CRASSSSHHHHH!!

Marielle, who was clearing the plates, had somehow let two of them fall to the floor.

'Sorry,' she said, looking ashen. 'That cardboard box. I nearly tripped over it.'

Rumbles also looked pale. 'It wasn't the linguine, was it? You feel OK, Harriett, don't you?'

'Tommy didn't have any,' said Woozie. 'Maybe it was something he read.'

Harriett, it turned out, had done a First Aid course and she pinpointed the problem to Tommy's arm.

'Them there puncture marks. Looks like he's been a-bitten by an owlaconda.'

'An owl-a-what?' asked Rumbles.

'They're hairy and hang out in garbage holds . . . By the looks of him, I'd wager he's got about half an hour to live. Maybe less. Unless we can find somethin' to suck the venom outta that there arm.'

Twenty minutes later and they'd tried Harriett's vacuum-cleaner and the one from Swiggy to no avail.

'He's getting weaker!' exclaimed Woozie.

'You just might be able to remove that there venom by suckin' on the arm,' said Harriett. 'But it'd be mighty dangerous. You'd have to be sure not to swallow none. A drop of venom in your belly is a heap more dangerous than having a cupful under your skin. You'd die in half the time.'

Summy and Woozie discussed ways of placing a balloon or a plastic bag in their mouth to stop the venom sliding down.

'Getting paler he is,' said Summy.

'There's a balloon under Swiggy's kitchen sink.'

'There ain't no time to get it!'

The desperation in Harriett's tone caused everyone to freeze. Everyone, that is, except for a certain someone who'd been standing silently away from the fray. A certain someone who pushed past her paralysed friends, knelt by Tommy's side, pressed her lips to his arm and sucked with all of her might.

Although she spat through the smashed cockpit window and rinsed her mouth with informaldehyde, Marielle ended up with a mild fever for the next two days.

And yet, the elquinine swore everyone to secrecy. Tommy was not to be told what she'd done.

27

Hairy Backs

'Two moored craft – side by side, sir.' This announcement was made into a microphone by the captain of *I-Headbutted-Your-Gran* (a spacecraft that looked vaguely like a shark-finned syringe and was registered to one Nack Jickilson). 'Should we approach?'

'No!' cried a voice, followed by the sound of a forehead whacking against a radio receiver. 'Stay well-hidden! Till I come down to the bridge.'

'Yes, sir.'

'If they see us, I'll have your arms chopped off and served to the crew for dinner!'

'Er, yes, sir.'

'And have some *good* music playing when I get there . . . I want to *savour* their *demise*.'

Even though the captain had no arms (instead he had a hand protruding from each of three tails), he made sure to keep *I-Headbutted-Your-Gran* well hidden from Swiggy and *There's-A-Funny-Smell*. For the moment, he was just feeling relieved that the tracer they'd planted on Swiggy when she was on Planet Skanger (as 'an unnecessary precaution') was still sending out a strong signal.

A hand reached out and pressed a button on the wall. 'Bring me my sherbet!'

The hand's hairy-backed owner frowned. *Tying me to a chair! Itching powder!? Aaiigghhh!! They think they can make a fool out of me – Nack Jickilson!*

Knock-knock! The door opened. Nack Jickilson snatched up a crossbow.

'Don't shoot!' exclaimed the entrant – a centaur, bearing a silver tray. 'Please sir. Your sherbet.' And he lowered the tray to reveal a small bag in its centre.

Nack snatched the bag, snorted half its contents up his nose and whumped his forehead full-force on to the centaur's back. *How stupid those kids were not to kill me. Because now, soon enough, I'll be killing them* . . . When he raised his head, he looked as though a pair of electrodes had been attached to his eyebrows. *And there'll be no elaborate ploy, offering the possibility of escape. Oh, no . . . Just a simple smack! – into a black hole for eternity.* His face stayed frozen like this for a time, only his eyebrows moving – wriggling and vibrating like a pair of demented caterpillars.

'Cos the sherbet powder don't work, it just makes things worse'
(famous lyric from a song by Le Vurve)

'Mind I don't toss sour-sherbet-powder at you and change your expression forever.' This is a favourite quote from fathers across the galaxies when kids pull silly or ugly faces. It's really just an old-husbands'-tale (quite like an old-wives'-tale), but it does give you some idea of how potent high-grade sour-sherbet-powder is. People have been known to eat too much in one go and to explode from what coroners term 'an overdose of fizzy sourness'.

28

Nooooooooo!!!

Marielle dipped her most treasured possession in cold water. It irked her that the object held such a special position in her heart – sometimes it enraged her! – but it just did. Three times she'd been on the verge of throwing it down Swiggy's garbage chute. On the last occasion she'd even let go of the object and then had a change of heart before pulling the flush lever. She'd ended up having to crawl down the chute to rescue it. After that, she resigned herself to keeping the object and always carrying it on her person. *To remind me of the past. Not to cling to it, but to face up to it and move on.* The object, a white silk hanky with red polka-dots, had *TLM* stitched into one corner in tiny letters. The previous year she'd thought this could – at a stretch – mean 'Tommy Likes Marielle', but in recent times she'd come to know that it meant 'Tommy Laments Marielle'.

She didn't blame Tommy's stutter or his poor co-ordination for the distance that'd wedged between them. No, she put it down to Tommy being 'over' her. For in truth, she always sensed the stutter and bad co-ordination were temporary aberrations. And she hadn't loved him in the first place for being the best scimmy fighter or the best jegg flyer, so when these skills fell away, she loved him no less. If anything they made her love him even more.

She looked down at the young human lying in the bunk. His complexion was paler than usual – light cappuccino, she'd call it. With a slight darkening under his closed eyes. She noted his long black lashes. 'Like a girl's,' she used to tease in those first laughter-filled months of the mission.

His hair was still spiky, even after hours lying in bed. A lock hung outwards, obscuring the scar on his right cheek-bone. She brushed it back so she could see the imperfection – a short, purpley-brown curving line. Touching it softly, it felt slightly raised, making her think of a solitary mountain range on a land of flatness. *What a silly thought.* Half embarrassed, half afraid he'd wake and catch her, she withdrew her finger and eased the damp handkerchief across his brow.

'Marielle, you should be in bed,' said Woozie. 'You've been sitting there since we got back.'

The young elquinine shook her head.

His nose – she'd never really noticed its exact slope from the side. Almost perfectly straight, then curving deeply into his nostrils. The very nostrils that'd flare whenever he became angry with her.

And the bow lips – a shade paler than their usual rich plum colour.

'How many more hours can you sit there?' asked the furry wibblewallian. 'I can do that. Look, you got a fever. You go rest.'

'Huhhhhhhhhhhhhhh.' It was the first sound to come from those lips.

'He's rousing.'

'OK, I'll go – on one condition.'

'Anything.'

'Don't tell him I sat here and looked after him.'

'Mum's the word.'

Marielle stood and exited. Twenty seconds later she returned, removed the handkerchief from Tommy's forehead, replacing it with a damp facecloth. Then she left the room. With the object that had that hateful hold over her.

Harriett was on the outside of *There's-A-Funny-Smell*, just inside the bubbles, checking the sealant on the new pane of glass in the cockpit window.

'Looks mighty fine,' she said.

Rumbles was floating nearby, holding a toolbox. 'You sure I can't make you anything else to eatskeys?'

'You're oh-so kind. But no, thank you, Rumbleys.' Harriett opened out one of the two doors on the dumptrux's bonnet, just below the cockpit window, revealing a large oily engine. 'This darn thang's liable to blow a gasket.' Marielle's ripping of the wires and the surge of voltage through Harriett's body necessitated a few repairs.

Rumbles watched admiringly as Harriett leaned over, elbow deep into the engine. 'My, oh-my, this StickyFingers™ massage oil's runnin' low.' (Many spacecraft run on massage oil as it's environmentally friendly.)

'You got any brothers or sisters?' asked Rumbles.

'Yeah, four sisters. All way more purdy than me.'

'I doubt that.'

'What? You think I'm a-lyin'?' Harriett looked up, angry. 'You think I got *five* sisters and ain't tellin' you 'bout one of them!'

'I just meant they couldn't be any prettier than you.'

But Harriett was face down in the engine again and hadn't heard. By now, her arms were covered in oil. Rumbles raised his voice.

'What's your favourite colour?'

'Oh, I don't rightly know. Amber, maybe. You?'

'Amber. Yeah, definitely my favourite, too.'

'Hmmm, my Lordus, most interesting, yes?'

Summy was sitting in Swiggy's Lounge with the three sheets of paper Marielle and Harriett had retrieved from the dumptrux. The young dinosaurus had just opened a silver case containing an interactive lesson from Crabble on the subject of *Interpreting Parchments*.

The monocled tutor had an enormous pipe in his mouth and was blowing a soapy bubble out its bowl end while examining the sheet of paper below.

save the girl & triumph

'A deceptively difficult yet obscure task, yes?' he exclaimed. 'Hmmm, yes, Madam Sum-Wun-Saurus, I predict this is indeedy the Deadly Scroll, hey ho!'

Earlier, Summy had opened two other *Interpreting Parchment* lessons – one from Wisebeardyface, one from Lady Muckbeff.

When he saw the first sheet, Wisebeardyface noted that the handwriting clearly belonged to a dreamer who'd never saved a girl themself. 'It is not the Deadly Scroll,' he declared.

Lady M thought it unlikely to be the Deadly Scroll and went off on a tangent about the merits of saving girls, since it was really boys who required saving.

When he picked up the second page, Crabble grew very excited. The page looked like this . . .

IF

If you can keep your mind when all about you
Are losing theirs and blaming it on you,
If you can trust yourself when all men doubt you,
But make allowance for their doubting too;
If you can wait and not be tired by waiting,
Or being lied about, don't deal in lies,
Or being hated, don't give way to hating,
And yet don't look too good, nor talk too wise:

If you can dream – and not make dreams your master;
If you can think – and not make thoughts your aim;
If you can meet with Triumph and Disaster
And treat those two impostors just the same;
If you can bear to hear the truth you've spoken
Twisted by knaves to make a trap for fools,
Or watch the things you gave your life to, broken,
And stoop and build 'em up with worn-out tools:

If you can make one heap of all your winnings
And risk it on one turn of pitch-and-toss,
And lose, and start again at your beginnings
And never breathe a word about your loss;
If you can force your heart and nerve and sinew
To serve your turn long after they are gone,
And so hold on when there is nothing in you
Except the Will which says to them: 'Hold on!'

If you can talk with crowds and keep your virtue,
Or walk with Kings – nor lose the common touch,
If neither foes nor loving friends can hurt you,
If all men count with you, but none too much;
~~If you can fill the unforgiving minute~~
~~With sixty seconds' worth of distance run,~~
Yours is this Earth and everything that's in it,
And - which is more – you'll be a Man, my son!

'Cripes! Double-cripes!' he cried when he put the page down. 'I've never seen the like, yes? Undoubtedly, hmm, *this* is the Deadly Scroll.'

Wisebeardyface's main comment had been to explain that knave meant a creature who isn't very honest, while Lady M had noted: 'I sayest that an eraser hast been used on the final line. Fie! Originally it didst read: " . . . you'll be a Woman, my daughter!" And, a few lines up, it didst surely read "walk with *Queens*".'

Perhaps, Lady M speculated, the crossed-out lines were due to be erased also, before the author threw it in the garbage and started again.

I should say that across the universe, 'man' was the word used to denote an intelligent adult male of any species (not just human); 'woman' denoting any intelligent, adult female. Incidentally, the word used to denote an unintelligent adult male was hornbeeper. The corresponding word for a female was PR-Executive.

Crabble picked up the third page and put it down glumly. 'Lordy-lord. This is definitely not it.'

The Triumph of Hope Over Reason

4 Tasks . . .

A. Climb Mount Neverrest Quomolanga in the HerAlayan Range
B. Sing '*The Hillocks are Alive with the Sound of Music*' in the Mos Eisely Cantina – without getting beaten up
C. Clean out all the dung from the Ageing-UnStables
D. Enter the Atole Maize and find the Holey Gruel

Could you perform ALL these feats in <u>less than 3 months</u>? If the answer is NO, then you should forget

Wisebeardyface and Lady M both concluded that this was certainly the first of two or more pages, but since it was only printed on one side, they had no idea what the next page might say. In any case, the next page was irrelevant in their opinion, since this was 'certainly not' the Deadly Scroll.

In this, all three masters were in disagreement with Tommy. For this page had been the one clasped in his hand when he whispered, 'Th-this is it,' before collapsing.

Because she could think of nothing else to do, Summy took the lorry puzzle out of her pouch and gave it to Crabble.

'Hmmm . . . No way to do it, hey-ho!' said the wild-blue-haired tutor after a few puffs on his guitar-sized pipe. 'A trick question, yes?'

'What I said exactly.'

Having made Crabble disappear, Summy wandered into the Boys' Dorm, the lorry puzzle in her hand, the other three pages in her pouch. She saw that much of the colour was back in Tommy's cheeks. It looked like he was asleep, having a bad dream.

'Better is he?'

Woozie nodded. 'Been mumbling these last minutes.'

'Hear can you what he's saying?'

'Rambling – 'bout his parents and the TFC. And he keeps saying *Marielle*. Must still be angry with her . . . That the lorry puzzle? Lemme see.'

Just then, Harriett arrived into the room carrying Rumbles.

'My, he's groggy. Hit his head, poor soul.' (Rumbles had leant into the dumptrux's engine to give Harriett a kiss and she'd lifted the 'second' bonnet door at that very moment.)

'Kissy-wissy,' said Rumbles, looking like he was half drunk.

Woozie came to give a hand and somehow the lorry puzzle got pushed against Rumbles's nose.

'12024561111,' said Rumbles.

'Huh?'

Rumbles repeated the number several times till Woozie realized the thunderbumble was staring at the numbers and symbols at the bottom of the lorry puzzle page . . .

$$\oint\{\Sigma(\pi \times e^3 \times \Delta(A + B) - \sqrt{63})\} = \text{'The number to call'.}$$

'Quick! Write down that number.'

'The phone number that is.' Summy grinned, removing a pencil from behind her ear. 'The prize to collect.'

Woozie explained to a confused-looking Harriett. 'Rumbles is brilliant at maths whenever she receives a bump on the head. But it only lasts a short time. Soon after, she has trouble with her six timestable.'

'Now need we the lorry problem itself just to solve.'

'What for?' asked Woozie. 'We gotta concentrate on the Deadly Scroll. That's far more important than a stupid lorry question.'

'Ayowatywus.' It was Tommy mumbling again.

'Where am I?' muttered Rumbles, coming to.

'What's nine times six?' asked Woozie.

'Hmm . . . forty-fourskeys?'

'OK, Rumbles is better,' laughed Woozie.

'Ay owa t-tyres.'

'He say something 'bout *tyres*?' asked Harriett, looking at the human in the bed. Woozie and Summy shrugged. 'All-righty, I'm gonna go take the dumptrux for a spin – make sure it's OK . . . You fine 'n' dandy, Rumbleys?'

'Oh, yes. I'll come with you!'

'Nah, you should stay and clear your head. I'll be back soon.'

Harriett gave Rumbles's third hand an extra squeeze, then left. Woozie and Summy craned closer to the sleeping Earthling who mumbled: 'Air outta t-tyres.'

'*It* that is! By Jupiter!!' Summy cried so loudly that Tommy opened his eyes with a start.

'Can you k-keep the noise d-down? I'm trying to s-s-sleep.'

'Hear hear!' exclaimed Marielle, who'd hurried in from the Girls' Dorm.

'To the puzzle the answer that is,' said Summy. 'With the answer Tommy came up.'

'Yeah!' exclaimed Woozie, realizing. 'If you let the air outta the tyres, the lorry'll fit under the bridge. Then you pump the tyres back up on the other side.'

Tommy realized where he was. 'Wh-what happened?'

'Bitten on your arm you were. Nearly killed you did the venom.'

'Till Marielle sucked the—' Woozie saw Marielle's glare. 'Er . . . Till Marielle sucked up all the linguini and then we brought you here for a rest.'

'The lorry problem we have solved.'

But Tommy didn't want to hear about the lorry puzzle. He wanted to read – again – the three pages in Summy's pouch.

'You feel OK now, Tommy?' asked Marielle.

Tommy nodded and, despite all that'd happened in the dumptrux, he gave the fevered elquinine a weak smile.

Summy left the Boys' Dorm where Tommy, Woozie and Rumbles were discussing the Deadly Scroll and made her way through the Lounge towards the Lobby.

She heard Tommy say: '*Enter the Atole Maize* . . . Hmmm

. . . And what on Earth's the *Holey Gruel*?'

'No idea – not a sausageskeys.'

'And all the tasks must be completed in three months, start to finish!'

The voices faded to nothing as the dragon girl reached Swiggy's liftwell, stepped into the diagonal lift and descended . . .

The SwotStudy's most striking feature was not Swiggapedia, but a beautiful set of French windows which took up an entire wall, providing a clear view out to space. Summy completely ignored this view as she shuffled in behind the cluttered wooden desk and pulled herself up on to the swing that hung from the ceiling. She reached through the papers and lumps of moon rock covering the desk, till she found a heavy, old telephone that had no buttons, just a circular dial with eleven numbers: 0–9 and ∞, the symbol for infinity. (Across most of the universe you call the emergency services by dialling 1-∞-1.)

Dipping into her pouch, she removed a few biscuit crumbs and the lorry puzzle – with the number Rumbles had calculated scrawled across it – and picked up the receiver. She dialled the number. After six rings, a voice answered.

'Hello, you have reached *ChAOS*™. If you are on a touch-tone phone, press *hash*. Otherwise please say the first word that occurs to you.'

'Antidisestablishmentarianism.' (Summy was always looking for any excuse to use this word – even though she had no clue what it meant.)

'Thank you . . . If you are an adult, please say *CrushedDreamsMortalityLooms*. If you are not yet an adult, please blow a raspberry.'

Summy blew a loud raspberry.

'Excellent. Now, please tell me the name and number of the challenge-puzzle you are calling in with.'

'Lorry 22.'

'Thank you. What is your answer to the puzzle?'

Summy paused and glanced out the French windows. A spacecraft glinted in the distance. Her mind was so focused, she wrongly assumed it must be Harriett, testing the dumptrux.

'I must hurry you if you want the chance of winning a super-duper prize. The deadline for this show ends in forty-six seconds. What is your answer?'

Summy was so excited that the only words she heard were *hurry* and *super-duper prize*. 'Oh, em . . . Let out from the tyres air,' she said, her voiced pitched higher than usual (she loved winning prizes).

The phone went silent and then, quite suddenly it made a noise like a slot-machine hitting the jackpot.

Harriett pulled back the throttle on the dumptrux. It was purring perfectly and that new window pane made everything so clear. She'd just shifted into third gear when she noticed something hurtling towards Swiggy. Despite its steel-hook tail and serrated-edge fin, it somehow resembled a syringe. She radioed Swiggy's cockpit but no one was there. (Tommy, Woozie and Rumbles were discussing the Deadly Scroll, Marielle had returned to bed and Summy was making a phone call from Swiggy's study.)

Too far away to intervene, Harriett watched in horror as the syringey craft accelerated. She saw its front 'needle' widen and spit out a floppy, studded, leather glove. Saw the back of the craft compress and the glove inflate to a giant, steel-studded fist. And knew its sole intention.

To wham Swiggy into the inescapable vortex of LitterLout*Wot!*.

Nack Jickilson stood on the bridge of *I-Headbutted-Your-Gran* and rubbed his nose. That sour-sherbet-powder had left a tingly residue.

'Nineteen seconds to impact,' said the armless captain.

Behind him, a stereo was playing 'Don't Halt Me Now' by QuEENie.

Tonight I'm gonna have myself a real good time . . .
And the world, I'll turn it inside out – yeah.

Through the large windscreen, Nack could see a silver Lancaster-like craft in the distance. There was no sign of the dumptrux, but no matter. This was his prey.

All the robberies he'd organized, all the counterfeit sherbet he'd smuggled, all the enemies he'd put in headlocks. At moments like this, all those pleasures flashed through his mind. Here he was – Nack Jickilson – rich beyond his dreams, with an army of willing henchmen and with the power to get the best seats for any circus performance across 600 galaxies. But none of that compared to the thrill of the chase. To those last seconds before an enemy disappeared forever. Especially one that'd eluded him twice before. *Revenge*, he thought. Revenge is a dish best served with a side order of sour-sherbet.

The captain had explained how they could ram Swiggy without any danger to themselves. 'If anything, we'll bounce backwards – away from the black holes.'

Nack thought momentarily of the centaur he'd just killed. How he loved the taste of centaur, seasoned with garlic and ground pepper. It was the combination of man and horse that gave it such a wonderful taste.

'Nine seconds to impact.'

Someone turned up the music.

I'm a shooting star leaping through the sky,
Like a tiger defying the laws of gra-vi-ty . . .

'Five seconds . . . four . . . three . . .' Swiggy loomed large.

Nack felt the rush. Couldn't resist emptying half a bag of sour-sherbet-powder down his nostrils. And slamming his head off the dashboard. *Agghhh!* Exquisite. Pain. How he loved it. A heady cocktail when mixed with the pending death of others.

Harriett shielded her eyes, expecting to hear an enormous bang. At the last moment, through her fingers, she saw Swiggy lurch backwards and *I-Headbutted-Your-Gran* flash by, missing the silver craft by inches, and ploughing on towards LitterLout*Wot!*.

Maybe I should open a chain of restaurants called 'Little Centaurs'.

This was the last thought that went through Nack Jickilson's mind before he realized that *I-Head-butted-Your-Gran* was heading straight for the black holes, the stereo bellowing:

Yeah, I'm a rocket ship on my way to Warz,[23]
On a collision course . . . I'm out of control.

23 Warz is a planet close to MercuryFredrick, a planet named after the person who wrote 'Don't Halt Me Now'.

A moment later, *I-Headbutted-Your-Gran* disappeared (weirdly vanishing long before it reached the black holes).

Harriett flicked her eyes towards Swiggy. Although the craft had avoided the attack, she started moving towards the black holes. *Why is it doing that?* It was still outside the vortex. It could easily escape the black holes' pull. Yet, if anything, Swiggy was accelerating towards them. The blur of silver shot towards LitterLout*Wot!*. And then, just before Harriett expected it to break into a thousand pieces, it too disappeared with a VVVRRRHHOOSSSSSSSSSSHHHHHHHHH!!

Harriett looked again. All she could see in the distant blackness was a faint trail of fire and smoke, the ghostly remnants of Swiggy. Wishful thinking, she told herself. That's all I'm a-doing. Surely I blinked at the wrong moment and missed it.

For Harriett had seen a billion, billion items fall into a black hole and none had ever returned. Yes, they're gone for all eternity, she finally told herself. Her grief came upon her so suddenly, she vomited all over the dashboard. Betelgeux burgers, cooked by that wonderful bear-like creature. Her eyes filled with tears. They seemed like nice people. And that Rumbles. Warm, smiley, furry, kind, a good cook and a great mathematician (when bumped on the head). Exactly the kind of fellow she'd always wished for.

'Nooooooooooooooooo!!!'

And if a cry could pierce the blackness of space, if a cry could fill its vast emptiness, then this was it.

29

Bad-Hair Day

The phone in her hand was making a sound like a slot-machine hitting the jackpot. 'Won have I!' cried Summy. 'Won have I!'

In her excitement, she dropped the receiver and failed to notice the syringe-like spacecraft speeding closer. Nor did she hear a new voice on the phone say: 'Please do not hang up. Your call is being traced. You will receive your *initial* prize shortly. If you are in a spacecraft, please buckle up.'

When Summy picked up the phone, all she could hear was cheesy music.

'Put me on hold they did.'

As soon as the music stopped and the voice returned, Swiggy began to shake.

'We have traced your spacecraft. Prepare to receive your prize.'

'A crossed line I think we have,' said Summy. 'Our spacecraft something is shaking.'

But the line had gone dead, Swiggy was shaking harder than ever and, behind Summy, a syringe-shaped craft was almost upon them.

Quite suddenly, pulled by an inescapable force, Swiggy zipped backwards, halted, then whooshed forwards, towards the black holes (in the direction the syringe-like craft had just taken). Two seconds before Swiggy should've disintegrated, the silver craft disappeared.

Officially, you see, the 'initial' prize for answering *Lorry 22* was to have a temporary wormhole constructed in your honour and its entrance placed directly in your path. (After it tried to ram Swiggy, Nack Jickilson's spacecraft flew into the edge of this *partially constructed* wormhole – extremely hazardous since it could 'materialize' *anywhere* between the wormhole entrance and its intended final destination.)

Why isn't *Worm* spelt *Wurm*?

Wormholes are the long-distance cousins of wigholes,[24] allowing people and objects to take 'shortcuts' when travelling around space. Wormholes have two mouths – you enter through one and exit through the other – and these mouths can be as wide as a football pitch or as narrow as the tip of your little finger. Whatever their size, wormholes are always one-way – you need to find another one to send you in the opposite direction.

In the twelve seconds it took Swiggy to make its way through the *Lorry 22 Temporary Wormhole*, it travelled almost 17,000 times the distance it'd covered in the previous three years, moving from the outer edge of the universe, to somewhere a good way closer to its core.

During the journey, the forces were so great that the IGGY Knights experienced a phenomenon known as *wormhole gurning* – their faces making a series of grotesque and improbable expressions. If you looked closely at Tommy, you'd swear that between impersonations of an agonized

24 Wigholes are pizza-sized holes allowing you to travel short distances. See *TS1* for more.

goat, Winston Churchill and a half-eaten gerbil, his face regressed to that of a baby, then accelerated through the years till he was an old man.

When Swiggy finally slowed, the FiiVe all sported paranoid expressions and for some reason, their hair and nails had grown to an extraordinary degree. Tommy's hair would've reached down to his bum, except that it spiked out in all directions.

Analogies Are Like Toilets Without Locks – Only Desperate People Use Them

If our universe were a hollow globe the size of Earth, then our galaxy (the Milky Way) would be a speck of dust about three metres down from the surface. When *Swiggy* entered the wormhole, it would've been the equivalent of 320m from this speck of dust. And when it exited the wormhole, it would've emerged deep inside the globe – about halfway to its very core.

Incidentally, wormhole-gurning-and-hair-and-nail-growth is easily preventable and only happens to unseasoned travellers. All you have to do is attach a tiny rubber tail to the back of your spacecraft (similar to cars on Earth with a little lead at the back, touching the road surface).

'What the squel happened?' cried Woozie, whose fur was so long he looked like a reddy-brown blur of candy floss. 'You look ridiculous, Tommy. Your nails are six inches long.'

'So are yours.'

Rumbles's fur always stays the same length from the waist up, but there are no such restrictions beneath her 'equator', so she looked as though she was wearing a dark grass skirt. She, Tommy and Woozie hurried up to Swiggy's cockpit to see where they were. Everything was black, except, in the distance, they could make out a set of bright lights floating in the middle of space.

'What's *that*?'

'I don't n-know. It's not a p-planet.'

'It looks unnaturalskeys.'

'I c-can't . . .' Tommy was trying to move the steering wheel and push the throttle (not easy with six-inch nails). 'It w-won't respond. We're being s-sucked towards that th-thing, whatever it is.'

Marielle arrived at that moment, almost tripping on her long ponytail.

'What happened?'

'Silly hair. That's what happened.'

Swiggy approached a platform crowded with seemingly 'mental' creatures. As it did so everyone took a turn at pushing Swiggy's controls to see if they could escape the vortex of this strange place – but only succeeded in breaking three nails between them; the FiiVe agreed that they'd 'more than likely travelled through one of those wormholes Lady Muckbeff told us about'; Rumbles was half-persuaded that Harriett was fine ('Her dumptrux is in good working order and has a full tank of massage oil'); Summy explained about calling to claim the lorry prize (although she couldn't hear what anyone said in reply because of the hair in her ears); and Tommy admitted to Woozie that he'd prefer to go ten weeks without showering than ten days without eating.

A voice boomed over Swiggy's internal intercom. 'Welcome to *ChAOS*™. You have one minute to prepare yourself and exit on to the Arrivals Platform.'

Thinking quickly, Marielle flicked Swiggy's segnitia

switch, slowing time within Swiggy – making one minute feel like fifteen.[25] As everything outside appeared to go into slow-motion, the FiiVe hid their most valued possessions and 'fixed' their hair and nails. By the time Tommy was finished, he no longer had mad, spiky hair.

'You skinned yourself!' laughed Woozie.

Tommy'd shrugged. 'I used a t-two-blade. F-felt like a n-new look. Wh-what did *you* do to your-s-self?'

'Rushing too much.'

The wibblewallian's fur was much shorter on one side than the other.

'We b-better go.'

Gathering by Swiggy's main exit doors, the FiiVe agreed on a course of action. 'No mention of the TFC. Not a word. We don't know who these people are . . . Let's just collect our prize and leave.'

25 Segnitia switches are fuel-hungry so the Knights used theirs sparingly. Segnitia switches appear frequently in *TS1*.

30

Failure is the Only Option

'Here they come!' announced FionaDeFridge as a door opened above the red letters spelling out *Swiggy* on the side of the silver craft. The crowd whooped, an inflatable slide unravelled and, one after another, five creatures slid head-first on to the Arrivals Platform. The small, furry creature who slid last got the biggest cheer, which may have been the reason he did a cartwheel as soon as he hit the platform and then skidded on his knees ahead of the others, towards FionaDeFridge.

'Welcome!' cried DeFridge. 'Can you tell viewers what question you answered correctly to get here?' And she thrust the can of hairspray into the furry creature's face.

Woozie was so excited and nervous, his mind went completely blank. 'Er, the TFC,' he said, fiddling with his dog tags and giving voice to any thought that entered his mind. 'Meaning the end of the universe.'

The crowd laughed as though Woozie had told the funniest joke they'd ever heard.

'Really?' said DeFridge, most amused.

'Yeah, we're the IGGY Knights and we're on a mission to save the universe from the TFC.'

‘Sorry,’ said Woozie. ‘I had a blank – didn’t realize what I was saying.’

The FiiVe were travelling in a hovercart towards a flat, white disk floating in the middle of space – DeFridge had called it the Selection Section.

‘You said exactly what we agreed we *wouldn’t* say.’

‘On *live* TV!’

‘Maybe no one noticed.’

‘Maybe no one *n-noticed*?’ cried Tommy. ‘D-did you hear what the c-crowd were chanting during the r-r-rest of the interview . . ? *The TF-suh-C! Please s-save me f-from the TFC! Whoa! Whoa!*’

‘They were laughing, at least,’ said Marielle. ‘They didn’t think he was serious.’

‘No, they thought he was n-n-nuts.’

‘OK! I said *I’m sorry*.’

Before jumping into the hovercart, they’d all introduced themselves to FionaDeFridge. She hurried them off because an unexpected ‘final-final contestant’ was arriving and then they got embroiled with two ‘technicians’ tasked with moving Swiggy to a ‘special parking place’. Tommy and Marielle were nervous about letting someone else fly Swiggy, but were assured that the technicians were ‘expert pilots’ and that Swiggy’d be returned as soon as they were ‘off’ the show.

The Selection Section had over twenty circles painted on its floor – most encompassing about four kids, though some held just a solitary kid and one looked to be holding no less than thirty.

Standing within their designated circle, the FiiVe watched

FionaDeFridge descend on a platform from the overhead rigging. 'Silence!' she cried into her hairspray (mainly directed at the raucous group of thirty kids). 'Or you'll forfeit any prize coming to you.'

This prompted a barrage of questions about the nature of the prizes on offer.

'We will give you two quick tests,' declared FionaDeFridge, giving everyone a silencing glare. 'If you fail the first test, you will be out of here in five minutes with a flask-vat of jelly and ice-cream as a prize. If you pass the first test and fail the second, you will be out of here in ten minutes with *two* flask-vats of jelly and ice-cream. And if you pass *both* tests, then you will stay on ChAOS as our guests for the next three weeks.'

The FiiVe exchanged glances. No way were they staying here three weeks.

DeFridge continued: 'And whoever gets the most votes from viewers during their stay on ChAOS gets the super-duper fame-and-fortune jackpot prize . . . Clear?'

No one had a chance to answer, for a blare of music sounded and DeFridge looked towards a camera. 'Viewers, welcome back from the ad break. And welcome also to ChAOS's most intelligent and loyal fans.'

A loud cheer erupted and Tommy saw that two tilted platforms, full of demented fans, had swooped in on either side of the Selection Section. Then caravan-sized helmets lowered from the rigging. Like all the other 'groups', the IGGY Knights ended up completely covered by one of the helmets. The cheering of the fans became muffled and the FiiVe's only view was straight ahead, through the visor, towards a huge orange screen that'd appeared at the far end of the Selection Section.

'The first test starts immediately,' announced FionaDeFridge, her voice piped clearly into the helmet. 'To avoid cheating, we have ensured that you can neither see nor hear the other participants.'

And with that, all the lights died, and the far orange screen turned white with a thick hair-flecked grey line cutting across it, bulging pointedly in the middle.

'This is a close-up, silhouetted picture. *But of what . . ?* You must nominate one person to step forward and give your answer within the next three minutes.'

Now they could talk in private, the IGGY Knights formed a loose huddle within their dark helmet. Once they'd voiced their bewilderment at the turn of events, Tommy piped up: 'So, wh-what you say . . ? We f-fail these tests on p-purpose and be on our w-way?'

'Sounds good,' said Woozie. 'We get to leave with a flask-vat of jelly and ice-cream.' (A flask-vat is a car-sized tub that keeps things hot or cold.)

'It'll fit in Swiggy's JeggHold,' said Rumbles.

'That's a dumb idea,' said Marielle.

'D-dumb?' said Tommy, hackles rising.

'Yes,' said Marielle. 'Much better to pass the *first* test and fail the second one on purpose. Then we can get cracking on Elza's challenge, with *two* vats of jelly and ice-cream in Swiggy's Hold.'

'Most brilliant!' exclaimed Summy.

And Tommy, like all the others, had to concede that she was right. Then all five stared at the image on the far wall.

'Hmmm, possibly a volcano with ears it is.'

'No, I think it's a very knobbly knee.'

'A knee like that when have you ever seen??'

'I dunno. It was just a guess!'

‘Maybe it’s someone in a party hat, hiding under a rug,’ offered Marielle.

‘Duh! That’s dumber than my suggestion.’

‘W-wait, no!’ exclaimed Tommy. ‘Marielle’s r-right . . . Couldn’t it b-be a creature inside s-s-something else?’

‘Inside what? A whalepython?

Tommy shook his head. ‘There’s s-something familiar . . . Those h-hairs . . . An owla-c-conda! Y-yes, it’s a c-close-up of an owlaconda’s b-body.’ He never thought he’d consider being squeezed by an owlaconda as a piece of good fortune, but momentarily that’s how he felt.

‘Don’t be silly. Owlacondas are flat. Not all lumpy like that.’

‘But it’s s-swallowed something f-funny.’

‘Maybe somebody wearing a party hat it swallowed.’

‘No, a p-party hat would s-squish. A c-c-crown, I’d say.’

‘Which means they’re a king or a prince.’

‘Or a queen or a p-princess.’

‘Or some nutter wearing a crown!’

‘Point very good.’

‘Whoever they are, they’d have to be pretty small to fit like that in an owlaconda.’

FionaDeFridge’s voice was heard inside all the helmets: ‘OK, contestants, we need your answer in the next twenty seconds.’

‘Go on, Tommy, you give the answer,’ said Woozie. The others murmured their assent.

Tommy stepped forward and a spotlight pierced through the visor, illuminating him. The black-clad Earthling tried to sound confident.

'Eh, we th-think it's an owlaconda that's s-swallowed a little p-p-princess.'

Nothing happened for a few seconds and then everything went pitch black.

'Who turned the lights out?'

'In the wormhole again we better not be.'

'Ow! Who's standing on my foot?'

The FiiVe could hear muffled announcements through the helmet and saw eight distant spotlights click on and off. Then the muffled cheering switched to a clear roar and the lights returned, accompanied by a burst of music. The helmets had disappeared. As had eight 'groups' – just thirteen remained.

'Those who got the question wrong have already left us,' declared FionaDeFridge. 'All together . . . Aaaahhh.' The crowd went *Aaaahhh*. 'The image you saw was a picture of an *owlaconda* that had swallowed a *little prince*. Although we accepted *little princess* as an alternative answer.' And behind the refrigerator robot, the far wall lit up with an image showing a cross-section of the owlaconda – and the little prince was clearly visible, standing inside.

The image vanished and thirteen garden-shed-sized boulders lowered from the rigging, settling in front of the remaining groups. Each had a sword handle protruding from its top.

'Behold the Arthurian Stones!' cried DeFridge above the din of the whooping fans. 'You have three minutes to perform this trial. Climb up on the rock and try to pull the sword free.' The set went dark before thirteen spotlights flashed down from the high rigging – one picking out Tommy. DeFridge's microphoned voice came from the darkness, cutting through the fans' maniacal screams. 'Whoever answered the last question for your group must perform this trial[26] . . . Your time starts *now*!'

Like the twelve other spotlighted individuals, Tommy began climbing on to the white boulder before him. Enjoying the feeling of full co-ordination, he considered how he should approach this test . . . *Pretend you can't pull the sword from the rock, but don't make it too obvious. Look like you're trying.*

Within sixty seconds, thirteen spotlighted creatures were crouching atop thirteen boulders, each pulling on a sword handle.

Pretending to pull, Tommy peered under his arm, at the creatures to his right. One, covered in suction pods, was holding its sword aloft already. Another was pulling at the sword handle with its teeth. And then there was a guy with rabbit-like ears, a waggly tail and a cast on his arm. All his veins straining, but the sword wasn't budging.

Out of curiosity (or pride), Tommy pulled a little on the sword. *I presume I could pull it out if I wanted? Just a little way – that'd tell me.*

He gave a few gently tugs. No movement. Glancing up, he saw two more creatures holding swords aloft. He turned to get a better stance and peered to his left. Pulling a little harder, he saw three creatures on this side were holding swords aloft. And still he hadn't got his sword to tweak an inch. All that training on Swiggy, all the martial arts, plus his returned co-ordination – and yet not the faintest movement. *This is ridiculous!* The sight of yet another sword being freed – this one by a delicate, bird-like creature – raised his frustration.

26 This was because the beer-belize union had stipulated that each of their spotlight operators would 'only illuminate one creature from each group for the two trials – in the absence of a 50 per cent salary rise'.

'Twenty seconds to go,' announced DeFridge from the darkness.

From that same blackness, deep in the heart of the universe, Marielle saw Tommy grip the sword handle with both hands and lean backwards. Nothing budged.

'Ten seconds to go.'

The human, dressed all in black, sporting his new sheared haircut, shifted his feet and heaved, veins standing out on his forehead. If nothing else, thought Marielle, he's a good actor.

'Aaaagghhhh!' cried Tommy, wrenching with all of his might. Every sinew screaming to the task. *Why won't it move!? Why can't I get it to move?*

As DeFridge and the crowd counted, 'Three . . . two . . . one,' Tommy gave the handle one last jerk – throwing everything into it. Next thing he knew, he was on his back on the floor. The sword still firmly wedged in the boulder.

Marielle surveyed left and right. Eight creatures had freed their sword. And before she could register their features, all thirteen spotlights switched off. The set was dark and silent, except for the panting of five creatures who'd failed to free the sword and a low whisper from Woozie: 'Fantastic acting, Tommy. Wow! Really looked like you were trying. Specially that dramatic fall at the end.'

Marielle wondered if two flask-vats of jelly and ice-cream would fit in the JeggHold. Fleetingly, she thought about the eight creatures with the freed swords. Where were their groups being taken to? What obstacles would face them as they lived out the next three weeks in the glare of TV cameras? And what was the super-duper prize . . ?

Then she thought of Elza's challenge and the need to stop the TFC. *Who cares what the jackpot is! If we don't stop the TFC, the universe and everybody in it will be no more!* And the blonde elquinine had a sudden realization of the vastness of their task – the very thought of it making her feel weak and exhausted all at once.

When the lights returned, the sword-freeing creatures and their groups had gone. And the cheering fans had been transported back in front of the glass structure near the Arrivals Platform. Tommy picked himself off the floor and was met by FionaDeFridge who asked him to repeat his name and those of his four friends for all the viewers. Then the vacuum-cleaner-tailed presenter intercepted the other four participants as they climbed down off their boulders, asking them the same question.

'Zestrella,' said a tall, beautiful, brown-haired girl in a yellow dress. She had a tentacle under both arms and two wiry antennae sticking up from her head with bobbly fluff on the end. The other member of her 'group', a guy wearing a maroon bandanna and sunglasses, was called Jay-T. A cross between a meerkat and a human, he was folding the edges of a ball of paper, looking as if he found the whole spectacle to be spectacularly boring.

'Yagoyurway AisleGomine CartonSydney,' replied the waggly-tailed guy with the cast on his arm. 'Most people call me Yago.' He was the only person in his group.

A girl with blue-black hair, glasses and a grey cape mumbled, 'Uladrack.' It was hard to tell because she was biting on her nails (with funny-looking teeth) and her hair hung down before her pale face. There were two others in her group, but before Uladrack could introduce them, the first – a many-armed, snow-haired girl – stepped forward and offered a hand to FionaDeFridge. The glamorous robot shook it with her salad-tongs hand and got such a shock that she dropped the hairspray microphone and her vacuum-cleaner tail leapt into action, sucking at her dress. 'Oldest one in tha book – ach aye!' laughed the snow-haired girl, displaying an electric buzzer couched in her palm. 'The name's Beryl . . . Beryl MacPairyl.'

'And this little fellow is Lillroysen,' said the other member of the group, referring to himself (yes, to himself!) as he picked up the hairspray. Sporting a short-trousered school uniform, he looked almost human, except that he had a pair of translucent wings folded under his arms and a wasp-like tail. 'Lillroysen prays you accept his apologies for Beryl's behaviour.'

Once DeFridge had recovered, the next person she approached looked like a girl except that 'she' had a very odd moustache. 'Bernard, yeah, Bernard's the name.' She sported a backwards baseball cap and was standing on a skateboard. Amazingly, she'd also been on the skateboard while up on the rock. The other member of this group looked like a pinkish polar bear and he had his head in his hands. 'Disaster,' he wailed. 'I knew we'd fail. I just knew it.' Maybe if Bernard had lost the skateboard she might've accomplished the task, thought Tommy.

The last 'participant' FionaDeFridge came to was a group of thirty people who took longer than everyone else to descend from the boulder. Tommy frowned. *I thought only one person from each group was allowed to perform the task.* It turned out the thirty people were actually *one person* called Charles Lemass – they all intoned the name together. (The LaTin term for such a creature is *Crowdidia Followus*.[27] The

27 The official names of all creatures in the universe are kept in a secure tin (known as LaTin) in the Biologique Galaxy where they can be accessed by botanists and the makers of a 'hair-raising' board game called Trivial Hirsute™.

tails of all the human-like people in the 'group' come together in a central 'knot' and everyone is attached to two others in the group, sharing an arm or a leg or maybe a bum. The entire creature, therefore, rarely takes up more room than a large elevator space.)

When she'd finished speaking to Charles, DeFridge turned to all the remaining contestants and spoke with a glum voice. 'I'm very sorry to say . . . that 99.99 per cent of people in the universe can free a sword from an Arthurian Stone. Only those who are gifted or special or covered in baby oil are unable to do so.' She paused, her sad expression matched by ones of bafflement on the faces of the contestants. 'So all I have to say to you now is . . . *Congratulations!*' This last word she cried out with all the excitement of a billionaire freeing himself from the eye of a needle. 'All of you present,' she continued, 'have therefore *passed* the second trial and will be staying here for the next three weeks as our guests with the chance of winning the super-duper fame-and-fortune jackpot prize!'

Apart from the IGGY Knights (who looked desolated), Uladrack (whose hair masked her face), the pink polar bear (whose head was still in his hands), Zestrella and her 'cool' friend (neither of whom showed any emotion), all the other contestants broke into whoops of joy.

31
Killing Me

DICTATED BY PI BARLOWE FARLOWE . . .

'I heard *something*.'

I'm sitting in the darkest corner of the seediest bar in the skankiest galaxy known to dog or beast. Opposite a snitch who goes by the name of UglyBear. A low-life who lives up to *half* of his name – he doesn't look much like a bear. More like a three-armed anteater with his sorry face shadowed under an oversized cap.

'Something?' I repeat above the din.

He shrugs. 'But I can't remember what it was.'

I take a slug of ZackSpaniels[28] and reach for my pocket. It's the same drill wherever. Only one cure for amnesia . . . I slide three Squalor bills[29] across the table.

'It's coming back to me, Farlowe,' he says. Surprise, surprise. Three more Squalors slide his way.

He cracks a smile. 'OK, I got it now.' No kidding.

Turns out he knows a bootlegger with a stash of videos showing the final moments of two dozen EARTHs. 'The first video's called TSC1, the next is TSC2, the next is—'

'I get it,' I says. 'TSC 1 – 24: the collection.'

28 A whiskey-like drink.

29 This is the common currency across a host of galaxies.

'Each shows a similar story,' he says. 'EARTH comes up with a piece of wisdom . . . Then it gets destroyed.'

'And could you get your mitts on a set of videos?' I ask. 'For little ole' me?'

He shakes his head. 'Not a chance.'

Ten more squalors into his grubby hand.

'Maybe,' he says. Ten more squalors. 'I'll see what I can do.' A fifty-squalor note leaves my paw. This is killing me. 'I'll get 'em for you,' he smiles and I see the greed fill his double-crossing eyes. 'But it's gonna take a few weeks . . . Maybe longer.'

That's when I lost my manners.

Seconds later and he's squealing, 'OK, OK,' his ant-eaty snout pressed into the table by an angry paw. 'I can get 'em to you *in a week*.' My grip tightens. 'Three days,' he squeaks. 'Two days tops.' I make like I'm gonna squeeze harder. 'OK, OK – take 'em now! No extra charge.'

I let him go and he gives me a case he's been hiding by his feet. 'They're all there,' he snivels.

I give him a hanky for his snout and feed him a fib. 'Pleasure doing business with you.'

I-Don't-Believe-Your-Alibi is one hell of a rustbucketty spacecraft, but it's *my* rustbucket and it can still make the jump to multiple-light-speed if you can get the spark-line to stay stuck to the hyper-line.

I wind a length of duct tape round the two wires and skedaddle the hell out of the galaxy I call Skank.

After a feed of sub-prime beef, I flick the jalopy to 'cruise control' and slide down the pole from cockpit to TV room. The remote control's busted, but – lucky me – the room's so poky, you can reach the TV from the couch. I insert the first video, turn on the TV and, hey presto, the picture comes on, but it's some dumb-ass show called *The Duckling* – where they take pretty females and turn them into super-ugly divas within three-months. I curse the heavens till I realize it's not the video. The damn thing's not playing cos it's not rewound. I hate that. You can always tell a low-life by the way they don't rewind videos when they've finished with them.

So the video's rewinding – meaning *The Duckling*'s still on – but I can't stand watching an 'expert' pump a lady's lips full of fishjuice. That's when I switch channels and see the craziest thing. A small, furry creature surrounded by four other creatures. I'm pretty sure one of them's a human. Seriously – *human*. And he looks genuine. The thing is, you only find humans on planet EARTHs. But that's not the craziest thing. The craziest thing is the furry, reddy-brown creature blabbing into the camera.

'Yeah, we're the IGGY Knights and we're on a mission to save the universe. We'll save you all from the TSC.'

Or maybe it was T-*F*-C. Whatever. Sounds too close to be a coincidence.

32

Mr Fourth-Last-Place

Floating in the middle of space, a short walk from the Arrivals Platform, the focal point of the ChAOS set was made almost entirely of glass and everyone in the know called it the Bowl. A curvy, irregular-shaped structure (looking nothing like a bowl) it had a high glass roof and was filled with couches, cushions, games and a swimming pool (with various diving boards).

Tommy sat on the highest diving board, some thirty metres up, hugging his knees and feeling peeved. Below, he could see the other IGGY Knights sitting on high stools, sipping tall glasses of some multi-coloured drink. They were eyeing all the other contestants, pausing to make a remark now and again. What irked him most was how relaxed they looked. Particularly Summy and Marielle. *Aaaaaggghhhh!* Didn't they realize the seriousness of the situation?

Most of the other contestants were lounging around, drinking or snacking, generally sticking to their groups. That pretty girl in the yellow dress with the silly name – Zisteria or Destrella or whatever – she was sitting on a huge cushion, staring calmly out the window at a bunch of pesterazzi ('photographers') flashing by in bubbles outside.

Some of the other kids were playing No-Gravity-Snooker, clambering round a heavy-duty bubble (twice the size of your average wardrobe), taking it in turns to prod long cues through its transparent wall and hit snooker balls floating about inside.

Tommy churned over the events of the last half-hour in his mind . . . Soon after they arrived into the Bowl, Swiggy'd been backed into the Basement below the Bowl so the FiiVe could pack some essentials (like everyone else before them). Marielle and Woozie tried to get Swiggy moving, but the technician who'd parked her had taken the one and only ignition key. (As Wisebeardyface had often reminded them: 'Make sure you don't lose it!') So while Tommy made sure the Vault containing all the lessons from the Masters of the Way was double-locked and well-hidden, Rumbles dashed down to the Kennellstables (leaving three weeks' worth of food for the nawhitmobs) and Summy made photocopies of the three pages they'd recovered from the dumptrux 'for each IGGY Knight, so Elza's challenge during our stay work individually on we can'.

Before disembarking, Marielle beckoned everyone into a huddle around their bags. She had a suggestion.

'We've been charging about the universe achieving very little for the last three years and all getting on each other's nerves . . . If – *if* – it turns out we're stuck here, three weeks isn't really that long . . . Why don't we just relax and enjoy a well-deserved rest? Use the time to consider the Deadly Scroll and how we can complete its challenges.'

Summy agreed. Woozie was unsure. Rumbles missed Harriet too much to have an opinion. But Tommy was resolute.

'W-we can't just t-take a holiday for three w-weeks! We've g-got to complete Elza's challenge and g-get back to Hells-b-b-bells.'

'But you think the Deadly Scroll is the third page and I happen to agree with you,' argued Marielle. 'The page says the challenge is to complete its tasks within *three months*, start to finish. So if we get going as soon as the show is complete, we could be back in Hellsbells with the challenge completed four months from now.'

'Hardly l-l-likely!' retorted Tommy, trying to keep his voice down. '*B-before* we even s-start, we've g-got to find out where Mount N-Neverrest is and wh-where–'

'I've done all that. Well, *nearly* all.'

'Wh-what?'

'On Swiggapedia . . . Three of the four locations were listed. With wormhole co-ordinates to each one.'

'Swiggy must've picked up all the info when she was parked outside Hellsbells,' suggested Woozie.

'The only one I couldn't find was Ageing-UnStables – the dung-cleaning task,' added Marielle.

Somehow this seemed to exasperate the young Earthling even more. 'This p-proves my p-point.'

'How so?'

Tommy shook his head. 'If we only complete three of the f-four tasks then we've f-failed and Elza w-won't help us.' His voice turned sarcastic. 'B-brilliant – the universe ends c-cos we took a three w-week holiday and failed to c-clean up some d-dung!'

Once they made it up to the Bowl with their bags, Summy proposed a drink and Marielle suggested playing No-Gravity-Snooker together to allow everyone to relax and 'cool off'. Having no wish to partake in either of these activities, Tommy headed for the diving-board ladder.

'OK, people. You have two minutes left to vote.' FionaDeFridge was talking to camera. 'You hardly know them, they've just arrived in the Bowl, but this first vote so often sets the trend for the rest of the competition. So get on the phones and vote for your favourite contestant! . . . If you want to vote for Bernard, dial 18005698214789563214580001. If you want to vote for Beryl . . .'

As she spoke, viewers' TVs showed fourteen headshots down the left of the screen and fourteen telephone numbers to the right.

Tommy looked out through the glass, towards the stage by the Arrivals Platform. FionaDeFridge was talking into a can of hairspray and hundreds of demented fans remained camped out there, most jumping up and down and screaming whenever they thought a camera was pointing their way – some had a banner declaring: '*Mob rules. Go, CharlesLeMass, go!*' The maniacal screams were dulled through the reinforced glass – much to Tommy's relief.

A voice cut through his thoughts. 'How ya doin'?'

Tommy looked round. The guy with the cast on his arm and rabbity ears was lowering his legs over the other side of the diving board, moving his waggly tail so he could sit down. 'All r-r-right,' Tommy mumbled.

'Want some?' The guy held out a packet of chewing gum. Tommy shook his head. The guy shrugged and stuck a piece in his mouth, looking down at the kids below.

'They all seem to be having fun.'

Tommy grunted. They sat, back-to-back, in silence till the guy said: 'I don't wanna be here.' Tommy made no response and the boy continued: 'My parents locked me in my room with a dumb puzzle. Said I couldn't leave till I'd done it . . . So I worked it out and here I am.'

'Huh.'

'My dad's crazy smart. Gets real angry if I don't measure up.'

'Oh, r-right.'

Tommy saw the other IGGY Knights pick up a set of cues and begin a game of No-Gravity-Snooker. Despite himself, he felt a wave of warmth and kinship towards his fellow Knights. Strange how difficult he found it to convey these feelings when he was actually up close and with them. How so often he ended up saying the wrong thing.

'I skipped school last month,' murmured a voice. Tommy'd forgotten about the guy behind him. 'Went fishing every day instead,' he continued. 'My dad found out and . . .' Looking round, Tommy thought the guy glanced at the cast on his arm, his face hardening to defiance. 'If I was home now, I'd go off fishing *again*!'

The guy had foppish sandy hair and a darkish face – in fact, he looked quite like Tommy apart from his hair and his rabbit-like ears and his ever-wagging tail (even when defiant).

He wasn't sure why – he didn't particularly like gum – but Tommy said: 'That g-gum s-still on offer?'

'Oh, eh, sure.' The guy produced a packet from a patchwork of (twitching) pockets within his coat and Tommy took a stick.

They sat there, just chewing. Until a voice came over the internal sound system. 'The first day's votes are in. Over twelve trillion viewers from all over the universe participated.'

A giant scoreboard appeared beyond the crowd of fans.

CHAOS LEADERBOARD: RUNNING TOTAL OF VOTES

RANK	CONTESTANT	SELECTED VOTER COMMENT
1	BERYL MACPAIRYL	LOVED DA HAND-BUZZ GAG!
2	CHARLES LEMASS	2'S COMPANY. . .
3	WOOZIE	GO SAVE DA UNIVERSE! HURRAH!
4	ZESTRELLA	FOXY LADY!
5	J/S YUSS	CAN'T B ALL DAT BAD, JOE!
6	LILLROYSEN	LITTLE LORD FAUNTLEROYSEN, MORE LIKE!
7	BERNARD BURNSIDE	IT'S SO OBVIOUSLY FAKE!
8	JAY-T	CAN I B AS COOL AS U?
9	MARIELLE	FEISTY!
10	RUMBLES	IF U WEREN'T SUCH A FATSO I'D CUDDL U
11	YAGO	GET SUM FRENDS!
12	TOMMY STORM	HEY, M-MISTER S-S-SERIUS!
13	SUMMY	BORING! XCEPT 4 DA TAIL PIERCING.
14	VLADRACK	SAY *SUMTHING*!

'Dumb voters,' said the rabbit-eared boy, looking out through the glass wall.

Tommy nodded, stung by the comment across from his name. 'You'd have to b-be pretty s-sad to care 'bout your p-position on that dumb score-b-b-board.'

'I'm Yago – otherwise known as Mister Fourth-Last-Place.'

'W-well, I'm M-Mister Third-Last.'

Yago looked at the scoreboard. 'I once had a tortoise called Tommie.' They both laughed a laugh that left mild embarrassment in its wake – a feeling that stayed till Yago said: 'You don't wanna be here either, huh?'

Tommy shook his head, then laughed. 'W-we're a miserable p-pair, eh?'

'Sad.'

'P-pathetic.'

'Losers.'

'OK, I w-wouldn't go quite *that* f-far,' said Tommy with a smile.

'Yeah, you're right. Let's stick with *pathetic*.'

Yago pulled a hamster-like creature from a pocket (a hamstar) and fed it a tiny lump of something before replacing it. Then he took a second lump and fed it into another twitching pocket. All the time, his own tail was wagging, wagging and making a whistling, swishing sound. Almost absent-mindedly Tommy scanned around for microphones – they appeared to be focused at ground level.

It was Yago who broke the verbal silence. 'So where you from?'

They chatted for a bit, Tommy explaining about Earth and the Milky Way, while Yago (who, it turned out, had been in the bubble that arrived after the IGGY Knights) described his planet, Casiothello. It sounded like Earth in the centuries before Tommy was born, except that its 'beautiful scenery' could easily be moved around (so everyone could live by the sea or by a mountain). And on Casiothello you weren't considered mad if you spoke to yourself. Some people spent more time talking to themselves in long-winded soliloquies than they did chattering with others. That's why Yago had found it so hard to make many real friends – unless you count little animals as real friends (which Yago did).

One thing they realized they had in common was sword (or scimmy) fighting. 'I'm not much of a brawler,' explained Yago. 'But on Casiothello everyone has a sword. I started sword fighting when I was three. And I've never lost a duel. I even beat Tybaltromeo in the Under12s final.' He cast his eyes down. 'Made me very unpopular . . . Everyone loved Tybaltromeo.'

The topic moved on to Tommy's four friends and, in his frustration, the young Earthling spent most of the time talking about Marielle. 'It's her f-fault, we're here. If we'd f-failed the f-first test like I s-said, we wouldn't be here now.'

'Sounds as if you like her,' said Yago, a gleam in his eye.

'N-no, I don't.'

'The way you been talking 'bout her—'

'*Complaining* 'b-bout her!'

'The way you been "complaining" makes me think you're crazy 'bout her.'

'I'm n-not crazy 'bout her. I hate –!' Tommy grabbed Yago by the lapels. 'And if y-you say d-different, I'll p-push you off this diving b-board!'

'OK, OK, only teasing.'

The Earthling released Yago's lapels. His fury spent. Embarrassment, shame, left in its place. 'S-sorry. I don't know wh-what . . .'

'Forget about it. I've forgotten already.'

Tommy sat back down on the diving board, searching for a change of subject. 'So y-you n-know anything about ChAOS – this sh-show we're on?'

Yago nodded. 'A new producer's taken over. Says he's prepared to do *anything* to improve ratings. He came up with the idea for *this* – a one-off *kids* edition of the show.'

'Yeah, but d-do you know what *h-happens* on the show?'

Yago shrugged. 'Saw it a few times. Contestants have to solve dumb challenges all over the universe.'

'Ch-challenges?'

Yago nodded. 'They take ideas from viewers and sponsors and whoever.'

Tommy digested this and, before he knew what he was saying, an idea fired from his mouth. 'D-do they ever let the c-c-competitors come up with the ch-challenges?'

Yago shook his head. 'Very rarely.'

'How c-come?'

'The show's organizers are looking for mad, difficult challenges.'

'So?'

'So, think about it . . . Contestants don't want to do anything tiring or dangerous. Most of their suggestions are like: *challenge us to eat a roomful of chocolate,* or; *challenge us to lie on a beach and do nothing for ten hours.*'

Tommy tried not to look excited – but inside his heart was thumping.

Once Yago explained how he could submit a 'challenge', Tommy crafted a set of words on to a slip of paper and the waggly-tailed boy disappeared with it, reappearing half an hour later. 'Done!' he grinned. 'We'll see if they go for it.'

They chatted on amicably and, when they came to the subject of parents, Tommy felt comfortable enough to tell his story. Then Yago explained how his parents had also died when he was a little boy. Tommy was surprised. 'But . . . I thought you said your f-father stopped you f-fishing?'

Yago stared at him. '. . . What?'

'D-didn't you say your d-dad found out about you skipping school last m-month and . . ?' Tommy glanced at Yago's cast.

'Oh, er, yes, I meant my stepdad. My guardian, I mean. Er, I call him *dad* out of habit.' Yago glanced down at the ground. 'Hey, looks like food's on the way. Come on, let's dive-bomb!'

Tommy grinned. 'It'd be rude not to.'

The two new-found friends leapt off the diving board, splashing into the pool, soaking half the contestants. The fans outside cheered wildly – some striking up a chant of: 'Tommy! Tommy!' ('R-r-ridiculous!' exclaimed Tommy when he heard them.)

After trays of vacuum-packed food were distributed and consumed, gravity was turned off in the Bowl and all the contestants began floating above the ground. Spotlights picked out fourteen wardrobes and fourteen giant sleeping bags affixed high up on the Bowl's circular wall. Everyone claimed a wardrobe, tried to unpack their things (difficult in zero gravity) and took it in turns to wash in one of the two bathrooms (even more difficult in zero gravity).

As the lights dimmed, Tommy lay back in his sleeping bag, wondering why he'd never tried to sleep like this before. Glancing down at the crowd outside, he saw a few Tommy banners now dotted among the throng. *('You made a splash in my heart, Tommy.')*

'Hey!' Marielle's voice cut through his thoughts. She'd floated over, composure returned after the pool-splashing incident. 'We had a chat,' she whispered. 'While you were up on the diving board. And agreed we should try to escape from here first chance we get.'

Tommy was surprised. 'I thought you wanted to s-stay and r-relax?'

'I've changed my mind – a girl's prerogative. You were right. We should do everything we can to leave asap.'

'Well, I m-might've changed my m-mind too.'

'What!? How can you—?'

A voice resounded through the Bowl, drowning Marielle's words.

'Contestants . . . As you should know, ChAOS stands for Challenges All Over Space. Except, for this edition of the show, it *also* means *Children* All Over Space . . . Now, you will be pleased to hear that the Schedule has been finalized. Please review it at your leisure . . . Then we'd advise you to get some rest before tomorrow's activities.'

A screen lit up outside the Bowl – the first column entitled *Days on ChAOS* with the numbers 1–21 listed below and a challenge or 'Sponsor Destination' listed beside each one. Tommy's eyes scanned the screen.

Yes! Opposite Day Eighteen were the words: *Ageing-UnStables Dung-clean Challenge*.

'How . . ?' Marielle was shocked and perplexed.

Tommy gave a self-satisfied smile. 'Just something I organized while you four were off enjoying yourself.' Yet as he pushed off the glass wall, he felt an immediate sting of regret at sounding so smug. He would've turned to offer a fuller explanation to the pretty elquinine, but he was already propelling across the Bowl. When he knocked into Yago he had to hug the sandy-haired boy to stop them both from twanging off in opposite directions. 'Thanks, buddy,' he said, clapping Yago's back. 'I owe you one.'

33

NO CHANCES

In an indeterminate corner of the universe, a creature named Dell, sporting two buck teeth and a wispy moustache, began writing on a piece of card.

Master,

I know you said NEVER to contact you unless it was an emergency, but . . .

I was watching a show on TV when a group of five contestants started talking about the TFC, saying they are on a mission to stop it. These five will be on the show for the next three weeks.

Mr O.

Dell, otherwise known as Mister Oodid, popped the card into a toaster, twiddled the toast setting back and forth as though it were a safe lock, and the card disappeared.

In an antechamber somewhere in the depths of the universe, a long-eared creature was painting a dog-like figurine when a beep began sounding. He set down his brush and reached around dozens of other doggy figurines to a toaster. As soon as he twiddled the setting back and forth, a square of card began working its way out. The creature read the message and a cloud crossed his face. He spat out an obscenity, took up a club and began smashing figurine after figurine after figurine. When he was spent, smashed porcelain littered the ground and a plume of dust hung in the air. He dropped the club, reached into his pocket and took out a crumpled bin liner.

Dell's fridge began making a loud humming noise. He opened its door and looked past the neat rows of carrots and mint sauce. An image blinked on the back wall. An image of a creature whose head was covered by a sad, tatty bin liner, with two holes cut out for its eyes and a small slit for its mouth. The image spoke with a weird, distorted voice.

'Mister Oodid.'

'Yes, Maaaaaaaaaaahster.'

'Please, call me A-Sad-Bin-Liner. We must stick to code-names . . . I am most perturbed by your note. These people probably don't know what they're saying. But we can't take any chances.'

'That's why I contacted you, A-Sad-Bin-Liner.'

The creature more generally known as Bin-Liner produced a club and smacked it into his hand. 'The TV programme they are on, Mister Oodid . . . What is it called?'

34
Otter Lunacy

Tommy was running – running fast through trees and undergrowth, chased by dozens of strange animals. Some were as small as tennis balls, others as large as mules. All were squeaking or barking or braying. He leapt over fallen tree trunks and ducked under waving branches, the foliage so dense in places that the three suns overhead could only wink at patches of the wood-chipped ground. And then he stumbled on a fallen branch. And shrieked. The animals were upon him in an instant.

Just half an hour earlier, Tommy'd been listening to FionaDeFridge as she addressed all the contestants in the Wigglery – a glass room beneath the Bowl. 'Welcome to Day Two,' she'd said. 'From now on, you'll travel back and forth from the Bowl by wigglehole.' She went on to explain that wiggleholes are 'like cheap wormholes – they can only transport a few people at a time and they can't carry spacecraft.'

Tommy noticed that one of the Wigglery's walls bulged outwards and seemed to be covered in a shimmering shadow, so the stars and lights beyond looked hazy. A sign over the shadow said, *Entrance*. On the opposite wall, was another shimmering shadow, over which a sign said, *Exit*.

'Over the next three weeks, you'll embark on many of your challenges and activities in pairs or triplets,' continued DeFridge. 'This morning you'll choose your partners for the next twelve days. I repeat: you won't be able to change partners till Day Thirteen . . . So, choose now, using the keypads we gave you!'

Fourteen young contestants began punching their keypads.

'Remember,' added DeFridge. 'The only sure way of being paired with the person of your choice is if you choose them *and* they choose you.' A screen appeared behind the female robot. 'Behold, the pairings and groups.'

Tommy breathed a sigh of relief. He was paired with Woozie. And Marielle, Summy and Rumbles were together. None of them noticed Yago fling his keypad aside, hurt and anger etched across his face.

'OK,' said DeFridge. 'Today's destination is Pavlov's Paradise – organized by one of ChAOS's proud sponsors. This is a treat. A chance to relax before the *challenges* you'll face on other days. But . . . One warning: don't – DON'T – scale trees or climb above ground level.'

DeFridge refused to explain the reason. Instead she pointed at the shadow beneath the Entrance sign. 'Now, time to jump through . . . In your pairs or groups – ten seconds apart.'[30]

When their turn came, Tommy and Woozie stepped forward, clasped hands and leapt towards the shadow under the Entrance sign. Everything went black, Tommy felt a rush of air and next thing he was sprawled across the ground in

30 Contestants had little choice but to follow ChAOS rules and instructions as their lives (food rations, comforts etc.) were completely under the show's control.

the middle of a forest. Woozie was lying in a heap across a fallen tree trunk.

'You OK?' asked Tommy.

'Yeah,' replied Woozie, settling on to the ground. 'Just knocked the wind out of me. Think I'll lie here a while. Didn't sleep well last night. I hate zero gravity . . . And why wake us by dunking us in the pool?' (Gravity had turned off gradually in the Bowl that morning, so everyone's sleeping bag had wafted down to the ground. Those sleeping over the swimming pool had received a dunking.)

Tommy smiled and took a quick scout round. When he returned, Woozie was fast asleep. So he removed his shirt and put it over his furry friend. Then he wandered off again to take in the shrubs and flowers and beautiful foliage. Within a short time, he'd come across a bunch of animals. Or rather, they'd come across him.

As the animals descended on him, Tommy's shriek was one of exhilaration, not fear. For as he lay on the soft, wood-chipped earth, surrounded by furry creatures, he was being licked, nuzzled and bounded across (by the small ones). 'Stop!' he laughed, picking himself up and petting as many wet noses as he could.

Wow! Because of Earth's climate change in the twenty-first century, he'd never actually been on a planet with trees and shrubs and flowers and one or more suns beating down. The air smelt clear and wonderful. He closed his eyes and imagined he was in a little corner of Earth. Apart from the animals, the only sounds he could hear were birds singing and breeze-rustling leaves – *until* . . . A musical jingle reverberated from the sky and all the animals stopped playing and began munching the ground (Tommy saw now that the 'woodchips' were actually small, brown biscuits). Voices crooned: 'Pavlov's Animal Cookies® – *eternal salivation* for your pets!' Once the singing had died, the animals stopped eating and returned their attentions to Tommy.

In another part of the leafy planet, Marielle, Rumbles and Summy were tramping through the undergrowth.

'See?' said Marielle. 'No TV cameras.'

'With all this foliage, cameras following us they can't have,' noted Summy.

'Exactly! This could be our best chance to escape.'[31]

'Escape?' intoned Rumbles, puzzled.

Marielle nodded. 'There's clearly something strange and sinister about this show. The Bowl's a fortress – and I don't like being trapped against my will.'

'But I thoughtskeys . . . now the show's including the Ageing-UnStables-dung task . . .'

The blonde elquinine set her hands on her hips. 'Oh, please! If this silly show can locate the Ageing-UnStables in a matter of minutes, it can't be all that hard to find.'

Rumbles shrugged and swung himself up onto an overhanging branch. 'Tommy and Woozkeys – we might see them if we climb a littleskeys.'

A sudden rustling overhead, a blur of approaching colour and Marielle was leaping though the air – 'No!' – grabbing a handful of the thunderbumble's fur. In a trice she was lying on the ground, Rumbles sprawled on top of her.

31 Marielle had a point. ChAOS rarely showed footage of contestants on Sponsor Planets – preferring to concentrate on showcasing Sponsors' products.

The blonde elquinine hauled herself from under the thunderbumble. 'DeFridge warned us not to climb above ground level!'

'Sorry – I forgotskeys!'

Elsewhere on the planet, Yago was standing outside a forest on a flat rock not far from a thundering waterfall. He'd lost his (non-chosen) 'partner' – the paper-folding boy known as Jay-T – and was glad of it. Here, he could give voice to his fury without fear of being overheard.

'How dare he! I – Yago – an honourable Cassiothellian . . . He owed me one – he admitted it . . ! I got his challenge accepted. I gave him my trust, my help, my loyalty and look how he betrays me – by *rejecting* my hand of friendship! By choosing that furry fool as his partner instead of me!' The floppy-eared boy spat into the river flowing by his feet. 'But, I'll make him see the mistake he's made . . . Oh, yes, I'll make him see.'

Yago turned, distracted by the sound of animals emerging from the forest. His snarl melted into a smile.

Having played with the wet-nosed creatures for some time, Tommy thought he saw a figure retreating through the trees. Out of curiosity, he hurried after it, in the direction of a faint rumble. Quickening his pace, still escorted by a flurry of animals, he caught brief glimpses of the figure – it looked to be a black-haired girl in a red smock. Yet no matter how much he hurried, she always stayed the same distance ahead.

As the rumble grew louder, the foliage grew less dense. By the time the trees parted and he found himself by a wide, frothing river, the rumble had become a mighty roar. His escort of animals began dipping their noses in the water and frolicking along the rocks that lined the riverbank. But Tommy was looking up – up at a waterfall, thundering down a sheer, rocky cliff-face. When at last he drew his eyes from the mesmerizing sight, he noticed a large animal standing on a rocky outcrop to the side of the waterfall. And another. And another. They looked like tigers, except they had eight legs and big fangs jutting from their mouths.

A movement on the far side of the waterfall caught Tommy's eye – an otter-like creature (an ottercudul) had skipped on to a huge rock jutting high out of the river and one of the fang-tigers was leaping towards him. *Another movement!* A figure on the far side of the river was scurrying across rocks – *Yago!* The waggly-tailed boy, leaving a legion of animals behind, was yelling something – but it didn't stop the fang-tiger snatching the ottercudul by the back of the neck.

'Yago, n-n-no!' cried Tommy, seeing the rabbity-eared fellow chasing up the rocks after the fangy creature. But his voice was drowned by the water's thunder.

Marielle, Rumbles and Summy came across Woozie laughing under a blanket of furry creatures. 'Geroff!' he giggled, trying to answer their questions.

'Tommy left you?' exclaimed Marielle, appalled.

'I was asleep,' explained Woozie.

'All the more reason . . .'

Once Woozie'd found his feet, Rumbles kept the animals at bay by throwing sticks while Marielle and Summy explained the plans for escape.

'First Tommy we find.'

'Then when the return wiggleholes appear to take us back to the Bowl, we *don't* jump through.'

'And what about Swiggy?' asked Woozie. 'We can't escape without her – leaving all the lessons and all our belongings behind.'

Hmmm. Good point.

Tommy was in the river, but the other side was so far away, he was powerless to do anything but battle against the current and watch as Yago scaled the cliff-face. The fang-tiger reached its perch, dropped the paralysed-with-fear otter-cudul on to the rock and peered down, growling at the approaching boy. As Yago drew near, unsheathing a sword, Tommy heard a roar rise above the waterfall's thunder. The fang-tiger was standing up on two legs, mouth open, teeth flashing. Yago reached the perch, ducked under a swinging claw and lashed his sword. The next moments were a blur of claws, teeth and glinting metal – and when it was over, Yago was still standing (the ottercudul quivering behind his legs) and the fang-tiger had backed away, leaping to a higher rocky outcrop.

Yago dropped his sword, snatched up the ottercudul and began petting it and kissing its nose.

'Watch out!' cried Tommy. The fang-tiger was creeping down, foothold to foothold. It was almost upon the Cassiothellian before he realized.

'WAAAAGGHHHHHHHHHHHHH!'

The waggly-tailed boy leapt off the outcrop, cradling the ottercudul. The pair flew through the air, landing in the river with a splash.

Fourteen 'return' wiggleholes appeared on the leafy planet and fourteen contestants appeared, one after another, through the Exit in the Wigglery. Yago was dripping wet, trousers torn, happy to have saved a tiny creature. And yet . . . The sight of Tommy reignited flames within him. He gave vent to the anger by bemoaning the loss of his sword.

Most of the other contestants were full of chat. Only Tommy was quiet. Not because he too was wet. But because he'd realized that Yago's ottercudul adventure had distracted him from the little girl in the red smock. He wondered where she'd got to.

35

Introductions

While the contestants were in Pavlov's Paradise, a wooden, rope-lined walkway appeared high above the Bowl's floor, in front of all the wardrobes.

Marielle stepped onto a rope ladder dangling at ground level and climbed up. Following the walkway as it curved close to the glass wall, the elquinine reached her wardrobe, removed a small suitcase and began unpacking (she hadn't unpacked the night before as she hadn't accepted they were stuck here).

'Hey . . . Dig the dungarees.'

Marielle looked around. A meerkat-like boy in a maroon bandanna and sunglasses was sitting on the walkway, leaning against the wardrobe next to hers, snipping the corners off a piece of paper with a tiny scissors.

'Thanks,' she said, folding half a dozen tops and placing them on her wardrobe's shelves.

'You should chill,' said the boy, licking an edge of paper.

'Sorry?'

'Three weeks to unpack – what's the rush?'

Marielle paused. He had a point.

'Jay-T.' The boy raised an arm and opened one of his palms.

'Sorry.'

'Jay-T – 'swhat dudes call me.'

'Oh.' Marielle realized she was meant to smack one of his palms with hers. Out of politeness, she did. 'Nice to meet you. I'm Marielle.'

'Very pretty . . . And I'm not just talking 'bout your name.' And he pointed a finger at her like his hand was a gun, before returning his gaze to the twisted paper.

Less than enamoured, Marielle decided to return to ground level.

With Marielle up organizing her wardrobe and Tommy seeking solitude (once more) on the high diving board, Woozie, Rumbles and Summy were thinking about a game of No-Gravity-Snooker when a girl on a skateboard careered by, almost knocking them over.

'Sorry!' she exclaimed, coming to a sudden stop. 'I'm Bernard.'

Bernard was an odd name for this creature as she was clearly a *she*. With a human-like face beneath a reversed baseball cap, she had aquamarine eyes and moustache that was obviously fake (seriously, you could spot it at twenty paces). She wore a purple vest, baggy shorts and the most unusual thing about her physique was that one of her feet was much longer and wider than the other, with four wheels (part of her anatomy!) on its underside. Her other foot being quite 'normal', she moved about like a permanent skateboarder.[32]

'I'm gonna fly off the Edge to the crashmat in the Basement,' she announced. 'So take cover!'

32 Bernard's real name was Cara-Bernadette and she was a tomtombuachaill – a species of female who act even more like boys than boys themselves (except that they're very fond of ponies).

The Edge was a hole in the floor of the Bowl that dropped past two floors to the Basement far below. Bernard retreated, then charged full-pelt towards the Edge and raised her 'paddle foot' on to the skateboard. At the last moment, she swivelled to the left, careering into a champagne-pink polar bear.

'Sorry, bro,' said Bernard, adjusting her moustache. 'I wasn't in the zone – had to snapback.'

'My schnozzle!' wailed the polar bear, blood flowing from his nose. 'I'm disfigured for life!'

Marielle had just alighted from a rope ladder and automatically took out her polka-dot hanky and held it to the bear's nose. 'Here, let me see,' she said, lifting the hanky. 'You just got a bang. Put your head back.'

'Might as well kill myself now,' sobbed the bear, tugging the handkerchief from Marielle and pressing it to his nose. 'My schnozzle will never sniff again and no one will ever find me attractive.'

'Hush. You're fine,' said Marielle, eyeing the handkerchief. *There's no need to panic. The blood will come out.*

The elquinine was so lost in thought that she nearly stepped on a small, moving lump of fur – a miniature, deep-burgundy polar bear who appeared to be attached to the larger polar bear (they shared the same tail and their colours were on opposite ends of the *wine* spectrum). The little fellow seemed to be sleep-walking, the tail acting like a leash.

Just then, an announcement sounded across the Bowl's sound system. 'Apologies for the frugalness of the meals to date. Tonight's dinner, however, is sponsored by BBQBliss™. Contestants wishing to eat should make their way to the Wigglery.'

If anything this made the champagne-pink polar bear look even more despondent.

'Your name is what?' asked Summy, thinking she might be able to distract the big bear from its woes.

'Joe . . . Joe Yuss,' sniffed the creature in reply. 'This show's gonna end badly. Wait'll you see. They're gonna kill us all. I have a feeling for these things.'

36

Mentaler Fundyists

Dell's fridge began to hum. He rubbed his two buck teeth, patted down his wispy moustache and opened the door. An image of a bin-liner-covered creature spoke in a distorted voice. 'Mister Oodid.'

'Yes, maaaaaaahster – I mean, yes, A-Sad-Bin-Liner?'

'I have tuned to this ChAOS programme and seen the five children you spoke of . . . You must deal with them, Mister Oodid.'

'You mean . . ?'

Bin-Liner nodded. 'Yes.'

Dell looked scared for a moment. Then a surge of defiance – nay, excitement – ran through him. This was his chance to kill five troublemakers and achieve some recognition – nay, infamy – at last. 'Up the Mentaler Fundyists!' he cried. 'Our mission . . . To save the universe from being saved.' Already he was making a mental(er) list of the ammunition he'd need – *chocolate galaxy-gateaux, chocolate brown-hole-brownies and choco-snowballs.*

Bin-Liner's voice cut through his thoughts. 'Not so fast . . ! We must pinpoint a time when they will be together and will be most . . . *vulnerable* . . . For the sake of the end-of-the-universe, Mister Oodid, we must not fail.'

37

Eyes Narrowing

The FiiVe landed on Planet BBQBliss, finding themselves in a fire-lit campsite beneath a starry sky. They were the last contestants to arrive and the place was already buzzing – figures hurrying, pots banging, cutlery clattering, fires crackling, all washed down with two tablespoons of shouts, yells and laughter. Only Uladrack, the girl with the hair-veiled face, seemed immune – she was crouching before a huge, open cooler-box, her cape outstretched, her back to everyone.

Beryl MacPairyl, many-armed and boggle-eyed, rolled a handful of marbles across the ground and three people fell over. Then she turned her attention to a stack of tins balancing by a flaming bar-b-q. 'A tin oopener! Someone find me a tin oopener!'

'In my pouch a penknife I have,' said Summy and disappeared into the melee.

'Anyone for more than three buffaleg burgers?' roared a chubby face in a crowd of people by another roaring bar-b-q. 'Yes!' cried a load of faces in close proximity to him, while a few made comments such as 'Uuughh! Don't you know I hate buffaleg burgers?' or 'How come you always get to do the cooking?'

Rumbles and Woozie approached the boy and put in an order for the IGGY Knights. Turned out he was just one of the faces and bodies that made up Charles Lemass. When Woozie introduced himself, all thirty of Charles's heads said, 'Pleased to meet you' at the same time and then thirty hands were thrust his way. It took a few minutes to shake them all – and then Rumbles had to go through the same rigmarole.

It appeared that all Charles's heads could talk separately to each other, but to others, they responded en masse. All the 'bodies' were male and humanlike – about thirteen years old – and most were wearing orange T-shirts with *Wolvereen Wanderers*[33] stamped across the chest.

Someone noticed that all the bottles of sauce in the cooler had disappeared, causing an outbreak of bickering among Charles's many heads and they forgot about Woozie and Rumbles and began singing, 'Why are we wai-ting? Why are we wai-ting? Oh, why are we way-ai-ting, oh why, oh why!?' Strange, since they were the ones doing the cooking.

Jay-T appeared beside Tommy and Marielle. 'Marielle! Beautiful. Slip me some skin.' He held out a hand and, not knowing what else to do, Marielle slid her hand against his. 'Mmmm,' said the sunglassed boy. 'Me likes your touch.'

Much to Marielle's consternation, Tommy disappeared into the throng. He'd spotted something.

'N-n-need help opening that?'

He was addressing a tall, beautiful girl in a yellow dress.

'No thank you, I'm fine,' she answered, fingers fastened round the top of a bottle – all colour bled out of them.

'I c-can do that in t-two seconds if you l-l-let me.'

33 A popular kneeball team on the plant Tribalmediocrity (Charles's planet). Kneeball is very like football except that players mostly use their knees.

The girl shook her head and squeezed with all her might. No budge. She tried, in turn, with a cloth, a tentacle and even an armpit! Still no budge. Finally, she placed the bottle on the counter-top. Tommy opened it with a twist of his hand. (His Milky Foo training enabled him to open really tight tops and lids.)

'Thank you,' said the girl, eyes averted, and she poured herself a paper cup of sparkling water and began drinking, the two tentacles under her arms curling round her back and tying themselves into a large bow. Tommy admired her long brown hair, held back with a black velvet hairband. He eyed the two wire-like antennae protruding from her head and wondered how the fuzzy, bobbly bits on the end would feel to the touch.

'Any ch-chance I could have a cup t-too?' he asked.

The girl poured another cup without glancing in his direction.

'Th-thanks,' said Tommy. He took a few sips and moved into the girl's line of vision. 'I'm T-Tommy . . . Tommy S-S-Storm.'

The girl gave him a withering look, antennae erect. 'So?'

So?? Tommy wasn't sure what she meant. 'I w-was one of the g-guys who leapt into the p-pool yesterday drenching that lot.' He motioned vaguely behind him.

'So?'

'S-so . . . So, n-nothing. I'm just s-saying. I'm T-Tommy Storm.'

'You said that before.'

Tommy was frustrated. He should've walked away from this unfriendly girl, but there was something intoxicating about her. 'Wh-what's your name?' he asked.

'What a boring question . . ! If I told you, you'd only say, *Where are you from?* – another boring question . . . So now

I'm going to go.'

And with that, she walked off.

The FiiVe sat at a long picnic table with Yago, Bernard Burnside and Lillroysen, the wasp-like boy in the school uniform (he used a different knife and fork for his buffaleg burgers than he did for his baked-beings). Joe Yuss, the miserable pink-champagne polar bear sat opposite Tommy, the tiny polar bear who shared his tail propped against him.

'Is he g-going to eat?' asked Tommy, referring to the sleeping burgundy bear.

'No, she doesn't eat when she sleeps,' replied Joe Yuss, adding: 'This is probably the last meal we'll get for weeks. Wait'll you see. They'll starve us. That's if this food isn't poisoned. Which it probably is. Do you have any tummy pains yet . . ? Have you made a will?'

Tommy didn't have a tummy pain, but his mouth and insides felt fiery (due to an unintentional gulp of locust-chilli-oil or 'lochoi' – Beryl had 'swapped' his cup of water when he wasn't looking). He glanced across at the second picnic table. The other contestants were dining there, apart from Uladrack who'd disappeared behind the cooler-box (she squawked loudly when Summy checked if she wanted more baked-beings).

At one point, Marielle leaned towards Tommy. 'You seemed to be talking to Zestrella Ravisham for a long time.'

'Who?'

'The pretty girl in the yellow dress.'

'Oh, *her.* I wasn't t-talking to her *for a l-l-long time* . . . How'd you kn-know her s-surname?'

'Jay-T told me.'

'The g-guy in the s-sunglasses?'

'Yes. He's her cousin. Says she has no heart.'

'Wh-what else did your new b-boyfriend tell you?'

'He's not my boyfriend.' And with that, the elquinine twisted away to speak to Lillroysen.

Tommy turned to Yago (who'd been feeding scraps to his pockets and listening acutely to everything), just as Bernard Burnside leapt up from the table. 'Uggghhh! Who put baked-beings in my pockets!?'

Dinner was finished – the FiiVe plus Yago, Zestrella, Bernard and Joe Yuss were helping to tidy up. Despite his broken arm, Yago cleared the tables with Rumbles, Woozie and Summy, asking them all about themselves. Then the waggly-tailed boy asked about Tommy and Marielle. He was so persistent and so forensic in his questions that he got the whole scoop – Rumbles, Woozie and Summy coming out with things they'd never even said to each other.

'I think they still like each otherskeys.'

'Admit it she won't. But the handkerchief she still treasures.'

'The what?' queried Yago, eyes narrowing.

'Oh, a present of a red polka-dot hanky a few years ago Tommy gave her. Of his love a token, I think.'

'Always has it with her,' added Rumbles.

''Cept right now,' interjected Woozie.

Yago cocked his head. 'What do you mean?'

They explained about Joe Yuss keeping it for his bloody nose – and had just finished doing so, when Rumbles spat out a mouthful of liquid. 'Uuughaaarrrghhhh! Someone put lochoi in my waterskeys!'

38

Don't Blink

Yago left Planet BBQBliss before everyone else, saying he had to get back for his nightly chat with the show's producers. These chats were held using big screen technology in the *BlahRoom*, two floors beneath the Bowl. As Yago'd explained to Tommy the first evening: 'They've asked me to represent all the contestants – to tell them if we need more towels etcetera. I'm like a nerdy class-rep.'

Later, some commentators would claim this was a lie. That the producers planted Yago in the show to 'spice things up'. Others would claim he'd been sent by the Beast. Whatever the truth, on the evening he returned alone from Planet BBQBliss, viewers heard nothing of Yago's request for the producers to supply him with a tiny motorized contraption and a remote control device.

Nor did they see any images of the Cassiothellian ascending to the Bowl, climbing to his wardrobe and hiding three items before the other contestants got back. For in addition to the two items the producers had given him, Yago needed to hide a certain something he'd pick-pocketed from Joe Yuss. Something white with red polka-dots.

The challenge on Day Three was called the ScaredyCat Run.

Once they leapt through the shadow in the Wigglery, the contestants were surprised to find themselves emerge on to a platform floating in space not far from the Bowl. And docked alongside was what looked like a three-seater toboggan with wings.

'You will take it in turns – with your partners – to pilot the tobogganer,' explained FionaDeFridge. 'On the far side of the Bowl is another tobogganer, piloted by Captain Blink . . . This sounds like him.' A small craft whisked past the fans standing by the Bowl and zoomed towards the contestants. In seconds, the craft was almost upon them. Tommy expected it to bank up, down, left or right, but it didn't deviate and flashed across the platform, just above his head, forcing everyone to duck, and slashing through a banner strung across the far end of the platform ('*ChAOS – probably the best TV programme in the universe*'). Now a section of banner was caught on the nose of the craft, some of it flapping over the pilot's head. Yet the pilot seemed unfazed. The craft did a loop-the-loop and zipped back towards the other side of the Bowl – the banner covering the pilot's face all the while.

FionaDeFridge resumed her commentary. 'Contestants – your tobogganer is set to take off at a fixed speed and to go in a straight line, directly towards Captain Blink's craft.'

The trio of Beryl MacPairyl, Lillroysen and Uladrack were ushered towards the tobogganer and began climbing into the three seats, one behind the other. Then Lillroysen seemed to change his mind and slid back onto the platform. Tommy noted how the school-uniformed boy had perfectly parted blond-and-orange-striped hair and, below his translucent wings, his lower-back became furry and bulbous as it extended out beyond his legs like a wasp's tail. 'Eh, sorry,' said Lillroysen. 'But Lillroysen isn't sure he heard correctly.

Did you say, *fly directly towards Captain Blink's craft?*'

'Yes,' replied DeFridge. 'And please don't push that stinger out when you're addressing me.' (The sting on Lillroysen's tail had protruded.)

'I can't help it – when Lillroysen's agitated—' The waspish fellow remembered he was being watched on TV by trillions of people. 'Apologies,' he said, his sting retracting. 'But flying directly towards another craft, it makes no sense.'

Lillroysen was an etonianwasp – a species with a double-deadly sting that can only be used ONCE in a lifetime. Etonianwasps die within minutes of deploying their sting – hence the term 'double-deadly'.

'As you'll see,' replied DeFridge, 'each seat on the tobogganer has a steering wheel. And as you approach Captain Blink, any one of you can steer the tobogganer away from its pre-set course.'

Lillroysen was persuaded to climb into the tobogganer – in front of Uladrack, whose face was shrouded by hair (so Tommy couldn't see if she looked scared), and behind Beryl, who was squirting water out of a fake flower she had pinned to her lapel.

'So,' continued DeFridge. 'The challenge is *not* to turn your steering wheel before Captain Blink turns his . . . Yes, the challenge is *not* to be a ScaredyCat . . . And might I add that if *any* of you succeed, you'll *all* enjoy a slap-up meal tonight. But if none of you succeed, bread and water's all you'll get.'

After a countdown, Beryl hit the 'start' button by her steering wheel and the tobogganer took-off, zooming towards the crowds by the Bowl. Tommy saw Captain Blink's tobogganer approaching from the far side (the banner now removed). The two craft were heading straight for each other and might've collided just across from the fans had the contestants' tobogganer not veered sideways two seconds beforehand. A slow-motion replay revealed – to the surprise of many – that Beryl had been the one to turn her steering wheel.

A few more pairs of contestants had a go and then it was the turn of Rumbles, Summy and Marielle. They didn't fare nearly as well as Tommy expected. Summy veered them off course a full second before they made it alongside the fans and although Rumbles remonstrated with the kangasaurus, Marielle – who seemed distracted – said nothing.

At least fifty trillion viewers were watching when Tommy climbed into the tobogganer in front of Woozie. 'Let's show this guy,' said Tommy (eager for another slap-up dinner after the meagre breakfast that morning). He hit the start button and the tobogganer took off, heading towards Captain Blink. Viewers saw Tommy and Woozie pass the point where Beryl had veered, pass the point where Summy had veered and flash towards the crowd. Just when it looked as if a collision might happen, the pair banked upwards, Captain Blink whooshing beneath them.

'He wasn't going to swerve!' exclaimed Woozie. 'We would've collided if I hadn't turned my steering-wheel!'

Yago and Jay-T went next. Yago, sitting in the second seat, didn't seem to be concentrating on the task at hand and so it was that Jay-T veered the tobogganer away some hundred metres before a possible collision. Tommy reckoned Yago was very brave – his strategy being not to look at Captain Blink, thereby reducing the chances that he'd be the one to veer. But what Tommy didn't realize, and what the cameras failed to pick up, was that Yago spent the entire time inserting something into 'his' steering wheel shaft. He looked very pleased with himself when he disembarked.

'OK,' announced DeFridge. 'Everyone's had a go now – and everyone's failed to beat Captain Blink . . . You have just two more chances to defeat him.'

In the next round, Jay-T and Yago came closest to Captain Blink, but still pulled out half a second before a possible collision. Marielle, no less distracted than before, added nothing to her team's chances. When Tommy climbed into the tobogganer, he turned to the wibblewallian behind him and said: 'Why don't you leave the steering to me this time?' Woozie nodded, yet when they were a full second from possible collision, the tobogganer veered to the left.

'Hey!' yelled Tommy.

'I didn't do anything!' cried Woozie. But the pictures showed that he'd been the one to swerve.

What the pictures didn't show was a certain sandy-haired boy standing back from the other contestants with a big smile. He had a remote control device couched in his hand. And the dial was turned hard to the left.

The next round saw similar results for everyone. This time Tommy and Woozie swerved nearly two seconds before a possible collision. 'You swore you'd leave it to me!' screamed Tommy. 'What were you thinking? We were miles away from him!'

Again Woozie denied it was his fault. Yet the pictures proved he'd turned the wheel. 'It turned in my hand,' claimed the wibblewallian. 'Without me doing nothing!'

Tommy was a tad surprised that his furry friend had chickened out so early, but told himself that anyone can find themselves unduly scared by something new. What really surprised – and disappointed – him was how Woozie lied about it.

Summy and Rumbles also seemed dubious of Woozie's claim, but their disbelief was rooted in humour. 'Thought of that excuse I wish I had,' chortled Summy. Marielle didn't seem to have any opinion – she was off discussing something animatedly with Joe Yuss.

'OK,' declared DeFridge. 'That's the end of the challenge – you all failed, so it's bread and water tonight.'

What Tommy did next has been put down to his row with Woozie. (Though some claim it was, in part, motivated by wishing to change the moans of the distant fans to cheers.) The dark Earthling leapt into the front seat of the tobogganer and hit the start button. The tobogganer took off, heading towards the Bowl. As though hard-wired to respond, Captain Blink's tobogganer began approaching from the far side of the Bowl. They shot towards each other . . . 800 metres away, 600, 200 . . . Sitting in the front seat of his tobogganer, Tommy's hands gripped the steering wheel, willing himself not to turn away. 100 metres away . . . The next fraction of a second felt like it was happening in slow motion . . . 50 metres . . . 25 . . . He and Captain Blink on a collision course just a stone's throw from the fans . . . 15 metres away . . . 10 metres . . .

There was less than a car's length between the two tobogganers when Tommy realized that Captain Blink wasn't going to swerve. By then it was too late. The two spacecraft smashed into one another – the crash almost drowned by the cheers and yelps of the nearby fans.

39
What a Schmuck

DICTATED BY PI BARLOWE FARLOWE . . .

Beginning to feel like a sicko-punk. Three times I've viewed TSC 1–24. That's seventy-two eyefuls of an EARTH getting kapowed. Sure, I'm gunning for clues – for something that can give me a lead – but you can't watch that many planets crushed to nada and not wonder about yourself.

Fourth time round and I spot something in TSC6. The gloved hand crushing all these EARTHs – when I freeze it and magnify a section – I can pick out the letter F on the topside of the glove, illuminated by a cluster of stars.

I go back over all the videos again, focusing in on the glove, frame-by-frame. In some, there are no letters visible, in others there's half a letter, maybe less. I piece them together and get 'ENI PF'. Then spend the next day and a half checking for likely places that go by the first three initials. Result – a whole lot of nothing.

Then I have a stroke of inspiration. And by stroke, I mean 'stroke of the pencil'. See, I doodle when I'm stumped. But I'm not what you might call *artistic*. So I scrawl 'ENI' on a napkin and underline it twenty times. And one of the underlines cuts through the bottom of the 'I' making it look like an 'L'.

Of course, I realize. What a schmuck!

'But . . . but . . . I thought you wanted me to get you a wormhole to that TV show you were on about!"

I'm on the blower to Max Bohr. He's not enamoured with the suggestion that I drop in on his workplace.

'*ChAOS*,' I says. 'I may not even have to go there now.' Time to give it to him straight. 'One of your colleagues is doing the destroying. The glove on the videos is marked *ENLPF*.'

He tells me that's ridiculous, impossible, all the insane adjectives he can muster. But I can tell he's wilting. Eventually he admits all the labs in El Nerdo Lostalmost Physics Facility are kitted out with rubber gloves. And they all have a logo on the back. (No prizes for guessing what it is.)

'But you can't come here,' he says. 'People would wonder who you are. Discretion, remember?'

That's when I laugh. 'You got what – fifty thousand people working in El Nerdo. You really think anyone'll notice one more ugly mug?'

40
Smoke and Mirrors

The SuperFabAir-Bags built into the tobogganer saved Tommy from certain death. Yet he was still unconscious when ChAOS's medical team zoomed in among the floating bits of tobogganer and carted him away. The fans cheered madly as the Earthling was bundled onto a stretcher and brought to a medical facility beneath the Bowl's basement. Captain Blink, it turned out, was actually a blind robot – incapable of swerving – and he'd automatically self-destructed on impact.

The other IGGY Knights were desperate to see Tommy, but were assured that he was fine ('No bones broken') and needed some rest 'without the intrusion of visitors'.

Back in the Bowl, the contestants were informed that although Tommy had 'not swerved before Captain Blink' (thereby succeeding in the challenge), his achievement had occurred 'outside the allotted number of turns' and so the challenge was still marked down as a failure and dinner for all would consist solely of bread and water.

Marielle approached Yago during the sorry meal. 'I was wondering if I could ask a favour . . ? I think I dropped something on Planet BBQBliss last night. Any chance you could ask the producers if me and my three friends could pop back there for a short while and take a look?'

There were no bar-b-qs burning when Marielle, Woozie, Rumbles and Summy landed back on Planet BBQBliss – just the flaming torches lining the fence around the campsite.

'And you think you dropped it here?' asked Woozie.

'No, I told you,' replied Marielle. 'Joe Yuss had it – for his bleeding nose. But when I asked for it back last night, he couldn't find it anywhere . . . We've both searched his clothes, his wardrobe and all over the Bowl – it's not there. He must've dropped it here.'

They searched everywhere, failing to find the precious handkerchief.

'Hey, there's still some food here,' declared Woozie, attempting to cheer everyone up. He removed a parcel of left-overs from the giant cooler-box. 'Probably only good till this evening . . . Can't hurt to help ourselves. And we could smuggle some back for Tommy.'

Tired and starving, the four dug into the food.

Marielle spoke up between mouthfuls. 'None of you mention any of this to Tommy . . . About the hanky or about us coming back here to look for it . . . Not a word . . . The hanky will turn up.' Adding, to herself, *it's got to.*

Tommy, having recovered consciousness, was in bed in the medical room, Yago by his side.

'The others didn't come with you?' he asked.

'Oh, I'm sure they will later,' replied Yago. 'They're probably just busy at the moment . . . Look.' He picked up a remote control, pointing it at the TV above Tommy's bed. 'They're probably making you a present or something.' The

TV came on showing 'ChAOS *Live* – Channell II' and Tommy looked up to see a close-up of Marielle, Woozie, Rumbles and Summy stuffing their faces full of food. 'Oh, er.' Yago flicked off the TV. 'I'm sure they *were* busy.'

When Marielle, Woozie, Rumbles and Summy arrived back in the Bowl they descended to the Basement, but the heavy door to the medical facility was locked – and they didn't have the key.

'Asleep anyway he probably is,' said Summy.

Rumbles nodded. 'Yeah, we'll see him in the morningskeys.'

And so they made their way up to the Bowl and put the leftovers reserved for Tommy in the fridge. While they prepared for bed, a certain waggly-tailed person took the leftovers, descended with them to the Basement and unlocked the door to the medical facility – winning a whole heap of gratitude from a very grateful Earthling.

Soon after Yago returned to the Bowl, gravity turned off. Within a short while everyone was floating in their sleeping bags and the lights had dimmed. A few contestants were on the verge of sleep when Lillroysen caused a rumpus – having found a load of breadcrusts in his sleeping bag, which he flung across at Beryl ('Lillroysen knows it was you!').

Marielle sighed and dodged a shower of crumbs. She was trying to put thoughts of Tommy out of her head (*he's OK*) and trying to get some sleep, but that fool Jay-T wouldn't shut up talking to her.

'Delicious PJs,' he said. 'You know, I see all my dreams in

blue. Light blue, dark blue, navy blue, aquamarine blue, powder blue—'

'OK, I get it! *All kinds of blue*. You might see your dreams in a few more colours if you took off those dumb sunglasses. Now, will you please be quiet! I'm trying to get some sleep.'

'Chill, sister . . . Gimme four.' He was holding his hand up for a high-four.

'Ssshhh! . . . And please move away from me – there's lots of room over *there*.'

'Hey – can't you just give a bro a high-four goodnight?'

'Will you shut up if I give you one?'

'Yes, indeedy. I'll go to sleep right here alongside you. I'll be a shield beside you, protecting you from everyone else.'

Dying to get to sleep and not wanting Jay-T sleeping alongside her, Marielle gave the sunglassed fellow a forceful high-four. Thankfully, this made his sleeping bag rise and hers descend. The elquinine gave the annoying boy a sarcastic wave as their sleeping bags floated further apart.

Alone in the medical facility, Tommy flicked on the TV. Again it came on showing 'ChAOS *Live* – Channell II.' He fiddled with the volume, but it was permanently mute.

The images on view were of the contestants floating around the Bowl in their sleeping bags. For a moment, the screen filled with what could've been a tent. (This was actually Charles Lemass – three of his heads poking out the top of the blue sleeping bag, the others all inside going, 'Sshh!'). Tommy was on the lookout for Marielle, but even as the tent drifted slightly, he still couldn't see her. One person he could see was that fool, Jay-T, in a shiny, gold sleeping bag – still wearing sunglasses! – half-turned, jabbering to someone. The sunglassed boy lifted his hand for a high-four and Tommy saw a petite hand rise to smack it. This smack caused Jay-T's sleeping bag to go up and a stripy sleeping bag to descend. Tommy felt a pang course through him. Marielle, her petite hand outstretched, was the stripy sleeping bag's occupant. And she was waving to Jay-T.

47
SKEWERED

Tommy saw the little red-smocked girl again on the afternoon of Day Four.

That morning, he ascended to the Bowl and heard a tremendous roar. It was the fans outside – now bearing many Tommy banners ('Tommy, we love you,' 'Tommy, you're the greatest,' 'Tommy, don't blink,' 'Marry me, Tommy'). Pleased that someone, at least, had missed him, the young Earthling went to the glass wall and waved down to the throng. They went bananas. And Tommy couldn't help feeling chuffed.

When his friends hurried over, Tommy felt there was something missing from their hugs and banter – particularly those of Marielle and Woozie. It didn't occur to the young Earthling that the cheering of the fans might be putting his friends off, and he'd no idea that they all felt weird not being able to mention their trip to Planet BBQBliss.[34] All he knew was that they ummed and ahhed when asked what they'd got up to the previous evening and lied to him about what they ate ('just bread and water') and made lame excuses for not visiting his bedside ('the door was locked').

It all made him feel rather sad.

34 Plus they were all a bit surprised by the disappearance of the left overs from the fridge, but couldn't mention this to Tommy cos then they'd have to explain the trip to BBQBliss.

Later, the contestants plopped on to Planet NofingersThruIt (which was full of blond puppies trailing rolls of toilet paper). Once again Woozie was tired (still sleeping badly in zero gravity) and Tommy encouraged the wibblewallian to snooze. Glad it was a 'sponsor day' rather than a 'challenge day', the young Earthling breathed in the air, revelling in the sunshine, the trees and the sound of distant puppies barking, mingled with happy music in the background. How good it felt to be alone on yet another planet that reminded him of Earth.

He was clambering over some rocks when he spotted Yago and Jay-T in the distance. He waved to Yago and thought the waggly-tailed boy saw him, but, no, he must've been mistaken, for Yago caught Jay-T by the elbow and ushered him behind some trees.

Tommy hurried after them. When he reached the trees he was surprised to see that he was almost upon the pair. Yago was kneeling by a stream and Jay-T was . . . Jay-T was . . . holding a white hanky with red polka dots.

Tommy stayed hidden for a time. Then he crept away.

So something was going on between Marielle and Jay-T! She wouldn't've given him the polka-dot hanky unless it was 'serious'. Tommy tried to tell himself he didn't care and tried to block the image from his mind by turning his emotions to anger. Anger at Woozie for swerving the tobogganer, for lying about it and for lying about stuffing his face on Planet BBQBliss.

Tommy's thoughts were disturbed by a figure in the distance. Was that . . ? Yes, the little red-smocked girl standing atop a giant toilet roll. He hesitated, recalling DeFridge's words before they left the Wigglery: 'Planet NofingersThruIt is perfectly safe – so long as you stay *inside* the perimeter fence formed by the giant toilet rolls.'

The little girl jumped – off the toilet roll to the far side of the perimeter fence. Tommy could see her no more. And so he began running, accompanied by two faint shadows (this planet had two suns, so everything had two shadows). Reaching the perimeter of giant toilet rolls, he pulled out his scimmy (when not hidden in the wardrobe, he kept it inside a protective sheath down his back, under his shirt) and stabbed the toilet roll, gouging out a foothold. Then he stabbed a bit higher up, gouging out a handhold. Repeating this procedure, he climbed to the top.

The view that greeted him was not what he expected. It was dark on the far side of the perimeter. The planet's two suns throwing almost no illumination out this way. He could see the outline of trees against the starry sky and . . . yes, he glimpsed the silhouette of a little girl heading further into the darkness. He sheathed his scimmy and jumped.

What made Tommy follow the little girl, he couldn't tell. Afterwards, he'd wonder if it was simply the sight of a small vulnerable person heading into possible danger. Or perhaps that first sheet of paper – the one that said, *save the girl & triumph* – perhaps its words had seeped into his head, along with the thought that it just might be the Deadly Scroll. Or maybe it was just a way to exorcise his anger at Woozie and put thoughts of Marielle and Jay-T from his mind.

His fall was broken by a thick bush, and he rolled out onto hard earth. Stumbling across the uneven surface, he hurried in the direction of the little girl, picking out a star in the sky by which to navigate. He chased into the darkness, an arm outstretched before his eyes. Whenever he felt the ground dip, he leapt; whenever a line of stars blinked, he ducked. But then everything went black, he whumped into something and fell to the ground.

Nothing broken, he thought, catching his breath, his face centimetres from the dry earth . . . He stood and felt the large object he'd run in to. It was hard and ridgey. Like a tree. He looked up. An explosion of branches and leaves was silhouetted against the milky cosmos.

Ooooh Aayyyy Oooooh! A low chant swam through the darkness. Eerie and unsettling, it grew in intensity till a young girl's voice cried out 'Nooo!' and the chant died. Tommy unsheathed his sword, feeling his way round the thick tree trunk – surprised to see a splash of light on a bush ahead. He looked up for the light source and saw a wide hole in the tree he was touching. Standing on his tippy-toes, he peered inside . . .

What he saw was a rocky, cavernous space, illuminated by flickering, orange light. With hundreds of people standing to attention on its floor, their backs to him, clothed in white hooded robes and all carrying spears, held point-up. 'Nooo!' cried a voice and Tommy saw the little red-smocked girl. Two purple-clad hooded figures were dragging her up an aisle between the white-hooded onlookers. The chant struck up again – 'Ooooh Aayyyy Oooooh!' Bestial in its fervour.

What to do? *If I jump in, they'll kill me in two seconds.*

So he stood, frozen, as the girl was dragged on to a stone platform. As soon as her feet touched its surface, the chant stopped and the two purple-clad creatures turned around with her, facing the onlookers. Tommy could see their faces were covered with hook-nosed, leering masks. And the little girl's face had turned extra pale. Her two captors held their spears out horizontally. The onlookers made a grunting sound and whipped their hands forward. Now all the spears in the cavern were held horizontal.

'Live or die?' intoned a loud voice.

After a pause, during which the little girl's sobs were audible, the onlookers grunted, then every spear thudded against the stony ground – point-down. Despite her screams, the two purple creatures dragged the girl towards a stone altar.

This was the moment that Tommy leapt through the hole in the tree and landed at the back of the cavern. 'Yeeeaaagggggggghhhhhhhh!' he screamed, charging up the aisle, scimmy aloft. The crowd turned, spears raised. Tommy kept running towards the altar even as a dozen creatures blocked his path. He charged straight at them, pirouetting and slashing his scimmy – cutting through two spears before landing amidst the creatures and scurrying along the ground beneath their robes. People began shouting, but he was through them, almost up to the platform. A spear and then another flew into the ground close by. He leapt onto the platform, two more spears hitting the stonework, sending sparks into the air. He saw the girl pinned down, a purple creature holding a spear to her neck. Another spear flew past, and another, then – AAAAGGGGHHHHHHH!!! – something skewered into his leg. He pulled at it, breaking away the long handle, the spike still lodged in his thigh. *No time!* He was almost upon the first purple creature when – AAAIIIGGGHHHHH!!! – another spear stabbed into his flesh.

This time just above his elbow. He broke off the handle and swung at the purple creature. But . . . *Noooo!!!* The other purple creature looked up, smiled and pressed the spear into the little girl.

Everything went black.

42
MANHATTAN TRANSFER

DICTATED BY PI BARLOWE FARLOWE . . .

El Nerdo's a good name for this place. It's full of eggheads. And full of offices and floors and laboratories and a giant-giant wall with thousands of screens showing images from EARTHs.

I'm sporting a white coat, trying to look incognito on a bench on the Ground Floor. Potted plants surround us. Tree-fronds overhang us. The place is bustling with people – none of them looking our way. Yet still Max Bohr is uptight. As a fish at a cat convention.

'This all of them?' I ask, scanning down a list.

'Yes, that's all the departments we have here at El Nerdo,' says Bohr, checking behind him.

Once he's sure no passing egg-head has a microphone or a face that says *Gotcha*, I tell him straight: 'Nothing jumps out at me.'

'Of course nothing jumps out at you!' he exclaims. 'You're wrong – no one here would've destroyed those EARTHs.' Then he's back checking for Gotchas.

'Hmm, what's this?' I ask, pointing to a footnote – * *The Manhattan Project is not a full department.*

'Oh, that's just Heimenopper,' laughs Bohr, letting his

tension fizzle out. 'He's a bit odd. They wanted to fire him, but couldn't, so they gave him an office on his own and told him to do "research". They call it the Manhattan Project just to make him feel good. But no one bothers with what he does. I reckon he plays video games all day.'

Turns out Bohr's happy for me to talk to Heimenopper as he's already confided in him 'bout the missing EARTHs. *You don't say?* 'Yeah,' he explains, eyeing passers-by. 'I had to tell *someone* – and I knew Heimenopper wouldn't have any colleagues to gossip to . . . Anyway, he'll tell you the same as me: no one at El Nerdo would've destroyed those EARTHs.'

43
Blown It?

Since viewers saw little of what contestants got up to on Sponsor Destination planets (the footage being focused on promoting sponsors' products), no one saw Tommy venture outside the toilet-roll perimeter on NoFingersThruIt. Therefore nothing seemed remarkable when thirteen contestants popped into the Wigglery one after another on Day Four, followed after the briefest of delays, by Tommy Storm. The boy-in-black sheathed his scimmy before anyone noticed, allowed Rumbles to give him a high four and stood there, catching his breath, while everyone filed out of the room. He'd a tear in his trousers and a hole in his shirt, but the flesh that peeped through was intact. No hint of a wound.

Arriving at the Bowl, he avoided getting dragged into any games and climbed the ladder to the top diving board. There he sat, pondering what'd happened . . . *After they killed the little girl and everything went black, I felt as if I was immersed in liquid. Then the universe blinked and I could breathe and next thing I found myself in the Wigglery . . . But my wounds . . . How did they heal . . ?* His mind drifted from such practicalities and he was hit by the full impact of the little girl being killed. *I failed her. I couldn't save her.* It was a very private grief – something he didn't feel like sharing. Some would say this was because he didn't want to announce his failure to the world. Others might offer a more charitable explanation . . . That Tommy felt he had no one to share it with. Woozie had so annoyed him of late and he didn't feel like talking to Marielle – not now she was 'with' Jay-T. And if he wouldn't speak to Woozie and Marielle, then he certainly wasn't going to open his heart to Rumbles and Summy. Yago was an option, but he didn't know the Cassiothellian quite well enough to discuss such a sensitive topic.

Then a thought hit him. What if the *first* sheet ('*save the girl and triumph*') was in fact the Deadly Scroll and now I've blown it? Because seeing that little girl and following her to her execution – in hindsight it all seemed like a set-up. As if that'd been *the* test. The *one* chance to perform Elza's challenge.

On top of the grief, this was almost too much to bear. And so Tommy hardened his mind. *No, the Deadly Scroll was the third sheet.* And he kept repeating this assertion till it was branded into his soul. *That's why I'm here on ChAOS – ready to perform the Ageing-UnStables-dung challenge on Day Eighteen.*

He refused to descend from the diving board and journey to Planet WhizzNoodle for dinner. When Woozie climbed up and suggested he join them, Tommy asked to be left alone. Marielle tried to coax him with fire – shouting up that he should stop trying to show off to the fans and stop being so silly. Tommy looked like he was on the verge of descending, but then the fans starting chanting super-loudly: 'Don't go! Don't go!'

To cheers of delight, Tommy stayed put.

44
Devious Deceptions

Smaller than a grain of rice, an RCTBonbon gives out electromagnetic 'buzzes' in response to the pressing of an RCTButton.[35] If an RCTBonbon is swallowed, these 'buzzes' are felt as 'extreme bursts of inner tickling' – but have the power to debilitate or even kill. RCTBonbons are hard to trace since victims usually flush them (unknowingly) down the loo within twenty-four hours of swallowing.

On the morning of Day Five, Yago pressed an RCTBonbon into a marshmallow, slipped the marshmallow into a pocket and checked the RCTButton couched in his hand. Then he left the BlahRoom.

Tommy and Woozie landed on a tree house with a view over fourteen billion precariously balanced dominoes. This was Planet Don'tQuake and it looked like a purpose-built, domino-infested assault course.

Like all the other pairs and triplets of contestants who'd plopped out on other tree houses dotted about the landscape, Tommy and Woozie were tethered to each other by a length

35 Short for RemoteControlTicklemeisterBonbon and RemoteControlTrigger-Button – both have been banned across much of the cosmos.

of chain attached round their waists. The tree houses formed a wide circle around a lookout tower, and the challenge for all contestants was to make their way to the tower. Those who made it would have feasts for the next two evenings; those who didn't would have nothing but tripe and turnips instead.

The route to the tower involved walking along moving beams, swinging from suspended rings and climbing over slippery obstacles with lots of leaping in between. Being tethered together made things more difficult for contestants. So did the dominoes. As FionaDeFridge had explained: 'If any of you knock over a domino then *your partners* will each receive a small electric shock for each domino that falls over as a result.'[36]

Tommy was happy to be faced with a challenge – partly because he was starving and wanted to win a feast, but mostly because he hoped 'success' would block out thoughts of the little girl he'd failed.

This should've been an easy task for Tommy and Woozie, trained as they were in Milky Foo. But half an hour in, they were in trouble. Twenty metres off the ground, Tommy was hanging on to a tightrope by one hand and Woozie was flailing about under him, his legs just missing a tower of dominoes. This was the second time Woozie'd fallen (for no reason, it seemed), almost taking Tommy with him.

'OK,' said Tommy. 'Try not to swing. Just grab my leg and pull yourself up.'

36 There were gaps between pools of dominoes, so they wouldn't all fall at once. (To put the 14 billion dominoes in perspective, in 2008 the world record for the highest number of fallen dominoes on Earth was 4.3 million.)

Woozie was on the point of doing so when he lurched to the side and knocked over a tower of dominoes. Tommy shook and yelled as thousands of mini electric shocks ran through him.

'No!' cried Woozie. 'Sorry! Don't know what happened!'

The other contestants were having varying degrees of success. Marielle and Summy had received a set of electric shocks when Rumbles sneezed next to a line of dominoes (Marielle managed to karate-chop her hand between two dominoes to halt their fall) – but apart from that, they were making good progress.

Yago and Jay-T were going well (though some commentators noted that their obstacles seemed easier than everyone else's). The only thing delaying them was Yago stopping now and again to look across at the forms of Tommy and Woozie in the distance. 'What're you laughing at, man?' asked Jay-T.

'Oh, nothing,' replied the sandy-haired boy, shielding a red-buttoned remote control from Jay-T's view. 'Just thinking about marshmallows.'

Jay-T nodded and smiled. 'That was cool of you to organize hot chocolate this morning and serve us all up mugfuls.'

'Thanks,' said Yago. 'I made sure no one went without.'

The hooter for the end of the challenge went at an unfortunate moment for Tommy. He and Woozie had almost made it to the lookout tower when Woozie fell again, knocking over yet more dominoes. Somehow, thanks to Tommy's lifting, Woozie had his feet on the tower just as the final hooter sounded. Tommy, two steps away was deemed to have failed the challenge.

'They did that on purpose!' cried Woozie. 'There should've been a warning hooter before the final hooter.'

Tommy had other thoughts on who'd done what on purpose. But he said nothing cos he knew his suspicions were crazy. *Why on Earth would Woozie sabotage me?*

Only Woozie, Marielle, Rumbles, Summy, Yago and Jay-T succeeded in the challenge and, while everyone else ate tripe and turnips in the Bowl (Tommy eating his alone on the top diving board, acknowledging the cheers of fans and a few new banners – '*You would've done it without Woozie!*'), the 'challenge achievers' were whisked off to PizzaParadizzo, a planet that was literally covered in 'a carpet of pizza' (you just pulled sods of pizza from the ground). Before they returned to the Bowl, DeFridge warned: 'You will all walk through a pizza X-ray machine before you jump through the wigglehole. Anyone caught smuggling pizza back for other contestants will go without food for the next *ten days.*' This was enough of a threat to put everyone off such a venture.

And yet, after he returned from his chat with the producers in the BlahRoom, Yago climbed up to the top diving board and presented Tommy with some pizza he claimed to have smuggled. Tommy was chuffed and hugely impressed. His so-called other friends hadn't wanted to take the risk.

Tommy was sitting with Yago, munching pizza, when the fans outside gave a roar. A giant scoreboard had appeared outside the Bowl.

RANK	CONTESTANT	SELECTED VOTER COMMENT
1	BERYL MACPAIRYL	PERIL MACPRANKSTER, MOOR LIKE!
2	CHARLES LEMASS	UR A PROPER CHARLIE
3	TOMMY STORM	THE B-B-BRAVEST TOBOGGANER – GIZZA KISS
4	YAGO	A TRUE FREND
5	JAY-T	SLIP ME SUM SKIN
6	WOOZIE	*AN IGGY KNIGHT* – HA HA, I LUV IT!
7	ZESTRELLA	I'D LIKE 2 UNKNOT UR TENTACLS!
8	RUMBLES	WOT'S WITH DA SILLY WORDSKEYS?
9	MARIELLE	STOP BEING SO CRANKY
10	BERNARD BURNSIDE	JUST JUMP!
11	LILLROYSEN	Y DON'T U STING SUM 1?
12	J/S YUSS	IT *IS* ALL DAT BAD, JOE!
13	SUMMY	A NERD A BIT OF U R
14	ULADRACK	EVEN *TWO* WORDS!?

'Hey, you've done OK,' said Yago, adding quietly: 'Though not everyone will be happy.'

'What do you m-mean?'

It took some cajoling before Yago (reluctantly) revealed: 'I overheard your friend Woozie saying how you're getting all big-headed and showing off to the fans when only a few days ago you were *a big unco-ordinated lump*.'

'He said *that*?'

'I'm sure he didn't mean it . . . Probably just jealous that they like you better.'

Tommy couldn't quite believe it. And yet . . . It explained a lot.

It took some effort, but Yago managed to distract Tommy from his thoughts. He even managed to make him laugh lots over the next hour or two. The Cassiothellian was very good at building up the dark Earthling's pride after its recent battering. 'Third place – that means billions of votes . . . And look at that placard out there.' (It said, *We ❤ u Tommy*.) 'And that one . . . And that one.'

When Tommy stood up on the diving board to get a better look, the crowd began cheering and waving. He beamed back at them. The cheering, the thought of all those votes coming in for him – they were like an anaesthetic, allowing him to forget about his failures, about his grief for a little girl, about the TFC, and even about four particular creatures down below. Yes, it was good to know that the IGGY Knights weren't his only friends in the universe.

45

Not Forever

A-Sad-Bin-Liner's face lit up the back of the fridge. 'It is all settled,' he said. 'Day Twelve. That's when you kill them.'

Mister Oodid, surrounded by chocolate ammunition, punched the air. 'Yehooo! Up the Mentaler Fundyists!'

But the cry and the sight of a 'choco ammo' belt expelled his excitement and he saw an image of his own gravestone – the words 'ChAOS – Day Twelve' etched across it. 'Well, then,' he said, touched by melancholy. 'This is goodbye . . . Forever.' And he rubbed his two buck teeth and patted down his wispy moustache as though preparing for a final photo.

'No, no. Not forever,' rejoined Bin-Liner. 'May you enjoy JB Kennell till I join you there one day . . . And please. Don't chew all the bones.'

Belly Dancers Wanted – No Experience Necessary

Mentaler Fundyists are a secret (and secretive) sect of people who believe if they die 'saving the universe from being saved', they will live out the rest of eternity in a figure-of-eight-shaped cave beyond the universe. Although potentially crowded, this cave, known as JuicyBone Kennell by creatures with canine DNA and as DangledCarrot Warren by creatures with sheep DNA, is said to have an inexhaustible supply of muffins, skinny lattes, carrots and juicy bones. Sect members worried about boredom can console themselves with the 'certainty' that '333 belly dancers continually entertain the kennel's (or warren's) occupants.' Bin-Liner's comment – 'Don't chew all the bones' – would've been considered a light-hearted joke, since the bone supply is, and ever shall be, inexhaustible (and, in any case, Dell would've been far more interested in the carrots).

Note: it's never been clarified whether the same 333 belly dancers keep going for eternity or if a much larger pool of belly dancers performs the task in shifts.

46

Betrayed by a Kiss

Tommy saw something on Day Eight that completely devastated him.

The two previous days on ChAOS had passed without major incident. Day Six was noteworthy only for the fact that Tommy was on breakfast duty and went out of his way to fulfil a special request from Zestrella, receiving nothing more than a cut-glass Thank You in return. It wasn't the rudeness that annoyed him most. No, it was the fact that he cared.

After a brief furore, caused by all the eggs mysteriously vanishing from the fridge, Day Seven's main event involved a trip to a moon which circled a barren planet called Hurricane-1-in-50trillion. Contestants had to take it in turns to 'create' objects on the planet by means of a giant interactive screen.

When it came to Tommy's go, he scrolled down a list of Possible Ingredients, ticking bits of wire, strips of fabric, fragments of metal, rubber, plastic, steel and so on. When he was finished, a giant dumpster poured tonnes of these 'ingredients' on to the planet. Then, when he pressed a button marked *Hurricane – Go!*, the clouds over the planet began whisking faster and faster and the screen showed all the ingredients being whipped into a frenzy. Every now and again everything would freeze and an object would (briefly) become visible on the ground. Tommy saw a rickety fence, and then a giant hairdryer, followed by a statue of a one-legged weasel. As DeFridge had explained: 'The storm whips the ingredients into over 50 trillion forms every second. Any time one of these forms takes up a recognizable shape, everything freezes so you can see the object. If this is the object you want to accept, then press the *Stop* button. If you don't press it on time, then the storm will restart, breaking up the object – so the whole process can start again.'

Tommy's final 'creation' was nothing more than an ugly, square-wheeled digger – which meant he forfeited dinner that evening. Yago tried to cheer him up, explaining: 'They made us use an old worn-out Hurricane-A-Go-Go today. If they'd given us the *latest* model, you could've created a masterpiece!' During the conversation, Tommy felt a wave of joy and relief. Not because of Yago's words, but because his stutter suddenly disappeared. ('Elza was right – it really is linked to travel sickness!').

Day Eight was another Sponsor Day, the contestants landing separately on Planet NoZits – another beautiful place, except that the ground here was dotted with small, puss-filled molehills.

Jay-T, following Yago's instructions, sought out Marielle. 'Hey, sister,' he said. 'Come with me and I'll help you find what you've lost.' Despite the fact that he wouldn't answer any questions, Marielle, still desperate to find her hanky, went with him.

They ended up in a clearing on a spot Yago had ear-marked.

Jay-T thanked the stars that he had Yago as a friend. The Cassiothellian had not only noticed how he fancied Marielle, but had offered to help him win her affections. Three days earlier on Planet NofingersThruIt, Yago had presented him with a hanky that he promised held a certain power over the elquinine.

And now Marielle was standing before him.'Hey, prettiness,' he said. 'I can procure for you a certain polka-dot hanky . . . *if* you plant one here.' Jay-T pointed to his lips.

Marielle was about to shout an obscenity and storm away, but something made her halt. 'A *red* polka-dot hanky?' Jay-T nodded. 'And you can *definitely* procure it?'

Unbeknownst to Marielle or to Jay-T, they were standing in a spot overlooked by a well-camouflaged camera. And at that very moment, Tommy was whisked from the planet back to the Wigglery – where a large screen was showing footage from NoZits. The sound was muted, but he could see Marielle and Jay-T standing before each other. White blobs started falling all around them and Tommy had his first inkling of how romantic snow can be (it was actually NoZitCream™ falling from the sky and, as it covered everything, the puss-filled molehills were fading to nothing).

Tommy saw Marielle and Jay-T move in close. He watched as Marielle leaned in, kissing Jay-T on the lips. Then the screen went dead.

What Tommy didn't see was Marielle jumping back quickly from the kiss and demanding: 'OK, now how can you get me my hanky?'

Jay-T removed a blood-stained polka-dotted item from his pocket. But if he expected some thanks or another kiss, he was in for a shock. For the elquinine snatched the hanky from his grasp and smacked him hard across the cheek. 'Aaaaiiiiiiggggghhhh!' she cried. 'I should've known!' And just before they were whisked away through a wigglehole to join the other contestants in the Bowl, she added: 'Don't you ever touch any of my things again or you'll be sorry.' The words carried such ferocity that Jay-T said nothing in reply and, from that moment forth, he ceased trying to win her affections.

Tommy spent much of Evening Eight up on the highest diving board with Yago. He found that laughing with the rabbity-eared boy or listening to his disc player or even standing up and making the crowds below leap and cheer were the best ways to forget about Marielle and everything else.

At one point Woozie climbed up the ladder towards them, hearing giggling as he made the ascent. But once he reached the top, where Tommy and Yago were sitting side-by-side – he was greeted with complete silence.

'Hey,' he ventured.

Yago was the only one to turn around – holding a tiny music disc-player – but he said nothing.

'What would you prefer,' said Woozie, 'to have to eat nothing but baked-beings for two years or to lick *all* of Charles Lemass's underarms?'

'Uugh!' replied Yago. 'Why would you want to do either? That's just weird.'

'It's a joke,' said Woozie.

‘So that’s what you climbed all the way up here to say?’ said Yago, feeding a corner of cheese into a pocket. ‘The best thing you could come up with after chewing on your girly dog tags for the last half-hour?’

Woozie was stung – for that indeed was the best he could come up with after half an hour ‘chewing’ in a corner by the pool. But what hurt him most was that Tommy said nothing and didn’t turn around.

‘Come on, let’s dive-bomb,’ said Yago. And, grabbing Tommy, he leapt off the diving board.

‘Noooo!’ cried Tommy, half-laughing, half-screaming as he fell through the air.

Woozie was left on the diving board – all alone – as Lillroysen, Joe Yuss and Charles Lemass were splashed to kingdom come. Unfortunately for the wibblewallian, he had no idea that Tommy’d been deaf to the world. For the Earthling had been wearing wireless earphones and listening to one of Yago’s favourite songs – *Live and Let Die*.

On Evening Nine, after visiting Planet Notcardboardy® Muesli (a mountainous place covered in a layer of dried fruit and oats), and after regaling the fans with somersaults off the Edge to the crash-mat in the Basement, Tommy found himself in the Wigglery with Yago, just as a scoreboard appeared outside the Bowl.

CHAOS LEADERBOARD: RUNNING TOTAL OF VOTES		
RANK	CONTESTANT	SELECTED VOTER COMMENT
1	TOMMY STORM	UR DEADLY – SO FABULOUSLY NAWTY!
2	YAGO	A LOOTENANT IF EVR DERE WAS 1
3	BERYL MACPAIRYL	I DINNA KEN Y UR FALLIN' DOON DA LEADERBORD
4	ZESTRELLA	Y DON'T U KUM UP & C ME SUMTIME?
5	CHARLES LEMASS	O, UR ALL VERY QUIET OVER DERE!
6	JAY-T	WOT A KISSER!
7	WOOZIE	U CAN SAVE ME ANYTIME
8	BERNARD BURNSIDE	IF U WON'T JUMP, LET US PUSH U!
9	LILLROYSEN	I WANT UR LUNCH MONEY – NOW!!
10	RUMBLES	56 MINS TO DO A NO. 7!??
11	J/S YUSS	NO USE CRYING OVER UNSPILT MILK
12	MARIELLE	UR IN LUV WITH HIM, RITE?
13	SUMMY	SAW U STUFING MUESLI IN UR POUCH!
14	VLADRACK	SUMBODY STEAL UR TUNG?

It wasn't the fact that he was leading that most affected Tommy. No, it was the comment next to Marielle's name (he presumed it referred to Jay-T). For it made his heart squeeze tight – even more than when he'd seen the elquinine kiss Jay-T. And he resolved to ignore the elquinine from then on.

And though a smattering of light acne had flared across his shoulder blades, the young Earthling told himself he should be happy. *My stutter's gone, my co-ordination's back, I've got great new friends and the public like me . . . This thing with Marielle is no big deal . . .* He even managed to convince himself that the episode with the little girl in the red smock had been 'just a dream'. *The chemicals on Planet NoFingersThruIt must've gone to my head and made me hallucinate.* And he clung more fiercely than ever to the belief that the Deadly Scroll was the third sheet – the one about Mount Neverrest and the Ageing-UnStables dung challenge. In a moment of weakness, he conceded there was a 'theorectical possibility' that it could be the second sheet ('the weird poem'), but one thing was *definite* . . . The Deadly Scroll was NOT 'save the girl & triumph'. No way had he, Tommy Storm, blown the one chance to perform Elza's challenge.

It was this thought, perhaps, that made the young Earthling do something slightly crazy. He jumped through the Entrance wigglehole.

As he flew through the air, the thought occurred to him that he could plop out somewhere dangerous with no way back. But in a way, he didn't care. In fact, the more dangerous the better.

No sooner had he disappeared through the Entrance than he flashed through the shadow below the Exit sign and skidded on his knees across the Wigglery floor. 'Weeee!' he cried. 'Yago, check out the wiggleholes' night-setting!'

He and Yago did so many raucous jumps that most of the other contestants came down (via the peg-pole lift[37]) to give it a go. Bernard was particularly keen, since she still hadn't managed to leap off the Edge to the Basement crash-mat.

Only Zestrella Ravisham, Uladrack, Woozie and Marielle refrained from joining in. Zestrella because it was 'too

37 This was a chain-like contraption with pegs sticking out of its side. It moved in a continuous circle between the Edge and the Basement, allowing people to be transported between levels – you just had to be careful jumping on and off!

boring', Uladrack because she avoided 'group' activities, Woozie because 'I don't feel like it', and Marielle because she was in a huff.

Whether it was charging down to the Wigglery or dive-bombing into the pool or acting all cool – Marielle felt Tommy Storm was showing off. She could've sworn he loved the fans' adulation and even placed some store in the silly, stupid scoreboard . . . But even worse, in recent days, she perceived another reason for his grandstanding.

Zestrella Ravisham.

She was some cold fish. Marielle struggled to get two words out of her and shuddered when she did. *And they call Uladrack the mute!* Zestrella . . . How Marielle dreamed of throwing a pie in that cocksure face and maybe a chocolate tart at that yellow, spotless dress.

Apart from the pathetic show-for-Zestrella, Tommy was spending more and more time with Yago, someone Marielle didn't trust. As a result, poor Woozie looked quite lost at times.

When she saw the scoreboard with its comment – '*Ur in luv with him, right?*' – Marielle presumed some fan had seen through her anger and was referring to Tommy. For some reason, the comment – its very question – made her sad.

47

A Brief Word about Three Contestants (and a duel)

One person who changed quite literally during his stay in the Bowl was Joe Yuss. On Night Nine, he climbed into his sleeping bag – the sleeping, miniature, burgundy polar bear who shared his tail tucked in at his feet. In the morning, Joe Yuss had disappeared, replaced by a large burgundy polar bear who bounced out of the sleeping bag with a smile. Attached to her tail was a sleep-walking, miniature, pink-champagne polar bear.

'What a beautiful day!' she exclaimed to everyone she passed. She became an instant hit.

Joe and Syri Yuss were actually one creature known as a bi-polar bear. One of them is always 'hibernating' (i.e. small and asleep) leaving the other one 'in the ascendancy' (i.e. big and generally awake). They hibernate alternately and each hibernation can last anything from two to fifteen days.

Someone who appeared to change little during her initial stay was Uladrack – she of the smoggy-grey cape and blue-black hair pulled over her face. Despite the veil of hair, it was just possible to make out that she was ever-so pale, wore thick-rimmed glasses and had an oddness about her teeth. Something you couldn't work out on first sight. Often she'd bite her nails and scratch her head as if expecting to find little creatures – strange, since her hair smelt fresh and gleamed in the moonlight. Whenever Beryl MacPairyl tried to pour something down her back or push her into the swimming pool, she'd squawk loudly. Much of the time she spent leaning into her wardrobe, cape outstretched, so you couldn't see what she was up to.

Tommy thought her very odd. Particular when he heard from Yago that she was a breed of vampire. 'She drinks blood,' he'd said. 'I wouldn't want to be the person sleeping next to her!'

Rumbles and Marielle had wardrobes either side of hers. The first time Marielle spoke to her, it was to ask if she'd mind swapping wardrobes – so she could move away from Jay-T. But the 'vampire' gave a loud squawk and climbed head-first into her sleeping bag.

Rumbles was a little afraid of Uladrack, but Marielle, who was always looking for an excuse to avoid Jay-T at bedtime, persisted in her attempts to engage the strange girl in conversation. She'd face towards her when gathering night things and make comments such as: 'How are we expected to sleep with that Charles Lemass snoring? I wouldn't mind but there are thirty of him!' After a few days, Uladrack started responding – in a low tone – to these overtures.

From then on, Tommy often spotted the elquinine and the 'vampire' in the Biblioteck setting mousetraps, but he never heard Uladrack speak.

'The Biblioteck's a good place for a mute!' laughed Yago. 'You know, I was in the Wigglery yesterday, looking through the floor, and I saw her sitting in the Biblioteck on her own – *eating dead mice*!' The Cassiothellian's eyes welled. 'How could anyone hurt a tiny creature like that?'

The Biblioteck was full of books, atlases, desks, chairs and mouse traps. It had a glass ceiling and was situated on the first floor above the Basement.

Lillroysen was another contestant who didn't so much change as gradually reveal himself. He positively buzzed with energy and was always asking others to join him in activities such as gammonback[38] (people usually refused) or leg wrestling (the school-uniformed boy generally lost).

On Day Ten, when he saw Zestrella was watching, Tommy accepted Lillroysen's third request (in as many days) for a fake-sword duel . . .

The reason? Well, only the previous evening Lillroysen and Bernard had fought a fake-sword duel – and Tommy'd noticed the thrill Zestrella got from watching fierce competition (her antennae criss-crossed and went super-rigid). Later, Tommy realized it wasn't *competition* she enjoyed watching. But a fight. Between two males.

Within seconds of the fake duel commencing, Lillroysen was doubled over, winded from a (blunt) blow.

As he knelt beside Lillroysen, checking the little fellow was OK, Tommy saw a glint of something – pleasure? – in Zestrella's eyes, antennae vibrating. She passed him with a half smile. 'You're good,' she whispered, antennae bowed. For the rest of that day (during the visit to Planet Shagadellic™ – a beautiful wilderness with every flat surface covered in thick woolly carpet), and for most of that night, Tommy replayed those words. *I'm good.*

38 A board game involving two pairs of dice and thirty 'checkers' made from dried pork.

48

Denial of Love

'Welcome back!' cried FionaDeFridge twenty-three hours before the tragic events of Day Twelve. 'To ChAOS – the best TV show in the universe . . . You are about to witness . . . not a challenge . . . not a sponsor planet . . . But *Inquisition Afternoon* – featuring the three contestants you voted to hear from!'

The next image TV viewers saw was that of Charles Lemass, Uladrack and Tommy Storm tied to three chairs in a dark room on some godforsaken planet.

The camera panned back to reveal a figure wearing a black tutor's gown and a black mortar board upon his head. With two thumbs hooked under his lapels, he was pinning the three unfortunates with a steely glare. 'I am an eagle-eyed-canine-sapian,' he declared. 'The name is Brother Mallard Murphy Roshviler . . . But you may call me *sir*.'

Roshviler had an eagle-like face that stood for no nonsense. 'Today I will be asking you questions sent in by viewers,' he continued. 'My role is simple – to *ensure* I get the truth.' He leant on a desk that was shrouded in darkness. 'Have any of you heard of VIVo?' Charles, Uladrack and Tommy shook their heads. 'It stands for VeritasInVino – the strongest truth-serum known to eagle-eyed-canine-sapian or beast.' And he brandished three hypodermic needles. 'Let's hope you all co-operate and we don't have to use it.'

Tommy tried to suppress a grin. After all the training on Swiggy, he reckoned he could beat a silly serum.

'Oh, and I will be aided by one other thing,' smiled Roshviler. 'We came across it on one of your spacecraft – it had marvellous instructions sellotaped underneath.'

A spotlight clicked on over the desk, illuminating a certain object. Tommy recognized it at once. The colour drained from his face.

'Yes,' said Roshviler, eyeing the Earthling. 'This is *PoF!*'

The eagle-eyed-canine-sapian approached the many heads that made up Charles Lemass. 'So tell me,' he said. 'Have any of you ever stolen food from one of your . . . *companions*?'

Charles's heads looked at each other and replied in unison: 'No! Never!'

PoF! gave two loud buzzes. It also buzzed when Uladrack denied having ever eaten mice. Roshviler tutted and came to Tommy.

'Mister Storm,' he said. 'I have a question about Marielle. You have just heard your two fellow-contestants lie. Are you prepared to tell the truth?'

'Er, yes,' said Tommy. *PoF!* buzzed.

'Such a shame,' said Roshviler. And his face filled with sadistic pleasure as he raised a hypodermic needle to the camera, demonstrating its pointiness. 'Yes, a shame none of you saw fit to co-operate.'

By the time viewers returned from an ad break, Charles and Uladrack were looking quite drowsy, Tommy a tad tired.

'So, Mister Lemass,' smiled Roshviler. 'Have any of you ever stolen food from one of your . . . *companions*?' Thirty heads looked up at the tutor, fighting to button their lips. 'Don't answer to me,' added Roshviler. 'Speak to your nearest companion.'

After a pause, one of the heads answered, 'Er, yes.'

'I knew it!' cried another head.

Then another head piped up: 'Me too – I've stolen food.'

Within seconds, every head had admitted to the same offence and was arguing with its nearest companion. The cameras focused in on a sleepy-looking Uladrack as Charles was dragged from the room – all his heads trying to head-butt one another.

'So, Miss Kownt,' intoned Roshviler. 'Do you eat mice?' (Kownt was Uladrack's surname.)

'Eh . . .'

'Come-come!' pressed the eagle-eyed-canine-sapian. 'Don't fight it!'

It seemed as though Uladrack was straining to say no, but gave up. 'Yes!' she cried, flushed from exertion. 'Yes! They're tasty, oh-so-tasty. Especially with sliced ginger. Or rosemary.'

After a few more questions, Uladrack had admitted to stealing eggs from the fridge and bottles of sauce from the cooler and was blathering: 'No, I don't need these glasses! I hide behind them. And behind my hair!'

And after yet more questions, she was yelling: 'Because I'm shy, OK? . . . Because I'm scared! . . . Please . . . *I DON'T KNOW WHY!* I don't know . . ! I don't . . .' She was in tears.

Roshviler turned to Tommy as the 'vampire's' chair was dragged away. 'Just you and me, Mister Storm . . . You've seen what happens when people try to resist . . . Are you going to co-operate?'

'Yes.' *BUZZ!*

Roshviler looked startled. He'd never heard anyone beat the serum before. 'Eh . . . Ah, yes, obvious . . . Not enough VIVo.' And he produced another hypodermic needle.

Two minutes later, Tommy looked a little drowsier. And Roshviler looked quite smug. 'So, Mister Storm,' he said. 'I can tell that *now* you are ready to tell the truth – right?'

After a pause, Tommy smiled. 'Yes.' *PoF!* buzzed loudly.

In ChAOS's TV control room, a producer roared into a microphone. 'He's beaten the serum! Tommy Storm's beaten VIVo!'

An astonished Roshviler pressed his earpiece, nodded and fiddled with the back of *PoF!*. 'Oh, sorry . . . a slight mechanical fault.' Once he was finished, his imperious manner returned. 'Where were we . . ? Ah yes . . . Mister Storm . . . Tell me how you really feel about Marielle . . . You fancy her, don't you? Or is it more than that?'

Tommy had a moment of panic. With everything that'd gone on, he didn't know how he felt any more. But what if he said he didn't love Marielle and *PoF!* buzzed? Then he'd look like an idiot . . . But the alternative – saying he *did* love her – was even worse. Plus it probably wasn't even true. Was it?'

An image of the elquinine kissing Jay-T reared up in his mind and he heard himself blurting: 'No, I don't fancy her!' No buzz. 'And I don't love her.' Still no buzz!

Tommy felt the silence with a relief he hadn't known in months. Hearing himself say that he didn't love Marielle and *not* hearing a buzz – it was balm on tender wounds. So she'd betrayed him, fallen for Jay-T – well, hey, it couldn't be all that bad if he didn't actually love the maddening elquinine.

And it emboldened him. How far could he push things before *PoF!* buzzed? He was as interested in these questions as the viewers and other contestants (who, unknown to him were watching on a big screen in the Bowl). Perhaps even as interested as a certain elquinine who was swimming in the pool, pretending not to be listening to every word.

'I never loved her,' continued Tommy. 'And I never thought about marrying her or one day having kids . . . I never, never think of times when we've laughed together or . . .'

Tommy continued the litany till Roshviler asked another question, twiddling with the back of *PoF!*.

'Zestrella Ravisham?' exclaimed Tommy. 'I've hardly noticed her.'

BUZZ!!

As Tommy was dragged from the room, neither he nor the viewers realized that *PoF!* had been switched off for all his comments about Marielle. And then switched on again.

49

Death by Chocolate

A variety of factors – not just Tommy's comments in the Inquisition – convinced Marielle that the IGGY Knights must leave ChAOS *immediately*. And so, without consulting Tommy (she knew he'd advise against), she made a decision. Yes, it was a risk, but Woozie'd already blurted about the TFC on live TV and, when the universe is at stake, some risks are worth taking. Surely, five other kids could be found to take the IGGY Knights' places on the show . . .

Having convinced Woozie, Rumbles and Summy of the merits of her plan, the elquinine led them below the Bowl. And so, while Tommy, Yago and others were jumping about in the Wigglery, the four Knights locked themselves in the BlahRoom, refusing to leave till they'd spoken to the producers.

Eventually, the wall opposite lit up with the head-and-shoulder image of a wolf-like creature wearing an expensive suit. 'I'm Wolfstain – the producer,' barked the image. 'Next time you pull a stunt like this, I'll have your sleeping bags sprayed with skunkmeister and all toilet paper removed from the Bowl!' Rumbles looked at Summy in consternation. 'You've got five minutes to say what you gotta say.'

‘Not a chance,’ said Wolfstain when he’d heard their explanation and pleas.

‘But we’ve got to get out of here!’

‘On it the future of the universe depends.’

‘Kids, you ask one more time – or even try to escape – and I’ll have your spacecraft busted. Then you’ll be stuck here for a lot longer than three weeks.’

‘But please—’

‘One more time!’ bellowed Wolfstain.

The four went silent, till Marielle piped up. ‘I’m not pleading, not asking you for anything, but didn’t you hear what we said – about the TFC, about the end of the universe?’

Wolfstain broke into a smile. ‘Every word. And, what a story! The audience will love it!’

‘But you agreed this is a private conversation!’

‘And this isn’t a *story*! It’s the truth.’

‘*The truth*. Ha ha. I love it,’ said Wolfstain. And the screen went dead.

Had the door to the BlahRoom not remained locked for a further ten minutes, Marielle, Rumbles, Summy or Woozie might’ve got to Tommy before a screen appeared in the Wigglery. It showed (edited) footage of the conversation with Wolfstain. Most of the contestants found it a hoot. But Tommy was wounded to the core. His so-called friends had gone behind his back. His so-called friends were prepared to leave the show without him (that’s what the edited footage was made to sound like). And his so-called friends had revealed to trillions of viewers what should be revealed to no one. They’d put everything in jeopardy.

'Good morning and welcome!' cried FionaDeFridge. 'To Day Twelve and the Yikes-Get-Back Challenge . . . The only thing the contestants have been told is that they must return to the Bowl *as fast as possible*. Last back gets no meals for three days!'

DeFridge eased closer to the camera. 'Viewers,' she whispered. 'What the contestants don't know is that they're not being sent to a remote planet. Oh, no – they'll emerge on this black circle behind me . . . Fifty-three metres from the Bowl entrance . . . Fifty-three of the longest metres they'll ever encounter.' She pressed her earpiece. 'And, yes, we're almost ready.'

She scuttled into a craft docked by the Arrivals Platform. It rose up and the barricades lowered into the ground. The fans poured forth, trampling over one another, heaving around the black circle, those on the edge pushing backwards, fearful of setting a foot inside.

And stuffed amongst them, looking like an ordinary fan, was a man with buck teeth and a wispy moustache called Dell. Counting down the seconds, he patted his bulky jacket. Yes, the chocolate 'goodies' were strapped tight. And none of the jostling idiots was aware that the object in his hand was a detonator. That all he had to do was squeeze and then everyone – *everyone* – within a three-metre radius would be killed outright (including Dell himself).

For soon he would be in DangledCarrot Warren Paradise.

Standing side-by-side in the Wigglery, the contestants were feeling tense. Would the Entrance take them to a fiery mountain-top or to an unforgiving void? Marielle, who usually displayed a healthy lack of interest in accomplishing ChAOS challenges, was coiled like a sprinter, studiously avoiding Tommy's eye. He'd so hurt her feelings with his cruel words during the Inquisition that she wanted to 'beat' him today and to banish all thoughts of the Wolfstain 'chat' from her mind.

Like Marielle, Tommy was primed. He too was eye-avoiding – avoiding those of the four people who'd betrayed him (he'd spent the rest of the previous evening on the high diving board refusing to listen to any entreaties from his so-called fellow Knights).

Roshviler lashed a whip against the wall – the starter signal – and the contestants were off. Leaping through the Entrance, they were packed close – Marielle and Tommy out front, Charles elbowing Woozie and others in the middle, and Rumbles, Lillroysen and Summy picking up the rear (Rumbles trod on Summy's tail piercing, causing them both to stumble, and Yago tripped Lillroysen – he'd taken to bullying the stripy-haired boy of late – always out of Tommy's sight, as if he knew it'd meet with disapproval).

The (surviving) fans and contestants would recall many different versions of the ensuing minutes, yet all remembered the contestants landing on the circle and springing in all directions to avoid 'the most demented leers, hands and tails.' Seconds later, something exploded and there was chocolate and limbs everywhere.

Thinking this was part of the challenge, the surviving contestants continued scrambling over, under and through the crowd, and the fans kept on grabbing, scratching and ripping – trying to snatch a piece of their heroes.

This was survival at its most basic. *Everyone for themselves.* Trying to find or help a fellow contestant would only draw more fans and worsen their plight (and yours). Those contestants who made it back to the Bowl alive were covered in cuts and bruises, and had a lot less hair, fur or clothing than before. Approaching a commercial break, the cameras panned in on two dead creatures on the ground. One had sandy hair, rabbity ears and the remains of a waggly tail (still twitching). The other was human, with a darkish face, short dark hair and black clothes clinging to its dismembered body parts.

50
Death a-Knocking

DICTATED BY PI BARLOWE FARLOWE . . .

'Mister Heimenopper!'

I'm on a balcony – one of hundreds hugging the inside of El Nerdo's elliptical-shaped wall – and pounding like a no-good punk on a heavy office door.

'I know you're in there,' I say, though in truth I know nothing. 'I don't know why you won't speak to me. Max Bohr called you, told you who I am . . . Why did you hang up on him, Mister Heimenopper?'

Still nada. I try another tack. 'I know about the TSC, Mister Heimenopper. I know you're behind it and if you don't talk me to now, I'll have no choice but to—'

The door opens quarter-way and a donkey-faced man brays out at me. 'What're you saying!? I have nothing to do with the TSC! You don't know what you're saying. Now, go away!'

One bluff and this guy's cracked. I try another. 'I know it's your hand's been doing the crushing.'

He looks real pale now. 'Don't know what you're talking about,' he brays, trying to close the door.

But as the wood hits my foot, I realize where I've heard

that deep donkey voice before. 'I am Death,' I say, all dramatic. 'Destroyer of worlds.'

He looks at me like I'm not kidding.

The office is cluttered and musty and lit by a single over-hanging light that leaves shadows crawling over the shelves. I half expect to see one of those typewriters you see in ancient museums.

'I've done nothing. You can't prove a thing!' Heimenopper keeps repeating these words as I give his office the once-over. A fish-tank-shaped object in the middle of the room covered by a sheet, a small portable TV on a high shelf (muted) showing hare-brained racing from Planet Mugzgame, a desk strewn with papers and pencil sharpeners and . . ! I pick up a stub that reads '$20,000 Mick-the-Miller To Win 3:55'. *BINGO!*

'Er, that's not mine,' brays Heimenopper.

My watch reads 15:54. The TV shows another hare-brained race is about to start. 15:55 – and they're off! Twelve hares chasing a greyhound round a track. Whichever hare passes the finishing line *last* wins the race.

'If this ain't yours then you won't care who wins,' I say.

He gulps. Shakes his head and tries to look calm. Twenty seconds later and nine hares have crossed the finish line. Three – including Mick-the-Miller – have come to a halt, metres short of it, nibbling leaves on the track. A minute later and they're still there, inching forwards.

Veins are popping in Heimenopper's neck. I think he's gonna bust a gut when he bursts out: 'Slow down! Slow down, you little beauty!'

And it looks like The Miller's gonna 'win', till some

steward throws a handful of nuts and he scurries across the line, ahead of the other two.

'Noooooooo!' cries Heimenopper, head in his hands.

'Not your betting slip?' I says. 'Mister Heimenopper, I don't know how you crushed those planets, but now I got *motive*.'

A Sure Thing

In hare-brained racing, the greyhound is dressed in a bus costume and the hares' brains are 'wired' (or 'brained'), making them think they're late for a bus. Hare-brained aficionados place bets on which hare will be *last* to 'catch the bus'. According to the strict rules of the sport, all hares should be given performance-enhancing drugs to make them go *faster*. This way, the 'true slow-coaches' can shine through. However, some hare owners have been known to give fake performance-enhancing drugs to their hares and, worse still, feed them half a bottle of Beaujolais and a bowl of sherry trifle just before the race (strictly against the rules of the sport). In the most extreme case, an owner was found to have switched the wires being plugged into his hare's head. Instead of thinking he was late for a bus when the starting traps opened, the hare thought he was a tuna sandwich and refused to budge. Three times he won the Gamblers Synonymous No-University-For-Your-Kids Championship before the authorities cottoned on to him.

He opens up like a bottle of Fizzaholic Crater Dew. Turns out he's in the hole for thousands of squalors. Has had a gambling problem for years. Some heavy by the name of A-Sad-Bin-Liner heard of his woes and offered to pay him handsome. All he had to do was build a contraption that could destroy planet EARTHs and keep everything secret. The sheet comes off the fish-tank and I see the Case of Death.

Each time he crushes a planet it's on Bin-Liner's express instructions and Heimenopper gets another injection of squalors into his bank account. Just not enough to keep up with his habit.

I'm about to read him the riot act when the TV flickers. They've gone from the 16:45 to a news bulletin. The pictures show an explosion scene and it's chaos. No, I mean, *it's ChAOS*. Looks like the human's been killed.

51
Deadly Serious

Slow-motion footage of the moments before the chocolate-atomic-explosion showed a buck-toothed man in a bulky jacket heaving forwards when the contestants appeared on the Arrivals Platform. He seemed alarmed (this was because the FiiVe were not packed close together) and made a lunge towards the circle. Perhaps there was a fault with his detonator, for he clenched his hand, looked down and clenched again. It took two more clenches before his explosives detonated.

In the time it took to make those clenches, three fans, furious at being pushed, grabbed the man by the ears and slung him over their shoulders. Had the Cocoa Detonator (as the meteortabloids dubbed him) not been flying through the air when his 'bomb' went off, many more could've been killed.

As it was, twenty-three fans and two contestants lost their lives – and dozens more were injured – in 'the tragic events of Day Twelve' (as FionaDeFridge repeatedly termed the incident).

The two contestants who 'copped it' were Beryl MacPairyl and Jay-T. As Pastor Pastrami put it in a televised service that evening: 'It's how Beryl would've wanted to go – in a violent "prank" . . . And as for Jay-T – he no longer feels any pain. But our thoughts are with those who miss him most and are feeling untold pain.' With that, he gave Marielle a significant look and the cameras panned to the elquinine's face and did a split-screen shot of Jay-T's coffin – covered in paper flowers and paper figurines (one of which looked to be a female elquinine).

Like many viewers who watched the explosion live, you're probably thinking . . . Wait . . . Didn't Tommy and Yago die in the blast? The answer is no. At least seven of the fans who lost their lives were wearing FooledYaBodySuitMasks™ made up to look like Bowl contestants (these victims included two Tommies, two Zestrellas, a Yago, a Jay-T and a Marielle).

'If I said you had a beautiful BodySuitMask, would you hold it against me?'
(line from a popular song across the cosmos)

FooledYaBodySuitMasks™ were a popular product across much of the universe and the manufacturer (SpittingALuggy-Image Inc.) made a point of rushing new suit-masks to market as soon as someone arrived into the public eye (Roshviler suit-masks sold well, for example – 'scary' characters always being in demand). Customers could also send in photos of regular people and body stats and have suit-masks made up especially. Suit-masks were banned in most schools (otherwise it was hard to pick out the real teachers) and they were the most cited 'excuse' in divorce cases – 'I wasn't cheating. She was, er, wearing a suit-mask and I, er, thought she was you.' (Invariably the divorce excuse would fail because even if you wear a suit-mask and look incredibly like someone else, you still have your own voice, your own size and smell, and the *visible* eyes are either your own or a set of 'dead' ones).

Tommy received more cuts and bruises than any of the surviving contestants. This was because, having almost reached the Bowl, he glanced around and saw Marielle so far behind that he felt sure she must be injured or trapped. Despite all the recent betrayals, he couldn't help but turn back, braving a crowd that showed him even more 'attention' than before (since all but the dead contestants had by now made it back to the Bowl). By the time he realized that 'Marielle' was in fact some idiot in a Marielle body-suit-mask, he was a long way from the Bowl and facing a super-frenzied crowd. When he eventually fell through the doors of the Basement, he wondered why none of his fellow Knights were there to help him (never mind why no one had come to *his* aid). What he didn't know – and never found out – was that every other contestant who'd made it back to the Bowl was informed that they were the very last contestant to make it back and were then locked in one of fourteen portable bathrooms to freshen up and recuperate 'until such time as order is restored' (hence every contestant felt abandoned to some degree by their friends).

In the aftermath of the explosion, there were repeated calls from intergalactic parent groups to call off the show, but they agreed to withdraw their demands in return for a free ad during Pastor Pastrami's remembrance service. Some of the contestants' parents got in contact with the producers to request the return of their 'precious babbas', but Wolfstain managed to change their minds. Having convinced them that another attack was 'extremely unlikely,' he'd add: 'That little explosion . . ? A *ratings explosion*, more like! Just think of the extra fame and adulation your precious can achieve if he wins.'

Until the 'Chocolate Bowl Massacre', those parents who weren't regular viewers of ChAOS had no idea where their kids had disappeared to (since most had been whisked to the show without warning). However, the explosion scenes were carried on billions of news networks, so the parents of all the contestants (apart from the FiiVe) came to know what'd happened to their precious babbas.

'We have some neck to call *this* news'
(RNN motto)

One of the most popular (and profitable) news channels was RNN (Rubber Neck News), part of the Slyfoxy Network. Its popularity and profitability stemmed from its policy of dispensing with real reporters and not 'wasting time and money on the facts'. Day and night, it showed live footage of accident and disaster scenes from all over the universe. When faced with footage of the Chocolate Bowl Massacre, RNN's 'Disastrous Expert', AlTot OxBoll, commented: 'We don't know precisely what happened, or how it happened or why it happened . . . But we're happy to report that it looks like many people died in tremendous agony.'

Tommy gave Yago's hand a squeeze as Pastor Pastrami pushed the two coffins into space. Afterwards, he felt a tad embarrassed – *Why did I do that?* – till Zestrella came up, antennae drooping, and asked for a hug. *Yes, a hug!* It was brief – the tall girl pulling away stiffly. Yet the fact was inescapable. *She wanted me to hug her!* It cheered him – as did the growing conviction that Beryl and Jay-T weren't dead at all. This was probably just a test to see how everyone would react. Yes, he told himself, no way would someone try to kill the contestants. And if they did, no way would the producers allow the show to continue.

52
A New Plan

Deep in the heart of the universe, a creature known to some as Bin-Liner stood in a cathedral-like cavity hollowed into the side of a dark, rocky planet. He was half-illuminated by a watery moon spilling through gaping, glassless windows, and silhouetted by a bonfire that crackled at the far end of the echoey floor, its smoke rising through a gouged-out hole in the roof.

'You may be dead, but you failed.' He was addressing a life-size painting of Mister Oodid. 'The five children still live. And I will make sure you pay in the next life – your carrots will be severely rationed!' He turned and knelt before an enormous teeth-bared mouth which was carved into the rocky wall. 'Oh, Canine-of-Canines, help me . . . Five disgusting children are imperilling the end-of-the-universe we wish for – trying to "save" the universe . . ! And I must stop them – by any means necessary.' His eyes rolled into their sockets and he seemed to be talking to himself. 'I *must* get to them before they leave ChAOS . . . Hmmm . . . If only Heimenopper's Death Case could crush the Bowl . . . but it's only set for EARTHs and their solar systems . . . Hmmm . . . Perhaps another bomb attack – on one of the sponsor planets when the kids are most vulnerable . . . Hmmm . . . Or bribe the producer to change one of the ChAOS challenges . . . If

I could work out these children's weakness . . .'

Two eyes opened behind two slits of bin-liner and a tongue licked a set of lips – pushing a bit of beard through the mouthy slit. 'Yes,' said the wispy mouth. 'Yes.'

And Bin-Liner lifted the picture of Mister Oodid, carried it down to the bonfire and cast it into the flames. 'Yes!' he cried above the crackles and hisses. 'Yes!'

53
Escape

'It's Day Thirteen,' declared FionaDeFridge. 'Time for the second and final partner-choosing.'

Twelve young contestants punched buttons on their keypads.

DeFridge raised her voice. 'Behold, the pairings and groups for the rest of the show!'

A screen appeared. Tommy breathed a sigh of relief. Yago had chosen him too.

'OK,' said DeFridge. 'Because of the trauma you all suffered with the explosion, the challenges for the next three days are being dropped – to be replaced with Sponsor Planet activities.'[39] A cheer rose from most of the contestants.

No one noticed the strange thing that happened that afternoon when everyone returned from Planet NoYou'reNotSad-EveryoneThinksYou'reReallyCool&Successful-Seriously (a beautiful wooded planet where slick automobiles swished through puddles on a lone curving road). Eleven contestants plopped into the Wigglery and then, fractions of a second later, Marielle joined them.

39 Critics claim this decision had nothing to do with concern for the contestants, but was a reaction to the rise in viewership after the explosion.

That evening, Tommy had two exchanges he'd return to many times in the future – wishing he'd reacted differently.

The first was with Woozie who followed him into the Bowl Bathroom.

'I don't know why things have gotten so bad between us, Tommy,' said Woozie. 'But whatever you think I did, I'm sorry. I want us to be friends again.'

Tommy looked at his old friend and let the silence wash over them – a pause to show Woozie that he wasn't accepting too easily, that he'd really been hurt by the wibblewallian's behaviour. But Woozie, uptight, stepped into the silence just before Tommy's hand extended for a handshake. 'And I should warn you about Yago,' he said. 'He's mean and he's a fake.' Tommy's face darkened and Woozie blurted: 'I saw him today on the car planet. He took off his cast behind a tree and scratched his arm. It's a fake cast. You can't remove a real one like that.'

'What a scurrilous thing to say!' riposted Tommy. '*A fake cast* – is that the best you could come up with!?'

And with that, the Earthling took off to join Yago in the Wigglery.

Hurt and upset, Woozie stayed in the bathroom for an hour, perfecting an impression of Yago – 'My name is Yago. I'm a fake.' Over and over he said it – fantasizing about doing it over the Bowl's sound system.

Tommy's second exchange was with Marielle. Cornering him as he emerged from the bathroom, she whispered: 'I fell through some kind of wormhole this afternoon. On the way back from the car planet.'

After all the lies and betrayals, Tommy was tempted to say something cutting, but he caught himself and mumbled: 'Can we talk about this another time?'

The elquinine blocked his path. 'I met a warm old man called OleSayjj. He says we can help him.'

'Marielle, I'm late. Yago's already—'

'He's on the Council of Wisdom – I saw where they meet. He knows about the TFC. Says wisdom is the only thing that can stop it. Says we need to get off this crazy TV show asap and he can help us.'

'Marielle, can we—?'

'Didn't you hear what I said?' The elquinine's voice heightened. 'Talk about warped priorities! We're supposed to be stopping the TFC and you want to show off to Zestrella and all your "fans".'

'You've a nerve to—' Tommy checked himself. 'An old man says he knows about the TFC?' Marielle nodded. Tommy looked at her, impatience colouring his eyes. 'Was he one of the forty trillion viewers who heard you blabbing all about it to Wolfstain?'

'That's got nothing to do with it! This man—'

'Marielle!' Tommy felt like screaming at the elquinine – disgorging himself of all the pent-up frustrations. But a part of him knew now was not the time. Not after her boyfriend had just been killed.

He stepped to the side and before Marielle could utter another word, he was gone.

On Day Fourteen, Marielle's return was fractionally delayed from Planet BecauseYou'reWorthTakingMoneyFrom (a place where all the shaggy animals had unnatural gleaming hair and unnatural pointy eyelashes). Yet when she tried to speak to Tommy about how she'd once again been with an old creature called OleSayjj, she got diverted to another topic.

'You've abandoned Woozie! What kind of friend—? And I don't trust Yago. He's either too nice, trying to win you over, or else nasty and aloof. Have you seen the way he bullies Lillroysen?'

The Earthling told himself that Marielle was losing it. For he'd never seen Yago bully anyone.[40] And as for Woozie – Tommy wasn't the one who'd abandoned *him*.

Contestants found themselves on Planet UCanNeverAv2-MuchInsurance on Day Fifteen – it was full of fancy dwelling places that kept catching fire or collapsing for no good reason (contestants had to stay well clear to avoid injury).

That evening Marielle cornered Tommy on the highest diving board. 'There are dark forces in the universe hell-bent on ensuring the TFC *happens*,' she whispered. 'They're out to kill us IGGY Knights – that's what that chocolate explosion was the other day.'

'What're you on about?' asked Tommy, jolted (he hadn't heard the term IGGY Knights in some time).

'OleSayjj told me. The old, bearded man. I saw him again this afternoon.'

'Not this again! Marielle, dinner's about to be served and I don't want to miss—'

'Aaaagghhh! If it's not Yago, it's the fans or your stomach. Listen to me for a moment and stop being so selfish and self-centred. I'm positive—'

'Selfish? I'm not the one who lied. I'm not the one who—'

40 Incidentally, TV viewers were also unaware of Yago's bullying – as it was either not shown or else depicted out of context to make it look like self-defence.

Marielle's anger rose and with it all plans to explain things in a logical way went up in flames. 'We're escaping tonight,' she hissed, jumping straight to the conclusion. 'OleSayjj can help us stop the TFC. And he can get us out of here. But it has to be *tonight*. This is the last wormhole he can send.'

'I can't think without food.'

'He says the TFC is due to happen in eleven months' time.' The elquinine's face was flushed. 'The whole universe to be destroyed . . . *in less than one year!* And he doesn't just *say* it – it's *definite*. He's shown me evidence.'

'Let's talk about this tomorrow.' Tommy stepped to the end of the diving board. The fans below gave a loud cheer. How they loved his dive-bombs.

Marielle grabbed the dark Earthling by the elbow, pressing her lips to his ear. 'No! We have to leave *tonight*.' Her voice quivered. 'Abandoning Swiggy.'

Tommy laughed. 'Leave Swiggy and all the precious lessons!'

'Sshhhh . . ! We have *one* chance. It *has* to be tonight. When the cameras are off.'

The black-clad boy retrieved his elbow, annoyed at being shushed. 'You can't be serious.' And to the delight of the fans he was gone – over the edge.

Later that night, when he was changing in his sleeping bag, Woozie, Rumbles and Summy tried to tell him about Marielle's plan. But this so annoyed him that he cried out: 'Leave Swiggy!?' – shutting them right up. So effective was it, that he yelled, 'Leave Swiggy!' on seventeen of the occasions that any of them tried to bring the subject up.

Once Woozie managed to engage him in whispered conversation, but the Earthling was adamant. 'You can't be serious. Don't any of you remember the Deadly Scroll –

Elza's challenge?'

'Tommy, there's no guarantee the Beast will even—'

'The Beast will *definitely* help us. I know it.' For hadn't he seen a vision of his parents over Elza?

But Woozie didn't look convinced. 'The challenge sounds difficult. And that's *assuming* we choose the right one.'

'We *know* the Deadly Scroll is the third page,' hissed Tommy. 'We've got the co-ordinates for all of the tasks except the Ageing-UnStables-dung task – and we're going to perform that – on this very show – in three days' time.'

'Marielle says it's *not* the third page! She's been studying the pages – says the Deadly Scroll is in fact page number—'

'She's wrong!' interjected Tommy, an image rearing in his mind of a little girl in a red smock with a spear to her throat. 'It's the *third* page,' he insisted, drowning the crimson image with angry conviction.

Woozie sighed. 'You should listen to Marielle, to what she's gotta say 'bout this Guiding Light.'

Tommy shook his head. 'Remember what Wisebeardyface said? Beware *false* Guiding Lights. *Be cautious.*'

'How cautious were you running into Hellsbells?' retorted Woozie. For a moment, Tommy had no answer, allowing the wibblewallian to add: 'Elza could be a false Guiding Light . . . I'm telling you, Tommy, this sounds a better way to go. And – did Marielle tell you? – we got less than a year till the TFC!'

Tommy'd had enough of this nonsense. 'Leave Swiggy!' he cried, causing the wibblewallian to push himself away with a shake of his head.

The very last attempt Tommy remembered was some time in the middle of the night. Woozie shook him and whispered: 'We gotta go.'

Later, he'd have a vague recollection of the other IGGY

Knights floating before him.

'Off are the cameras.'

'Last chance.'

'We're seriouskeys.'

'Are you coming?'

'We could bop you over the head and take you.'

'But not right would that be.'

'This has got to be a choiceskeys.'

'A true leap of faith.'

'Because wrong we could be.'

'No, I know I'll see Harriettskeys again. See you guys down in the Wigglery. I've got to dash for the looskeys.'

'Tommy . . . The TFC is due to happen in under a year. *Less than twelve months* . . . If we have to leave you behind, we will . . . The future of the universe is more important than—'

'LEAVE SWIGGY!?' cried Tommy.

Then everything went blank.

54
The Mastervill

DICTATED BY PI BARLOWE FARLOWE . . .

We're still in the office when Max Bohr enters. I give him the skinny and motion to the Case of Death. 'Case closed.'

He's not happy. 'But you didn't find the missing EARTHs! They're still gone.'

''Course they're gone,' I says. 'They were destroyed. My job was to find out what happened, not magic them back. Now you know the story – case closed.'

He turns to Heimenopper. '*How could you?*' And grabs an electric chainsaw from one of the shelves. 'Aaaarrrggghhh!' he yells (or something like it) and lurches towards the Case of Death. 'No more EARTHs shall perish!'

While I'm pondering the health and safety standards of El Nerdo – a chainsaw? Seriously? – Heimenopper jumps in front of the kangalarsen. 'No!' he shouts. 'You'll destroy them *all*!'

Above the gurgle of chainsaw, Heimenopper explains that the specks of dust we see in the Case number almost five million and represent all the EARTHs ('Er, less the forty thousand I, er, crushed'). And if anyone damages the Case, all the EARTHs will be destroyed at once. 'When I want to destroy a single one, I pick out its co-ordinates and it magnifies and its sun and surrounding planets appear. All the other specks of dust – EARTHs, I mean – move to the inside edges of the glass.'

Using colourful language, Bohr suggests casting the Case into deep space.

Heimenopper shakes his donkey-head. 'No use. Bin-Liner has the mastervill.'

'*Mastervill*?' Too late I realize the question's come from me. What am I doing? This is none of my concern.

A flicker of pride crosses Heimenopper's face. 'The mastervill looks like two bits of crystal – a dark piece and a clear piece – clasped together to form one banana-sized crystal. It's beautiful. And it's unbreakably linked to the Death Case. I designed it. At Bin-Liner's request.'

'Clever I'm sure,' I say. 'But what does it *do*?'

'Bin-Liner can separate the two "crystals" at any time, no matter where the Case is located and all the EARTHs will explode. The only reason he doesn't is because he's wanted to hear the pieces of wisdom the planets come up with. And the mastervill can't destroy just one EARTH at a time – it's all or none.'

'So if you get the mastervill back from him . . .' says Bohr.

'Then the Case can be destroyed without harming a soul.'

Right on cue, Heimenopper's toaster starts buzzing and a note pops out of it. The old limbs are still working, so I get to it before he does and read aloud: 'Must talk to you *now*. Bin-Liner.'

Heimenopper's eyes fill with fear. 'You have to leave,' he says. 'Both of you.'

'I'm not going anywhere,' I tell him.

55

Bye-Bye, Swiggy

'Welcome, early-morning viewers!' cried FionaDeFridge into a camera. 'To Day Sixteen of ChAOS . . . And the big news . . . Contestants are still asleep but they *will* be allowed to have pancakes again this morning . . ! And the even bigger news . . .' Her face turned sour. 'Last night three cowardly contestants left the show. The sneaky sneaks chose the one hour of the day we're off-air and crept down to the Wigglery. They jumped through the Entrance wigglehole and, before emerging through the Exit, they somehow caught themselves a ride on a temporary wormhole.'

She looked directly to camera. 'You three . . . If you're listening, you've got two hours to get yourselves back here or . . .' Behind the vacuum-cleaner-tailed robot, Swiggy cruised into view. 'Yes, when you came on the show, like everyone else, you became bound by certain Terms and Conditions, allowing us to do *whatever we wish* to your property if you break the rules.' Viewers saw Swiggy fly into an enormous armour-plated 'box'. Then a huge cannon-ball-like object with the longest fuse you've ever seen drifted in after it.

'*Two hours* from now,' said FionaDeFridge. 'Be back here . . . Or else.'

Tommy was stunned when he awoke. Marielle, Rumbles and Summy had left the Bowl. Vamoosed . . . He'd never thought they'd actually do it!

And to make matters worse, his jaw felt stiff and sore.

'That's where she hit you,' whispered Woozie in the Bowl Bathroom. 'You cried out, Marielle hit you, a few people woke up and when they dozed off again, the four of us crept down to the Wigglery. Took a while in zero gravity, I can tell you.'

'Wwhhorrrr duhhh daaah gwwoh?'

'Huh?'

Tommy removed his toothbrush from his mouth. 'I said, where did they go?'

'Oh . . . To join the Guiding Light.'

'But that's mad! Leaving here, leaving Swiggy!'

'Ssshhh! . . . Hey, where's my toothpaste?' Woozie scanned the bathroom shelves. 'Someone's stolen it! *All* the toothpastes are gone.'

Tommy nodded in irritation. Woozie shrugged, dispensed a blob of handsoap and began brushing.

'*Elza's* the Guiding Light,' said Tommy in a low voice. 'Not some idiot who nabbed Marielle during a stupid explosion . . . When'll they be back?'

'Duuhhr nawwwt—' Woozie removed his toothbrush. 'They're not coming back.'

'*What?*'

'The Guiding Light – OleSayjj – told Marielle he could arrange a one-way wormhole. But if they came to him, *that was it*. An irreversible leap of faith. They'd end up halfway across the universe – with no wormhole back . . . They're gone for good.'

Tommy digested this. 'But that's mad! Leaving here,

leaving Swiggy! Elza's challenge—'

'Ssshhh!!'

'Well, I don't care!' He rubbed his jaw. 'Good riddance!'

'Ssshhh! . . . You don't mean that.'

Tommy brushed his teeth with renewed ferocity then spat into the sink as though his mouth were filled with poison. 'So how come you're here?' he hissed.

'Huh?'

'Why didn't you go with them?'

'Oh, er, turned out it was a very small, very temporary wormhole. Could only carry three people. Rumbles, Summy and I drew lots to see who'd stay . . . I lost.'

The Bowl was buzzing with excitement over breakfast. Since the last time the group had tucked into pitter-particle pancakes, two contestants had been killed and three had disappeared.

'Five down, nine to go,' as Yago put it, holding Lillroysen in a headlock behind the fridge and pouring moople syrup in his earhole.

'You don't think any more of us will disappear or be killed?' asked all thirty of Charles Lemass's heads at once.

'We'll probably be dead this time tomorrow,' said Joe Yuss. 'All of us . . . Can't see any reason they'd let us live.' (His jolly alter-ego, Syri Yuss, was back in hibernation – shrunken and asleep on the end of his tail.)

'Nothing's gonna happen to any of us,' interjected Bernard Burnside cheerfully. 'It's an awesome day.' (Only two evenings previous, after the burial service, she'd thought *what-the-hell* and skated off the Edge, landing safely on the crash mat in the Basement. She was still on a high.)

'Lillroysen will sting you with his stinger if you don't leave him alone!' cried a high voice behind the fridge.

'Yeh right,' laughed Yago. 'And my dad's the Count of Monte Crispo.'

Yago's confidence stemmed from knowing that Lillroysen would die within minutes of deploying his sting. (Incidentally, unbeknownst to Yago, his dad actually WAS the Count of Monte Crispo – but that's another story.)

Not registering this exchange, Tommy tucked into his pancakes and sidled up to Zestrella. Just being near her helped push the crazy images of Marielle, Summy and Rumbles from his mind. 'Nice pancakes,' he said, with a tentative smile.

'I've had better,' said Zestrella and walked off.

'Well, *I* think they're lovely,' said Woozie with a look of encouragement.

Unfortunately for the wibblewallian, his face now reminded Tommy of the very people he wanted to forget. Tommy harrumphed. 'I've had better.' And he swallowed a mouthful and moved away.

'Thank you,' said a voice aimed at Woozie from down the table. 'I made them – the pancakes.' Woozie looked over and saw the pale visage of Uladrack. 'Don't worry,' said the wild-haired vampire, seeing a cloud cross the wibblewallian's face. 'There's no mice in them.'

'Hey!' cried a clatter of voices from the far side of the room. '*There's* one of *us*!' Thirty Charles Lemass arms were pointing through the glass wall to the Arrivals Platform below. Turned out, one fan (or group of fans) had procured a Charles-Lemass-suit-mask. It truly looked like the many-bodied fellow was waving his arms in two places at once.

'And *there* are two Lillroysens,' said Lillroysen, clearing out his ear with a finger and licking it. 'Jolly handsome, eh?'

Woozie took a quick peek and saw three Woozies, six Tommies and a smattering of other contestants. For some reason the spectacle depressed him and he returned to the table.

'Hey – the latest scores!' cried another voice.

Sure enough, a giant illuminated board was visible through the curved window (the first time it'd appeared in days).

CHAOS LEADERBOARD: RUNNING TOTAL OF VOTES

RANK	CONTESTANT	SELECTED VOTER COMMENT
1	BERNARD BURNSIDE	WEH-HAY! YOU DA GAL!
2	J/S YUSS	NO USE CHUCKLING OVER SPILT MILK[41]
3	YAGO	WILL U B MY LOYAL FREND 2?
4	TOMMY STORM	UR BETTER OFF NOW DEM 3 AV GON
5	ZESTRELLA	GO ON – GIZA HUG
6	CHARLES LEMASS	UR GUD AT KISSING (GLAZGOH KISSES)
7	ULADRACK	R U A KLEPTOMANIAC?
8	WOOZIE	FAKE CAST? UR JUST JELUS OF YAGO
9	LILLROYSEN	LOSER!

'A mistake!' cried a high voice. 'There's obviously been a mistake in the vote counting!' Lillroysen stamped his foot. 'And Lillroysen is not a loser!'

Woozie looked down at his pancakes. Uladrack had moved away, mistaking his surprised look (*She spoke to me!*) for one of unfriendliness. The wibblewallian felt utterly alone.

41 This comment referred to Syri Yuss who'd been 'in the ascendancy' for the previous few days and was very popular with voters.

When Tommy saw the leaderboard, he felt a sense of relief. It actually felt good not to be out in front, beating everybody else. Joe Yuss was on washing-up – 'Pancakes *never* come off frying pans' – and Tommy thought he'd give him a hand. *Where am I? What am I doing?* These questions descended upon the young Earthling for the first time in weeks. Holding a stack of plates in the Bowl's Kitchen, somewhere out in the cosmos, he had a sudden sense of being lost.

The other three have gone. Really, really gone!

He looked about for Woozie and saw his old friend playing No-Gravity Snooker with Charles Lemass and Lillroysen. The wibblewallian was lifting Lillroysen so the waspy boy could push his cue through the top of the bubble that held the coloured balls.

Is there a chance the TFC's due to happen in under twelve months' time?

If the sense of being lost opened up a hole in Tommy's crusted armour, then this new question drove a dagger to his heart. Right there, right then, he thought about running over to Woozie and giving him the biggest hug – a hug that almost certainly would've ended in tears. Tears for the three Knights who'd vamoosed. Tears for Woozie. Tears for the red-smocked girl who'd died at the end of a spear (*due to my failure!*). Tears for the universe. Tears for everything.

And he might've given that hug had a certain screen not chosen that moment to appear outside the Bowl. It showed a shot of the inside of an armour-plated box, housing a spacecraft and an enormous bowling-ball-like bomb with a small flame running up its fuse.

'Swiggy!' cried Tommy.

FionaDeFridge's face swam on to the screen. 'Marielle, Rumbles and Summy . . . We gave you two hours' warning

. . . Now, if you're not here in . . . sixty-three seconds . . . Say bye-bye to your spacecraft.'

The next sixty seconds were a blur of movement, stillness, noise and silence. Woozie stood paralysed atop the N-G Snooker bubble. Tommy, smacking his hands off the Bowl's glass wall, cried out a hundred variations of 'No! No! Don't!'

But nothing stopped DeFridge from uttering the final: 'Three . . . two . . . one . . .' And nothing stopped the bowling-ball bomb exploding.

Tommy watched as the inside of the armoured box became a roaring swirl of smithereens. And Swiggy was no more.

56

Back-Up

DICTATED BY PI BARLOWE FARLOWE . . .

Heimenopper is trembling. 'Please! If he finds out—'

He's silenced by an image of a bin-liner-covered face that's just appeared on the office wall. I can see Bin-Liner's eyes and they show shock, then sudden resolution. A weird distorted voice says: 'So, Heimenopper, you have betrayed me! In that case . . .' He disappears and returns with a bread-roll-sized object that looks like it's made of black crystal on one end and clear crystal on the other.

Heimenopper, who's been mouthing off about betraying no one, exclaims: 'The mastervill!'

'Yes,' says Bin Liner. 'And you two, whoever you are . . .' He's addressing me and Bohr. 'I'd like you to witness what your meddling has caused.' He eyeballs Heimenopper. 'No more money for you . . . It's time I split these two crystals apart.'

'No!' cries Heimenopper. 'No, please! I don't care about the money! Please – don't destroy all the EARTHs!'

'Why ever not?' asks Bin-Liner, enjoying the moment.

'Because, er, well . . . Some of them still have wisdom suggestions to send.'

'I'm not bothered any more about their stupid suggestions,'

replies Bin-Liner. 'There's less than one year to go to the, em, er, nevermind. The point is: if the EARTHs haven't come up with a killer suggestion by now, they're hardly going to come up with one in the next eleven and a half months . . . So I can stop worrying.'

Hmmm. What's gonna happen in eleven and a half months? Before I can ask, Heimenopper jumps in: 'But think of all the people you'll be killing! And there are three witnesses here to testify to your crime. You'd be put away for life.'

Bin-Liner seems to smile. 'Two things,' he says. 'One, you don't know who I really am or where I'm located . . . And two, if I separate the mastervill, it's the Death Case that does the killing – which was created by you, Heimenopper. Technically, *you*'ll be the one doing the killing.'

All three of us know he's right. He lifts his elbows and sets himself to pull the crystals apart.

'Wait!' Once again, I'm startled (and not a little cheesed-off) to realize that *I'm* the one who's spoken. But now I've started . . . 'Wait, please. What do you achieve by destroying these EARTHs? Not much, I reckon . . . Surely there's a way we can convince you to return the mastervill? There must be something you need, something we can help you with.'

He pauses and I can see he's thinking. He thinks so hard his eyes roll back in their sockets and we're left standing like no-good losers till they roll back down and he fixes me with a look. 'If Day Seventeen doesn't go as planned,' he says, relaxing his elbows and lowering the mastervill. 'I'm sure it will . . . But just in case . . . You could be back-up.'

'Day Seventeen?' I ask.

'Tomorrow,' says Bin-Liner as if we should've guessed.

57
Chaos Aplenty

'On account of the disappearance of three contestants last night,' announced a voice over the Bowl's internal sound system, 'a few changes will be made to life in the Bowl . . . Firstly, your free time will be curtailed – Brother Roshviler will give classes every day for the rest of the show. And secondly, today's visit to a Sponsor Planet will be delayed till this afternoon while we ask each contestant to come down to the BlahRoom for an "interview".'

Tommy wasn't really listening to the message. Having just witnessed the destruction of Swiggy, he'd scaled the highest diving board and was slumped there, head in hands. When Woozie came up, Tommy cried out: 'This is your fault! For letting them go.' Woozie tried to explain that Marielle, Rumbles and Summy would've gone no matter what he said, but it was no use. Tommy wasn't listening.

When the Earthling finally came out of the foetal position, the fans outside cheered. This seemed to have some effect, for Tommy leapt off the diving board, dive-bombing into the pool. The crowd went berserk. 'Tommy! Tommy! Tommy!' And Tommy sort of went berserk too – charging up to the diving board again, then leaping off. He repeated this at least twenty times before he finally collapsed, exhausted.

Lying there, he became aware of a giant screen outside the

Bowl. It was playing a clip over and over. When he tuned in, he could just hear what was being said. 'When ChAOS ends on Day Twenty-One, one person will sit atop the leader-board. One person, chosen by you – the viewer – will win the ChAOS jackpot super-duper prize of fame and riches.'

Then it was Tommy's turn to descend to the BlahRoom. He refused to answer any questions and shouted at the screen. 'Swiggy was my property too! How could you destroy her? How *could* you!'

After the interview, Tommy realized that silence and stillness were his enemies. The only way he could contain his grief and bubbling feelings was to throw himself more than ever into the activities and challenges of ChAOS (and if this helped him win more 'looks' from Zestrella and more cheers from the fans, so much the better).

That afternoon, on Planet Oooh-The-Hunkiest-DisposableRazor-Ever, the young Earthling surfed high waves, and skied down steep slopes, surrounded by giant mirrors – always with Yago by his side.

Afterwards, Roshviler gave a class in the AlmaAnteMatterRoom, beneath the Wigglery, on the extra-exciting topic of collective nouns (a *herd* of cattle, a *stompede* of eagle-eyed-canines, a *lowestcommondenominator* of humans). To the delight of sixty-three trillion gormless TV viewers, Tommy managed to enrage the strict tutor – first by being cheeky, then by dodging Roshviler's lashing cane.[42]

An enraged Roshviler ended up storming out of the class-

42 In fact, Roshviler actually hit *himself* on one occasion as he tried to strike Tommy.

room with a cry of: 'Some day, Storm! Some day – I *will* have your guts for garters!'

Later, on the top diving board, the fans outside cheered their loudest yet. And Tommy almost allowed himself a smile. Already he felt better than he had that morning. He told himself he'd complete the Ageing-UnStables dung challenge in two days' time and surely he'd be able to get his hands on a spacecraft after the show. Then he'd complete the other 'third page' Deadly Scroll challenges and make it back to Elza.

'Sure – 'course I can win and claim the super-duper ChAOS prize.' Tommy looked up. The voice had come from yet another screen outside the Bowl – showing images of Bernard Burnside (an excerpt from her interview in the BlahRoom that morning). 'I'm stoked!' she added. 'If I can jump over the Edge, I can do anything!'

This was followed by other interview clips. In one, Zestrella Ravisham said: 'I like winners. So yes, I'd definitely date whoever tops the leaderboard at the end of the show – unless the winner is *me*!'

Hmmm. That made Tommy think . . . *So if I were to WIN the super-duper ChAOS prize . . .*

It was this very evening that Woozie stopped trying to engage Tommy in conversation – for he found the monosyllabic responses cut him to the core and, in any case, Tommy was now rarely without Yago by his side. This made the wibble-wallian miss Marielle, Summy and Rumbles all the more. What he wouldn't give now to hear Marielle bossing him or Summy saying something nerdy. Heck, he'd even be prepared to forgo the last of Swiggy's choco-snowball supply just to have half an hour larking about with Rumbles.

But no amount of wishing would solve his woes, so Woozie was forced to seek out new friends.

He found Lillroysen to be a surprisingly witty fellow and, after Roshviler's first class, he demonstrated self-defence manoeuvres to the little waspy boy in the AlmaAnteMatter Room. Then they played nearest-coin-to-the-wall – the wibblewallian winning most games till the stakes got super-high and Lillroysen's eyes gleamed and he fired a 'wonder throw' – *skill or fluke?* – and Woozie lost his entire stock of coins. (Luckily, he later found a coin and used this to win some back.)

And Uladrack . . . Having apologized for his look of surprise at the breakfast table, Woozie drew her into conversation and they ended up in the Biblioteck, discussing everything under the suns. 'Why is eating mice any different from eating a chicken or a shepherd?' asked the pale girl. And Woozie had to agree. (Shepherd's pie is a big favourite across the cosmos.) She went on to explain, 'I'm not a vampire, I'm an irevamp . . . Yes, I enjoy blood. But only when cooked.' Black pudding, it turned out, was her favourite dish. When Woozie asked why she'd stolen from the fridge, she explained: 'I've always collected things, like stamps and coins, and then when I hit my teens, I started stealing. Just to get a thrill. I don't even want the things I steal. I feel horrible afterwards. I'm trying to stop – I haven't stolen anything for two days . . . *Four days* if you don't count the toothpastes in the bathroom.'

And the strangest thing . . . Despite all the bad things that'd happened of late – Woozie felt a new, indescribable sensation . . . No, it wasn't possible, was it? A wibblewallian falling for an irevamp?

On Day Seventeen, Tommy once-again delighted in infuriating Roshviler during class, and then it was off to Planet Phool's-No-1-Comb-over-Cream – a place full of bald-backed animals whose long 'side-fur' had been combed over. Here, Tommy spent his time catching animals and 'revealing their true baldness'. He was riding on the back of a toupéstallion close to some other contestants when a rabbity creature rushed towards him from the bushes. The toupéstallion jumped sideways, the rabbity creature tripped and next thing an explosion went off. It was hard to know exactly what happened because eight of the contestants found themselves plopping back through the Exit in the Wigglery.

Many viewers with slow-motion action-replay technology claim the rabbity creature exploded in a hail of chocolate, taking Charles Lemass down with him. The official version, however, given to viewers and contestants alike, was that the 'explosion' was merely an optical illusion caused by a malfunction with the wigglehole taking contestants back to the Bowl. Charles, it was claimed, had not returned to the Bowl because four of his heads had come down with severe tonsillitis and had to be operated on right away. This was made more believable by a (doctored) video that appeared outside the Bowl, showing Charles sitting in bed eating ice-cream.

And so it was that life continued pretty much as usual that evening, with Tommy backflipping off the Edge with a towering armful of plates (only one broke on landing), wincing as his increasingly inflamed shoulder-blades hit the crash-mat. And though the fans roared, Zestrella gave no sign of being impressed (antennae paralysed, tentacles still knotted in a tight bow, face unmoving). Yet if anything, this lack of reaction made Tommy determined to go for everything all the harder.

58
A (New) Cunning Plan

DICTATED BY PI BARLOWE FARLOWE . . .

Bin-Liner comes back to us two days later. 'There might be something you can do for me . . . In return for the mastervill.'

I can't resist commenting. 'Day Seventeen didn't work out quite as you planned?'

He fixes me with a stare. 'You – you're a private investigator?'

I nod. 'Farlowe's the name.'

'Farlowe,' he repeats, the distorted voice making it sound like Faahhrrloowwe. 'I presume you're a disinterested party here.'

'Whadya mean?'

'I mean, I presume your job is done – now you've found the Death Case.' I shrug and he continues: 'Therefore, it's none of your concern what happens to these EARTHs.' Again I shrug and he adds: 'Meaning you could be a kind of referee in these proceedings.'

I'm not sure I like where this is going. He smiles and says: 'You see, there is one big problem with a deal to hand over the mastervill . . . What I want is big and I won't hand over the mastervill *before* I get what I want – to ensure I'm not double-crossed.'

I pitch in: 'And no one's gonna hand over what *you* want – specially if it's *big* – *before* getting the mastervill. Else *they* might get double-crossed.'

'Precisely, Mister Farlowe . . . So we need a solution that ensures no one can be double-crossed. A solution that leaves no room for error.'

'That what you meant about me being a *referee*?'

'In a manner of speaking.'

As though it explains everything, Bin-Liner describes how he's had some weird contraption built – housed in a capsule floating in deep space. Its image appears on the office wall and we see it's within shouting distance of a certain TV set.

'I paid the producer so much money,' he says. 'No one from the TV show will bother you.' Then he fixes me in his stare. 'By which I mean, no one will bother *you*, PI Farlowe.'

59

Dam-It

On Day Eighteen, Roshviler enjoyed a victory of sorts. During class he exclaimed: 'Ridiculous comment! You, Tommy Storm, are a complete idiot.' The boy he was addressing was dressed in black, with short dark hair and a darkish face.

'Funny that . . .' said the boy, releasing a waggly tail behind his back and pulling a wig off his head – revealing sandy hair and rabbity ears.

'Because,' said a boy beside him (who looked like Yago, but sounded like Tommy), '*I* am Tommy Storm.' And he removed a sandy-haired wig and fake rabbity ears, plus a fake tail behind his back. He smiled self-contentedly. For he had indeed made the silly comment – having leaned across Yago to make it when Roshviler's back was turned.

For a moment Roshviler was taken aback. It was remarkable how alike the two boys looked when you ignored hair colour, tail and rabbity ears. Then the tutor smirked. 'But irrespective of your ridiculous outfit, boy, *you* still made the remark, did you not?'

'Eh, yes,' replied Tommy, smile waning.

'Ergo, my statement stands – no matter whom I happened to be looking at when I made it . . . You, Tommy Storm, are a *complete* idiot.'

FionaDeFridge made an announcement at lunchtime. 'The See-How-Long-You-Can-Go-Without-Weeing-After-Drinking-Three-Litres-Of-Tea Challenge – which was scheduled for Day Twenty-One – is being dropped and replaced with the ForkInStewpit Challenge, as Mister Wolfstain, the producer, was persuaded it would be more exciting for viewers.'

Since none of the contestants knew much about either challenge, they gave the issue little thought.

Afternoon Eighteen was what Tommy had long waited for – it was his strongest reason for staying on ChAOS and refusing to escape.

'Contestants,' announced DeFridge. 'Your task will be to clean the Ageing-UnStables of three million years of animal dung. At the end of the challenge, your sleeping bags will be dragged through the UnStables. So your forfeit for failing this task is quite clear.'

The contestants leapt through the Wigglehole Entrance, landing near the precipice of a canyon on a cloudy planet. It smelled like one giant cowpat. And when they looked over the precipice, they saw why. The valley below, about twice the size of Luxembourg, was covered in a thick layer of manure.

'*That* must be the Ageing-UnStables,' said Bernard, pointing down.

Amidst the sounds of disgust, Lillroysen noticed nine mops and nine pails of water close by. 'How're we supposed to clean *that* with these?'

While some began arguing, refusing to even try, Woozie grabbed two mops and ran off down the pathway towards the valley floor. Tommy meanwhile had spotted something else. He took off, running along the edge of the canyon, towards an odd-looking wall at one end of the valley. It was hundreds of metres high and, unlike the high canyon walls, it looked man-made.

After half an hour of running, he was on top of the weird wall – at its midpoint – next to a large tap and a sign that read *DAM YOU IF YOU TURN THIS TAP*.

He turned the tap.

'Welcome back from the ad break,' cried FionaDeFridge to camera. 'The contestants are back in the Bowl enjoying a hearty dinner – apart from Woozie who's still in the bathroom trying to clean dung off his fur.' Behind her, the crowd gave a series of whoops. 'And yes, that cheer is for a certain someone who's waving out the Bowl at us – a certain someone who succeeded brilliantly in cleaning the Ageing-UnStables. If you missed it, Tommy Storm opened up the sluice gates of the Dung-oh Dam and fifteen gazillion litres of water did the rest.'

Inside the Bowl, Tommy was feeling pleased with himself. Zestrella was almost certainly glancing his way and he'd managed – in one afternoon – to complete a quarter of Elza's 'third page' Deadly Scroll Challenge.

Yes, he'd admit, it was unfortunate that Woozie'd been down in the valley when the water ran through it, but the wibblewallian was a trained Knight, so he'd managed to extract himself before things got 'too hairy'.[43] Tommy didn't think an apology was necessary since he had, after all, single-

43 This was Tommy's phrase – he thought it quite appropriate considering Woozie ended up with dung all over his fur.

handedly completed part of Elza's challenge. All he'd said to Woozie when they returned was: 'You see? It'll be no problem to finish off the Deadly Scroll tasks.'

But Woozie's response had been the very opposite of what he expected. 'You don't think that was a bit too easy, huh? Turn a tap and challenge done. If you ask me, today *proves* the third page is *not* the Deadly Scroll.'

Tommy waved to the fans and convinced himself that Woozie was deluded or just jealous. Jealous he didn't think of turning the tap and jealous that the fans didn't love *him*.

And for the rest of the evening, while Woozie sat in the Biblioteck with Uladrack, Tommy wowed the fans and kept glancing over at Zestrella and saying things in silly voices. For, yes, he wanted to impress Zestrella, but now he also wanted to make her laugh, to crack that mask-like face that held her in a prison of seriousness.

That night, Tommy dreamt that Zestrella was locked in a tall, dragon-guarded tower, staring out of the window, with ridiculously long hair. Then he, Tommy, appeared and slew the dragon. Antennae humming, Zestrella threw down her chestnut hair and he climbed up the tower's walls, clinging to the soft strands, anticipating her whoop of joy. Yet as he approached, her face was shrouded in shadow – the only sound, the hum of antennae. And the tower began stretching, for no matter how fast he climbed, he could never reach the window. And the antennae's hum became a tinny distortion, then chalk on a blackboard. And then, quite suddenly, the silhouetted girl leaned forward, shook her head and her hair came right off. And he was falling, falling.

He only just had time to look up, to see her face, before he woke up shaking in the depths of his sleeping bag.

For the face that looked down on him had blonde hair. It was the face of Marielle.

60
The Dummy

DICTATED BY PI BARLOWE FARLOWE ...

One day and one wormhole-journey later and I'm docking the ole rustbucket up against the capsule. *Bingo* – you've guessed it . . . Against my better instincts, I've agreed to Bin-Liner's suggestion that I play 'referee' for the exchange of the mastervill. How dumb is this? I wonder.

Following his earlier instructions, I make my way inside the capsule. Apart from the pair of steel boots welded to the middle of the floor and hooped by a ring of steel, it's a basic steel chamber, with a large window and a level of gravity that makes me feel twice my normal weight. Either that or I downed more pies than I thought at El Nerdo.

I bolt the inside of the door and a deathly noise fills the capsule. It's a horrible, creaking bending-of-steel sound, like an ocean liner sinking to the bottom of the sea. Then I see the reason. Four words have punched their way into the thick, heavy hunk of steel that is the far wall – *IS THE BUG DEAD?* Hmmm. Odd question.

And below it, on the floor, is what looks like a clunky projector. But then I see the logo *PoF!* and realize this is the 'truth machine' Bin-Liner mentioned (he said he saw one on TV and just had to get his own). I plug it in and not only does it come on, but it's like I flicked some switch in the capsule – the place starts humming and the steel boots are resonating like a tuning fork.

Through the window I can see the front bumper of *I-Don't-Believe-Your-Alibi* and, beyond it, in the distance, the glass 'Bowl' belonging to the TV show known as ChAOS (the very show where I saw those kids blabbing about the TFC – coincidences round here are two-a-penny!).

OK, I'm ready to do this . . . Donning a microphone-head-phones-set, I step into the vibrating steel boots, lift up the ring of steel and hoop it round my neck. Soon as I click the boot clasps, the insides start swelling till I can't move my lower legs and the steel ring shrinks round my neck till I'm nearly choking. Two chains fall from the ceiling and whip like snakes, attaching themselves to my neck ring and pull taut, up towards the ceiling, so I'm having to stand on tippytoes, 'cept my feet are still jammed into humming steel boots! My hands are clasped together like the instructions said when two more chains whip out, right and left, and loop round my elbows – pulling tight towards the capsule walls. And then it's there, I don't know how, a bread-roll-sized crystal right in front of my hands. And a bleeping noise that somehow tells me I've got two seconds to take it or it's gonna fall to the ground and break apart. I grab it – a hand at either end – and the bleeping stops. I can just see the words *Dummy Mastervill* printed across it and feel that it's really two pieces wedged into one another. Now my arms are straining to keep my hands in place and keep it together. Plus my neck hurts, my back hurts, my legs ache and I'm beginning to feel like a schmuck who's been tricked into some sort of masochistic game. Sure, Bohr said he'd pay double time for every day I'm here, but this kinda ****'s gotta be worth triple. Maybe even quadruple.

I glance across – least my eyes aren't manacled! From this angle there's no sign of the Bowl or my rustbucket through the window. Just the bottomless pit of space. My headphones start ringing – the sound of a long distance call – and then the call answers automatically and the unmistakable distorted voice of Bin-Liner fills my ears. 'Ah, Mister Farlowe. I take it you're trying out the Exchanger.'

I don't share his good humour. 'Can we get on with this, Bin-Liner?'

'Of course . . . All you have to do is repeat out loud the question on the wall. Then everything's set to go.' I flick my eyes to *IS THE BUG DEAD?* 'Once the Exchanger is primed,' he continues. 'It will release you if you answer *Yes* – truthfully – in response to the question on the wall.' Then as an afterthought. 'Oh, and the Exchanger will also release if the mastervill comes apart – if you drop it or let your hands break away . . . You see, this way we have our solution to the problem of exchanging the mastervill. No one can be double-crossed.'

I have a question. '*Is the bug dead?* – what does that mean?'

'Check out the window.'

I look and the view is totally blocked by a giant bug crawling up the inside of the window. 'What the—!?'

Bin-Liner laughs. 'When we do this for real, with the actual mastervill, the bug will be replaced . . . By something else . . . But that might not be for some days. So you have lots of time to learn just how the Exchanger works.'

He hangs up and I hear my voice say: '*Is the bug dead?*'

In response, a spotlight flicks on, illuminating the giant insect. And it must be shining through a magnifying glass or something, cos the bug starts sizzling.

'Yes!' I cry. 'Yes! Yes!' – not cos I think the bug's dead, but cos I *want* it to be.

PoF! buzzes three times and I'm still stuck here, limbs straining. And then the bug falls to the floor, dead as a dead bug. But now I'm feeling mean and, like my old Ma used say, I've gotten me an angry notion . . . This Bin-Liner bum is playing me for a patsy. I'm not gonna say Yes. No way.

Two minutes, five minutes, ten minutes pass. And I'm still holding out – arms like jelly, legs like mincemeat and a back that wants to fold up and die. *I won't say Yes, I won't say Yes!* Even as the mantra fills my head, I can feel my arms giving way, hands slipping, slipping. Till yeeeaarrrghhhh! The chain rips my arms wide apart and one end of the dummy mastervill's in my right hand, the other end's on the floor.

Suddenly the chains on my neck-ring release, the steel boots unclasp and I'm free.

Great, wonderful – I didn't say Yes. 'Cept if that were the *real* mastervill, five-million-odd EARTHs would be mashed to nothing right now.

61
Crazy Universe

On Day Nineteen the contestants plopped separately on to Planet Virtualosity™. Tommy spent the afternoon just trying to stay alive – dodging bullets and fleeing monsters – till he was 'caught' by a grizzly beast and realized it was nothing more than a virtual projection.[44]

After dinner, he lay on the top diving board, too exhausted to show off to Zestrella or the fans. It wasn't as relaxing as expected because he came to realize that all the frenetic activity of the last few weeks had been a great way to avoid thinking. And now his mind was filling with thoughts and visions he'd rather just forget. Eventually, when Woozie's words began repeating in his head (*You don't think that was a bit too easy? Turn a tap and challenge done*), he stood up (to loud cheers) and swan-dived into the pool.

That night, he dreamt that he climbed Mount Neverrest, sang 'The Hillocks are Alive with the Sound of Music' in the Mos Eisely Cantina (a bar) and found the Holey Gruel in the Atole Maize – all in a single afternoon – and was celebrating the ease of the Deadly Scroll tasks when he saw the little girl in the red smock running towards a gate. He chased after her into a graveyard and followed her to a mound of earth which

44 Virtualosity manufactured 3-D games. The company's slogan was: *Every spoilt kid should have one!*

she passed through like a ghost. Then he saw the gravestone – *Here lies the little girl that TS failed.*

After Roshviler's morning class on Day Twenty, the contestants plopped on to Planet Chah-chah-chariteeeeee. It was full of three-legged centaurs, overgrown dwarves, bandageless zombies, mermaids unable to swim, broken-horned unicorns and piles of ash with signs saying they could become phoenixes if only a donation were made. Aircraft flew overhead, tracing out phone numbers in the sky for viewers to call with donations. Tommy came across a dragon that couldn't blow fire, a werewolf afraid of the dark and a poltergeist allergic to loud noise. He also saw many broken wings (on gargoyles and griffins), plus a blind Cyclops and two blind oracles. He spent most of his time talking to starving creatures, completely gutted that he had no food to hand over. They explained how they came from planets where there was more than enough food to go around, but a small number of powerful, rich creatures hoarded all the food for themselves.

Back in the Bowl, Tommy sat alone, showing-off far from his mind. In a way he'd been feeling sorry for himself over the previous few days and weeks and, if truth be told, over the previous few years (moaning about his stutter and lack of co-ordination). For a brief time, he realized how lucky he was to be healthy, well-fed and surrounded by people who loved him. OK, maybe not quite *surrounded* by people who loved him, but Yago was a good friend and Zestrella cast a beauteous eye his way now and again. And of course there were the fans.

The young Earthling crawled to the end of the diving

board and hooked his legs around it, then eased himself backwards off the board. He hung there, upside-down, to the cheers of the madding throng.

Yes, he tried to convince himself. I am *surrounded* by people who love me.

While Tommy was wooing the fans, Woozie was down in the Biblioteck doing a little wooing of his own. He persuaded Uladrack to take off her glasses, then pushed back her curtain of hair.

'You're beautiful, you know. You shouldn't hide your face.'

Uladrack blushed, her pointy eye teeth visible, and gave a low squawk. Woozie'd quickly come to love these noises and to appreciate the irevamp's soft voice (way preferable to the look-at-me voice of someone else he could mention). He leaned forward, lips puckered. The irevamp's breath brushed his face before . . .

KWAAAAAWWWWW!!

Uladrack leapt backwards with a loud squawk. Luckily they were in the Biblioteck, so no one else had heard (unless you count the thirty-six trillion viewers).

'I'm sorry,' said Uladrack when she'd recovered.

But Woozie wouldn't look at her. He was sitting, head hung between his knees in shame and embarrassment.

'I'm just not . . .' Uladrack was unsure of the right words. She put a hand on Woozie's arm, but he swivelled out of reach. The irevamp's voice turned soft. 'I'm sorry,' she repeated. 'But I don't feel that way about you.'

'Cos I'm ugly and not clever like you,' retorted Woozie. And these words – *something* – opened a vault within the wibblewallian, for he poured forth: 'And I'm not cuddly like

Rumbles or graceful like Marielle or brave like Tommy.' A tear and then another dripped on to his furry cheek. 'All my friends've left me. And no one's ever fancied me. I never had a girlfriend . . . I'm ugly, aren't I? Repulsive and stupid.'

'No, no.' Uladrack squeezed the wibblewallian's hand, holding it till his tears petered out. 'You don't really love me,' she murmured. 'You just miss your friends.'

'Not true,' mumbled Woozie through sniffs. And Uladrack wiped his fur dry with the hem of her cape. 'Sorry,' said Woozie when he'd recovered. And they both laughed at the strangeness of the situation.

'I think you're handsome and funny and kind and thoughtful,' said Uladrack. 'I hope *I*'m your friend.'

But the wibblewallian held up his hand. 'I'm OK – you don't have to make things up to make me feel good.'

'I'm not,' replied the irevamp. 'I like being with you. I don't want our conversations to end because of this . . . incident.'

'But you don't fancy me?'

Uladrack shook her head. 'I would, Woozie, if I were that way inclined, but . . . I've fallen for another . . . Another contestant.'

'Really?' said Woozie, surprised. He couldn't think who.

The irevamp nodded. 'Marielle,' she said. Now there was a tear in her eye.

It turned out that most male irevamps fancy boys, while female irevamps fancy girls. Only thing was, Marielle hadn't felt the same way about Uladrack. 'She said her heart was with another,' explained the dark-haired girl. 'And before she disappeared, she claimed her heart was broken.' Uladrack admitted she'd never win Marielle's heart, but that didn't stop her loving the elquinine or being prepared to do anything to know she was safe.

'And then I go and ruin it all by saying something stupid like, *sneeze at me*.'
(popular love song across the galaxies)

In most galaxies outside the Milky Way, it was far more common for females to marry females, or for males to marry males, than for inter-marrying to happen between the sexes – perhaps because many of these creatures can create babies merely by eating a type of buttermilk pancake that's been sneezed on by someone else. Indeed, one of the universe's most popular churches, the Cattle-Prod Church, claimed that it was 'unnatural' for males and females to marry 'because they are so different' and that allowing such 'abominations' would 'undermine the happy marriages of same-sexers'. (The Church's superiors used electric cattle-prods to keep its flock of followers in line – you'd get a poke in the arm if you broke a minor Church rule, such as claiming that planets are flat rather than round. Cattle-prods were inserted in much sorer places if you were caught cuddling someone of the opposite sex.

That night – the final night – a voice over the tannoy system announced: 'After you return to the Bowl from the ForkInStewpit Challenge tomorrow, you will all be free to leave – except for the contestant at the top of the leaderboard – *the Winner* – who will have to stay to collect the jackpot super-duper prize.'

62

Choosing

Bin-Liner knelt before an enormous teeth-bared mouth carved out of the rocky wall. Behind him, a bonfire cackled and crackled, echoing across the chamber.

'Oh, Canine-of-Canines,' he incanted. 'There may still be two "Knights" left on ChAOS, but, I tell you, they may be nothing but a distraction, and we should be looking to other battles.' His eyes rolled up into their sockets. 'For wisdom is the only thing that can save the universe and if these "Knights" are not wise then they pose us no threat and we can cease our attempts to kill them.' His eyes rolled down, fixing the rocky teeth in their stare. 'And so, you should know that I have put in place a scheme – to discover if either Knight has the potential for wisdom and to destroy him if he does.'

Bin-Liner prostrated himself before the rocky mouth. 'Oh, Canine-of-Canines,' he continued, 'if I destroy one of these Knights, the beauty is that no one will suspect a thing and *nothing can go wrong* – no mistakes, no last-minute escape or trickery. Because I'll make him *choose* to die.'

When Tommy awoke on the morning of Day Twenty-One, he was delighted to hear a voice proclaiming: 'Last day . . .

They're probably going to kill us all – *very slowly*. Except for the overall winner. They'll die quickly – that'll be the *super-duper prize*. Wait'll you see.'

He was *delighted* because this meant Joe Yuss was still 'in the ascendancy'. (Syri Yuss was very popular with voters and if she'd appeared overnight she could've harmed his chances of winning.) He changed out of his pyjamas – keeping the spots on his shoulder-blades well hidden – and, after an uneventful breakfast (apart from Yago covering Lillroysen's food in pepper when no one was looking), an announcement rang out: 'The ForkInStewpit Challenge will begin in thirty minutes . . . Contestants will be dropped *individually* on to Planet Stewpit at a fork in the road. One road leads to a miserable pit of "stew". The other road leads to "treasures". You must choose a road and follow its path.'

'But how will we know which road to take?' cried Lillroysen.

'*That* is part of the challenge,' replied the voice over the speakers. 'But you will have help . . . Identical twins live in a house by the fork. One twin *always* tells the truth. The other *always* lies. You may knock on the door and ask any *one* question of whoever answers. If you say or ask *anything* else, you will immediately be transported to a pit of gloopy stew.'

Uladrack raised her voice, shielding her face with a hand. 'But how will we know which twin we're talking to – if it's the one who always lies or the one who always tell the truth?'

'You won't,' said the voice over the speakers. 'Which is why your question will have to be particularly clever . . . Oh, and anyone caught deciding on the road to take by means of Eenie-Meenie-Minie-Moe will be whisked to a pit of gloopy stew.'

'He who *baggzed* the peppercorn, gets the peppercorn – even if he hates pepper and throws away the corn.'
(one of the universe's most famous legal quotes)

Lots of important decisions (particularly government decisions) are made across the cosmos using the Eenie-Meenie-Minie-Moe method. Indeed, many disputes and court cases are settled in the same way – though rows can continue afterwards if the 'losing' party insists they thought it was the 'best of three'. Other methods for settling disputes in courts of law include:

★ *One-cuts-the-other-chooses* – used in cake or pizza-sharing disputes
★ *Who-'Baggzed'-It-First?* – used in disputes over items that cannot be shared
★ *Who-Bribed-The-Judge?* – prevalent across many EARTHs

The contestants began emptying out their wardrobes. As Tommy leant into his, stuffing belongings into a backpack, he came upon a package buried beneath his things. And written upon it, in familiar handwriting, was: *Tommy*. He almost opened it – *What would Marielle leave for me?* – till he realized that it could break his concentration and put him off the final challenge. In fact, he told himself, it would be disrespectful to open it now with everyone milling around, when he couldn't give it his full attention. Whatever Marielle had left, it could wait till later.

Tommy plopped on to Planet Stewpit. The light was murky, but he could make out two identical roads ahead of him, each bordered by high bushes. One was labelled *Prickly*, the other *Thorny*. The house containing the twins was right beside him. He ran up, knocked on the door and a completely nondescript creature answered. 'Yes? Can I help you?'

Tommy's mind was still racing – as it had been for the last thirty minutes. If he simply asked which road he should take to the 'treasures', one twin would say *Prickly* and the other would say *Thorny* – and since he'd have no idea if he was talking to the liar or the truth-teller, he'd be none the wiser.

Then the Earthling had a brainwave (one of the few he'd ever claim to have had). 'What road would *your twin* say I should take to the "treasures"?' he asked.

'Thorny,' replied the creature and closed the door.

Yes! thought Tommy. If that twin was the *liar*, then her twin would really say Prickly and that would be the truth. And if the twin I spoke to was the *truth-teller* and she says her twin (the liar) would say Thorny, then the real road is Prickly. In either case, the right road is Prickly!

And so he set off down the road called Prickly – the high, thick bushes closing in behind him so he couldn't change his mind.

After a time, the road petered out and he was faced with three caves. Raucous music and rich smells floated out of one. Soft lighting and warm steam spilled out of the second. And the third was dark and silent – something about it made Tommy shudder.

He was about to step towards the first cave when he halted – a memory jangling in the back of his brain. Lady Muckbeff . . . What was it she used to say?

The treasure thou seekest dost be in the cave thou fearest most . . . But that was just a silly saying, right?

He might've been able to ignore Lady M's words if it

hadn't been for a nagging thought weighing heavily on him, no matter how much he tried to suppress it – *I failed the girl in the red smock. I may have blown my chance.*

He couldn't afford to blow another. No matter how slight. And so he stepped into the third cave – its entrance sealing behind him.

'Ah, Mister Storm . . . We've been expecting you.'

Tommy swivelled towards the distorted male voice and saw a flickering image on the inner cave wall. It looked to be a creature covered in black plastic . . . with holes cut out for its eyes and mouth. And, behind him, a snarling mouth carved out of a rocky wall.

Apart from Tommy, only Yago and Uladrack correctly *deduced* (as opposed to *guessed*) that Prickly was the correct road and made it to the caves. Yago opted for the loud, rich-smelling cave and had himself a mini-banquet; Uladrack plumped for the soft-lit, steamy cave and enjoyed relaxing in a warm, embracing infinity pool. The other five contestants ended up swilling about in a pit of gloopy stew for the next few hours.

Tommy, meanwhile, had to endure a lengthy monologue from the creature who called himself Bin-Liner. The Earthling heard how the Death Case had been responsible for the destruction of forty thousand EARTHs and how Bin-Liner could destroy nearly five million more with a device called a mastervill. 'If you want to verify any of this,' concluded the slit-eyed figure, 'a wigglehole at the back of the cave will take you to proof.'

Shocked, sick, dazed, broad-sided – Tommy didn't know what he felt. This was all so sudden, so out-of-nowhere. 'Who are you?' he cried. 'Why do want to cause such killing and destruction?'

Bin-Liner laughed. 'The real question is, why am I telling *you* all this?'

'Well?' said Tommy, irritation colouring his voice. 'Why?'

Bin-Liner seemed to smile. 'Because all the EARTHs could be saved . . . if I get a certain something.'

'If you get what?'

'*You*, Tommy Storm . . . Your life in return for five million EARTHs.'

63

O Champion My Champion

The wigglehole at the back of the cave brought Tommy to a cluttered office where a donkeyish creature called Heimenopper and a kangalarsen called Bohr were expecting him. After the introductions, they confirmed Bin-Liner's account and showed him the Death Case.

'I asked Bin-Liner to let *me* die – rather than *you* – to save the EARTHs,' explained Heimenopper.'

'Er, me too,' said Bohr. 'I *also* asked him to let *Heimenopper* die rather you.'

'But he wouldn't hear of it,' said Heimenopper.

'It'd be a real shame to see you die,' said Bohr (in a tone intended to cheer Tommy), 'but one boy dying is better than trillions of innocents.' Then his eyes turned curious. 'Why does he want *you* to die?'

Tommy shrugged. 'He wouldn't tell me . . . I think he watched ChAOS and heard I want to save the universe and for some reason he wants the TFC to happen. He's obviously a nutter – a powerful nutter.'

'TFC?' brayed Heimenopper. 'You mean T*S*C – Terrifying Slaughter Countdown. That's what we call it whenever we destroy an EARTH.'

Tommy shook his head and explained about the TFC, adding: 'TFC-TSC – sounds too close to be a coincidence.'

Then he thought of something. 'Could the Death Case destroy the universe?'

'No,' replied Heimenopper. 'Only EARTHs and their solar systems.'

Hmmm. Was there a connection between Bin-Liner and the TFC or was Bin-Liner just a nutter-psycho who happened upon the similarly sounding TSC? Was he linked to the Beast . . ? Somehow Tommy was sure he wasn't.

'So,' said Bohr, interrupting Tommy's thoughts. 'How does Bin-Liner want you to die?'

'Oh, er, on TV,' replied Tommy. 'In front of trillions of viewers.'

'And . . . are you going to go through with it?'

Tommy said nothing for a time, then shook his head. 'No. No way. This guy's a terrorist. He's killed billions and is prepared to kill trillions more. He wouldn't give up the mastervill if I died. He'd break his word. And my death would be for nothing.'

'But . . .' Bohr looked at Heimenopper.

'What?' asked Tommy.

Heimenopper cleared his throat. 'Bin-Liner must've known you wouldn't trust him . . . And, at the same time, he doesn't trust you. He thinks you could try and trick him – pretend to die or get out of dying at the last minute.'

'What do you mean?'

'That's why he had the Exchanger built. That's why he asked PI Farlowe to be a "referee".'

Heimenopper flicked a switch and an image of a bloodhoundy man appeared. He seemed to be in some kind of capsule. 'Glad to sort-of-meet-you, sonny,' he said, addressing Tommy. 'I wish it could be in different circumstances.'

Farlowe explained the workings of the Exchanger. 'If you

decide to do this, then you and I will have a phone conversation some minutes before your execution. I'll have the mastervill in my hands by then and will confirm that to you. If for any reason I don't, then the deal's off.'

'We'll place a wigglehole behind you after you come off the phone,' said Heimenopper. 'It's expensive and not easy to do, so it'll only be there for two seconds. If Farlowe doesn't have the mastervill then you can jump through it and land back here . . . escaping execution.'

Tommy didn't speak for a time, until eventually he gave four sneezes. 'Sorry,' he said. 'High anxiety makes me do that.'

Tommy plopped back into the Wigglery (via the dark cave) half a second after the other contestants. Yago looked stuffed, Uladrack looked extra-relaxed and all the others – including Woozie – were dripping with gloopy stew.

While some took showers, Tommy stood in the Bowl, leant against the glass wall and stared out at the depths of space. He remained like this, transfixed, despite the appearance of a dazzling structure in the distance. It looked like a casino-hotel with *Wolfstain Plaza* writ large in neon lights.

And even as the fans cheered, waving dozens of *Tommy* banners, and a tobogganer dragging a huge baseball mitt zoomed over their heads, the young Earthling continued staring into nothingness. He didn't even glance across at the final leaderboard when it materialized outside the Bowl, accompanied by a blaze of fireworks.

CHAOS LEADERBOARD: RUNNING TOTAL OF VOTES

RANK	CONTESTANT	SELECTED VOTER COMMENT
1	TOMMY STORM	BOLD, BEWTIFUL . . .& BRAVE
2	ZESTRELLA	PLEEZ B *MY* GIRLFRIEND
3	YAGO	U LUK LYK TOMMY – BUT NOT AS NICE
4	BERNARD BURNSIDE	NOW TRY BAKWARDS OFF DA EDGE
5	ULADRACK	IT SPEAKS!
6	J/S YUSS	GRUMPY GIT. BRING BAK SERI!
7	LILLROYSEN	KEEP UP DA FITE TRAINING
8	WOOZIE	ME NO LIKE U[45]

'Tommy Storm – champion of ChAOS!' declared a booming voice. 'Hurrah!'

Next thing, the glass wall Tommy was leaning against gave way and he was falling, falling . . . Till *ssscchmacckkkk!* He whacked against the passing tobogganer, caught his leg on its radio aerial, and was whisked towards Wolfstain Plaza.

Of the contestants, only Uladrack and Yago saw what happened. 'No!' cried Yago. 'No.' Tears were streaming down his face – though whether this was because he feared for Tommy's health or because he was upset at not being the champion of ChAOS was hard to tell.

'Lemme see him!' cried Woozie.

'He's in the Champion's Suite – recuperating,' replied FionaDeFridge. 'You can't go there.'

'But he's my friend! He's injured!'

'It's not our fault,' declared DeFridge. 'We meant him to land on the mitt.'

45 Recent editing had made Woozie look unpleasant to viewers.

They were in the Bowl (off-air), surrounded by luggage, *PoF!* and six other contestants – four of whom were eyeing the dazzling Wolfstain Plaza, while Yago (who'd stopped crying) had Lillroysen in a half-nelson.

'But I gotta see him!' cried Woozie.

'I'm sorry,' replied DeFridge.

'Yeeaaagghhh!'

Distracted by Lillroysen's yell, the wibblewallian looked over to see Yago gripping the little fellow in a headlock. 'No use leaving all this moople syrup here,' declared the Cassiothellian, brandishing a squidgy bottle.

Woozie caught Lillroysen's eye and motioned a digging manoeuvre. The stripy-haired boy breathed in, then drove a hand, shovel-fashion, in under Yago's ribs (careful to miss the bulge of a guineahog). The Casiothellian lurched and released the headlock. Lillroysen swivelled and kicked him hard in the bum. Yago toppled to the floor, still gasping from the dig.

'Lillroysen concurs,' said the little fellow, picking up the bottle of moople syrup. 'No use leaving all this here.' And he emptied its contents over the prostrate bully. (A sea of excited, licking mouths darted out of Yago's pockets.)

For the first time since arriving at the Bowl, Woozie saw Lillroysen give a full and hearty smile. It was only now that the little fellow could truly believe Woozie's assertion during all those self-defence lessons: *bullies can't deal with someone standing up to them*.

'Don't know what you lot are looking so pleased about,' spat Yago, wiping syrup from his eyes. 'Everyone on Cassiothella knows I can't brawl for toffee . . . But I'd beat any of you in a sword duel. Just try me.'

Woozie noticed that *PoF!* (charging by his luggage) made no buzz.

After Yago disappeared to wash his hair and change his clothes, Woozie returned to DeFridge. 'So what's the jackpot prize Tommy's won?'

'Wait and see,' replied DeFridge. 'Wait and see . . . Now, it's almost time for the seven *losers* to officially exit the Bowl.

Various spacecraft appeared at the end of the Arrivals Platform (now called the Departures Platform) as the 'losers' walked down the steps and through the aisle between the (still) baying fans. Yago and Zestrella apart, most exchanged hugs. ('You hate me, don't you?' declared Joe Yuss with every embrace.)

Uladrack and Lillroysen, it turned out, were orphans with no spacecraft – the one they'd arrived in was owned by Beryl MacPairyl's parents and they'd reclaimed it after she died. So the irevamp and the etonianwasp joined Woozie aboard a small, grubby craft that'd been donated by a sponsor[46] for anyone left without transport. It was little bigger than a bathroom inside, with a dashboard that looked like a cooker, three rickety bunks and a cabinet at the rear that served as toilet and shower. Powered by a lawnmower engine it had a maximum speed of 23 kmh.

'All contestants are entitled to a *consolation prize* of a *return wormhole*[47] any time over the next two weeks,' explained DeFridge. 'This should facilitate those wishing to hang around for Tommy's super-duper-jackpot-prize-giving-ceremony.'

Woozie bade DeFridge farewell and turned the

46 Karl's-Kosmic-Salvage-Yard®.

47 Returning them to the place they were originally whisked from.

'Lawnmower' towards Wolfstain Plaza. It took forty minutes to make the journey and when they attempted to dock at the Plaza, security guards turned him away. 'You have to be one of the two people chosen by Tommy Storm,' they explained. 'Or else be on the official party invite list.'

Tommy had banged his head on the tobogganer and cut his leg. So he was feeling groggy and sore when a screen lit up in the Champion's Suite of Wolfstain Plaza.

Greetings and congratulations, Mister Storm,' barked the sharp-toothed face of Henry Wolfstain, ChAOS's producer. 'I'm here to finalize your jackpot prize . . . It's up to you to choose a big event to boost your fame and celebrity and we'll pay for it. Then we'll take half the proceeds from the ticket sales, TV rights, sponsorship and merchandizing. And you take the other half. You're going to be rich and famous, Mister Storm!' Wolfstain spoke in a rapid-fire stream – a car salesman crossed with a machine gun. 'Now what would you like us to organize?' he continued. 'A concert? You probably can't sing, but no matter. We can still sell thousands of tickets and get a fortune for the TV rights before anyone realizes . . . Or we could kidnap someone – maybe one of your fellow contestants – and you could cover them in gloop and creepy crawlies . . . We can do pretty much anything, so long as it promotes your future fame and helps to sell merchandise . . . Do you have any suggestions?'

'Yeah.' Tommy looked up at Wolfstain's grey-furred face. 'An execution.'

The decision to die – Tommy'd made it quickly, maybe too

quickly, but he *knew* it was the right course and he feared he might back out of it if he considered the question for too long. Two factors had settled it.

The first was the five million EARTHs . . . How could he not give himself up to save trillions of others? Especially with PI Farlowe and the Exchanger making it *certain* that Bin-Liner couldn't renege on his promise (and making it impossible for Tommy to double-cross Bin-Liner!).

And secondly . . . Tommy now felt certain that the third page was *not* the Deadly Scroll. No way would Elza's challenge be so easy. And he could no longer suppress the conviction that he'd failed Elza's challenge when the little red-smocked girl died at the end of a spear. And so, the best way he could help save the universe was by completing Bea's Way. Those words he'd sought to suppress for so long came back to him forcefully: *If you sacrifice yerself, then the Beast will help yer fellow Knights wi' the TFC . . . Sacrifice – meanin' you allow yerself tuh be killed tuh save someone else. Not pretend-killed where yuh're revived later or turn up in a new guise. But dead-forever-killed.*

Once Wolfstain heard what Tommy had in mind, the sharp-toothed producer was ecstatic. 'This is wild! We'll make a fortune! You'll be super-rich, Tommy. And super-famous. All right, you might not be around to enjoy it, but hey – minor drawback . . . Obviously we'll send your half of the money to whoever you want – friends, family—'

'You can keep all the money,' replied Tommy.

'All?' Wolfstain was astounded (and even more ecstatic).

Tommy nodded. 'On condition you do two things for me. *And* allow me a last-minute phone call.'

When Tommy had finished explaining, Wolfstain nodded. 'I will agree to the phone call and your two conditions,' he said. '*If . . . if* you agree to submit yourself to my security regime. I'll want every precaution in place to ensure no rescue plan is hatched by your friends.'

Tommy nodded. 'Agreed . . . But the two things I asked for – you must do them *now*.'

Dragging an enormous armour-plated box in its wake, a spacecraft flew towards the 'Lawnmower' and docked against it. A door opened and FionaDeFridge emerged. 'Woozie,' she said. 'Mister Wolfstain would like to offer you a special prize for coming last on the leaderboard. If you wish, your two friends here can join you.'

Woozie, Uladrack and Lillroysen plopped on to a moon circling Planet Hurricane-1-in-50trillion. They walked over to the giant screen showing the planet below and watched as the armour-plated box emptied its contents over the planet.

As DeFridge had explained: 'There'll be nothing on the surface of the planet except all the exploded fragments from Swiggy. Take as long as you like . . . We'll keep you fed and watered. Hopefully you can get your spacecraft back.'

Woozie pressed the button marked 'Hurricane – Go!' and the clouds over the planet began whisking faster and faster.

As the fragments on Planet Hurricane-1-in-50trillion coalesced into a one-legged clock tower and then into a helicopter encased in a slipper, a deluge of food, seeds, gardening books and cookery books rained down on Planet Chah-chah-chariteeeeee. This was followed by a shower of bandages, first-aid kits and prosthetic limbs. Then a cloud of leaflets floated to the ground. These apologized for 'sending no fish,' but promised to go 'two steps better'. As they explained: 'The seas and streams of Planet Chah-chah-chariteeeeee are full of fish. Below are some instructions on how to fish in a sustainable manner . . .' Then a hail of nets and fishing rods fell to the ground – injuring many one-legged and blind creatures (but luckily there were lots of bandages to go around).

64

Nightmare Kiss

It was finalized. The execution was scheduled for fourteen days' time.

Tommy would stay in the Plaza till then, with 'celebrity' parties organized each evening to celebrate his ChAOS win and his upcoming execution. He was allowed to invite two people to join him in the Plaza – they'd be put up in swanky rooms and, like him, not allowed to leave the hotel till just before the execution.

He might've invited Woozie to be one of the two, but Tommy felt the wibblewallian had a greater task trying to recreate Swiggy and, in any case, the very sight of the wibblewallian still hurt him. What's more, he knew Woozie would only try to talk him out of 'sacrificing' his life – and there was no turning back now.

The first person Tommy 'invited' to join him was Zestrella. When she arrived, true to her word, she agreed to be his girlfriend. 'But be warned,' she said. 'I've no heart.' (Tommy didn't believe her.)

The second person was Yago. If anyone could cheer him up in this last fortnight, thought Tommy, it was his waggly-tailed friend. But when Yago arrived, he fell to his knees. 'Oh, Tommy,' he wailed, tears streaming down his cheeks. 'I'm so sorry . . . *So* sorry.' (Yago assumed Wolfstain had told Tommy about the underhand schemes he'd perpetrated during the show. Surely this was why Tommy'd summoned him. What other reason could there be?)

Tommy stooped and embraced the Casiothellian. 'It's OK, my dear friend . . . Don't worry.' (*He* assumed Yago'd already heard about the execution). 'Why don't you check into your room and prepare for this evening's party?'

Woozie took a break from monitoring the creations appearing on Hurricane-1-in-50trillion and handed over to Lillroysen. He joined Uladrack who was nibbling on a snack and sitting in front of a TV (no longer wearing spectacles). She was half-watching a show called *ChAOS – The Aftermath!* and FionaDeFridge's face was taking up the whole screen.

'Yes,' exclaimed the vacuum-cleaner-tailed robot. 'I can announce that Tommy's two invites to the Plaza are . . . Zestrella and Yago!'

Woozie turned and walked away.

Two days in, Zestrella Ravisham allowed Tommy to kiss her. It was a cold kiss – Tommy felt nothing. Yet he consoled himself that these things 'can take time', deciding the fault lay with *him* because he'd moved 'gingerly' (protecting his inflamed, spotted shoulder blades). The tall, tentacled girl had the room below his and she joined him for extravagant breakfasts every afternoon (he needed to sleep-in after the late-night parties) and they watched movies together on a big screen.

By day five, Tommy was enjoying the fact that he could kiss her 'whenever I want' and told himself it was just greedy 'to expect all these kisses to be the kiss of the century'. He had quantity if not quality.

On top of the kisses, Tommy revelled in the lavish parties thrown every evening in his honour. They were full of 'celebrities', yet all the pesterazzi wanted was shot after shot of him with his arm around Zestrella. *Wow!* He'd never felt more wanted, more loved or more alive. All the celebrities seemed oh-so excited to meet him and sacks of fan-mail were deposited in his suite every morning (he only read three letters – each one asking to marry him[48]). He even had a coterie of servants to prepare his meals and cater to his every whim.

And yet . . . And yet . . . He found it harder than ever to be alone. Parties, milling people, 'romance' – they all helped blot out a looming darkness. Seeping thoughts of Marielle and Woozie threatened to *unblot* everything and so he pushed them back.

The eighth day on the moon over Planet Hurricane-1-in-50trillion was bitter-sweet for Woozie. The bleary-eyed wibblewallian was monitoring the Swiggy-forming task when he heard DeFridge's voice waft over from the TV. He tuned in – only to hear the robot announce that Tommy was to be executed in six days' time – supposedly his 'jackpot prize'!

As Uladrack looked over with a cry of: 'It must be a mistake!', Woozie turned away (his two hearts lurching) and saw a half-recognizable form whisk into view on the hurricane planet. Without thinking, he smacked the Stop button by the Creation Screen.

48 They were from two women and 'an Alfabull ice-hockey player' called Gary.

'What an odd-looking craft!' declared Lillroysen when he saw it. This was about the thirtieth space-craft-like object they'd frozen and this thing looked stranger than many of the others and not nearly as sleek as the perfect jumbo jet they'd rejected that very morning.

Hmmm. Woozie blew his nose and stared at the object. It looked like Swiggy, except its paintwork was all funny (there were splodges of different colours all over the silver hull) and one of its wings was turned the wrong way and its 'tail' jutted down from the underside of the cockpit. And what looked like a giant bowling ball was bulging out from one side.

'Can you check whether this thing flies?'

Lillroysen pressed a few buttons below the screen. 'Yep,' he replied. 'It says here this craft can travel at up to sicko-warpo-speed . . . Not bad. But it's pretty ugly. If we keep going for another week, Lillroysen is sure we could come up with something better.'

But Woozie shook his head. 'No time. This is what we're going with.'

'We?' said Uladrack.

Woozie nodded. 'Yeah, forget the Lawnmower. Join me – the both of you. Please. We could drop you somewhere . . . when Tommy joins us. Or you could travel with us for a while.' Then, looking at Uladrack: 'You might even be able to help in tracking down Marielle.'

By night nine, Tommy's enthusiasm for his new life began to wane. The celebrities and hangers-on who laughed at his jokes and gave him hugs, laughed with their mouths not with their eyes, and hugged with their arms not with their hearts. Worst of all, the parties were losing their effectiveness at blocking out thoughts of Woozie and Marielle and of the fate that was to befall him in five days' time.

Inside, the 'new' Swiggy was similar to the 'old' Swiggy, except the furniture was all rearranged, half the rooms had mad, stripy denim wallpaper and the horn now sounded like a piglet squealing. She certainly flew much the same as ever and all the MoTW interactive lessons appeared to run as normal (they were made of extra-strong kryptonite, so perhaps they'd never been harmed by the explosion) and the nawhitmobs seemed fine – even if they'd become luminous and, rather than barking, they now made a fizzing-fuse noise when excited.

Once they'd taken control of the 'new' Swiggy and returned to the vicinity of the Bowl, Woozie gave Uladrack and Lillroysen flying lessons and taught them as much as possible about Swiggy, while making numerous attempts to visit Wolfstain Plaza.

'Ten times we've been refused entry!' declared Woozie after two days of trying. They were 'parked' some distance from the gaudy hotel.

Lillroysen nodded. 'All the windows in the top suites are blacked out.'

'And armed guards patrol every possible landing spot,' added Uladrack.

By now they knew the routine. Every evening, a line of limocraft would arrive at the Plaza's front entrance and vomit out the latest batch of 'celebrities'. Security-patrol-spacecraft would call out over loudspeakers mounted on their wings, urging Swiggy and other voyeuristic spacecraft to stay back.

'They're keeping him captive against his will,' said Woozie.

'And if we don't save him within the next four days—'

'Woh!' interjected Lillroysen. 'What's that?' He was pointing to a floating structure – newly arrived – under the Plaza. Woozie hurried to the viewfinder and peered through. A sign over the structure read: *Super-Duper-Prize-Giving Location*. And it looked like four stadium-like stands were being erected round its edges, with enough seating for thousands of fans. And . . . Woozie tried to focus in. Something hulking stood at the centre of the structure – the light too poor to discern precisely what it was.

But from one angle, Woozie thought he saw a gleaming ridge, like a great razor-blade.

It's night-time, the air thick with darkness and fog. Tommy finds himself walking through a raging storm, cupping a lighted candle with his hands. He looks behind and sees a gigantic, dark figure following him, and he hurries on, through the shrieking wind and rain, cradling the candle, knowing – knowing with every fibre of his being – that all will be lost if it goes out. He glances over his shoulder. The dark, hulking figure is *still* following him. And so he begins to jog, shielding the candle, its flickering more erratic. Yet still the figure looms behind him. And so he begins running. But still the giant figure is there, close behind him. And now he's sprinting, sprinting – *Aaaaaagghhh!!*

Tommy sat bolt upright. Panting. Sweating. Shoulder blades smarting. Alone in his suite in the Plaza.

If anything, the parties were making things worse. With three days to the execution, Tommy told his servants that he'd miss the next party. They told him this would be impossible. The guests and magazine photographers had all been booked and couldn't be disappointed. Plus Zestrella would be expecting him.

And so he redoubled his partying efforts, outwardly holding it together – smiling and exchanging inanities as required and going to bed even later. And yet, still, he could only manage a few hours' sleep before the first nightmare. And then he'd be up – putting on a movie, doing press-ups, scrubbing the pristine bathroom. Counting the time till Zestrella would appear and he could have that first mind-blotting kiss.

He'd expected Yago to lift his spirits, but the sandy-haired boy seemed permanently upset and remorseful and was unable to get out of bed between parties. Only Zestrella's company cheered him.

Actually, that's not entirely true . . . The *anticipation* of her company cheered him. Those five minutes before she came through his well-guarded door were the best five minutes of the day. For, in truth, he never felt happy by her side. Every kiss they exchanged – however inexhaustible the supply – felt empty, only adding to his sense of isolation.

The twelfth lavish party at the Plaza was marked by an argument. Tommy got into a heated debate with the 'actor' Hustin Doffman, finally calling for Doffman to be 'thrown out'. Having received a mild beating and been thrown into a waiting taxi, Doffman was discovered half an hour later tied up in a floating bubble, claiming to know 'nothing' about the argument and denying he'd ever been at the party. Journalists put this down to Doffman's 'weird acting methods' and presumed he was merely preparing to play a 'psychopathic liar' in his next movie role.

The real story was a little different . . .

'I'm *ecstatic* to meet you,' Doffman had said when he met Tommy in the ballroom. 'I'd like to talk to you about a project I'm working on – *Tommy Storm: The Movie*.'

Those within earshot clapped at this news. 'Great!' exclaimed Tommy, soaking up the applause.

'Can we talk . . . *more privately*?' asked Doffman.

Tommy nodded. 'Please,' he said to the onlookers. And they melted away. 'So what kind of movie is it?'

'An *escape* movie.'

'Escape?' Tommy was perplexed.

'Yeah . . .' added Doffman, his voice changed. 'We can get you out of here.'

Tommy stared at Doffman like a dummy. His eyes were telling him one thing, his ears another.

'It's me . . . *Woozie*,' added the strange figure and winked – in Woozie's unique way. 'Good BodyMaskSuit, eh?'

'What are you doing here?' whispered Tommy, looking about. The nearest party guests seemed involved in their own conversation.

'You could sound more pleased,' said Woozie. 'You know how much trouble this took?'

For a moment Tommy did indeed feel pleased. Pleased that someone had gone to such effort to see him. Then a figure with sandy hair interrupted and Tommy had to make the introductions.

'*Doffman*, this is Yago – a *loyal* friend.'

'I love your work,' said Yago to 'Doffman'.

'Thank you,' replied 'Doffman', adding with a cheery smile: 'You strike me as a pretty good actor yourself . . . In fact, you strike me as a phony . . . A back-stabbing phony.'

During this exchange, Tommy saw Zestrella beckoning from across the room. *Time to do it for the cameras.* He could almost feel the kisses – knew every one would eke a little more from his heart. And yet, like an addict miserable after every cigarette, he couldn't bring himself to stop.

Perturbed by Doffman's comment, Yago skulked off.

'I'm here to rescue you,' whispered Woozie.

'I don't need rescuing.'

'They're gonna kill you,' hissed Woozie. 'That's the super-duper prize. The guillotine – in front of trillions of viewers. Just take a look at what's floating under the Plaza.'

Tommy seemed unmoved by this 'revelation'. 'I don't need rescuing.'

Woozie was astounded. 'You – Tommy Storm – are happy to die!?' Tommy made no answer. Thewibblwallion's eyes boggled. 'The TFC, the whole universe due to be destroyed in less than eleven months now, and you're happy to lie down and die. You're an IGGY Knight and we—'

'The IGGY Knights,' blurted Tommy. 'That's a laugh! Marielle, Summy and Woozie abandoned me and then—'

'They didn't abandon you. *You* abandoned *them*!'

'Rubbish!' exclaimed Tommy, turning purple.

'True! You've forsaken your friends, betrayed all your principles—'

'And you,' interjected Tommy, seemingly shaking with anger. 'You . . . What kind of friend have you been?' He pressed his finger into Woozie's midriff. 'Sabotaging me during the challenges, jealous of my new friends.' Tommy's fury appeared to be so great, his breathing had become laboured, his eyes all red.

'I never—'

'I don't need saving from anyone. Least of all from you!'

And before he summoned the bouncers to throw out 'Doffman', before he scurried over to Zestrella for his camera-clicking fix of kisses, Tommy's voice seemed to crack with fury. '*Don't* – I repeat – *don't* ever try to save me again.'

Quack-Quack

Many scholars have attempted to interpret Tommy's 'candle-in-the-storm' dream. Some say the gigantic, dark figure was the TFC and the storm was Tommy himself. Others say the storm represented Earth. However, the famous Quaxpert,[49] Jarl Kung, maintains that the candle was Tommy's soul and that the dark figure following him was nothing but his *own* shadow, cast by the candle. This shows, according to Kung, that deep down Tommy realized his own soul was his greatest treasure – and yet – that he, Tommy, was the one who could do it the most damage. Particularly if he allowed himself to be executed.

49 A Quaxpert is someone who analyses people's minds – so called because their main task is to help people not to 'duck' the truly important issues in their lives.

65

If Only

Back in his suite, after the Doffman incident, a screen lit up with an image of Wolfstain. 'Just to let you know . . . We're stepping up security to ensure no 'slip-ups' . . . Tommy Storm BodyMaskSuit detectors have been installed everywhere – anyone caught wearing one will be executed . . . Now, get some sleep. You'll want to look your best for the cameras!'

Whether it was due to Wolfstain's words or Woozie's visit, alone in his room, Tommy was hit with the realization: *I'm to die! In less than thirty hours!*

This 'awakening' had been threatening to break through for days. Imprisoned in party-hell, he was hardly sleeping at all, relying on extra-strong sleeping pills for those scant few hours of unconscious relief. The shadows were closing in. For he couldn't escape the fact that he'd lost the other IGGY Knights. He couldn't but see that Zestrella would never love him and that, in truth, he'd never really loved her. The kisses he gave her were as empty as the ones he got back. For he really wanted to kiss someone else. The only person in the universe he'd ever truly loved. Maybe that's why he couldn't get enough.

Tommy sat on his bed, staring at the blank wall.

Eventually, he went to a wardrobe, pulled out a rucksack and rummaged through the socks to a package underneath. Ripping it open, he found a letter from Marielle with another page attached and a small disk. First he read the letter.

Dear Tommy,

I don't know what to say. I'm writing this really quickly because I never thought we – I – would leave you. But now we are and I have no choice. Saving the universe is bigger than my selfish wants.

To be honest, leaving you tonight is easier than staying because it feels like I've lost you already. I don't know what I did wrong. Was I so mistaken?

I think our lessons on Swiggy have all had the same underlying message – *at some stage in this mission, we have to take a leap of faith . . .* Now, I'm taking that leap of faith. I think this is the way to save the universe. I've met a Guiding Light I can believe in.

You think Elza's challenge is the way to go and maybe you're right. I've pored over 'the three pages' every night in this Bowl and in the afternoons when we've been on those awful Sponsor planets (I'm sure you have too). I even took Uladrack into my confidence and discussed it with her and she agrees with me (and she's smart, Tommy). We think it's the second page (see attached). Now I see it, it's obvious. I was wrong before when I thought it was the third page.

Seems I've been wrong about a lot of things.

~~If only~~ Sorry, time's up . . . Got to run.

Please, Tommy . . . Whatever you do, wherever you go, do know that I won't forget you.

Marielle
x

P.S. I made this disc for you some time ago. Never had the courage to give it to you.

The page attached was the poem entitled 'If'.

Tommy removed the disc. Scrawled across it were the words: Marielle plays clarinet. The memory of the last time he'd heard Marielle playing came to him and his heart lurched. For a moment he saw it all so clearly. How selfish, how cruel, how stupid-stupid-stupid I've been! If only—

KNOCK! KNOCK!

'Is sir awake yet?' intoned a voice. 'Should we summon Zestrella and bring in the brunch?'

'Ten minutes!' replied Tommy, gathering himself. 'Gimme ten minutes.'

He hurried in to the shower and blasted cold water in his face. I lost it there, he thought. I let her get to me . . . She even made me feel like I abandoned HER? Hah! . . . She abandoned ME!

He felt a new pain, a bruised heaviness deep in his chest. And it angered him to feel so softened. He ran back into the bedroom and removed three pages from a zip pocket at the front of his rucksack – the three possible Deadly Scrolls. Oh, how he'd feared it was the first page – 'save the girl & triumph'. But now, as he read and reread the poem 'If' – the one page he'd dismissed – he saw that yes, Marielle just might be right.

And yet . . . What did it matter? He had to save the EARTHs. And the Beast would help his friends if he 'sacrificed' himself.

He dressed and stuffed Marielle's letter along with all the pages into the depths of his rucksack. He was about to do the same with the disk when he hesitated. He looked over at the disc-player by the bed.

KNOCK! KNOCK!

'Miss Ravisham is here, sir!'

Tommy shoved the disc into the rucksack and pushed the rucksack under his bed. 'OK . . ! Let her in!'

66

Determined to Die

A battered figure climbed out of a spacecab and in through a doorway in Swiggy's side. Moments later, a 'hotel bellboy' emerged from the corkscrew lift in Swiggy's Lobby.

'You're back!' cried Uladrack (her hair pulled back in a rubber band). 'You look hurt.' In truth, he looked worse than when he'd returned as Hustin Doffman the night before. 'You OK?'

The bellboy nodded and the irevamp led him into the Lounge and helped peel off his clothes and his very skin, revealing a furry creature underneath. 'These body-mask-suits are a nightmare to remove,' said Uladrack.

Now that he looked himself once more, Woozie fell back into a giant cushion. He looked utterly depressed.

'Didn't work?' asked Uladrack. Woozie shook his head. 'But you had the voice perfect. That's what separates you from all the regular dummies who put on body-mask-suits.'

Woozie sighed. 'The disguise worked perfectly . . . I even got into his room this time. Got him on his own – no celebrities or staff hanging about.'

'But . . ?' coaxed Uladrack.

Woozie touched his swollen eye. 'We were arguing and he says: *What do I have to say to make you stop trying to save me?* I says: *Tell me our friendship is over.*'

'You said that?'

Woozie nodded. 'So he looks at me and says: *Consider our friendship over.*'

'No!'

'Yeah! . . . He was either really angry or really upset, cos his eyes were all watery and he turned away. And I says: *You don't mean that. If you meant it you'd punch me.* And his shoulders were shaking and I think maybe he's crying. I think, at last I've made him see sense. So I says again: *If you really meant that you'd punch me*. And just when I think he's turning round to hug me, he whips round quick as lightning and gives me one. Right in the eye.'

'He punched you?'

'A real smacker . . . And while I'm lying there, he says he's gonna die no matter what. Says he's gonna save five million EARTHs. Says I should forget about Elza's challenge and just get to Hellsbells. The Beast will *definitely* help me stop the TFC . . . Then before I could protest or ask a question he had me thrown out.'

They fell silent for a time. 'He's lost it,' said Woozie eventually. 'He's due to be executed tomorrow and he seems *determined* to die! He's not—'

Woozie was interrupted by a cry from the cockpit. It was Lillroysen. 'Woh! A rickety, rustbucket coming close! I think it's trying to dock with us!'

At the urge of Uladrack and Woozie, Lillroysen had managed to stop referring to himself in the third person ALL the time. In return, he got them to do something for him. 'I've always wanted to be known as Roysters,' he explained. And so 'Roysters' he became.

Woozie hurried to the cockpit and donned a set of headphones. 'You've made a mistake. This is Swiggy. Please disengage your craft.'

'No mistake, kid,' retorted a voice. 'Let me in. I got the scoop on your buddy.'

'Who are you?' asked Woozie, suspicion colouring his voice.

'I'm the keeper of promises and the breaker of dreams – or was that my ex-wife?'

Middle-aged, with big floppy ears, the new arrival had strange and startling news.

'I been in and around that capsule yonder,' he said, pointing to a dot floating beneath Wolfstain Plaza. 'Lotsa time to kill – I saw you "recreate" this spacecraft on *ChAOS – The Aftermath!* Then out my window, I saw you flying and scooting round. And I told myself, PI Farlowe, these guys are up to something – probably trying to save their friend, Tommy Storm. Am I right . . ? So I thought I'd have a word, as I feel kinda bad – cos of my role in all this.'

Farlowe gave them the low-down on the EARTHs and Bin-Liner and the Exchanger.

Woozie was angry. 'Why didn't he explain it to me properly? I thought Tommy was making up a story!'

'His life is due to end *tomorrow*,' replied Farlowe. 'He probably can't explain how to make a cuppa coffee right now.'

Uladrack's mind was on to practicalities. 'This Exchanger – is there some way we can rig it?'

The blood-houndish man shook his head. 'No, I've tried everything. It's foolproof. Unless Tommy dies, five million EARTHs will . . .' He mimed a gun to his head.

'What if I came into the capsule with you? If we tried to—'

Farlowe cut Woozie off. 'Can't be done. There's three sets of doors to get in. Soon as you go through one set, the other locks behind you. Each set opens by reading *my* iris and checking *my* paw prints and doing an Enclosed Space Scan to ensure I've got no one and nothing with me.'

Frustration got the better of Woozie and he turned on Farlowe. 'So what are you here for? Eh?'

'Like I said, I'm sorry for your friend. Just wanted you to know . . . Plus I need to kill some hours before the execution – sorry! – poor choice of words.'

Once Uladrack had calmed Woozie somewhat, they invited Farlowe to stay and eat. Over bowls of spaghetti carbon-R-aahh, Farlowe answered more questions about the mastervill, and Woozie (who couldn't eat) gave a lengthy explanation of the TFC and the IGGY Knights' mission.

'Listen,' said Farlowe. 'I saw there's a reward for finding your three friends.'

'Marielle, Summy and Rumbles?'

'Sure. The Big Universe Missing Kids Organization – BUMKO – are offering ten million squalors. It's a publicity stunt – they don't expect anyone to find them . . . But *I* reckon following the TFC trail might just lead you to them.'

'What're you saying?' asked Woozie.

'I'm saying, after – I mean, *if* – Tommy dies, I'd be happy to hitch my trailer to your wagon for a while.'

Woozie frowned. 'If you're saying what I think you're saying, you should know that we won't be hanging round here . . . If Tommy says we should go to Hellsbells, then that's where we'll be going!'

'Fine with me,' replied Farlowe.

The blood-houndy detective fell asleep on the couch after dinner.

'What if we handcuffed him and kept him here?' suggested Woozie. 'Then he wouldn't be able to perform his Exchanger function and the execution might be called off.' When he saw Uladrack's appalled expression, he added: '*I know* – it wouldn't work and it wouldn't be right. But you can't blame me for thinking it!'

The wibblewallian spent the next while going over ideas with Uladrack and Roysters – but they came up with no way to save Tommy *and* save the EARTHs. 'Maybe if I talk to Tommy again,' said Woozie at last, glancing at the snoring figure of Farlowe. 'We might be able to come up with *some way*.'

The wibblewallian fetched another body-mask-suit. 'I could dress up as his butler.'

'Why don't I accompany you?' suggested Uladrack. 'I could be a chambermaid . . . Maybe he'll listen to the reasoning of a female.'

Two hours later, a spacecab screeched to a halt alongside Swiggy, depositing something (or some *persons*) in through a side door. It whizzed off just before a swarm of security craft swooped in, missiles firing. Swiggy revved up and started moving. Most of the missiles missed, but two landed – one on the wing, one near the tail-fin – waking Farlowe and making the Lancaster-like craft rock before she pulled away and disappeared into space.

Inside the cockpit, Roysters tugged on the steering-wheel, crying, 'Where are they!? Have we lost them!?'

'Outta sight, sonny,' said Farlowe from over the waspish boy's shoulder.

They flicked on the automatic pilot and descended to the Lounge. Woozie was kneeling on the carpet, half divested of his butler body-suit-mask, holding a chambermaid in his arms.

'She got whacked,' he said.

'Whacked?' said Farlowe, miming a gun to his head.

'Not that kind of whacked,' replied Woozie. 'The bouncers roughed us up. She got hit on the head before we escaped.'

'She's ever-so pale.'

'She's always pale!'

As if unpeeling a banana, they opened up the body-mask-suit and eased Uladrack out. A pile of shampoos and soaps fell out of the pockets of the chambermaid suit.

'Golly!' exclaimed Roysters. 'Did she steal all those?'

Farlowe held the irevamp by the wrist and searched for a pulse.

'You didn't get through to him?' asked Roysters. 'Tommy, I mean.'

Woozie shook his head. 'If anything it was worse than before . . . He flew into a rage when he realized it was us. Gave me a flurry of punches.'

The wibblewallian wandered to the shelves outside the Boys' Dorm and picked up the Tommy action-man that Rumbles had made so many months ago. He twisted its arms and stared into its face.

'Say, what if you dressed up as Wolfstain?' suggested Roysters.

Woozie squeezed the action-man and hurled him across the room. He smashed into pieces against the far wall.

Farlowe appeared from the Girls' Dorm with a stethoscope

around his neck. He glanced down at the broken figure, then up at the two young men. 'She'll live,' he said. 'She's getting some shut-eye.' Then the bloodhound-like man walked across the room. 'Now, if you'll excuse me, I presume my rustbucket's still down in your docking bay?'

Woozie nodded. 'Sorry for that . . . escapade – while you were asleep.'

Farlowe gave him an unreadable look. 'I better get going . . . Got a job to do.'

When he was gone, Roysters picked up the pieces of the broken action-man. 'Five hours till the execution,' he ventured, the sting peeking out of his tail. 'You can't intend to sit here and do nothing?'

Woozie slumped on the couch. 'I've had my fill of persuading,' he said. 'I'm not gonna put Swiggy and everyone else in danger again.'

'But Tommy's—'

'Screw Tommy Storm!' snapped Woozie. 'Marielle was right! Saving the universe – or, in this case, saving five million EARTHs – is more important than the life of one person. *Whoever* that person may be.'

67
Fornax!

It's a strange thing knowing you've only ninety minutes to live. You realize all that will never be.

Sitting alone in his suite, Tommy felt the press of time like never before. It pushed at a door deep within him. Yet he stared at his own reflection in a mirror. Impassive. Ignoring the bruised heaviness in his chest. There is honour in death, he told himself. My parents – they chose to die to save others.

These thoughts, meant to seal the door deep within him, whirled and pulled the other way. He stared in the mirror and saw his mum and dad hugging Marielle and Woozie. *But that's crazy – they're dead! Dead!! And this is just a mirror!*

With a cry of 'Fornax!' he punched the mirror, smashing it. And the door within him burst open.

'Fornax! Fornax! Fornax! FORNAX!!'

Why? Why!? WHY!?

He smashed a light. And a chair. And crumpled to the ground. Gasping, he crawled to his rucksack and pulled out the envelope. He read Marielle's letter. Then read it again. And again. And again. No tears, just uncontrollable shaking – through his body, through his soul. *If I'd listened . . . If I'd done this . . . If I hadn't done that . . . If I'd just . . . If only . . . If . . . If. IF!!*

He took the disc and crawled to the disc-player by the bed.

He pushed it into the slot. The anticipation of the pain that'd flow, of the door still locked that could open, of the deepest demons that might be released . . . His finger tremored, over the *Play* button. And tremored.

I can't!

He snatched the disc and stuffed it into his inside pocket together with the letter. Then he ran into the bathroom and threw water on his face. *I'm due to die . . . in seventy-eight minutes . . ! By lunch-time, I'll be dead!*

Woozie. An image of the wibblewallian came to him. *I want to see him.* Woozie was the last contact with his beloved IGGY Knights. *And the terrible things I said to him!* Things he'd only said to ensure the wibblewallian wouldn't try to save him. *I have to see him!*

'Sorry,' replied Wolfstain's image on the big-screen. 'There's no time before you enter the Execution Arena.'

'Yes, but he could visit me in the Arena. You said I could have visitors in the minutes before I die.'

'Yes. *Two* visitors. You chose them days ago.'

'But can't I add *one* other?'

'Impossible,' barked Wolfstain. 'Security would throw a wobbly. Not to mention the advertisers.'

'But . . .' Tommy looked desperate. 'If I can't *add* someone, can I *swap* one of the two I've chosen for someone else?'

Wolfstain shook his head. 'Too late.'

68
The Chop

'Thirty three minutes and counting!' boomed a voice over the speaker-system.

The forty thousand fans crammed into the circle of stands that made up the Execution Arena went nuts – whooping, screaming, flinging rolls of toilet paper, and performing an inverted Mexican wave.[50] High above them, the base of the Plaza. Below, in the centre of the stadium, a raised platform with two structures upon it. The first, a wooden hut with no windows. The second, a ghoulish monstrosity that struck fear and nervous giddiness in all who glanced its way.

The voice through the speakers was announcing a special price on *Tommy* scarves and hats when a lift-like contraption descended from the Plaza and the doors opened. The crowd went berserk.

'There he is!'

'He looks scared!'

'Rubbish! He looks excited!'

'Don't you throw toilet paper at me!'

Tommy, surrounded by an entourage of bodyguards, was almost at the steps leading up to the platform when a wolfish-looking man appeared from behind the lift with a hairspray-

50 Formed by lines of people sitting down briefly in a stadium where everyone else is standing.

microphone. 'My name is Henry Wolfstain,' he proclaimed. 'And I'd like to announce a change of format to this execution.'

What that change was supposed to be, no one ever found out, for a spectator leapt from the crowd and charged. An explosion rang out – sending fragments of chocolate, limbs, hats, scarves and toilet rolls everywhere. When the chocolate settled, Wolfstain was dead, as were six bodyguards and fourteen fans.

The charging spectator (the bomber) was one of the 'fans' to die. He had no link to Bin-Liner's Mentaler Fundyists. As the note he left sellotaped to his seat explained, he was merely staging a protest against 'the cruelty of staged executions'.

Fortunately (or unfortunately) for Tommy, he was unhurt and still surrounded by a crew of bodyguards who squeezed in tight while the dead were scraped from view.

Tommy was scared – very scared – as he approached the platform steps. Yes, he was set on this course of action, but that didn't mean he wasn't frightened by the prospect of pending death.

But the fear – though aching and tangible – was no longer all-consuming. For Tommy now understood the zits on his shoulder. *They only come when I'm being untrue to myself.* And in the last forty-eight hours they'd begun to clear from his shoulder blades.

He could take some comfort from that. He was definitely doing the right thing.

The black-clad boy was led up the steps of the platform, past the ghoulish monstrosity and into the windowless hut in the centre of the stadium. Then the bodyguards took up posts around the hut – some even climbing under the platform to guard it from below and some scrambling up on its roof.

'Thank you, ladies and gentlemen,' boomed the speakers. 'We apologize for that interruption to proceedings and are pleased to announce that the execution will proceed on time . . . In twenty-two minutes . . . And please remember that Tommy Storm T-shirts are still available for purchase from stalls all over the stadium.'

There was a roar from the crowd as a troop of Tommy look-alikes paraded on to the platform in chains.

'Behold, the people caught in Tommy Storm body-mask-suits,' exclaimed the loudspeakers. 'Now, as a taste of the proceedings to come, they will be executed.'

Two groups of archers appeared, one on either side of the platform. Thirty seconds later, the look-alikes were dead (as were three archers, six fans and two bodyguards – the archers weren't great shots).

A phone was brought up to the platform on a silver tray. 'The last phonecall,' bellowed the speakers and the crowd seemed to understand, for they hushed as the hut door opened and Tommy emerged. He took the phone, punched a set of numbers and, after a pause, spoke into the receiver.

'Hey, this you? . . . I need to be sure. Last time we spoke, you gave me the low-down and then I sneezed. How many times did I sneeze?'

In an impenetrable capsule floating high above the stadium, a blood-houndy man stood in a pair of humming metal boots, a set of headphones on his head, a metal ring around his neck (pulled upwards by a chain), two sets of chains hooped round his elbows pulling his arms outwards, and a bread-roll-sized crystal – dark at one end, light at the other – held within his trembling hands. And, punched into the wall beside him, was a question: IS TOMMY STORM DEAD?

'Gotta admire you, kid,' he said into the microphone before his lips. 'Great thinking. Making sure it's really me and not some Bin-Liner stooge pretending to be me . . . The answer is four – four sneezes . . . Yeah, I can confirm, I've got it in my hands, right now. The mastervill – the real thing . . . I can see you on the platform through the window here . . . You're doing a good thing – a great and brave thing. I only wish it didn't have to be this way . . . You, too, kid . . . So-long.'

Viewers and fans saw Tommy hang up the phone and, for a brief few seconds, a shimmering shadow appeared behind him.

'It's a wigglehole!' cried one of the fans. 'He's going to escape.'

Tommy looked over his shoulder. The guards were hurrying towards him, yet he could easily jump through before they made it over. The Earthling closed his eyes just as the wigglehole disappeared and the guards grabbed him. They shoved him into the hut and closed the door.

'Now,' bellowed the speakers. 'The first of two visitors chosen by Tommy to share his final moments.'

The sandy-haired figure of Yago stuttered up the steps of

the platform and grasped a microphone.

'I'm sorry,' he cried, between tears. 'I never wanted Tommy to die. I don't want my friend to die. What've I done?'

He crumpled into a heap and two bodyguards helped him to his feet and half-carried him to the door of the hut. They opened the door and he collapsed through it. Then they shut the door and allowed the two boys to have three minutes of privacy.

'Time up!' boomed the speakers and the crowd roared as the door opened and Yago collapsed to the ground. He was removed from the platform by bodyguards (no one wanted the TV pictures ruined by such overt signs of grief).

Then it was Zestrella's turn. She waved away the hair-spray-microphone when it was offered to her and entered the hut. When the speakers boomed 'Time up!' she failed to emerge. A bodyguard flung open the door and warned her to exit. In the end, he dragged her out and shut the door. She stood before the crowd, looking shaken, two fingers touching her lips. Someone handed her a can of hairspray and the crowd hushed.

'I've never felt so . . .' She stared at her fingers, then touched her lips again. 'What is this?' she mumbled, dream-like. 'This strange feeling . . .' She turned pale then flushed. 'Let him out!' she yelled. And she lunged towards the hut. 'Don't let him die! Don't kill him! Don't—!'

A hand was clamped over her mouth and Zestrella was bundled from the platform, kicking and struggling.

The crowd loved it. Almost as much as the advertisers.

The technical term for the ghoulish monstrosity upon the platform was a kah-plonk-chopper-in-halfer (kah-chopper for short). It looked like a giant guillotine with coils and funnels and pendulums and weird-shaped objects stemming like a jagged tail from the raised blade. This 'tail' wound its way back and forth across the platform till it reached the ground in the form of a long tube. Kah-choppers are activated by rolling a marble into this tube – which sets a series of dominoes falling, releasing another marble which plops into a beaker of acid, causing an explosive puff to ignite a length of tinder wire, which in turn sets a pendulum swinging. At the end of the process, the Doom Marble is set rolling. When this hits the Guillotine-Release-Hair-Trigger, two tonnes of razor-sharp steel drop fifteen metres, chopping whatever lies below.

Two things need to be done correctly to ensure that 'the chop' happens. Firstly, the kah-plonk mechanism must be set up perfectly by the K-P Mechanic so that all the processes will happen. Secondly, the Doom Marble must be rolled accurately by the Executioner. This isn't too difficult – the marble is the size of a gob-stopper, the Tail Tube opening is wider than a waste-paper basket and the Executioner 'releases' the marble less than an arm's-length from the tube opening.

'Let's hear it for Tommy!' boomed the speakers.

The crowd roared and Tommy Storm appeared from the hut. For a second it looked like he might make a run for it, then he strode to the centre of the platform (which was completely surrounded by bodyguards) and picked up the microphone. The crowd hushed.

'Death,' he said. 'Is it the end?'

'It is for you!' cried a spectator and a smattering of people laughed.

Tommy ignored them. 'I don't know the answer to that question,' he said. 'All I know is that what I'm doing today—' His voice cracked and he had to stop speaking. Again some people giggled. The young Earthling gathered himself and found some inner strength for when he next spoke it was with a voice of exhortation: 'What I do today – choosing to die – I do because I believe it gives our universe, my universe, the best chance of being saved from the TFC. And saves a lot of planets.'

A few titters rang out from the crowd in response to this and a group began chanting *TFC, TFC* half-heartedly – giving up when no one else joined in.

Tommy continued in a softer voice: 'I've made many mistakes in my life . . .'

'That's for sure!' cried another spectator (who looked embarrassed when he didn't get a laugh).

'. . . And I've done some mean things I'm not proud of . . . There's one friend particularly that I've hurt and never meant to. For I can see now, in these final moments that I love him with all my heart – no matter what darkness has passed between us these last five weeks . . .' Again his voice cracked and he turned away. The crowd was now so silent that everyone could hear the sobs emanating from the young Earthling. Some hung their heads and looked at the floor. Others craned forward to get a better look at his tears. The dark boy seemed to recover. He cleared his throat and turned around. 'As for Marielle, Rumbles and Summy—'

But no one heard what he said for a technician cut the microphone (a big sponsor had called in to say 'Cut the chatter. Get on with the main event!').

When the young Earthling had finished saying whatever it was he had to say, he put down the microphone, walked to the centre of the kah-chopper and lay across the chopping block. A number of bodyguards stepped forward and bound him to the block with 'unbreakable' tinderwire. Tommy couldn't move.

'Now, let's hear it for the K-P Mechanic!' boomed a speaker. A creature on the platform, bowed, slipped on his tail and fell into the crowd. 'And now let's hear it for our guest Executioner! . . . Someone who needs no introduction.'

An elderly man with an eagle-like face, strode up the steps of the platform, acknowledging the applause. He wore a black mortar board on his head and a black tutor's gown. He approached Tommy, crouched and said something. (Lip readers claim it was: 'You may think I don't like you, boy, but you'd be wrong . . . You see, I like feisty boys the best. For, I enjoy the battle . . . So I'm sorry to see you die. Truly . . . And yet I can enjoy this moment. Because it means, at long last, I *will* have your guts for garters. Quite literally.' At this point he put a hand on Tommy's cheek and supposedly said: 'Make peace with yourself before you go.')

Roshviler stood back, a drum rolled, the fans did a count-down and then the eagle-eyed-canine-sapian rolled the marble.

69
My Everything

Some hours before the execution, Woozie took Roysters up to Swiggy's cockpit and set out the plan for getting to Hellsbells.

'If you press this code into this keypad, it'll activate the 'return wormhole' we were given by ChAOS. We were close to some black holes when we first came through to the show and Swiggy'll reappear through the wormhole in the same spot – travelling in the opposite direction, away from the black holes. But still, it's probably best to have Swiggy travelling at max-speed when going through.' The wibblewallian smiled. 'Let's just hope Swiggy doesn't get hit by a shower of gunge and dead squirrels when it rematerializes.' He touched a screen on the cockpit's ceiling. 'And these are the directions for getting to Hellsbells.'

224 trillion viewers watched *The Ultimate Tommy Execution Extravaganza*. Roshviler rolled the marble perfectly. Dominoes fell, puffs of fire lit up and pendulums swung. Nothing went awry – even the sparks that fell towards Tommy missed the tinderwire binding his hands.

As the Doom Marble bobbled towards the Release-Trigger, Tommy cried out: 'IGGY Knights, my friends, my family, my love, my universe!'

The guillotine dropped.

Tommy Storm was chopped in half.

In the capsule floating above the stadium, Farlowe saw the whole spectacle.

'Yes!' he cried in answer to the question punched into the wall beside him. 'Yes – he's dead!' No buzz came from *PoF!*.

The chains unfastened, the metal ring around his neck fell loose and the humming boots unclasped and fell silent. The floppy-eared man was left standing, tears in his eyes, with the precious mastervill – intact – held within his hands.

70

No More Goodbyes

Clasping the precious mastervill, Farlowe exited the Exchanger capsule and entered his rustbucket of a craft. A newly minted wigglehole was waiting for him and he jumped through – landing in Heimenopper's office. Heimenopper slid the mastervill into a slot in the side of the Death Case and then Max Bohr (with the aid of a chainsaw) destroyed the Case for ever.

After hugs and thanks were exchanged and Max confirmed Farlowe's fee was winging its way to his bank account, the blood-houndy detective landed back in *I-Don't-Believe-Your-Alibi* (via another wigglehole). He set the rust-bucket on a course and docked inside a certain (bigger) space-craft.

Not twenty minutes after the guillotine fell, Swiggy flashed through a wormhole and materialized travelling *away* from the black holes of LitterLout*Wot!*. She continued for four and a half days before arriving at the force field surrounding Hellsbells. There she sat till the force field was lifted and the silvery-splodgy craft entered the inner sanctum. A lone jegg[51] rose from Swiggy, towards the exposed 'skull side' of Hellsbells, landing near its ear. A

51 Its metal was bleached of colour and one of its wings stuck out at a jaunty angle.

figure emerged and a giant three-headed dog charged at him, then skidded to a halt and sat still while the figure walked slowly into the cave.

The figure didn't re-emerge for three days. And when he did, he looked a little older, as if he bore a great weight across his shoulders. His jegg rose up and whizzed away, slowing momentarily to examine a huge dumptrux now floating next to Swiggy.

It took another twenty-four hours before the force field lifted and Swiggy flew towards the pale moon. And disappeared into sudden blackness.

Much happened in those nine days between the execution and Swiggy flying off from Hellsbells in a new direction.

Once the guillotine had fallen and Tommy Storm had been chopped in half, the crowd went bananas and a volley of fireworks exploded over the stadium. The price of Tommy hats and scarves tripled and a chant of 'Tommy! Tommy!' rose over the arena.

Amidst the revelry, one fan noticed something odd. Tommy Storm's short black hair had slid from his head, revealing foppish, sandy hair and rabbity ears. The fan looked to the lower half of the corpse, searching out a folded tail when – CCRRRRAAACCCKKKKKKKKKKKKL!! – the last of the fireworks showered sparks all over the stadium. The next thirty seconds were a blur of screams and activity (many of the fans had flammable fur – or feathers in the case of Roshviler) and, next thing, the corpse was on fire and the kah-chopper was in flames (tinderwire having ignited in both cases). Even though firefighters blasted it with jets of water, the corpse continued to burn bright for a day and a half –

long after the kah-chopper had disintegrated into a heap of damp, smoky ash.

However much ChAOS's (new) producers protested ('Impossible! That was *definitely* Tommy Storm.'), the fans and the viewers took a new hero to their hearts – best illustrated by the fact that Tommy memorabilia found its way into charity shops, while the most expensive garments across a host of galaxies were those bearing the name or likeness of one Yagoyurway AisleGomine CartonSydney.

Eventually, ChAOS's producers relented ('We knew it was Yago all along. The *Yago Switch* was our idea.'), claiming to own the rights to all memorabilia bearing Yago's name or likeness.

What transpired inside the hut during Yago's pre-execution visit would become the subject of folklore and the basis of a number of religions. But only a few people have ever seen the actual events unfold (as captured by a secret camera). Here it is, described in full.

> Yago collapses through the door of the hut. Once the door is closed, he gets to his feet.
>
> 'Hey,' says Tommy, helping him up. 'You OK?'
>
> 'Yeah. Fine.'
>
> 'I didn't know if you'd come.'
>
> 'You doubted me?'
>
> 'Well . . .'
>
> Yago interjects: 'In your hour of need, I'd travel to hell and back to be with you.'
>
> A tear appears in Tommy's eye. He wipes it away, removing a letter from his pocket. 'Do me one favour . . . Please make sure this gets to Woozie.' Yago pockets the

letter and Tommy adds: 'I never thought . . .' He's unable to finish the sentence.

For a moment, Yago looks as if he too might succumb to emotion, but he gathers himself and says: 'If you get out of here, you must save the universe . . . You have the skills and the courage to stop the TFC. First, go straight to Hellsbells. Don't turn back for anything.'

Tommy looks at him with puzzlement. '*If I get out of here?* . . . What're you on about?'

Yago opens his arms. 'I love you. As much as anyone can love a friend.'

They hug. Trying to freeze time with an embrace.

'Don't fool yourself,' Tommy whispers into the rabbity ear. 'I die today.'

When the hug is over, Tommy turns his back and walks away. 'Now go,' he says. 'Just go. No more goodbyes.' Suddenly, he halts. 'Hellsbells? How do you know about Hellsbells?'

But Yago has taken something from his pocket and is already upon him, gripping him in a headlock, pressing that something against his nose and mouth – it's a handkerchief (*doused in chloroform?*). Tommy flails, striking Yago's arms and ribs, but he cannot break the life-or-death resolve and, in seconds, he's on the floor, unconscious. Yago works quickly. Fixing wigs and swapping clothes and rabbity ears and tails. (It's truly amazing how alike the boys look if you take away the tail, floppy ears and different-coloured hair.) As the speakers outside boom, 'Time up!', Yago wipes a tear, lifts his lifeless friend and kisses his cheek (it's the tenderest kiss you've ever seen). Then he opens the door and pushes him out.

Before the execution, the unconscious 'Yago' was taken from the platform by bodyguards to a medical area beneath the stands. There, they handed over the slumped figure to an officious-looking 'doctor' in a white coat with a sting peeking out of his tail. With the excitement of the execution to come, no one noticed 'Doctor Lillius Roysterson' bundle 'Yago' into an empty ambulancecraft and fly away.

When Tommy awoke in Swiggy, the silvery-splodgy craft was half a day into its journey towards Hellsbells. It took the young Earthling a few moments to realize where he was because he was lying on a bed in a room he hardly recognized. It looked like a bank vault. He jumped up, hitting an intercom button on the wall.

'Yup?' said a voice.

'Let me out!' cried Tommy. 'Where's Yago? How did I get here?'

'Roysters doesn't know the answer to those questions.'

'Let me out! Why am I in the Isolation Cell? Take me back to the Plaza!'

'Sorry – Woozie's orders,' replied the voice. 'You're staying put till we reach Hellsbells.'

' . . . *Roysters?*'

'Aka Lillroysen. Or just plain *me* . . ! Say, I'm sending you a present down the chute.' Three pages landed at Tommy's feet. 'Woozie said you should take some time to read them. Make your mind up once and for all which one is the Deadly Scroll.'

Tommy tried to process all this, then turned purple. 'Put Woozie on the intercom!!' But the intercom went dead. And stayed that way. But that didn't stop Tommy hitting the button every few hours and ranting, demanding to be released. By the second day, his rants had petered out (partly because he'd smashed the intercom button).

He didn't need anyone to tell him. He knew what Yago had done. Knew that his friend was dead. And he knew now that he loved Yago. For his sandy-haired friend had shown a loyalty and a selflessness beyond belief. *To think I wanted to lose him as my visitor and have Woozie instead!* He felt guilty. And the guilt warped into blame. *That was Woozie's fault!* Blaming felt so much better than guilt. And the blame fed his anger. *What am I doing on* Swiggy? *Why am I locked down here? Woozie's behind this. He's ruined everything. Wait till I get my hands on him!*

On the third day of captivity, Tommy experienced a sense of being free from some deadly drug (later he'd realize this drug was Zestrella). He'd spent some hours reading and rereading the three pages (what else was there to do?) and had come to a final-final conclusion on the Deadly Scroll. It made him feel a little better.

Then he caught himself. *Don't let go of the anger – not before you get your hands on Woozie.*

71

A Tail of Two Slitties

As soon as Swiggy had come to a standstill, Tommy's cell door opened. He hurried up to the Lounge, surprised to see Uladrack and Farlowe with Roysters (not to mention the complete rearrangement of furniture).

'Hey, kid,' said Farlowe. 'Thought you'd died. Looks like we were both tricked. The EARTHs were saved, at least.'

'You'll be pleased to hear we're hovering outside Hellsbells' force field,' announced Roysters, launching into a breathless explanation. Tommy cut him short.

'What do you mean Woozie's not on board?'

'He said he'd make his own way to Hellsbells.' Uladrack held up a note as if this explained everything.

'Make his own way!?' exclaimed Tommy, snatching the note. '*How*?'

'I don't know,' replied Uladrack. 'I was asleep, recovering from a knock, when he went off. I assumed he knew of a wigglehole.'

All were standing, bar Farlowe, who was sitting in an armchair, fingers steepled. The young Earthling read the note. It left orders to head for Hellsbells as soon as he arrived on board Swiggy – and to keep him (Tommy) locked in the cell till they got there – ending:

Don't wait for me. Woozie x.

'I think he departed Swiggy wearing a Wolfstain body-mask-suit,' said Roysters. 'And Yago was involved. He called us and informed us how you'd be dressed like him and where to collect you.'

'There's something else . . . He said this is for you.'

Tommy thought he detected sadness in Uladrack's eyes as she handed him a lunchbox-sized octagonal object. It was one of Swiggy's time-lock safes. The flickering digits indicated it wouldn't open for another three and a half days.

SSCCCCRRREEEEEEEESSCHSSSS!!

No matter how hard Tommy hit it with his scimmy, the safe stayed firmly shut. Eventually, he gave up, collapsing on the ground.

'If he's made it to Hellsbells, he won't be floating about outside,' said Tommy. 'We'll have to go in.' He corrected himself. '*I*'ll have to go in.'

Tommy landed his jegg, making it past ThreeHeads (who sat obediently), and on through the cave into the flame-lit passageway. When the torches extinguished, he began running, running – ducking and leaping till his lungs burnt. And then he was out in the hot canyon, striding along the beam of ice. It melted after him, giving way as he caught the hanging rope. He ignored the crater belching magma at his soles and sulphur at his nostrils, and pulled his sleeves down over his palms. Despite the protestations of his lungs, he began climbing, climbing, climbing – up, up towards the teeny disc of rock above.

Eventually, the heat turned cool and the sulphur dissolved to nothing. He felt tired – really, really, really tired. And his hands bled. Progress was slow now. Measured in centimetres. Every nerve and sinew trembled. Yet still the disc of rock was a floating penny high above. 'Hold on,' he murmured, blocking out the pain. 'Hold on.'

Three times, depleted of strength, he came close to quitting and letting go. But each time, he found some inner reserve – a brute determination. At last, his body stretched past breaking (and yet unbroken), he touched the disc of rock and hauled his very soul upon it.

'Well, I'll be . . .' declared the voice of an old woman. '*Made it to the top of the rope* . . . Congrats! . . . Yuh have the challenge? . . . Completed?'

He saw his hand pull a sheaf of paper from somewhere. Saw blood seep across a word – *If*. Then nothing.

He awoke – *I'm back in that other canyon on the island of rock!* – and realized that his hands had been healed when – KUUUKKLAMM! A spotlight clanked on, piercing the darkness, blinding his face. A female voice, deepened through a microphone, intoned: 'You made it up the rope . . . The very first to do so . . . And brought the challenge – the correct one. That's a test in itself.'

'Yes,' replied Tommy.

'But, alas,' continued the voice, 'you have not completed the test, have you?'

'No, I haven't, but I hoped–' Tommy tried to shield his eyes from the light. 'Please, where's my companion? Let me see Woozie?'

There was a pause and Tommy thought he heard whispering

in the darkness and a slight laugh before the voice spoke again. 'You climbed the rope, held on through the pain, *just to see a companion*?'

'Where is he?'

Again there was a pause and a murmuring and the voice said: 'The Beast should know.'

'Oh, good!'

'Not so fast . . ! The challenge has not been completed . . . The only reason you haven't been thrown out of Hellsbells is because we're mildly impressed with how you were prepared to lay down your life to save the EARTHs . . . But that was not the challenge . . . The Beast is unlikely to see you.'

'Oh, please! I'll come back when the challenge is complete. For now I seek only my fellow Knight.'

There was a pause and then: 'How worthy are you to see the Beast?'

'Worthy enough,' replied Tommy. 'At least, I hope I'm worthy enough.'

'Hmmm,' intoned the voice. 'And how much do you know? How knowledgeable are you?'

'Quite knowledgeable.'

'*Quite?*'

'I mean, I know a reasonable amount. Quite a bit.'

'Aahh . . . And are you *better* than a lot of people?' pressed the voice. 'In general.'

'I suppose.'

'You *suppose*?'

'Er, yes.'

After more murmuring, the voice asked: 'Who is your best friend? Dead or alive.'

What a strange question, thought Tommy. And he wondered if he should say Woozie since it might help in his quest to find the furry fellow. But then he determined the best strategy would be to tell the truth.

'Yago.'

KUUUKKLAMM! The spotlight clanked off. And all was dark – till, quite suddenly, one whole side of the canyon was illuminated with footage of Marielle, Woozie, Rumbles and Summy beneath the Bowl – floating in the Wigglery.

'You hit him hard!' said Woozie.

'He shouted,' retorted Marielle. 'He'd have woken everyone.'

'No choice had she,' said Summy.

'I don't like leaving him any more than you do, Woozie,' said Marielle, putting a hand on the wibblewallian's shoulder. 'But what choice do we have?'

'He's changedskeys,' added Rumbles. 'He's not the friendskeys he once was.'

'But it's just a phase!' exclaimed Woozie. 'Can't you see? He's been ensnared by all the fame and adulation. He's not himself.'

'I'd like to believe that,' replied Marielle. 'And I don't want to leave him either.'

'Let's ask him againskeys.'

'No,' said Marielle, tears in her eyes. 'He's made it clear – he's not coming.'

Summy looked at her watch. 'To intercept us, ready will be the wormhole in six minutes.'

Marielle unhooked her rucksack, took out some paper and a pen, hovered cross-legged and began writing. The others floated in silence, contemplating the momentousness of what they were about to do. Marielle folded the letter and stuffed it into an envelope together with something else she removed from her bag. 'I'll just dash up and put this in his wardrobe,' she said.

'No time is there,' said Summy. 'Twenty seconds and counting.'

'Sugar!' exclaimed Marielle. 'I could leave it here. No one else would open it, right? It would get to him.'

'Twelve seconds,' said Summy, taking Rumbles and Marielle by the arm. They braced themselves against the floor, so they'd be able to leap. 'Come on Woozie.'

'Er, I . . .'

'What?'

'I'm not coming.'

'*What?*'

'You *have* to!'

'No.'

'Woozskeys!'

'Four seconds.'

'*I*'ll give him the parcel.'

'But—'

'Go!'

After a momentary hesitation, Marielle, Woozie and Rumbles disappeared through the Entrance, leaving Woozie floating alone, holding the package from Marielle. The 'movie' died. Tommy was left in darkness.

KUUUKKLAMM! A spotlight clanked on and the voice intoned: 'Wormhole too small – wasn't that the excuse he gave you . . ? Tell me – who is your best friend? Dead or alive.'

Tommy hesitated, then: 'Yago . . . I told you already.'

KUUUKKLAMM! Spotlight off. One side of the canyon lit up with an image of Yago pickpocketing a polka-dot handkerchief from Joe Yuss on Planet BBQBliss.

'That's Marielle's hanky,' said Tommy, to no reply.

The footage showed the truth behind the whole Hanky Episode – Yago giving it to Jay-T, Jay-T forcing Marielle to get it back and Marielle smacking Jay-T across the face. The next footage showed Yago with a remote control – manipulating Woozie's steering wheel on the tobogganer. This was followed by images of Yago inserting an RCTBonbon in a marshmallow and serving it to Woozie, then activating it on Planet Quake. The final footage before the 'movie' died showed Yago removing his cast and scratching his arm. Tommy was left in darkness.

He felt . . . He didn't know what he felt! Yago – had he really told all those lies and done all those things? . . . But that'd mean Marielle had been true to him all along. That he – Tommy – had doubted her and maligned her and betrayed her . . . And Woozie . . ! He'd never set out sabotage him. And he'd been right about the cast . . .

No, no. Something's wrong here. Yago wouldn't – couldn't – have—

KUUUKKLAMM! A spotlight clanked on and the voice intoned: 'Who is your best friend? Dead or alive.'

'Yago,' declared Tommy, defiance in his voice. 'I don't care what you showed me! He gave up his life for me!'

KUUUKKLAMM! Spotlight off. One side of the canyon illuminated with an image of Yago dressed as Tommy inside the hut just before the execution. Eyes closed, sitting cross-legged, on the floor. I'd've been fooled, thought Tommy. He looks so like me.

The door opens and Zestrella enters. She looks stiffer than usual, the tentacles in a tighter knot behind her back. Looking at the ground, she says: 'I'm going to have to break up with you . . . Sorry.'

'Tommy's' eyes remain closed. He seems to smile momentarily. 'Best news I heard all day.'

Zestrella clearly wasn't expecting this response, but

recovers her poise. 'Because you *hate* me at this moment, right? You *despise* me.'

'I don't think anything of you . . . Now go, Zestrella. Leave.'

'What? . . . Don't talk to me in the manner.' Zestrella's voice heightens. 'Look at me!'

'You're a cold, repulsive creature,' says 'Tommy', eyes closed.

'So you *do* hate me!?' Zestrella looks triumphant.

'Tommy' shakes his head. 'Just stating facts.'

'Facts?'

'Just ask yourself, Zestrella . . . If you'd never been born, would the universe be worse off?'

The tall girl looks a little taken aback, then: 'Aahh, I see . . . Being offensive because I'm breaking it off.'

'I'm delighted you're breaking it off,' replies 'Tommy' with evident sincerity. 'If you hadn't got there first, *I*'d've broken it off with *you*.'

'You're just saying that,' says Zestrella, less certainly.

'Tommy' gives a dismissive snort. 'Why would anyone want to go out with *you*? Think about it . . . 'I've met nawhit-mobs that show more affection than you.'

'I warned you,' retorts Zestrella, fire in her voice. 'I told you, I have no heart.'

'Tommy' laughs. 'Pathetic excuse!'

'It's true.'

'You're just scared.'

'Yeah, right.'

'You act all tough, Zestrella, but you're just frightened.' 'Tommy' stands, eyes closed.

'Very funny . . ! Open your eyes! Look at me!!'

'How did you turn out this way, Zestrella?' 'Tommy' faces

Zestrella, eyes still shut.

'I don't know what you mean.'

The black-clad boy approaches the tall girl. 'Did someone do something really horrible to you as a child?'

'Shut up!'

'That's it, isn't it!?' says 'Tommy', realizing. 'Someone did something to you as a child.'

'I said SHUT UP!!'

The tentacles behind Zestrella's back untie, flail and wrap themselves into a knot once more. She punches 'Tommy's' midriff. But his face shows no reaction. Instead he presses the question. 'What did they do to you?' Then twice more – 'What did they do to you?' – Zestrella showering him in a hail of weakening punches, her tentacles unravelling. 'SHUT UP! Shut up! Shut up. Shut . . .' Her words dissolve into tears, her fists bouncing off 'Tommy's' thighs, his knees, his shins, his feet, till the blows die to nothing and the brown-haired girl's form is heaving, curled on the floor.

The organizers must've allowed Zestrella far more time with 'Tommy' than they did Yago – for she remained sobbing for some minutes. 'Tommy', eyes open now, standing over her all the time.

In Hellsbells, Tommy saw a change of expression in 'Tommy's' face as he stood over the broken girl's tears. More than a softening, it was a *yielding*, infused with fear. As if he'd just realized that the hand of death was almost upon him.

Zestrella's sobs die out and the fear in 'Tommy's' face drains to sadness. The young girl staggers to her feet, not looking at 'Tommy'. 'Time up in twenty-eight seconds,' boom the distant speakers. She prepares to leave – her tentacles have tied themselves into a bow – when 'Tommy' says: 'Kiss me.' She looks at him, surprised. 'Please,' says

'Tommy', a tear in his eye. 'Before I die . . . No one's ever truly kissed me.'

She looks at him oddly – *no one ever truly kissed you?* – then steps forward for a functional, dutiful kiss.

Tommy in Hellsbells had never seen a kiss like it. It started cold as an iceberg and began melting, flowing, sweeping somewhere quicker and warmer. And on – on somewhere urgent, somewhere fiery. Two creatures ripping at their tethers and finding them broken. Searching for that *other* and finding it.

For one moment.

'Time up,' boom the speakers.

It's 'Tommy' who breaks away. They stand there flushed, gasping like swimmers. Saying nothing. Just their eyes meeting. Two creatures alone in a hut in the centre of the universe . . . The door opens, throwing light across the room. Zestrella's face turns quizzical. *You're not Tommy,* it says. *Now I see!*

'Come out now before I drag you!' A gruff bodyguard stands silhouetted in the doorway.

'Tommy' nods at Zestrella and turns away. Uncomprehending, shell-shocked, Zestrella stands frozen, fingers to her lips, tentacles swinging loosely. Then the bodyguard drags her out by the arms and shuts the door.

The movie died.

KUUUKKLAMM! A spotlight clanked on and the voice intoned: 'Who is your best friend? Dead or alive.'

'Er, em . . . Yago,' replied Tommy, head spinning. Who cared if his friend had kissed Zestrella? What did that matter?

KUUUKKLAMM! Spotlight off. One side of the canyon illuminated with an image of Yago inside his room at the Plaza. A knock sounds and Wolfstain enters with a rucksack on his back.

'Why are you locking the door?' asks Yago.

'This is why,' replies Wolfstain and he plucks a roll of tape from his rucksack, tears a strip and fastens it across Yago's mouth. Yago looks at him in shock – a look that magnifies when Wolfstain rips off his face, revealing Woozie underneath. Yago bolts for the door, trying to remove the tape. But Woozie is too quick. He intercepts the Cassiothellian and the pair fall to the floor in a tangle of grappling limbs. The body-suit and the rucksack impede Woozie, for he takes half a minute to overpower the sandy-haired boy and begin tying him up.

When Yago is secured, the wibblewallian locks him in a cupboard, rips off the last of the Wolfstain costume and removes a bundle from the rucksack – it's a pair of height-boosting shoes and a *Yago* body-mask-suit (the most expensive version available, including 'a tail made up of two slitties'). Woozie puts on the suit and shoes and removes a black, short-haired wig from the rucksack, stuffing it into his pocket. Then he says a few words in a Yago voice, produces a walkie-talkie and dials a number.

'Hey. That Swiggy? . . . Yago here. From ChAOS . . . I've been speaking to Woozie. He's arranged a way to get Tommy out of here.'

Woozie gives rendezvous instructions, concluding: 'So Tommy will be dressed as Yago. Don't give away nothing to the bodyguards . . . Be sure to wear the doctor costume . . . And remember – stay in character!'

The movie went blank.

Tommy stood, paralysed. 'You mean . . ?' He couldn't finish the sentence. 'It's not true!' he cried. 'It's not true! It's not true!!'

How many times he screamed the assertion, no one knows.

But at some stage, it morphed ever-so slightly . . . 'Tell me it's not true! Tell me it's not true!' Hours passed with no response to his screams. When at last he slumped to his knees, he found he couldn't stand up again. And, when he tried to call out, he couldn't speak.

72

Diddly-Squat

'Woozie, not Yago, died to save you,' said the voice from the darkness. 'To get round the Tommy body-mask-suit detectors he 'became' *Yago*. Then disguised his *Yago* persona as you.'

The canyon lit up with scenes from ChAOS – times when Tommy'd ignored Woozie or been rude to him or allowed Yago to be rude. And times when he, Tommy, had been too hurried to listen to Marielle or had otherwise been mean to her. He saw himself denying love for the elquinine three times and how *PoF!* had been turned *off*. Watched himself punch Woozie and declare: 'Consider our friendship over.' (To this he screamed: 'I didn't mean it! I told him in my letter. I was desperate to stop him trying to save me . . . Did he read my letter? Please! Did he read my letter!?' – And received no reply.)

No matter how often he screamed for them to stop, the scenes kept coming. No matter how hard he pressed his hands to his ears, the stinging words cut through – *Consider our friendship over*. And no matter how hard he shut his eyes, the scenes kept on searing through his soul.

And then the worst scene – the execution – played again and again and again.

When it was over, he felt as though he'd been pounded into

the rocky ground. Yet still the scenes kept playing in his head. He tried to block them out with thoughts of happy times. But these proved even more painful. Rocketblading with Woozie; foodfights; late-night chats; 'Would you prefer to eat a thunderbumbles' undies or . . .'; misbehaving during Lady Muckbeff's lessons; meeting for the first time in the Milky Way . . . Too many memories too count. Each one another nail through his being.

And in the background he heard an echoing voice. *Real or imaginary?* 'I WILL DRAG YOU DOWN TO THE SEWER AND I WILL BREAK YOU. I WILL STRIP YOU DOWN TO NOTHING, AND I WILL RIP YOUR HEART RIGHT OUT OF YOUR CHEST.'

The voice spoke out of the darkness: 'It is nearly done . . . You need time to absorb and time to rest.'

And the canyon lit up with a flickering image of an EARTH. For half a second Tommy thought he was going to witness another destruction and might've shouted 'No!' but he was beyond speech. The image zoomed through the EARTH's atmosphere and past juddering wisps. Then it veered away from large continents to a vast, wrinkling ocean. As the ocean grew, a speck appeared – a tiny island, covered in trees and beaches. Like the sky itself, the sea and trees upon it seemed to flicker.

'The flickering you see is night and day,' said the voice. 'A year on this planet is a handful of seconds in Hellsbells . . . The island you see is uninhabited by humans.' A shimmering outline materialized beside Tommy. 'This wigglehole will take you there,' continued the voice. 'Another wigglehole will return you here – when you are ready . . . Take your time.

However long you take will be but seconds . . . Ensure you are ready. For when you return, you will have but one chance to prove the Beast should see you.'

Tommy sat motionless in the darkness for some minutes. Then, scimmy sheathed to his back, he climbed to his feet and staggered through the wigglehole.

He re-emerged seconds later, darker, slightly taller and more gaunt. His trousers now shorts, his black shirt but a T-shirt, and his hair (once again) long, wild and spiky.

Tommy never spoke much of his 'six months' on the EARTH island, except to say that he learned 'how to survive in the wilderness' and that, having carved a headstone for Woozie and set it on a high promontory overlooking the sea, he spent long stretches 'doing nothing but thinking'.

He looked up into the blackness. 'I want to see the Beast,' he said, gripping his scimmy. 'And I want my revenge . . . Woozie's revenge.'

'You must purge yourself of vengeful wishes before you see the Beast.'

'Hah . . ! Vengeful wishes can't just disappear!' And the youth's tone darkened and his eyes turned steely. 'I want vengeance.'

'Then you must seek it *before* you see the Beast.'

The canyon was illuminated by an image of Yago standing bare-chested in the centre of a crowded arena, swishing a sword. Five creatures, all wielding weapons came at him from different directions. Yago threw his sword high, leapt in the air to catch it and, within moments, had slain the five. The crowd roared at first, but in seconds they were kneeling, bowing to the sandy-haired boy as if he were a god.

'This might help,' said the voice. Something soft fell to the rocky ground.

'What is it?' asked Tommy, feeling the strange and furry bundle in the darkness.

'And this may help too.' A shimmering wigglehole appeared. 'If you survive there will be another one to return you here.'

Just then, the pale moon passed overhead. And Tommy saw that the furry bundle was a body-mask-suit.

Some time after it'd stepped through the wigglehole, the furry form of Woozie reappeared on the rocky island in the heart of Hellsbells. The figure staggered towards a candle on the ground casting its light on a jug of (holey) water and a roll of bandages. It peeled off its furry suit with faint groans. A torso gleamed, save for an oozing wound slicing across a midriff. The (revealed) young man washed and dressed the wound, then fell into a deep and troubled sleep.

'How worthy are you to see the Beast?'

Tommy, recuperated from sleep, thought before answering. And when he did, his head was hung low. 'I'm not worthy,' he said. 'Not worthy at all.'

'Hmmm . . .' replied the voice. 'And how much do you know? How knowledgeable are you?'

'I know so little . . . Compared to all the knowledge and wisdom in the universe, I know nothing. Diddly-squat.'

'Hmmm . . . And are you *better* than a lot of people?'

'No.'

'Please elaborate.'

Tommy raised his eyes to the blinding light. 'I've been trained and am lucky to have certain skills and to be entrusted with a mission. But I've made mistakes – big mistakes – and I'll continue to make mistakes. I've got weaknesses and traits I'm not proud of . . . I'm worth no more and no less than any man or woman.'

This response was greeted with soft murmurings and then the voice asked: 'Who is your best friend? Dead or alive.'

RRRRRRAAAAGGGGHHHHRRRRRRR!!! The roar made the air quake. And the ground shook with an approaching BOOOOOMMMM! . . . BOOOOMMMM!

Tommy Storm stood tall, licked silver for an instant by the pale moon streaking by. And then the breeze carrying the BOOOOOOMMMM! BOOOOOOMMMM! became a gale, and the rocky island shook so much, he had to sit to stop from falling.

Then peace, until – 'FEE FI FO FUM. MUSTARD, PICKLE, TOASTED BUN.' The fleeting moon cast its silver on red eyes the size of office blocks, jagged teeth the height of skyscrapers and three ivory horns the length of jumbo-jet runways. 'WHAT DO YOU WANT?' thundered the voice.

'I want you to help me stop the TFC. And find my friends.'

'WHAT DO YOU WANT?'

'Are we going to go through this again – you repeating and repeating the question?'

'WHAT DO YOU WANT?'

'Because if you're going to do the whole bun and pickle thing, just get on with it. Go on! Bite me if you have to. Eat me if that's your thing. But the answer will always be the same. *I want you to help me stop the TFC and find my friends*.'

There was a breathy pause from Beashto and Tommy thought he heard whispers.

'WHAT ABOUT WANTING EVERYONE TO LIKE YOU AND TO THINK YOU'RE GREAT?'

'I don't care about that now.'

'HMMM . . . BUT YOU SAID YOU WANTED TO DO GREAT THINGS. TO SCALE WILD HEIGHTS . . . HAS THAT CHANGED TOO?'

'Yes. No. I mean . . .' Tommy thought about it. 'I still want to do those things. But not to make people like me . . . The only great things I want to do now are to stop the TFC and to find my friends . . . And if I ever scale other wild heights, it'll be for *me* – for the fun of it. Or to see how far I can stretch myself.'

More whispers and then: 'THERE IS ONE OTHER THING YOU WANT, ISN'T THERE?'

'No,' replied Tommy. 'Nothing . . . Nothing that I know of.' And he begged and begged for help in stopping the TFC and finding his friends.

Beashto shook his head. 'EVEN IF WE SET ASIDE THIS OTHER WANT, YOU HAVE ONLY COMPLETED *PARTS* OF THE CHALLENGE . . . ONLY A FEW MORE LINES CAN BE CROSSED OUT.'

One side of the canyon lit up with an image of the poem.

IF

If you can keep your mind when all about you
Are losing theirs and blaming it on you,
If you can trust yourself when all men doubt you,
But make allowance for their doubting too;
If you can wait and not be tired by waiting,
Or being lied about, don't deal in lies,
Or being hated, don't give way to hating,
And yet don't look too good, nor talk too wise:
If you can dream – and not make dreams your master;
If you can think – and not make thoughts your aim;

If you can meet with Triumph and Disaster
And treat those two impostors just the same;
If you can bear to hear the truth you've spoken
Twisted by knaves to make a trap for fools,
Or watch the things you gave your life to, broken,
And stoop and build 'em up with worn-out tools:

If you can make one heap of all your winnings
And risk it on one turn of pitch-and-toss,
And lose, and start again at your beginnings
And never breathe a word about your loss;
~~If you can force your heart and nerve and sinew~~
~~To serve your turn long after they are gone,~~
~~And so hold on when there is nothing in you~~
~~Except the Will which says to them: 'Hold on!'~~

If you can talk with crowds and keep your virtue,
Or walk with Kings – nor lose the common touch,
If neither foes nor loving friends can hurt you,
If all men count with you, but none too much;
~~If you can fill the unforgiving minute~~
~~With sixty seconds' worth of distance run,~~
Yours is this Earth and everything that's in it,
And - which is more - you'll be a Man, my son!

'Realization spread across Tommy's face. 'So . . . The two lines that've always been crossed-out at the bottom – those are the bits completed last time I was here!' Beashto nodded. 'And the four newly crossed-out lines – they're cos I climbed the rope to the top this time?' Again Beashto nodded. 'But . . .' Tommy stared at the poem, his mind racing.

'SO I'M SORRY, BUT—'

'Wait . . ! What if, er . . . What if . . .' Then it hit him. 'What if it's *not* just about me?'

Beashto paused. 'I DON'T FOLLOW.'

'What if it applies to *all* my fellow Knights?'

'I STILL DON'T FOLLOW.'

Tommy's voice was filled with excitement. 'We came to Hellsbells *together* seeking your help to stop the TFC. So why not consider us *together* when weighing up how much of the poem has been achieved?'

Beashto growled.

'*Can't you see . . !?*' cried Tommy, scanning the poem's lines. 'Marielle was lied about and didn't deal in lies . . ! And Woozie waited and didn't get tired of waiting. He was hated and didn't give way to hating! And you can't say he looked too good or talked too wise.'

'HMMMM.'

'And Marielle didn't lose her mind when lots of us in ChAOS were losing ours and blaming it on her . . ! And she had the truth she spoke twisted, trapping a fool like me! And Woozie trusted himself when he was doubted and he made allowances for *my* doubting! And, and . . . Swiggy and everything in her – we've given our life to it and we saw it broken and Woozie built it up with worn-out tools – that hurricane planet was a cheap, second-hand model.'

'HMMMM.'

'And me – I've learnt not to make dreams my master. Or thoughts my aim . . . And I've learnt about Triumph and Disaster, I swear!'

'AND PITCH AND TOSS?'

'Well . . .' Tommy recalled scenes from ChAOS shown on the canyon wall. 'Woozie played nearest-coin-to-the-wall with Roysters and others in the Bowl. Didn't he ever lose all his winnings?'

'HMMM . . . YES . . . YES, HE DID.'

'And did he complain about his loss?'

'MMM . . . NO.'

'And he started playing again. And, and . . . he never

pandered to the crowds of fans, did he? He kept his virtue . . ! And as for kings, I don't know, but we've met a lot of important people on our travels and Woozie has always been himself with them – very down-to-earth.'

Beashto cleared his throat, thinking.

'And I tell you,' continued Tommy. 'All creatures count with me now. But none too much! Yes, perhaps, Marielle more than others, but not *too much*. It could never be too much with her.'

'AAHH,' intoned Beashto. 'BUT FOES AND LOVING FRIENDS CAN CLEARLY HURT YOU.'

'Yes, yes, that's true,' replied Tommy, scrambling for an answer. 'And that may always be true, but . . . but foes can only hurt me by hurting the people I love. And as for my *loving friends* . . . I don't think they can hurt me more than I've been hurt already . . . Compared to Woozie dying, nothing can . . .'

The young Earthling turned away, unable to finish the sentence. Standing in the darkness, he ignored the lengthy murmurings above and tried to cry. But no tears came.

At last Beashto spoke. 'YOU HAVE MADE AN ARGUMENT . . . I SUGGEST A COMPROMISE.'

'What is it?'

'THE BEAST WILL ONLY HELP SOMEONE WHO PUTS *EVERYTHING* ON THE LINE – THEIR LIFE, THEIR SPACESHIP, EVERYTHING.'

'I don't understand.'

'THE BEAST WILL HELP YOU . . .' A spotlight picked out a violin. '. . . IF YOU PLAY BETTER THAN BEA.'

My violin! He'd forgotten all about it. Had he left it here all this time . . ? Had he really not played since that last fateful performance . . ? He looked up at Beashto with worried eyes.

'And . . . if I'm not as good?'

'YOU HEARD . . . *EVERYTHING* ON THE LINE.'

73
Bea-Elza-Bobbi

The old woman appeared on the rocky island. Once again, she stood like a (decrepit) ice-skater, tail poised over the violin. When she'd finished (sinking to her knees, exhausted), the air still shook with the memory of her notes. So moved was Tommy by her playing that he went to help her and, as he did so, he kissed her on the cheek without thinking and whispered, 'So beautiful.'

In a heartbeat, the woman's lips unshrivelled, her face unwrinkled and her figure stretched. When Tommy stood back, the young girl – Elza – was there before him. 'You're not touching the tree,' he said, forgetting momentarily that the exquisite music had almost certainly consigned him to death.

Elza looked into his eyes. 'I'm sorry to hear your friend, Woozie, died . . . Truly, I am.'

Given this strange turn in events, Beashto (prompted by Elza) agreed that Tommy need not play his piece till 'THIS TIME TOMORROW.'

'In that case, may I make a request?' asked Tommy, recovering from the shock of Bea's transformation. Beashto raised a quizzical eye. 'I understand that I will die and Swiggy will be destroyed if my playing is not as good as Bea's, so please, let me play on board Swiggy – I play best there and, if we are both to be destroyed, I'd like us to go together.' Beashto said nothing. 'You have the technology to hear from here,' Tommy added. 'And we'll be inside the force field. It's not as if we can escape.'

'Bea and I are one person,' Elza explained back in the 'bright' canyon as she chopped the tree stump. 'Poor woman had to hack at this for hours every day. Something that'd take me thirty seconds.' Tommy wasn't sure he understood. 'I've been around a long time,' added Elza. 'Almost since the universe began.'

'So you're really as old as Bea *looks*?' ventured Tommy, glad of a subject to distract him from thoughts of TOMORROW. 'But when you touched the apple tree, it made you young?' Elza nodded. 'And a kiss acts in the same way?'

'If I ask for a kiss and receive one, it makes me young again for hours, sometimes as long as a day.'

'So you'll be Bea again soon?'

Elza shook her head. 'An *unprompted* kiss has longer-lasting effects.'

'How long?'

The young girl shrugged. 'A hundred, two hundred years.'

Elza explained how she often used to have people in Hellsbells kiss her 'in the last billennia,' but their kisses began having less effect, 'eventually lasting only seconds.' And Tommy learnt that her full name was Bea-Elza-Bobbi.

'Bobbi?'

Elza plucked a leaf from the apple tree, ate it and promptly disappeared. Tommy felt something stamp his foot. He looked down to see a little girl, swimming in Elza's clothes.

She snatched something red from a pocket, disappeared under the tent of clothes and, after some wriggling, stepped into the open, wearing a red smock.

'You!?' exclaimed Tommy.

And as his mind raced to make sense of things, a chant echoed behind him 'Ooooh Aayyyy Oooooh!' He turned. Over a hundred hooded creatures were standing, spears raised, by the cave entrance.

The girl giggled and pulled at a bow in her smock. It released a forked waggly tail – the signal it seemed for the hooded creatures to file into the cave. In seconds they were gone.

'I thought they'd killed you!' cried Tommy. He knelt and grabbed the girl by the shoulders. 'I tried to save you!'

The little girl looked as if she might throw up, shook off Tommy's hands and disappeared under Elza's tent of clothes. Before Tommy could go after her, the tent began to swell. Next thing, Elza was standing before him, adjusting her apron.

'That was Bobbi,' she said.

Tommy looked at her uncomprehending.

'That scene you came across with all the hooded creatures looking like they were about to kill Bobbi,' smiled Elza. 'We were just playing with you . . . But you can't say we were unfair – we dipped you in holey water and healed your wounds before returning you to the Bowl.'

'But . . .' Tommy tried to say 'Why?', but no sound came from his lips.

'Choosing which page was my challenge was half the test,' continued Elza, reading his expression. 'And we were trying to make your choice more difficult . . . We thought you might go for that ridiculous page, *save the girl & triumph*.' She laughed. 'But you weren't that stupid.'

Tommy tried to digest this. 'So Bobbi is your younger self? You become her if you eat leaves from this tree . . ? And Bea is your older self?'

Elza nodded. Tommy had so many questions – about the apple tree and the waterfall frozen inside it, about Elza's long life and the tree stump she kept chopping – but something in the washergirl's eyes made him think of the end of the universe, and with it flooded thoughts of TOMORROW.

He cried out: 'Why all these stupid games? Why does the Beast want me to die? Why won't he just help me? To find my friends, to stop the TFC – why won't he *just help*!?'

The word *help* echoed round the canyon, dissolving to nothing. Elza, picking up her mop, stepped into the silence. 'Maybe the Beast—'

'I don't want *maybe*!' snapped Tommy. Then, seeing Elza's surprise: 'I didn't come all this way, risk my life to talk to some girl with a mop!' Elza's look turned to hurt and Tommy saw himself as if in a mirror. 'Sorry,' he said, shame colouring his face. 'I shouldn't have said that . . . But I'm to die tomorrow and – worse – the TFC will happen in such a short time . . . Sorry . . . Forgive me.'

Elza looked him in the eye. 'Don't ever speak to me like that again.' There was a steel and an authority to her voice that Tommy had never registered before.

Tommy nodded. 'I won't.'

'Good . . . Consider yourself forgiven.'

'Thank you,' said Tommy, realizing what'd been bugging him since he'd kissed Bea – Elza's accent was different. No longer uncouth. 'What were you going to say?' he added. 'Before I interrupted you.' Elza eyed him and he wondered how he'd never noticed the silent power in her look. 'Please,' he pressed. 'I'd like to hear.'

Elza held him in her gaze as though deciding something. Eventually, she spoke. 'Maybe the Beast knows the answers to these things, but the Beast can't just hand you the answers.'

Tommy considered this. 'And why might that be?'

'What if the Beast made an oath to herself not to *tell* anyone how to stop the TFC – yet she'd still like to help someone worthy to find out the answer for themselves. And what if she knows where your friends are, but thinks that *just telling you* would impede your chances of stopping the TFC.'

Herself . . ? *She* . . ? 'Wait . . .' Tommy's mind was racing. 'Beashto . . . He's not the Beast, is he?'

Elza shook her head. 'He's actually the warmest, cuddliest fellow . . . But he has a wonderful ability to scare people. And he's happy to say what he's told to say.'

'So the Beast is . . .' Tommy was slightly stunned. 'The Beast is really . . .'

Elza nodded.

74
Without Trust

'My-my, if it ain't Tommy Storm!'

'Harriett!'

Emerging into Swiggy's Lounge with his scimmy strapped to his back, his violin under one arm and a leather box under the other, Tommy was surprised at how pleased he was to see the bulky form of Harriett Steptoe. Maybe he saw a shadow of Rumbles in her, and she saw the same in him, for they hugged far more tightly than might be expected of two people who hardly knew each other.

'I saw y'all on telly,' she explained. 'But I couldn't find me a wormhole to the Bowl, so I got me a permanent transfer to the Hellsbells route. Kept hopin' you guys'd return . . . Then when Rumbles and the others disappeared . . .' She wiped a tear. 'I jus' kept on hopin'.'

Harriett hurried off to find a tissue and Uladrack gave the young Earthling a hug of her own. 'Crikey, we thought you might've died in there.'

Tommy hadn't noticed before, but Uladrack looked changed. Yes, she still wore those smoggy-grey clothes, but she'd ditched that cape and her blue-black hair was pulled back, and gone were the thick-rimmed spectacles. She looked almost beautiful.

Roysters held his thumb and index finger a centimetre

apart. 'We were *this* close to jolly-well going in there and saving you.' And as he clapped the Earthling on the back, a distant buzz sounded. (*PoF!* had been left *on* in the GalleyKitchen.)

Farlowe shook Tommy's hand a little formally. 'Glad to have you back, kid . . . Did you crack our case? Cos, if not, I'm ready to go in there and knock some heads together.'

'I wouldn't advise it,' said Tommy with a grimace.

'Me neither,' declared Harriett, entering the room, recovered (a smear of chocolate on her face). 'If their refuse is anything to go by, it's a mighty dangerous place . . . They're good recyclers, mind.'

'Er,' said Tommy, looking solemn. 'We all need to have a talk.'

Uladrack burst into tears when she heard that Woozie was dead. 'I had a feeling he was gone,' she murmured through sobs. 'But I tried to ignore it.'

After hankies had been passed round and memories of Woozie discussed, Harriett made a pot of tea and Tommy continued his account.

'So Bea, Elza, Bobbi – they're all the same person!' exclaimed Roysters. 'They're all the Beast?'

Tommy nodded, going on to explain: 'She says she knows where Marielle, Summy and Rumbles have gone – even claims to be an enemy of OleSayjj – but can't tell me how to get there.' His face turned grave. 'And she confirmed the TFC's due to happen in less than eleven months.'

'Do you believe her?' asked Roysters. 'How would she know?'

Tommy nodded. 'Apart from all her TV channels, she

seems to have a window into so many galaxies.' He thought of the hole in the apple tree and the weird tree stump, adding: 'Maybe even into other worlds.'

He was going to mention the holey water too – show them how it'd healed the wound across his belly, when Farlowe cut in. 'And did you ask the skinny on the TFC?'

Again Tommy nodded. 'I asked her was she behind it. She said no.'

'No!?' Roysters looked doubtful. 'I bet she's linked to Bin-Liner.'

Tommy shook his head. 'She claims to be his enemy.'

'Him *and* OleSayjj?'

Before Tommy could answer, Uladrack leapt in. 'What about those EARTHs she showed you being destroyed on your last visit!?'

'She said she has gazillions of clips from around the universe. And she chose to show me the EARTH footage for three reasons. One, she knew it'd 'break' me. Two, she hoped it might somehow lead to my thwarting her enemy, Bin-Liner. And three, it was her way of helping me.'

'Helping?'

'She said some of what I learnt from the whole *EARTHs experience* could help in stopping the TFC.'

'Huh,' mused Harriett. 'So what did you learn?'

'I don't know yet.'

'But . . .' Uladrack was confused. '*We are all in the gutter* . . . Marielle told me you gave the Beast some wisdom and then two people said it before their EARTH was crushed.'

Tommy shrugged. 'It was a recording of an EARTH crushed years ago. As Elza put it: *Forty thousand EARTHs destroyed – you don't think we could find one in the archives that came up with similar wisdom to you?*'

Farlowe stepped into the fray. 'So what did she say about the TFC *specifically*?'

'Just that wisdom is the only thing that can stop it. And that OleSayjj *wants* the TFC to *happen*. She says he intercepted wisdom suggestions from EARTHs – to *prevent* any good ones making it to the Council of Wisdom.'

'But Bin-Liner was doing exactly the same thing!' interjected Farlowe. 'Heimenopper told me.'

'So they're in league, together?' asked Roysters. Tommy and Farlowe shrugged. 'And why would anyone want the TFC to *happen*?' Two more shrugs.

'I don't get it,' said Uladrack. 'How could intercepting wisdom suggestions make the TFC *more* likely to happen?'

Apparently,' replied Tommy, 'if they can get their hands on *the ultimate wisdom*, the Council of Wisdom could use it to stop the TFC.'

This prompted a barrage of questions, such as what and where was the Council of Wisdom and how might a piece of wisdom stop the TFC and why was Elza an enemy of OleSayjj? – questions to which Tommy had no answers.

'So she wouldn't tell you anything else?' exclaimed Uladrack. Tommy shook his head.

'Did you press her, kid?' asked Farlowe. 'We're talking the end of the universe!'

''Course I pressed her!' Tommy's mind went back to the fear he'd felt not three hours previously . . .

'Be careful child,' Elza had said, moving to the tree stump, 'lest I not help you at all.'

'Enough games! Just tell me how to stop the TFC! The whole universe is at stake!'

'Hush.'

'And tell me where my friends are! Where's OleSayjj!?'

'Hush!'

'No, I won't *hush*. No more games! The whole universe is—?'

RRRRAAAAAARRRRRWWWWWRRRRR!!!

Elza let out a roar, except she wasn't Elza any more. She'd slipped her hand into the cracking fissure in the tree stump and all at once she'd flushed and towered thirty metres high. *SSSSHHHMMAACCKKKKK!!* Her forked tail whipped against the rocky ground and she roared again – this time a blast of flame shot from her mouth, hitting a corner of the plateau. The rock turned molten and poured itself down, down into the abyss.

'I haven't done that in 600 million years,' said Elza (herself once more). 'Pray you don't make me do it – *or worse* – again.'

'And I can't believe she's still making you play the violin!' exclaimed Uladrack.

'We made a deal,' said Tommy. 'And I agreed to it.'

'She wouldn't kill you though – if you play worse than she did. Now that she knows you.' It was more a question than a statement.

'She's been waiting a long time to help someone. She needs to know I'm worthy.'

'That doesn't answer my question.'

'Uladrack,' replied Tommy. 'I want to apologize to you if I was ever mean to you in the Bowl. And you too, Roysters. I'm sorry I didn't see Yago bullying you and help put a stop to it.' Before Roysters could reply, the irevamp retorted (with a touch of impatience): 'What's that got to do with anything?'

Tommy sighed. 'All of you . . . I'd like to thank you for your help in getting Swiggy to Hellsbells. And I know Woozie was very fond of some of you, and Rumbles of you, Harriett. But however I play tomorrow, I'll be saying goodbye to each of you in the morning.'

'What do you mean?'

The young Earthling explained how two wormholes would appear either side of the pale moon the next day. The one on the left would lead to somewhere that'd help him in his quest to stop the TFC (Elza wouldn't say where). The one on the right would lead directly into a black hole. 'I'll have to pass remote control of Swiggy to Hellsbells,' continued Tommy. 'Then, when I'm some way into my violin performance, they'll lift the force field and start Swiggy moving. Which wormhole they send her through will depend on whether I play better than Elza.' He stood up and walked towards the Boys' Dorm. 'So you see . . . None of you can stay on Swiggy. Because, if you do, chances are you'll die in a black hole with me.'

'I don't care!' Tommy looked over. It was Uladrack. For some reason she'd stepped up on to the coffee table. 'I'll stay with you on Swiggy . . . If the universe is going to end in less than eleven months anyway, then what's the difference . . ?' She looked at Tommy and saluted. 'You're the captain of Swiggy, Tommy. Consider yourself *my* captain.'

'I'm a-stayin' too.' It was Harriett. And she stood up on a side table. 'This is the only way I'll find Rumbleys.' She looked at Tommy. 'Captain . . . You're my captain.'

'Captain, my captain.' Now Roysters was standing on a little table that held a plant. 'I'll jolly well stay too . . . Almost certainly . . . Probably.'

The three on tables looked at Farlowe. He cracked his knuckles. 'I dunno. I'm my own captain. And Tommy's talking a lotta sense. I might take that dumptrux and seek out the missing three from another angle, so to speak.' He looked at Harriett. 'If that's kosher with you?'

But Tommy looked resolute. 'Sorry, but I refuse to be responsible for the deaths of anyone else.'

'You wouldn't be,' replied Uladrack. 'Staying would be *my* free choice.'

'Mine too!'

'No,' said Tommy, forcefully. 'No one's coming through the black hole with me.' And he opened the shelves through to the Boys' Dorm.

'But . . .' Uladrack was calculating. 'What if we, em, if we . . ?' Her eyes had glazed over.

'So,' said Tommy with an air of farewell. 'If you pack your things and—'

'Of course!' Uladrack's eyes were bright. 'What if we got into the dumptrux and attached it to Swiggy so we'd be dragged along behind?'

I don't see how that'd—'

'Once Swiggy gets moving, we'll be able to see which way she's going. If she's heading to the left of the moon, then we stay attached and come through the wormhole with you.'

'Yes, siree!' exclaimed Harriett. 'A hoot 'na holler behind you!'

'And,' continued Uladrack, 'if Swiggy's heading to the right, we hit the *release* and you go through to the black hole on your own.'

'A mighty fine idea!'

Tommy shook his head. 'Who knows how fast Swiggy will be travelling. You may not be able release in time.'

'We would!' declared Uladrack.

'Yeah.'

'Harriett, do you have a tow-rope strong enough?'

'Naw, but surely there's one on Swiggy.'

Four people started chatting excitedly about the merits and practicalities of the idea. Tommy smacked his hand against the shelf to get their attention. No one noticed. He smacked again. Nothing.

'You're NOT getting the tow-rope!' That got their attention. Tommy looked at them gravely. 'Even if I flew through the *good* wormhole – a big *if* . . . I don't really know any of you. Or how much I can trust you. I need to trust anyone travelling on with me *with my life* . . . So I'm sorry. I'd like you all to leave in the morning.'

Just then, Roysters's table gave way. He and the plant crashed to the floor.

75
One Question

Alone in the Boys' Dorm, Tommy watched the seconds counting down on Woozie's time-lock safe. A knock disturbed his thoughts. 'Howdy,' said Harriett, peeking round the door. 'OK to come in?'

'Eh, sure.'

There were clothes and belongings all over the floor and Harriett stepped on the corner of something. 'My!' she exclaimed, leaping backwards. 'Didn't see that.' She crouched low – to a long, curved leather case. 'Hope ole klutz here didn't break nothing.' She ran her finger along its side. 'Say, ain't this the case you brought back from Hellsbells?' Tommy nodded. 'What's inside?' Harriett put her hand to her mouth. 'Sorry, I'm such a nosey-boots. Pa was always sayin' so.'

'No, it's fine,' said Tommy. 'See for yourself.'

Harriett looked to see if he meant it, then opened the box. Inside was a violin – a beautiful specimen, made from different shades of wood. 'It looks a heap more delicate than that there one.' Harriett was pointing at Tommy's electric one, leaning against the bed.

Tommy nodded. 'It's a Straddlevarious. Its wood straddles various billennia. Bea made it from the wood choppings and Elza gave it to me as a farewell present.' His voice turned sarcastic. 'Wow, thanks for the *ancient* violin.'

'May I?' asked Harriett. Tommy shrugged. Harriett lifted out the violin, picked up the bow and drew it across the strings. It made a wailing sound. 'Can't play to save my life,' she laughed – then stopped abruptly, looking aghast. 'Oh, my, I didn't mean . . . I'm sure you'll save *your* life when you play.' She set down the violin. 'I only popped by to ask you if you want to eat somethin'. Roysters is a-making omelettes.'

Tommy said no and Harriett hastened out of the room.

Three seconds, two seconds, one second . . . And then Tommy was in the safe. Removing an envelope and a set of dog tags.

Over and over he read the letter, expecting – wanting – to burst into tears, but none came. He never spoke of the letter's contents, except to say that his best friend (alive or dead) spoke highly of Uladrack and Roysters ('let them join you'), and that his best friend had explained how he'd attached a special little rubber tail to the back of Swiggy which he'd purchased off Swiggapedia. Not only would this tiny tail prevent wormhole gurning, but it should also ward off all symptoms of travel sickness from the occupants of the spacecraft it was attached to.

Oh, and one other thing the young Earthling once let slip . . . The PS at the end asked whether he'd prefer to eat a bucketful of boogers or to be locked in a room with Rumbles for thirty days with no access to shower facilities.

Tommy was lying on his bunk, chewing on the dog tags, when Farlowe entered the room. 'Hope I'm not disturbing you, kid.'

'No,' murmured Tommy.

The burly detective placed something by Tommy's feet, then pulled a bag out from under the bunk and zipped it up. He was about to leave, when he looked at the young Earthling. 'I, too, used to find it hard to trust new people.'

Tommy gave a bitter laugh. 'I don't have that problem . . . I trusted Yago, didn't I?'

'And now you'll never trust anyone again?'

'I didn't say that!'

Farlowe shrugged and was halfway out of the door when he said: 'You know, I heard about you losing your parents very young.'

'What's that got to do with anything?'

Farlowe stepped back into the room and shut the door. 'My parents croaked it soon after I was born. It's a long story. All my siblings too.'

'And?'

'And Uladrack and Roysters – they're orphans too. And Harriett doesn't seem to have anyone. She baked that for you, by the way. She was upset when she came out of your room.'

Following the line of Farlowe's finger, Tommy saw a large pie sitting by his feet. He looked back up at the blood-houndy detective. 'Your point being?'

'My point being, you got a lot on your plate, sonny. Saving the universe, finding your friends . . . If I had good people offering to join me, ready to put their lives in danger – *to die* if necessary – I think I'd sort out my trust issues and not be so darn picky.'

No tears. Nothing. No matter how many times he read and reread Marielle's letter.

'Hello,' said a voice.

Tommy shot upright, covering the letter. And a disc – with the word *Tommy* scrawled across it – fell off the bed. It rolled across the carpet, stopping by a clumpy grey boot. 'Sorry,' said the voice of Uladrack. 'I did knock.' And she picked up the disc.

'Oh, er.' Tommy was caught off guard.

The irevamp filled the awkward silence. 'This your music?'

'Uh-huh.'

'I always think you can tell a lot about someone by the music they listen to . . . Can I?' She was motioning towards a thin slot beneath a line of buttons in the corduroy wall. Tommy shrugged and Uladrack pushed the disc into the slot. She was about to press a button.

'No, wait!' Tommy leapt off the bunk. Alarmed. Frightened even. 'Sorry, that's a disc of Marielle playing the clarinet.'

'Oh.'

Again an awkward silence. Tommy, trying to look nonchalant, ran a hand through his hair. He gripped a tuft. Fingertips turning white.

'I've never heard her play,' said Uladrack eyeing him curiously. 'Do you mind if I listen?'

'No!' exclaimed Tommy, bounding closer. 'I mean, no, not now . . . I can't have any other music played. Not with my violin performance tomorrow. It could put me off my technique.' He placed his hand over the buttons on the wall. 'Was there something else you wanted?'

Uladrack tried to hide her puzzlement. 'Er, I just wanted to check what time you perform tomorrow. And what time we have to leave.'

Tommy stared at the corduroy walls of the Boys' Dorm. After what seemed like an age, he sat up and began writing (telepathically) into his hologram diary. There was one question he couldn't bring himself to write. He kept starting and breaking off. Then he had a brainwave. *Maybe I could write it backwards?* Ten minutes later, he fell back, panting – as though he'd swum a great distance underwater.

76
Too Late

'It's jolly good,' said Roysters.

'Good?' said Farlowe. 'It's great!'

'Hmm,' said Uladrack. 'It needs to be *exquisite*.'

'It ain't quite *that*,' said Harriett, flicking a dial on a small safe and hinging open its door. '*Dreamchoco* support – anyone?'

All four were in the dumptrux cockpit, surrounded by bags and belongings, listening to Tommy (via radio link) playing violin in the Bellepoch Studio. The dumptrux was still floating alongside Swiggy, but wasn't attached in any way. It'd be left far behind once Swiggy started moving.

Not thirty minutes earlier, they'd bade the Earthling a tearful goodbye. Actually, Farlowe didn't cry (he just looked grim) and Roysters claimed not to have cried (but even now his face looked tear-stained). And Tommy'd still found himself incapable of shedding a tear.

By now, the technical people in Hellsbells had taken over Swiggy's controls (remotely) and two dark patches had appeared either side of the pale moon ('Wormholes if ever I saw 'em,' Harriett had announced, a telescope to her eye.) In nine minutes' time, Tommy would have to start playing his piece for real.

Harriett looked at Uladrack and swallowed a mouthful of

chocolate. 'He's gonna die if he plays like this, ain't he?'

Uladrack shook her head, but the tear welling in her eye told a different story.

'I'm a-goin' back!' declared Harriett.

'You can't! We promised we wouldn't sneak onto Swiggy.'

'I'll make it back here – to the dumptrux – afore he starts a-playin' for reals.'

'No!' squawked Uladrack. 'If you're delayed and Swiggy goes through the black hole . . .'

But Harriett was already gone.

They heard the violin music stop. And voices.

'Harriett!? The hell are you doing here? You promised—'

'You left this in your room.'

'What're you doing with that!?'

'Elza wouldn't've gifted you a Straddlevarious 'less she thought it could help.'

'I'm not using that ancient thing. *This* is my trusted violin.'

'I'm just tellin' you . . . Your playin's not good enough with that. If you trust the Beast, then put *all* your trust in her . . . Sometimes you gotta let go of ole things and put your faith in new ones. I'm a-tellin' you – use this here violin and quit your stubbornin'.'

'Harriett, you've got to go!'

'Yes, siree, I'm a-goin'. But I'm a-leavin' this here Straddlevarious on the floor – 'n case you get sense.'

The room went quiet, except for a door opening and closing. By the time Harriett made it back to the dumptrux, there were three minutes till Tommy's 'real' performance, and a new sound carried into the cockpit – notes sharper, higher, lower than before. The good ones warmer, more colourful than earlier. But – alas – like walking a tightrope on a thinner rope, Tommy was hitting more off-notes. And these were magnified out of all proportion.

'He should stick with the violin he knows,' said Roysters. 'This sounds inferior.'

Harriett shook her head. 'The Straddlevarious may be harder to play, but if he gets it plumb, it just might be *exquisite*.'

'Balderdash!' exclaimed Roysters. 'He doesn't make mistakes with the other one. Those bad notes sound *yikes*! I tell you, he's definitely going through the black hole hitting *them*.'

'Well he's definitely a-goin' through the black hole if he plays with the aim of *no mistakes*. Mistakes are a sign of passion. And he's gotta play with all the passion he's possessin'!' The side-burned lady bit into another *Dreamchoco* bar.

'He's a smart boy,' said Farlowe, steepling his fingers. 'He'll figure the best one.'

At that, the music stopped. Then resumed.

'He's a-dumped the Straddlevarious!' exclaimed Harriett. 'Gone back to his *trusted* violin.' She made *trusted* sound like a dirty word.

'The violin isn't the problem,' said Uladrack.

Before anyone could question her, she was gone.

'Beside the dumptrux – that's them . . ! *Is it?*'

A shark-finned, syringe-like craft drew closer to Hellsbells, its steel hook-tail glinting in the pale moonlight.

'Aye,' said Captain Roger, lowering his telescope. 'Looks a bit different, but I can make out the name *Swiggy*. And the homing device confirms it. Unfortunately they're *inside* the force field.'

A very stubbly, sticky-haired Nack Jickilson gave a bad-breath smile. 'Nearly six weeks since they somehow flung us to the middle of nowhere . . . Been travelling in circles like idiots since then – run out of food provisions, outta hot water and cleaning products.' He smacked his forehead on the cockpit dashboard. 'Aaaiigghh! . . . Look at that – it's filthy . . . And we all stink, don't we!?'

The captain nodded. 'Aye, sir – I mean all of us do, except you, sir.'

'Inside the force field, you say, eh?' Nack's eyebrows began wriggling like electrocuted caterpillars.

'Aye, sir.'

'Well, I'll tell you something.' Nack's voice turned crazed. 'We-Are-Gonna-Wait-Here – Till-Hellsbells-Freezes-Over-If-Necessary – Till-They-Come-Out.' His eyes rolled into their sockets. '*And-When-They-Do* . . .' The hairy-backed fellow went to smack his forehead against the wall, accidentally whacking his nose. 'Eeeeigghh!' he cried, blood spurting down his T-shirt and water suddenly spraying from the ceiling. 'Shyyyysen . . ! Who put that button there!?'

A braying wail filled the air.

'That's the fire-alarm button, sir.'

Nack snatched Captain Roger's cap and held it to his nose. 'Just be ready to attack *whenever* they exit the force field!' Then, as an afterthought: 'Any *mistakes*, any *oops*, *they escaped*, and I'll have you ground into little pieces and eaten with fava beans. That clear?' He raised his head. Water sprayed into his eyes. 'And that better not be the last of the water!'

A clock counted down in the Bellepoch Studio. Forty-two seconds, forty-one . . .

'Stay out of things you don't understand!' cried Tommy. He looked nervous and flushed. 'You didn't hear Bea play. I did! It was . . . *stratospheric* . . . It's *my* life on the line.'

'Exactly,' replied Uladrack, standing by a row of buttons in the wall. 'And everyone else's life – if you're the only one who can stop the TFC.'

Tommy paused at this. Twenty-two seconds to go. 'I appreciate your help, but my technique's got to be perfect – *perfect* – if I'm to get anywhere near Bea's playing. I can't risk putting myself off. I can't risk—'

'*Can't risk!?*' The irevamp gave a shrill squawk. 'Listen to yourself. You can't risk the Straddlevarious, you can't risk me pressing these buttons, you can't risk trusting us. Tommy, you're risking *everything* here. Whether you like to admit it or not.'

Seven seconds . . . six. Uladrack gave Tommy a hard look, squawked and bolted for the door. The Earthling remained fixed to the spot as the clock ticked down to zero. Hellsbells was visible through the semi-domed glass outer-wall.

A voice echoed through Swiggy. 'Tommy Storm, please begin your performance.'

Tommy ran to the door and opened it. 'The tow rope's under my pillow! Take it if you like. I trust you, Uladrack. I trust Harriett. I *could* trust the others. But I'm not playing that disc. Trust isn't the issue. My technique is the issue!'

'Mister Storm,' repeated the voice. 'Please begin!'

Tommy came back inside, took up his trusted violin and began playing.

'They're hooking a tow-rope from Swiggy to the dumptrux.'

Captain Roger heard the sound of a body part being smacked against something hard and then a voice fizzed through the intercom. 'Aaaaiiggghh!! . . . That means something's gonna happen! I'm coming to the bridge. Have my sour-fizzy-sherbet ready and put some music on. *This time* we're gonna get 'em!'

When Nack appeared, he demanded to know why classical music was playing throughout the ship. 'I HATE the violin!' He smashed his foot into a panel of winking buttons. ''Specially violin solos! HATE 'em! HATE 'em! HATE 'em!'

'Apologies,' said Captain Roger. 'I thought you might be interested. It's on the local radio station and our monitors tell us it's originating from Swiggy.'

He went to change channel just as the violin moved from sweet melody to something more explosive. Nack punched an array of dials – blocking Roger's path and sending glass fragments into a puddle of water on the floor. Nack's eyebrows were wiggling like speared snakes and he seemed to mouth a *No*. Which Roger took to mean, *No, don't change the station.*

'Er, it looks like Swiggy's moving, sir.'

And Swiggy *was* moving. Dragging the dumptrux along behind her.

'The force field is up, sir . . . They're both through it . . . Shall we charge them now . . ? Sir . . ? Mister Jickilson . . ? Shall we charge them . . ?'

Nack Jickilson, spittle foaming at his mouth, was looking more demented than usual. Boy, thought Roger (realizing his employer hadn't snorted any sherbet yet), he must *really* hate the violin. Or else he really, really wants to kill these IGGY Knights.

'Sir, if we don't charge them soon . . . They're heading towards the pale moon. Looks like they're going to the right of it.'

Swiggy was moving at a smooth pace, allowing Tommy to see the direction they were headed, even as he threw his energies into playing his beloved electric violin.

To the right? At the black hole! No! No!! I'm not playing well enough!

And he redoubled his efforts. A nose faster, a tad more oomph. *This note, that note, these notes, together, up, down.* Through the labyrinth – not one out of place. He'd played *fury* to perfection. Now he was giving *happy* the same treatment. Yet Swiggy didn't deviate from its course.

'Nearly . . .' said Farlowe.

'Say when!' cried Harriett, eyes closed, finger hovering over a red button.

'You'll have to release it soon!' exclaimed Roysters. 'Yes, you jolly well will. Else we'll *all* be dragged through. To our deaths.'

The music died.

'He's stopped playing!'

'No wait . . . He's back! The Straddlevarious!'

Now the music was sharper, stronger. Tommy must've been going on adrenalin, for he was walking the thin tightrope with aplomb – hardly any agonizing notes.

'It's way better!' cried Harriett.

Captain Roger was in a bind . . . Nack Jickilson hadn't answered any of his questions. Instead he'd sunk to his knees amid the floating glass shards and was bonking his head against the wall. Temporary insanity, thought Roger. Then he checked himself. *Temporary*?

His thoughts veered back to the present. *Should I take the decision myself? But I'm not authorized! Hmm . . . but what if they escape?* An image of fava beans simmered through this mind. 'Yes, we're going to charge!' he announced. 'Cut them in two with the fin.'

The violin music stopped. Then started again. 'Beautiful,' mumbled Nack, blowing snots out his nose on to the floor.

'Yes,' said Roger, pushing the throttle with a swell of authority, thrusting *I-Headbutted-Your-Gran* forward. 'But it's not quite . . .' He searched for the right word . . . 'Exquisite.'

'It's made no difference!' cried Roysters. 'We're still heading to the right.'

'Say when!' Harriett's hand quivered over the 'release' button, tears streaming down her chocolate-smeared face.

'Almost . . .' rasped Farlowe. '*Almost.*'

Uladrack let out a yell to wake the very soul of a black hole. 'DO IT!!!'

Harriett hit the button. And the music stopped.

'Fourteen seconds from impact . . .'

'My father . . .' Nack blubbered. 'He played the violin.' The sorry fellow was crumpled in a heap on the floor. The music stopped for a second time. Then started again. 'He used to play it to lull us to sleep . . . Every night. Before he left us . . . Left us . . . Left us . . .'

'Eight . . . seven . . .' Roger and the rest of the crew braced themselves. Swiggy loomed large. As did the pale moon to their left. 'Three . . . two . . . one . . .'

In the cockpit of the dumptrux, they hadn't heard the music restart.

'The tow-rope,' cried Harriett. 'It ain't released!'

'Did you press it hard – *jolly* hard?' roared Roysters.

'Yes!'

'I didn't mean *you*!' squawked Uladrack in utter despair. No one knew what she was on about. '*DO IT!* – I meant *Tommy*!'

'But . . . How could he hope to hear you?'

'Too late now,' declared Farlowe, his life flashing before him, an unexpected feeling of peace descending on his soul. He closed his eyes and heard the music of heaven.

Just before it reached the dark shadow, Swiggy slowed a mite and the shadow seemed to wink shut, then open again. The high fin atop *I-Headbutted-Your-Gran* sliced in front of Swiggy at a cross angle. Inside, Roger cried, 'Missed!' followed by, 'Wha—!? How—!?' as the craft was hauled sideways.

Anyone looking through a telescope from Hellsbells would've seen Swiggy, followed by the dumptrux, zoom through the dark shadow to the right of the pale moon and disappear. And – its hook-tail caught in the tow-rope – *I-Headbutted-Your-Gran* passed through with them.

77

Come (To Me)

Squeezing perfect notes from the Straddlevarious, Tommy saw the dark shadow approaching, saw it only as a black hole. And knew: *This Is It*. Somewhere in the depths of his mind he heard an incantation. *DO IT!* Was this his very soul calling? Or a cry from Marielle? Or just some interference over the airwaves? Whatever it was, he knew what he had to do. *Even though it's too late.*

He stopped playing. And hit a button by a slot in the wall.

A clarinet croaked to life . . . Soft, gentle notes, whiskering into the air like a rabbit peeking out its warren. They frolicked onwards, a touch louder, before Tommy recognized . . . *Adagio Formaggio*. As the music swooned to sadness, he felt his heart squeeze with it. Time seemed to slow – everything slowed – and he saw an image of Rumbles and Summy bouncing on a trampoline. And Woozie . . . Woozie wearing rocket-blades, willing him to race.

But Marielle . . . Where was she?

A vision of his hologram diary appeared – its last entry flashing large. *Again her see ever I will?*

Without realizing, his hand took the bow, teasing it across the Straddlevarious's strings, like a tear across a cheek. Down, down, sank the clarinet, towards depths of despair, the Straddlevarious chasing her all the way. Images roared out of the blackness – times when he'd hurt Woozie and times when he'd been mean to Marielle. The clarinet and the violin – pushing, pulling each other further, further towards the darkest reaches. Tommy, swimming through blackness, chasing something precious. Something lost. He saw himself denying love for the elquinine three times. Saw himself punching Woozie and declaring: 'Consider our friendship over.' Heard his own voice: *Again her see ever I will?* The clarinet and violin wailing in unison. And then the execution. Repeated from a dozen angles. *Woozie's dead! Woozie's dead!* Like a scalpel, the clarinet and violin sawing to the heart of darkness. *Pain! Pain!* And just when he couldn't bear it, the clarinet and violin twisted deeper. Pain soared. *AGONY!!* And his heart cried out. *WILL I EVER SEE HER AGAIN?*

At that very moment, the clarinet and violin struck the bottom, spearing an image of blackness. And the spearing stained it white, till it was black *and* white, with smudged corners. Till it was a photo. Of Marielle, side-on, looking out at the stars.

And the clarinet was skipping upwards. The violin hesitated, then chased after her – past images of lessons from Wisebeardyface, of pillow-fights with Rumbles and Summy, of late-night chats, of flippety-flapjacks cooked by Woozie, of foodfights in the Lounge.

Tommy never saw the dark shadow almost upon Swiggy wink closed. Nor did he see it wink open again, looking lighter than before. As though it could never lead to a black hole. For the music soaring from the Straddlevarious was brighter and darker – more exquisite – than anything Bea or Elza had ever played.

And the clarinet continued soaring – up, up towards a place we call *joy*. And before it reached there, it lingered, waiting, at a height just below. Tommy's arm was ghosting slower. As though looking back down to the gloom.

And when the clarinet could wait no longer, it cut a quivering note. Tommy raised his head, tears running into his mouth, salting a pair of dog tags. The violin died and sounded a note of lamentation – *Goodbye*. The clarinet called for him again. And again the violin cried out, sadder still, *Goodby*e. Outside, the dark shadow rushed to greet him. The young man biting down on dog tags.

The clarinet cried out a third time. *Come!*

Tommy dropped his head, the dog tags fell from his mouth and a single tear splashed the edge of the Straddlevarious. And, just as the clarinet turned to scale the heights of possibility, Tommy's arm sliced forward.

The violin swam up. Up to join her.

EPILOGUE

When Yago appeared in public two days after his supposed execution, he was declared a god by thousands of galaxies. He acquired an agent who soon realized that Yago's only outstanding skill was swordsmanship. Thus the *Sword-God Roadshow* was born – with Yago travelling the cosmos, defeating (i.e. *killing*) skilled swordfighters before ginormous crowds.

At only his second 'Deity Duel', Yago was standing bare-chested in the centre of an arena, five dead bodies at his feet, the crowd worshipping on their knees, guineahogs, hamstars and other tiny creatures surrounding the stage, when a wibblewallian materialized from the ether, wielding a slightly curved sword. Those close to the stage heard Yago exclaim, 'What . . ? How . . ? But you're dead!'

'It must be another god,' whispered a large portion of the crowd.

'No, it's that loser Woozie – from the last ChAOS,' argued others.

Whoever he was, this creature was a fine swordfighter, for he launched an attack on Yago that had *Yagod* (as he was now termed) defending with all of his skill. 'But look!' yelled some. 'Yagod's getting the upper hand!'

And, sure enough, the sandy-haired boy had stopped

retreating – he was beginning to edge the wibblewallian backwards. 'You're not Woozie,' he hissed. 'That sad body-mask-suit fooled nobody. Woozie was too much of a loser to last two seconds in a duel with me. Who are you? Reveal yourself before I take your life like all the others.'

The mention of Woozie breathed new fire into the wibblewallian and he slashed forward, knocking Yagod's sword to the floor. 'Would you prefer a scimmy through the throat,' he asked, 'or to eat a bucketful of boogers every day for the rest of your life?'

'Tommy!' exclaimed Yagod, recognizing the voice. 'It's me, *your friend* . . . I knew it was you all along. I'd never have hurt you.'

'Answer the question,' said the wibblewallian, the point of the scimmy pressed into Yagod's neck.

'Er, em, the bucketful of boogers.'

'Too bad . . . Cos I *don't care* which you prefer.'

And just as it looked as if the wibblewallian would drive home his scimmy, there was a blur of movement and the furry fellow fell to the floor. Yagod stood over him, a bloody dagger in his hand. 'Cockiness,' he rasped. 'It's always been your fatal flaw . . . And when I say *fatal* . . .' He laughed, took up his sword and sliced it towards the wibblewallian's neck – where it was stopped by a last-moment scimmy block.

'So you're going to make it interesting,' laughed Yagod as his foe stumbled to his feet. 'Think about it . . . In a way I'll have had a hand in killing *two* Woozies.'

Once again, the mention of Woozie fired up the wibblewallian and he seemed to forget about his wound. Back and forth the two fought – slashing, thrashing, leaping, twirling – until at last, the wibblewallian knocked Yagod to the floor and stood on his sword. He pressed his scimmy to the Casiothellian's throat.

Leaning close to Yago's face he said: 'This is for Woozie.'

In response, Yagod spat in his face. The spittle hitting the wibblewallian's eyes, nose and cheeks. The wibblewallian paused, lowered his scimmy and kicked Yagod's sword off the stage. He said something in a low voice then turned, walked through a shimmering shadow and disappeared.

Yagod would later claim that the figure said: 'I won't kill you – cos I know you'll only rise from the dead and be yet stronger . . . You are the greatest of all gods.'

And yet, from that day forth, the numbers attending Yago-Deity-Rallies began to dwindle (within eight months, *Yagoanity* had fallen out of the Universe's Top Twenty-Million Religions[52]). The reason . . ? Word spread that what the wibblewallian really said was: 'Thank you . . . You've made me see. It'd dishonour Woozie's memory to give you an honourable death.'

As Tommy, Swiggy and the others flashed through the wormhole left by Elza, a creature known to some as Bin-Liner knelt before a teeth-bared mouth carved into the rocky wall.

'Oh, Canine-of-Canines,' he incanted. 'Yes, Storm escaped . . . But no matter. Whatever I said before, be thou assured that he cannot trouble us. He may be smart, but he is young and callow and obviously lacking in the wisdom of the gods. We can forget him.'

The plastic-sheathed creature stood and genuflected. 'In any case, it is time for a change of strategy . . . Instead of working to *prevent* the universe from being saved, I will focus

52 The universe's most popular religion – by some distance – remained MyInvisibleFriendism.

on *precipitating* its destruction . . . In less than eleven months, oh Canine-of-Canines, we will be in dangled-bone paradise.'

Bin-Liner strode purposefully across the echoey cathedral space, pausing only to throw something into the spitting bonfire. An opening appeared in the wall and he stepped through. Here, in a hidden vestibule, surrounded by dog-like figurines, he removed a voice-distorter from his throat and pulled the black bin-liner off his person, revealing an elderly creature covered in reddy-grey fur who looked half-man, half-spaniel – with a smidge of fox thrown in for good measure. Bearded, with a bushy tail, the fire in his eyes might've been madness or the twinkle of round-the-corner laughter.

From the vestibule, he hurried along a series of tunnels before coming to an indentation in the tunnel wall. Reaching in, he lifted away a rectangular object and climbed through the resulting hole. He was now in a warm, hearth-lit room. He fixed the rectangular object back on to the wall, obscuring the hole from view. Then he unbolted a heavy wooden door on the far side of the room, tossed a log on the hearth-fire, sank into an armchair and placed a blanket over his knees. No sooner had he done so, than a knock sounded on the door and a voice spoke up: 'The three children to see you, Master OleSayjj.'

The old, bearded creature glanced at the rectangular object on the wall – a blackboard full of notations, perfectly in place. He settled his eyes into a warm twinkle and took a book on to his knee. The voice that rose from his throat was deep and trusting. 'Send them in, Balwick . . . Send them in.'

Zestrella Ravisham signed a deal with Tellall Publications to write her memoirs. Refusing to return to her planet

(Neuterdafekers), she holed up in an interplanetary motel for six months, producing a 666-page tome entitled, *What My Uncle Did*. She turned up at a Yagod Deity Rally some time after publication and managed to kiss him several times – yet despite this and despite having numerous high-profile boyfriends, it's claimed she never recaptured the 'rapture' of that special moment in the 'execution hut'.

Bernard Burnside became an extreme sports TV presenter. At the behest of the show's sponsors she grew her hair long, took to wearing slinky dresses and (the point of most contention) removed her moustache. She died (strangled) three months later when a strap on a frock she was wearing got tangled in the reigns of a pony that was an unwitting contestant in the *Catapult* segment of a show called *So-You-Think-You-Know-How-Far-A-Non-winged-Animal-Can-Fly?*

Joe Yuss and Syri Yuss ended up dying penniless 'in a place of squalor'. Things started well – Joe became a successful stand-up comedian while Syri Yuss had a series of fruitful relationships. Things turned sour however when Joe's stand-up gigs began falling on days when Syri was 'in the ascendancy', while Syri's boyfriends kept organizing weekends away, only for Joe to turn up. Joe's drinking problem and Syri's gambling habit (she was 'clinically over-optimistic') only accelerated the decline.

On the subject of gambling habits, Bobby J. Heimenopper quit his job, gave up betting on hare-brained racing and became a geography teacher. His only 'lapses' involved the occasional game of strip-poker 'but not while correcting homework'. Max Bohr went on to become President of the El Nerdo facility. His 'misplacing' of just over forty thousand EARTHs was never noticed.

EXTRA BITS NO. 1

EARTH SCENARIOS (A SAMPLE)

Scenario (difference to earth)	Outcomes
Humans have perfect memories	Childbirth levels plummet. Human race dies out early – indeterminate date.
In 1919, Beth Finegold accepts A. Hitler's invitation to go on a date	World War II never happens. Instead, Germany is ruled by Fitsov Lavfter, a comedian dictator (1933–47), who decrees that all citizens must wear lederhosen 'with sausage-filled pockets'. On the plus side, *The Sound of Music* is never made and *The Great Escape* features a cast who work in a frankfurter factory and dream of wearing Bermuda shorts.
The 1969 moon landings are faked in a TV studio	No difference.
Men, rather than women, get pregnant and give birth to babies	Nightclubs have 'free-for-men' nights and women buy all the drinks. Football jerseys sold in three versions: Home, Away and Maternity. Costs of childbirth soar as men choose to have three-month-long epidurals. Morning sickness recognized as a life-threatening condition. (Note: most of this 'outcome' has been censored by the publisher.)
Judas Iscariot is rich from birth	Main emblem of a certain religion is a bed and dodgy shellfish rather than a cross.

Scenario (difference to earth)	Outcomes
James Joyce does *not* lose the 'punctuated' transcript of *Ulysses*	The book is never hailed as a masterpiece, but is made into the 1936 movie *Another Bloomin' Day*, starring Errol Flynn and Marlene Dietrich as Leopold and Molly Bloom.
All voting machines function perfectly in the 'policeman-of-the-planet' nation	The 43rd President of this nation pronounces 'nuclear' correctly. (Note: most of this 'outcome' has been excluded due to the Fish-in-a-Barrel principle.)
Woody Allen is tall and attractive	Woody works his entire life as a tennis coach – makes no movies.
Albert Einstein does *not* bump his head on a window sill in January 1905	The US Air Force drops 5 million cheeseburgers and 15,000 franchise agreements over Hiroshima and Nagasaki in 1945. Japan surrenders two years later, the entire nation suffering from type two diabetes.
Humans have no selfish gene	Unrecognizable outcome.
Enormous meteorite *never* hits Earth	Dinosaurs rule the planet having evolved the ability to speak intelligently and iron a pair of pants. Humans, having existed for a short time, are now extinct, exhibited in museums (skeletons only) and appear in sci-fi movies. Baby dinosaurs' favourite TV show features a truly annoying purple 'human' called Bernie.
The moon is made of cheese	Neil Armstrong dies of obesity at the age of 40 and for six days every month, the planet smells of old socks.

Scenario (difference to earth)	Outcomes
Humans 'believe' things and live their lives based on evidence and reasonable likelihood rather than on what they *wish* were true	The number of wars, silly outfits and level of guilt is reduced by 98 per cent. Cartoonists and desert-based mini-skirt retailers flourish.
Lakes, rivers and seas consist of beer rather than water	Humans remain forever in the Neolithic phase of development. Attractive people have little advantage over unattractive people.
All humans have IQs of 150+	The number of wars declines, unemployment falls, late-night talk-show radio disappears, professional wrestling dies as a sport, tabloid newspapers go out of business, commerce grinds to a halt as 95 per cent of the adult population work on PhD theses involving topics such as *The Influence of Parody in a Post-Colonial Landscape*, unemployment then rises, alcoholism increases, late-night talk-shows and tabloid newspapers reappear, the number of wars starts to rise. (Pro wrestling remains extinct.)
Humans use no more than 10 per cent of their brain capacity	No discernible difference.
All humans are encouraged to carry licensed guns and the death penalty applies everywhere for those convicted of murder	The murder rate soars (adolescents have a 52 per cent chance of making it through high school alive) in line with a rise in the instances of inbreeding. Customers feel it necessary to tip waiters at least 25 per cent.
Politicians eschew corruption and make *long-term* decisions for the good of the country with no thought for re-election	Unrecognizable outcome.

Scenario (difference to earth)	Outcomes
In Santiago, on 7 June 1985, a butterfly beats its wings 9,456 times rather than 9,455 times	The Iron Curtain never falls, Maggie Thatcher remains Prime Minister of the UK till 1999 (when she dies after being 'body-slammed' by Luciano Pavarotti while participating in *It's A Knockout – The Millennium Celebrity Extravaganza*) and Monserrat wins the 2004 World Cup, beating Brazil 7–0 in the final.
Sliced bread never invented	Toasters are all oval and 'that's the best thing since flattened pancakes' becomes a common phrase.
Human noses grow visibly longer whenever their owners tell a lie	The Inquisition, the 'witch-hunts' of the Middle Ages and the McCarthy hearings of the 1950s are far more boring to spectators. Politicians can smoke cigarettes in the rain without getting them wet. The following phrases are dispensed with: 'The cheque is in the post.' 'Coffee – nothing more.' 'I have to work late.' 'I can't work, I have the flu.' 'No, your bum doesn't look big in those trousers.' 'The WMD could be ready for launch in 45 minutes.' 'The dog ate it.' 'It meant nothing.' 'We woz robbed!' 'I don't know how it got up there, doc.' 'I . . . will to the best of my ability, preserve, protect and defend the Constitution of the . . .' 'I'll call you tomorrow.' 'I do.' 'Please, Mum – Dad says I *can*.'
No drugs in sport	The World Records for the Men's 100m and Women's Shot-put stands at 11.32 seconds and 426 cm respectively. The Tour de France takes three months to complete and rugby players look human.
No alcohol on Earth	The number of car crashes, fist-fights, broken families, literary masterpieces and unprompted hugs fall drastically. Total volume of human vomit over planet's life reduces by 10^{23} litres. The planet's three superpowers are Ireland, Scotland and Vladivostok. Pubs sell nothing but peanuts and flamenco dancing lessons. AA stands for Apoplectics Anonymous. Childbirth levels plummet. Human race dies out early – indeterminate date.

Extra Bits No. 2 Some Answers

Before this book had a fancy cover, it was read by a bunch of detective-like young readers. They had lots of questions on the background to this book, including:

- The first sheet found in the dumptrux – 'save the girl & triumph' – where did this come from? And how did Elza know about it?
- The third sheet found in the dumptrux, the one about Mount Neverrest and the Holey Gruel – what was that?
- Did Uladrack manage to stop stealing things by the end of the book?
- If the holey water in Hellsbells was so good at curing things, why didn't Tommy take some with him on either of his 'visits' there?
- If there's no night and day in space, how did the IGGY Knights regulate their time on Swiggy?
- Why do the IGGY Knights need to cook aboard Swiggy? I ask this because in TS1 they ate *favo-fant*[53] which tasted of whatever they wished it to taste of without needing to be cooked. Favo-fant would seem to be an ideal food to bring on a trip.
- Is it true that the most common location for truth

53 Stands for 'FAVOurite FANTasy food'.

serums in the universe is on public transport? (I heard that spacecraft conductors are armed with cans of truth serum spray which they spray over passengers whenever an SBD Warning Light goes off – indicating that someone has farted.)

- I liked hearing about the lessons given to the IGGY Knights by the Masters of the Way. Can you tell me more?
- Hmmm, I thought Swiggy was supposed to look more like a Spitfire than a Lancaster bomber?

The answers to these questions can be found at www.tommystorm.com. Just click on the *Secret Bit* tab and input the password, 061106. This will take you to a section reserved for people who've read this book to the end. So keep the password to yourself!

As there were so many questions about chocolate explosives and their manufacture, I'll deal with that opposite.

War . . . Hah!! What is it good for . . ? Absolutely *lots*.'
(advertising jingle for ACE Inc.)

Atomic Chocolate Explosives Inc. (ACE) was one of the most successful companies in the universe. Originally, the company sold only to customers 'who use our products for self-defence purposes and for the betterment of the universe'. But after 300 million years of zero sales, they modified 'betterment of the universe' to 'profit of the universe' ('since they sort of mean the same thing') and 'redefined' *self-defence purposes* to cover anyone who paid cash. The company, which always claimed its stockholders were 'loving, pious folk', suffered a scandal when a whistleblower revealed how the stockholders '*burst into tears* any time peace descends on war-torn parts of the universe'. But the company saved its reputation by releasing a statement admitting that yes, the stockholders did indeed burst into tears on such occasions, but this was 'almost certainly for reasons of joy'.

Can Tommy find Marielle, Rumbles and Summy and stop the TFC?

Find out in *TS3*